"I'm absolutely crushed, my dear. While I thought my charm had won you over, it was only your infernal pragmatism."

Genevieve leaned back in his arms and, despite herself, smiled at his foolery. "You are truly an incorrigible rogue, Mr. Cormick, and quite full of yourself, too, I might add. Now release me, if you please."

"It hardly pleases me." He grinned. "You're quite delectable, you know."

She blushed to the roots of her chestnut curls. "Is confusing me at every opportunity your greatest delight?"

"No." Mischief danced like a blue flame in his eyes. "But this is."

Dipping his dark head, he kissed her, expertly fitting his mouth against the softness of hers . . . and was instantly lost.

If you've enjoyed this story by
Suzannah Davis
Be sure to read

DEVIL'S DECEPTION
DEVIL'S MOON
OUTLAW HEART

DANCE OF DECEPTION

SUZANNAH DAVIS

An Avon Romantic Treasure

AVON BOOKS NEW YORK

For Gordon Nelson,
Master of Blarney and Storyteller Supreme
Thanks, Daddy.

DANCE OF DECEPTION is an original publication of Avon Books. This work has never before appeared in book form. This work is a novel. Any similarity to actual persons or events is purely coincidental.

AVON BOOKS
A division of
The Hearst Corporation
1350 Avenue of the Americas
New York, New York 10019

Copyright © 1992 by Suzannah Davis
Excerpt from *Only in Your Arms* copyright © 1992 by Lisa Kleypas
Inside cover author photograph by Terry Atwood
Published by arrangement with the author
Library of Congress Catalog Card Number: 91-93014
ISBN: 0-380-76128-9

First Avon Books Printing: March 1992

AVON TRADEMARK REG. U.S. PAT. OFF. AND IN OTHER COUNTRIES, MARCA REGISTRADA, HECHO EN U.S.A.

Printed in the U.S.A.

RA 10 9 8 7 6 5 4 3 2 1

Chapter 1

"**P**ox and perdition! The king's drunk again!"
    The words fell like a curse from the death-white lips of the ancient hag. She shook her polished yew walking staff in impotent rage while jeers and catcalls from the audience chased the hapless monarch across the stage.

"I'll grind his bones for bread!" Her coarse gray locks slithered over the rough black sacking of her voluminous robe. "I'll use his entrails for fish bait! I'll—"

"Shhh! He speaks," admonished the stout little woman at her side.

Crown askew, words slurring, the king stumbled toward the footlights, only to reel backward under a hail of over-ripe tomatoes, assorted garbage, and derisive hoots.

"Arrgh! 'Tis too late. We're ruined!" the hag moaned. "Quickly! The curtain! The clowns!"

A skinny Harlequin, two dancing milkmaids, and a hook-nosed dwarf juggling oranges galloped out of the wings as the dusty curtain closed over the players' igno-minious retreat. A pair of grim courtiers dragged off the king and tossed him into a corner, where he instantly be-gan to snore in a drunken stupor.

"Oh, la! What's to become of Claude?" the stout woman asked, wringing her hands.

"He can sleep there till doomsday, for all I care! He's finished!" the hag raged. She scanned the painted and

1

costumed thespians waiting for their turns. "We're in need of a new king. Who will unseat my sodden monarch? Come, there must be a man among you! Has no one the mettle to seize the opportunity?"

The distant, raucous roar of the audience was her only answer.

Whirling in an ominous billow of black cloaks, she stormed through the musty, ill-lit maze of ropes and canvas panels until she came to a room in the rear. Pausing just over the threshold, she stared at the cracked mirrors and mysterious apothecary of pots and jars glittering in the light of a single greasy candle. With a screech of frustration, she flung her staff to the floor, but no legion of hellhounds responded to her fervent wish to wreak vengeance on gin-soaked Claude. Genevieve Maples heaved a dejected sigh, and her shoulders slumped beneath the weight of her heavy costume.

"Did you really expect the earth to open up?" a deep, amused voice asked.

Genevieve jumped, startled by the tall stranger's sudden, soundless presence, and turned on him with vast irritation. "If this entire benighted playhouse collapsed of its own weight, 'twould undoubtedly be a blessing to the British Empire! What do you want?"

The man blinked, taken aback as much by her vehemence as by her wrinkled, scabrous visage. "I—ah, that is, do I have pleasure of addressing Miss Maples?"

"Yes—" It was her turn to blink as realization dawned. "Were you backstage? This is about Claude's part, isn't it? Wonderful!"

The tilt of her shoulders straightened as her manner became businesslike. Taking up the candle, she lit a lamp, then turned her mossy gaze back to her visitor. "Well, don't just stand there. Come in and let me have a look at you."

"By all means."

Again there was an amused, sardonic inflection in the gravelly timbre of his voice, but he dutifully stepped into the flickering circle of lamplight in the tiny dressing room, ducking his ebony head to miss the low beams.

Her robes rustling about her ankles, Genevieve circled the man, studying him carefully, frowning to herself.

He was of a height and broad-shouldered enough beneath his sturdy blue wool jacket to suit her purposes. The well-cut coat had once sported the braid and insignia of some horse regiment, but now only the remnants of poorly picked threads traced the outlines where they had once gleamed. His comfortable workman's trousers and military boots had seen better days, too, but even as Genevieve nodded to herself, she felt her heart sink with disappointment. Since Napoleon Bonaparte's surrender and exile to Elba in the spring of this victory year of 1814, scores of discharged soldiers drifted along the English highways looking for a return to a life that in many cases had disappeared completely. This man could hardly be the reliable replacement she needed.

Genevieve's frown deepened. Indeed, this fellow had the look of a gypsy about him. Despite his educated accent, there was something wild and untamed in the raven's wing sheen of his thick, shaggy hair and a raptor's predatory gleam behind his smiling affability. A ne'er-do-well if ever she saw one. Her instincts said he'd be nothing but trouble. Still . . .

Her glance scoured his angular face, searching the high cheekbones and dramatic hollows beneath. Straight, thick eyebrows framed piercing blue eyes surrounded by sooty lashes. His nose, though straight, was a bit too long, she thought critically, but balanced the width of his mouth and the squareness of his beard-shadowed jaw. Now the corners of his mouth quirked faintly upward at her scrutiny.

"Would you care to examine my teeth?" he asked gravely.

"I'll take your word they're sound." Rubbing the side of her bulbous nose, she mused aloud. "A bit too comely, perhaps, though that may draw the ladies, but the bearing is regal enough. Aye, you might make a king."

"I'm flattered to hear it."

With a start, she came out of her reverie, the impropriety of discussing a man's attributes as though he were a prime bit of cattle impinging on her consciousness at last. Added to that embarrassment was the sudden realization that her own attributes were scarcely at their best as she still wore the raiment from *Macbeth*, performed earlier in the evening by the company as part of a typical night's varied and extensive offering. As her hands flew to her face, her tone turned sharp.

"Have you any experience at this kind of thing?" she demanded.

"A bit." His answer was laconic, but edged with amusement.

Exasperated, Genevieve glared at him while deftly peeling away the bulging mass of her nose. "Has anyone ever told you that you're less than forthcoming, sir?"

His eyes widened as she laid the molded waxen nose on the cluttered table, then delicately scratched the end of her newly revealed proboscis, a feature that was short, straight, and aristocratic. She rapidly turned her attention to the removal of the hair-tufted wart that graced her round chin.

"Extraordinary," he murmured, then gave her another smile. "Actually, I'm usually quite glib when I'm at my best, which is to say when I've had a bit of the grape."

Alarm sparked suspicion in her green eyes. "You're not a drunkard too, are you?"

"Only when the circumstances warrant it." He chuckled, then raised a hand to forestall a heated rejoinder. "Calm yourself, Miss Maples. I assure you I can hold my liquor and that I've troden the boards often enough. I daresay I'd be adequate at any role you'd have me play."

"We can't pay much," Genevieve warned. She took a handful of oily lotion from a fat earthenware jar and slathered it over her face and hands, then reached for a linen towel, shrugging. "But then it isn't much of a part, is it? Only a minor king in the melodrama and a few small bits here and there. However, though we cannot boast a Siddons or Kean or one of the newer names like Cormick or Ingram, you'll find there is a certain amount of prestige involved in being a member of the Maples Company."

His tone was mild, but his blue eyes gleamed as she scrubbed her face. "There is?"

"Most assuredly! Such experience will see you in good stead should you decide to pursue the profession. As it is, you will have to learn while on the job, for we leave for our next engagement at Sadler's Wells tonight."

"So late?" His surprise showed.

"Actually, it will be early, once we're packed and on our way," she explained seriously, pausing in her greasy ablutions. "You may ride with the other members in the coach I've engaged."

" 'Tis a dangerous time of day to begin a journey. Whose idea is this folly? Yours?"

"Stuff and nonsense! There's nothing to fear. Are you such a coward, sir?"

His white grin flashed. "I admit it candidly. 'Tis my cowardice that's kept me alive. French infantry can scarcely hold a candle against our determined English cut-throats."

"You were with the Peninsular Campaigns?"

"For a time." His words were suddenly clipped.

"I've heard much—" she began curiously.

"Forgive me, Miss Maples, but I'm not given to reminiscences. Too bloody painful for a cowardly fellow like me, you know."

"Oh. I see." And she did, perhaps more than he wished.

Though he couldn't be older than thirty, experience beyond his years etched his tanned face. While the fullness of his lower lip hinted of latent sensuality, there was strength, even implacability, in the thin mobility of his upper lip. Whatever hardships he'd endured during the war, there were evidently painful memories attached. To hide her discomfiture at stumbling into his private sorrows, she reapplied her towel, mumbling from behind it.

"At any rate, I'll help you learn the part, for it's not overlong. You can try out before Grandpapa when we break the journey at midday."

"Miss Maples, if you'll just—"

"It's not that I doubt your ability to perform the part," she interrupted, folding the towel into precise squares with an efficient snap of her wrists. "But we can ignore neither Grandpapa nor tradition."

Reaching up, she plucked a trio of ivory pins from her hairline, then dragged the matted gray horsehair wig free. Cascades of autumn-hued ringlets spilled from their confinement, a fall of glorious, unruly chestnut curls that tumbled about her shoulders in an opulent display. With a sigh of relief, she tossed the wig beside the false nose and raised her face.

Bare at last of all artifice, the peaches-and-cream porcelain of her complexion glowed in the lamplight. A pronounced jawline and wide-set green eyes beneath decisively arched brows made her square face more striking than fashionably pretty. But it was the lush promise of her perfectly formed mouth that caught a man's attention, for it was richly curved and rosy and hinted at pleasures heretofore only imagined. The man standing before Miss Genevieve Maples suddenly found that he could imagine quite a lot.

"So if you want the job, you must agree to an audition," she continued. His look was so intent, her hands hesitated on the fastenings of her robe. "You do want it, don't you?"

Shifting his feet, he dragged a hand through his black hair and gave a wry grimace. "Well now, there's a question—"

"For if you don't," Genevieve interrupted severely, hesitated, then decided to lie through her teeth, "there are plenty of others who do."

"Oh, I'm certain of that."

"I dislike your tone, sir. We've had experience with other out-of-work drifters of your sort."

"And what sort is that?"

"The sort that begins in a blaze of glory, then when the work is hard, or the hours long, decides to disappear! I must have someone reliable. You see what a debacle Claude has caused this evening with his drinking. Why, he turned the melodrama into pure farce and completely overshadowed the success of the Scottish play! Thank God this is our last performance here. I told Claude if it happened again he'd get the boot—and this time I'm making it stick!"

"You seem to have rather a lot of authority around here."

"My grandfather has complete faith in my abilities as manager of the company," she returned stiffly. "I assure you we have traveled to Ireland and the most remote provinces this summer season under my direction without the slightest difficulty."

"Except for the importunate Claude." One dark eyebrow lifted, and he jerked his head slightly in the direction of the stage.

"Well, yes." Having to admit that to this gypsy-browed stranger changed her sweetly carved mouth into a mulish pucker.

If he only knew! A drunken actor had been the least of her troubles during the past grueling months. Grandpapa's ill health, the paucity of funds, one headache after another. This invitation from Sadler's Wells so near the end of the summer season was a godsend as far as Genevieve was concerned. She would be heartily glad to be back in London, no matter that they would be hard-pressed to make the journey from Dunstable's rustic provincial playhouse to Sadler's Wells with any time to spare before they opened. At least once in London she might have a chance to catch her breath and make some plans.

But arriving at London meant mounting a full complement for every performance, and that entailed replacing drunken Claude, admittedly something she'd tried to avoid, for where was she likely to find a replacement in the provinces? Taking a chance on this drifter might be a mistake, but time was short, she was desperate, and if she bullied him a bit, perhaps he'd stay the course. If only he weren't quite so perceptive!

With jerky, irritated movements, she shrugged out of her enveloping robe. The pale yellow muslin gown she wore beneath the costume was unadorned but deceptive in its simplicity, artfully cut to show off her lissome form while its high waist accentuated the rounded fullness of her bosom. She struggled to lift the heavy costume to a row of hooks that held an assortment of theatrical robes and gowns. "Blast!"

"Allow me." Reaching past her shoulder, he lifted the robe onto the hook for her.

Though it was nearly September and approaching the midnight finale of the evening's slate of performances, the day's heat lingered inside this shabby theater, and moisture dewed Genevieve's hairline. Suddenly aware of the man's closeness and the scents of shaving soap and musky male skin, Genevieve flushed and stepped away. Fanning her face with her palm, she gave a short, self-deprecating laugh.

"Thank you. Every time I play one of the weird sisters, I nearly smother!" Her wry grimace indicated her familiarity with such roles. To her way of thinking, she had inherited amazingly little of her famous progenitor's theatrical talent, so she hid that galling trick of fate behind roles that demanded heavy makeup, broad characterization, and only a modicum of lines. Thankfully, her true talents ran to other areas. She pointed at the bulky costume.

"That cloak must weigh a full stone! The next time I construct a witch's gown, I'll make certain it is as gossamer as a spider's web."

"You designed this?" His hand lingered on the rough sacking. "It's very effective, despite your complaints."

"Yes, I know." Everyone knew the Maples Company had the best wardrobe of any traveling troupe, and she would not be falsely modest about an accomplishment of which she was most proud. "I design all the Maples Company's costumes."

He flipped through the hanging wardrobe. "Impressive."

Though praising her work might only be a ploy to gain the job, still it gave Genevieve a pleasurable warmth to hear the admiration in his voice. To counteract its effect, she shrugged and made her tone brisk. " 'Tis but part of my job, though my favorite, I admit. Now, sir, your answer, if you please. Do you intend to join us or no?"

Coal-black brows drew together in thought. "Sadler's Wells, is it?"

"For a month's engagement. Then we'll see."

"But could a drifter abide that long in one place?" he asked lightly.

"That's one thing about the theater, you're hardly ever in one place long enough to take root." Though her words were just as light, there was a small, betraying catch in her voice.

"Still, I'd hate to disappoint you. Perhaps I'd better think on it, Miss Maples."

It took all of Genevieve's acting ability to keep her disappointment from her face. She should have known replacing Claude couldn't be this simple.

"As you wish. If you should change your mind, we leave on the hour. But if you miss this chance, you may not get another, and you look as though you could use the work," she pointed out, her gaze on his tattered coat.

His slow smile was somehow both charming and infuriating. "Your concern touches me dearly. I'll bear it in mind."

He turned to go, but she put out a hand to stay him. "Wait. If you're hungry, there's usually a supper basket after the performance. You're welcome to join us before you go . . ."

"Lovely and kind as well," he murmured.

Genevieve shifted uncomfortably under the warmth of

his gaze. "Though you're foolish to turn down honest employment, I'll not send one of the king's soldiers away in need."

"Thank you, I am well fed today."

"If you're certain, Mr.—I don't know your name!"

He hesitated, then the full force of his smile returned. "Call me Darcy."

Genevieve's eyebrows drew together. "Darcy? Darcy what?"

Bowing over her hand with surprising elegance, he pressed his lips to her knuckles. "Just Darcy, *chérie*."

"I've fired Claude."

"Hmmm?" Everett Maples raised his large, leonine head, smiled vaguely at his granddaughter, then bent his silvery pate back to the task that occupied him at the inn's crudely fashioned desk. "That's fine, my dear."

"A fine kettle of fish you mean!" Maebella Smythe snorted.

The Maples Company's wardrobe mistress stood half in and half out of the large trunk she was hurriedly packing. Her faded butter-colored curls escaped from under the ruffle of her mobcap as if they had a mind of their own. At two score and ten, she still had the smooth complexion and boundless energy of a woman half her age, despite a tendency to gain too much flesh. Placing a chubby hand in the small of her back, she stretched, her coffee-brown eyes bright with her usual no-nonsense pragmatism.

"Even sotted, Claude was a warm body on the stage. Now what will you do?"

With a quiet sigh, Genevieve folded the last of Everett's shirts, stroking the crisp, starched fabric in an automatic gesture of pleasurable appraisal before tucking them into his satchel. "Play the role myself, if worse comes to worse, I suppose, and shuffle the others around to accommodate the change."

"Breeches parts!" Maebella sniffed. " 'Tain't fittin' for a young lady."

"At twenty-four, I'm hardly an ingenue anymore," Genevieve said with a laugh. "Not that I have it in me to play Ophelia or Juliet."

"Nonsense," Maebella disagreed loyally. "Your grand-papa discourages you from playing more roles only as a poor means of protecting you from those young bucks who think an actress's virtue is fair game." She looked up from her packing in mild exasperation, hands full of unidenti-fiable bundles of old cloth, feathers, mismatched buttons, and leather patches. "And must I pack and repack this rubbish of yours?"

"You mustn't be so critical of my little treasures," Genevieve said with a laugh, giving her a hand at stowing away the articles. "You know full well how handy these bits and pieces come in from time to time."

"Never saw a child with such a penchant for collecting trash, and that's the God's truth! A regular magpie, though I'll admit you can do more for a costume with a scarf and a bit a fluff than any tailor can with an entire bolt of silk. I just wish your ingenuity ran to conjuring up sober actors when we need them."

"Don't worry about King Harold," Genevieve said. "Something will turn up. Why, I nearly hired a replace-ment this very evening."

Maebella slammed the lid on the trunk and flipped the latches. "Why 'nearly'?"

"He wouldn't have suited. A former soldier, with too much of the wanderlust in him."

To her supreme disgust, Genevieve found herself un-consciously rubbing the spot on her knuckles Darcy had kissed. So what if he was attractive in a rough-hewn way and could be almost charming? And so what if she was patriotically sympathetic toward a homeless former sol-dier? It was still best to steer clear of such a rogue and just as well her offer of employment hadn't tempted him. She already had enough problems. Determinedly, she put Darcy out of her mind, snapped Everett's satchel shut, then moved to the old man's side.

"Grandpapa? Are you ready? The coach I hired will be here soon."

"Don't bother me now, gel," Everett boomed in the bass voice that had first made him famous on the Dublin stage. "I've almost got it."

With utmost care, he rearranged on the desktop the contents of a small chest. There, a line of jeweled necklaces; here, a pile of gaudy brooches and pewter buckles; a precision arrangement of blunted daggers; a small pyramid of gilded crowns and diadems. They were worthless trinkets all, a collection of props used by the Maples Company, but of late they'd become her grandfather's growing obsession.

"But it's almost time to go," Genevieve said briskly. Accustomed throughout her lifetime to Everett's successive eccentric interests, she'd paid this one little attention, certain it would go the same way as had his insistence that snakeskin garters prevented joint pain, an experimental diet of ale and raw eggs, last year's intensive study of famous magicians and sorcerers, and his belief that the Holy Grail was buried under the obelisks at Stonehenge.

"Can't you see I'm busy here?" Everett demanded. His spiky silver brows drew together into a ferocious line over his beaky nose. He looked down at his piles in consternation. "There's something wrong, if only I can find it . . ."

Genevieve exchanged a helpless, puzzled look with Maebella. Usually Everett's hobbies were harmless, but lately his moods had been erratic. Tonight Everett had been Macbeth incarnate, never bobbling a line, never missing a cue, but off stage his preoccupations were making him vague and sometimes even irrational. Genevieve had depended on Everett since losing her parents to smallpox when she was only seven, and the possibility that her once robust grandfather might be failing physically frightened her.

Although Everett was the most fondly affectionate grandfather, growing up between boarding schools and holidays spent on tour with the troupe had made Genevieve's a vagabond life without roots. The company's fortunes were always uncertain, some years fat, others lean, according to the public whim, and Everett's skills as manager were questionable at best, even with Maebella's help. That was why Genevieve had left school at seventeen to take over the everyday responsibilities of running the company. Even when she was that young, her practical skills and sensible nature had proven a valuable asset. Now, seven years later, she was suddenly aware that, at sixty-three, Everett was finding life increasingly hard. The push of the summer tour had made his lapses worse.

If they could only get settled in London and establish a routine, then he'd get better, Genevieve assured herself. For an instant she allowed herself to hope he'd agree to retire. Their carefully hoarded savings, on deposit at a London bank, might be stretched to purchase a modest cottage in a quiet suburb of the metropolis. With her flair for design and Maebella's skill with a needle, they could open the small dressmaking establishment she'd dreamed of and settle down at last. London was her beacon of hope.

"Don't fret, Grandpapa," Genevieve soothed, massaging the old man's neck in an affectionate habit of long standing. "You can't think because you're tired tonight, but you'll be able to sleep a bit in the coach, won't you? You've always been able to do that."

"I know there's something wrong," Everett muttered again, staring at the assortment of jewelry. "Damned ruffians! Someone's been in my things again!"

"Might a wee dram of the innkeeper's best brandy relax the master?" Maebella suggested.

"Yes, that's a good idea," Genevieve replied, handing the older woman Everett's satchel.

"I'll just be fetching it then," Maebella said. "I'll call when the coach is ready."

Genevieve shooed Maebella toward the door, then turned back to Everett, her tone bracing. "Grandpapa, if you could tell me what the problem is, then perhaps I could help."

Unaccountably, the old man's hazel eyes began to water. "No, darling Genny, there's no help for it, none at all."

"I'm sure it's not as desperate as you think," Genevieve replied, alarmed.

"But nothing belongs, don't you see?" His ruddy face became more and more florid with his growing agitation and her failure to understand his meaning.

Genevieve normally paid little attention to the contents of the box, so she couldn't be sure if certain pieces were new or merely unfamiliar, but she helped sort through the jumble as best she could. "This brooch goes here, and you wanted to separate the chains, didn't you? And where did these come from? Have you been shopping for new trappings for us?"

She picked up a surprisingly fine strand of fake pearls, a tarnished chain attached to a bell-shaped stamp covered with old wax, a magnificent bracelet of paste diamonds, and a set of shiny bangles so bright they were obviously made of brass.

"They aren't mine," Everett said, his voice strained.

"But they're in the box—"

"I tell you I've never seen any of it before!" Everett jumped to his feet, the legs of his chair scraping discordantly across the rough plank floor. "Take it away, I say! Take it all away!"

"Of course I will, but don't you think—"

"Away, blast your eyes!" With a snarl, Everett swept everything off the desk. Daggers and chains, crowns and beads smashed to the floor in a tangled heap. Everett sank his broad hands into his silvery mane and tugged madly, his face contorted with anger and desperation. "Cursed be this empty noggin! Ye fates may as well take my tongue as my memory! Either way I'm a dead man!"

Amazed and horrified by her grandfather's violent outburst, Genevieve fell to her knees and hastily scraped all the offending trinkets together. She shoved everything into the small painted chest, then closed the cracked and splintered lid on the falsely glittering mass and stashed it in the waiting trunk. Rising, she hastened toward Everett in an attempt at pacification. "There, Grandpapa, it's all right now. They're gone."

Everett's lower lip trembled, and he opened his arms to her. She went to him immediately. Though now her medium height nearly matched his, she fitted herself against his broad chest and comfortably rounded belly just as she had when she was a little girl. But who took more comfort from the embrace she couldn't be certain.

"Ah, Genny," he said in a gruff tone, stroking her bright curls, "you're a good girl, you are. I love you best, you know that, don't you?"

"Yes, Grandpapa. I love you, too."

"I'd never do anything to hurt you, would I?"

"No, Grandpapa, never."

"That's all right, then." He exhaled on a deep, gusty breath, relieved by her assurances. As he sank down heavily in his chair again, Maebella appeared with a tankard and the hostler's sleepy-eyed son.

"They're ready to load the master's trunk now," she announced, and pushed the tankard into Everett's hands. "Here, sir. Something to warm you on the way."

"I thank you, Bella."

While the hostler's son manhandled the trunk away, Everett quaffed the contents of the tankard with lusty enjoyment. When he finished, he smacked his lips and looked at the two women expectantly.

"Well?" he boomed, his voice strong again. "Are we going to London or ain't we?"

Still shaken and now disconcerted by his quicksilver mood swing, Genevieve nevertheless made good use of it, grabbing up her gloves and her precious sketchbox and tying on her straw summer bonnet. Handing Everett his cane, she hurried him down the narrow stairs and through the taproom where, despite the lateness of the hour, the proprietor was doing a boisterous business.

In the courtyard, two shabby hired coaches waited in the flare of torches. Milling nearby were the other members of the troupe: Arthur and Betty Donegal, the young couple who played the romantic leads; Winfred Farnham and Peter Hite, the tragedy boys; Audrey Lincoln and Penelope Johnstone, the comediennes; Mike Murphy, the young stagehand who filled in wherever he was needed. This complement formed the backbone of the company, and from its members in their various guises came everything from Shakespearean tragedy to burletta to melodrama. Now, with yawns and mumbled complaints, they waited to board the coaches.

Worried that in the rush to leave, something essential had been forgotten, Genevieve double-checked their luggage, making certain the trunks of costumes and props were on board. In her usual efficient manner, she spoke to each player, jollying the grumpy along, cajoling the stubborn, placating delicate egos until each had found a seat that suited within the first vehicle. Under the dour, impatient glares of the drivers and coachmen, she got Everett and Maebella settled in the second, with young Mike atop with the driver. Breathless from the rushing, she prepared to mount the coach step herself. But the step was high and treacherous and the narrowness of her skirt rather impractical for such a maneuver, so she stumbled, reached for the coach door, and grabbed a handful of linen shirt instead.

"Easy, Little General, I've got you." Hard hands closed around her waist, lifting her easily from the brink of disaster.

"I beg your—Darcy!" Genevieve found her footing and hastily released the death-grasp she had on the front of his shirt. His sudden, catlike appearance disconcerted her yet again, and she hid her fluster in an irritated show of brushing aside his hands. "Thank you, sir, but I'm quite capable of entering a carriage under my own power."

"Indeed, 'twould have been a sight to see if you'd tumbled in upon your pretty—er, nose." His laugh was quick and soft, and his provocative glance took in that part of her anatomy upon which she would have undoubtedly landed.

"You are not a gentleman to say so." Her voice was stiff as she fussed with her skirts and straightened her gloves, more unnerved than she wished to admit.

Under the moonless heavens he looked even larger than he had in the tiny dressing room, all long legs and broad shoulders, utterly masculine in every cord and sinew. Genevieve refused to acknowledge a thrill of secret, feminine pleasure at seeing him again.

"I'm forced to agree," he replied, his tone amiable. "But I can also testify that I've never seen a lady marshal her troops with such flair as you. A regular Wellington of the fairer sex!"

"Such compliments must surely keep you from all company but your own," she replied tartly, turning again toward the step. "I extend my sympathies for your unfortunate lack of wit, but as you can see, we're on the point of leaving so if you'll excuse me . . ."

"Might there be room for a sorry excuse of an actor?"

Genevieve froze, then turned slowly back. "I have no time for games, Mr. Darcy. Have you something to say?"

"Only that I've been giving your proposition some consideration. If I and my man"—he raised his hand, and a balding, pug-faced man in a workman's rough tweed coat led a pair of surprisingly fine-blooded horses out of the stable's shadow—"may ride along, perhaps we can come to some agreement."

"A simple yes or no is all that's needed," Genevieve said, angry heat building along her cheekbones. "If you're trying to use this as an excuse for a free passage—"

"You've heard that there's safety in numbers, Miss Maples. And, as I happen to be going in your direction, what harm is there in a little friendly companionship? After all, I've never served under so fair a general, and I might be persuaded to join you if you use all your charm. I know how badly you need my services."

Genevieve nearly choked. "Of all the insufferable, insolent—"

Everett Maples rapped his cane imperiously on the coach roof and leaned out to interrupt her. "Genny-girl, are we going or staying? And who's this fellow?"

Genevieve's jaw snapped shut, and she ground her teeth around her answer. "No one of consequence, Grandpapa. I'm coming."

Darcy stepped past her and offered his hand to Everett. "I've been speaking to your granddaughter about taking Claude's place, sir."

"What? Splendid!" Everett took the proffered hand and wrung it soundly. "Do step aboard, young man. We'll discuss this as we ride, eh, Genny?"

"But Grandpapa—"

"You heard your grandfather. Don't argue with your elders," Darcy ordered with a smirk that made Genevieve's palm itch with the need to slap it off his handsome face. He turned to his companion. "Taffy, tie Diable and your gelding to the rear, then perhaps you can find a place in the bonnet for a nap."

Taffy saluted. "Aye, Cap. I'll take a chance to rest me peepers any day!"

"Shall we go, Miss Maples?" Darcy asked politely, indicating the open coach door.

Genevieve looked at her grandfather's expectant face and shuddered at the thought of causing a scene that might bring on another one of his mystifying tirades. For his sake she could swallow her aggravation, at least for a time. Forcing a smile past her tight lips, she nodded and allowed Darcy to hand her into the coach. When he took his place beside her on the seat, however, she inched into the opposite corner and tucked her skirt beneath herself in an effort to show her disdain. Whatever his motives, he would find no satisfaction from her! And just as soon as they reached Sadler's Wells, she'd make it her business to discover what kind of game this rascal was really playing.

But as Everett introduced Maebella, then proceeded to

carry on a desultory conversation with Darcy, ranging from the latest victory festivities to the price of a good bottle of Madeira, Genevieve could find no fault in her unwelcome passenger's manners. Aside from adjusting his long legs to provide her more room, he barely addressed a word to her, and soon the sonorous conversation and the swaying of the coach combined with the lateness of the hour to lull Genevieve into a light doze.

She came awake with a start to find herself leaning heavily against a solidly male shoulder.

"Oh, I—I beg your pardon!" Mortified, she straightened abruptly, thankful that both Everett and Maebella had also dropped off and now continued to snore quietly in the opposite seat despite the bumping, lurching ride.

"There's no need, Little General," Darcy said, gazing down at her with only the reflected gleam of the coach lanterns to light his blue eyes. "You may presume on our friendship any time you choose."

"You say the most presumptuous absurdities." With a glance at their sleeping companions, she made her voice low. "I see nothing that can be termed friendship in our acquaintance."

"Yet."

His single word was a warning and a promise warmed by the heat of his languid smile. At a loss, she stared at him. The bald statement of his interest set up a frisson within her, a shiver of physical excitement, fascination, and fear. She knew nothing of this man! How could she feel such strong attraction for a virtual stranger? Aghast at the turn of her thoughts, she drew back even further into the corner.

"You're crushing your bonnet." He teasingly tugged the satin ribbons knotted under her chin. "Wouldn't you be more comfortable with it off?"

In a daze, her green eyes wide with confusion, she slipped off the bonnet and laid it in her lap.

"You see?" he asked gently. "We are not destined to be at odds at every turn."

She flushed. "You may mock me as you will, Mr. Darcy, but I take my responsibilities seriously. I'm trying to keep this company together as well as I can, and I fear that hiring a homeless vagabond who cannot make up his mind, much less keep a commitment, may not serve our best interests."

"Who said that I was homeless?"

"But—" She looked again at the thread-picked coat, her practiced eye taking in the once-fine cut and quality of the garment, now worn with age. "I assumed from your appearance . . ."

"A woman who can play *Macbeth*'s witch knows better than most that appearances can be deceiving," he chided.

"I beg your pardon. But if you're not without a place to go, as are so many returning military, there is even less reason for you to throw your lot in with a group of traveling players."

"Ah. Are you always so suspicious?"

"I prefer to think of it in terms of self-protection. Well?"

He lifted his shoulders in a half shrug. "Perhaps after having seen the world, I find the life of a farmer stultifying. Not everyone finds his home a pleasant place, Miss Maples."

"Perhaps if you'd never had one, you'd be more appreciative of your good fortune, Mr. Darcy." The longing in her voice surprised them both.

Darcy's dark countenance sobered. Reaching out, he touched a ringlet of her bright hair as it fell forward over her shoulder. " 'Tis ironic, is it not? Home is a prison to me, yet you would exchange your wings, your freedom, for those bars."

"There are worse fetters."

"Such as?"

"I should be ashamed to admit I neglected my responsibility to those who care for me. Does anyone need you at home, Mr. Darcy?" Her words were breathy with the effort it took to remain calm as he absently toyed with her hair.

"Thank God, no. To be honest, my father, for all his good intentions, is most relieved when my visits come to an end. He's never known quite what to make of his prodigal, you understand."

"I understand very well," Genevieve muttered fervently, sympathizing with the elder Mr. Darcy. She reached up to push his hand away. "Stop that."

"Be easy, sweet Genny," he whispered, bending close. "You have nothing to fear from me."

"Yet." The ominous overtone of her murmured response was lost as his mouth softly covered hers.

Genevieve had been kissed before, but only groping, adolescent experiments in the backstage shadows. This melting, seductive sweetness was totally new to her. The shameful and very real possibility of discovery mingled with the taste of him to produce a surging excitement that made her heart leap almost out of her chest. In terrorized wonder she raised her hand to his stubble-roughened cheek, not knowing whether to push him away or pull him closer. When he lifted his head, her fingers remained in the deep groove beside his mouth where his pulse throbbed in time with hers.

In the near-darkness, his eyes glittered, and he breathed her name, "Genevieve . . ."

The shrill neigh of a horse, a harsh shout, and the jolt and jingle of a coach being brought up short broke the spell. The sudden jostling woke Everett and Maebella. In something of a panic, Genevieve flung herself at the window.

"What in heaven's name—"

A pistol shot cracked, and above the melee came the hollow demand: "Stand and deliver!"

Maebella shrieked and threw her apron over her head. "God preserve us—bandits!"

"Laugh's on them," Everett grunted, more concerned

about the state of his wrinkled waistcoat. "Ain't' got a copper farthing betwixt us, right, Genny-girl?"

"They've stopped the first coach," Genevieve reported. "What shall we do? Darcy—"

She swung around in complete astonishment as Darcy vanished out the opposite door, leaving behind only the echo of a low whistle. "What? Darcy, where are you going? Don't leave us!"

But he'd disappeared into the night, soundless as a shadow, and outside, the highwaymen ordered their driver down to open the coach door. Genevieve's surprise gave way to fury at his abandonment. She was the worst kind of a fool to think a single kiss made a man a hero. After all, Darcy had claimed he was a coward. Unexpectedly, she laughed.

Now she believed him.

Chapter 2

How the bloody hell did I get myself into this?

Bryce Darcy Cormick cursed silently and inched himself on his stomach through the brambles and muck that mired the bottom of the roadside ditch. Thorns raked his cheek, and something reptilian hissed a threat and rustled through the tall dark grass. Bryce mouthed another silent obscenity. No doubt about it, the price of a bit of flirtation with Miss Genevieve Maples was rapidly becoming too dear.

Though he'd come direct from his father's home at Huxford's insistence to seek out the Maples Company, he'd never expected to find a chestnut-haired costumer beneath a witch's guise. He'd left Clorinda behind only a day ago, yet her brown-haired prettiness faded in his memory, a pallid comparison to Genevieve's vibrancy. And those luscious lips . . .

He didn't intend to accept Genevieve's offer, but he couldn't resist temptation in the form of the most kissable woman he'd ever seen, either. And besides, a man who was contemplating matrimony deserved one final fling, didn't he? Well, it looked as though the Almighty was punishing his impudence.

Slowly, painfully, Bryce wormed closer to the second of two sentries guarding this strip of wooded highway. Beyond the guard, the pair of coaches with their nervous horses and the clump of frightened passengers blocked the narrow road. At this point, it was more a tunnel through the black Epping Forest than a thoroughfare, and a place so perfect for an ambush Bryce might have chosen it himself on another occasion. One bandit held the victims at gunpoint while two others methodically plundered the heaps of tumbled baggage. From the other side of the overhung road, there came a low night bird's call.

Taffy, Bryce thought in relief. *God bless his skinned head!*

There wasn't a better man in a pinch than Taffy McKee, and they'd been through enough close scrapes over the years together to prove it, first on the dusty Spanish plains and later under the nose of the emperor himself. Sometimes Bryce thought the wiry Welshman could read his mind. Giving a low answering whistle, he fervently hoped this was one of them.

Bryce closed his eyes to clear his night vision, simultaneously fighting down the incipient nausea that clenched his gut before every battle. God, he hated this! It was too reminiscent of dark things he was trying to forget. Opening his eyes, he carefully kept his gaze focused away from the coach lamps and toward the rough-looking individual scuffing the gravel of the roadbed not two feet away. The ruffian clutched his huge horse pistol carelessly, more interested in the panorama of actors handing over their pocket watches and weeping actresses stripping off their rings and beads than on his assignment.

Everett Maple's deep voice boomed through the heavy night air. "By God, you villains! Unhand my valuables!"

Genevieve's melodious tones interrupted her grandfather, the words too low for Bryce to understand, but her angry demands clear enough. The twit was in a dispute with the hulking leader of this desperate band over a small, battered chest he'd just removed from a fractured trunk.

Bryce stifled a groan. Who the hell did she think she was, some sort of bloody Joan of Arc? Didn't she have better sense than to try to play heroine against hungry men who had nothing to lose? At least he could make use of the distraction she was causing.

With a stealth he'd learned as a boy on the wharves of Marseilles, he felled the guard soundlessly with a blow to the back of the neck. Bryce caught the man before he hit the ground, grabbed his pistol, then rolled him into the shallow ditch. He sensed a flicker of movement on the other side of the coaches and knew Taffy had succeeded in a similar operation. Oblivious, the bearded leader of the band continued to argue with Genevieve while one of his cohorts held his pistol on the timorous group.

"I told you it's all worthless!" she insisted as the bandit leader clawed through the contents of the chest, growling his disappointment. "Paste and tin, all of it! You have everything else. What harm will it do to let an old man keep his trinkets?"

"Don't try to bargain with these thieving monkeys!" Everett shouted, lunging forward with his cane. "*En garde,* you fiend!"

The lead highwayman hastily dropped the chest at Genevieve's feet, his look one of comical consternation at Everett's Falstaffian challenge. He narrowly missed being hit by a clumsy swipe of the cane. "Hey!"

"I'll teach you—" Everett grunted.

The leader snatched the cane out of Everett's hands, then used it to punch the old man in the chest. As Everett fell, Genevieve shrieked and launched herself at her grandfather's tormentor.

Bryce heaved a disgusted sigh. *Oh, great. Enter the hero, stage right.*

Stepping out of the shadows, he fired the pistol, rather surprised but thankful it was properly primed and loaded. The ball hit one robber in the shoulder, toppling him over like a Punch and Judy puppet. With a surprised roar, the bandit leader cuffed Genevieve to the ground and swung on this new threat, pulling his own pistol from his belt. The remaining thief raised his weapon at Bryce, but was

flattened the next moment by young Mike's flying tackle
and an avalanche of furious actors.

"Stand where you are!" roared the hulking highwayman over the confusion, training his weapon on Bryce.

"I wouldn't advise it, friend," Bryce returned amiably,
steadily advancing.

"Oh, ye wouldn't, would ye now?" A snaggled grin
flashed behind the bandit's scraggly beard. "Carp! Twig-
gins! Get over here!"

"I'm afraid your friends are out of commission. Best be
calling the whole thing off," Bryce advised.

"Hold, I said!" The leader's smile faded, and his
weapon wobbled betrayingly. At his feet, Genevieve
moaned and struggled to her hands and knees. "Impudent
bastard, ain't ye? What's to keep me from plugging you
here and now?"

Bryce paused a few feet away, the spent pistol held easily at his side. "Maybe the fact that my friend has a gun
pointed at the back of your skull this very moment?"

"Haw! You expect me to believe that rubbish?"

"Believe it, laddie." Taffy's words echoed from out of
the darkness, followed by the ominous click of a pistol
being cocked.

Panic flickered behind the bandit's black eyes, but with
the resourcefulness of a desperate man, he saw his chance
and took it. Reaching down, he caught the back of Genevieve's neck in one meaty paw and pressed his pistol to
her jugular.

"Back off, I said, both of you!"

Bryce froze. "Easy, friend. All we want is to be on our
way. Accept you've caught the worst of it tonight, and
we'll call it a draw and leave peacefully."

"Draw, my arse!" The bandit spit in the dirt, then
waved his weapon at the rest of the terrorized passengers.
"Get around there, all of ye!"

Reluctantly, they complied, Winfred and Arthur helping
Mike to his feet, leaving a very battered and unconscious
thief bleeding in the dust. At Maebella's frantic urgings,

the women assisted a dazed Everett. On her knees with
her back to the bandit, Genevieve winced and cried out at
the cruel pressure of his fingers on her slender neck. As
the others moved into the indicated position, Bryce met
her frightened gaze.

Now what, hero? his inner demon jeered. For once, his
recklessness promised the direst consequences.

The bearded bandit squeezed Genevieve's neck even
harder, evoking her whimper, his hard eyes never leaving
Bryce. "Tell your friend to come out where I can see him.
Now!"

"Taffy." Bryce gave an imperceptible nod. Silently,
Taffy appeared on the outer rim of the group.

"Now drop that pistol and kick it to me," growled the
bearded one.

"Aw, Cap!" Taffy protested, deeply chagrined.

"Now." The bandit pointed his pistol at Bryce's forehead.

"Do as he says," Bryce ordered grimly. On the edge
of his senses, he knew that Genevieve's fingers were
clenching and unclenching in the dusty gravel. Her pain
pierced him like a blade, but outside he retained an icy
aloofness that let him meet the bandit's black gaze unperturbed. "Now release the lady, friend."

"The gun first."

Taffy shrugged, then lobbed the pistol in a high arc
toward the woods. Everyone's eyes followed its path, and
only Bryce saw Genevieve swiftly twist and plunge a dusty,
blunted dagger into the highwayman's lower thigh. Before
the bandit truly registered her unexpected attack, Bryce's
fist smashed into his mouth, cutting off his cry of pain.
Genevieve wrenched free as the two men fell together,
grappling for the gun.

It was really no contest, for Bryce had the superior
training, the greater will . . . and he fought dirty.

One swift knee to the bandit's crotch, then an uppercut
to the jaw was all it took to double the thief over and
dispatch him completely.

Bryce rose to his feet over the prostrate villain, and a ragged cheer went up from his audience. Flexing his sore knuckles, Bryce pivoted, seeking his next victim—and jerked Genevieve to her feet.

"That was a damned foolish stunt!" His voice grated like broken glass.

"I—I—" Shivering with reaction, she swayed drunkenly, gulping for breath. Bryce pulled her against his chest, supporting her with one arm, neither one of them caring if the mud and filth on his coat ruined her yellow gown.

"You're all right?" he demanded gruffly. "He didn't hurt you?"

"No, not really." She shuddered. "But I was so frightened."

"Nonsense. I've never seen such a cool head. Where'd you get that knife?"

"Grandpapa's box of props. It was on the ground . . ."

Incredulous, he snapped at her. "You tried to stab that bastard with a *fake* knife? Are you crazy?"

She drew back, meeting his irate gaze without flinching. "Well, I had to do something, didn't I? He was going to shoot you!"

Her tone was so indignant, he laughed and shook his head in disbelief. "General, I didn't know you cared."

"I—I misjudged you, Darcy," she confessed softly. "When you left, I thought the worst. But you saved us all. Mayhap I've been mistaken about other things, too."

Oh, hell. Genevieve's expression of dawning adoration played havoc with the tattered remnants of Bryce's conscience.

"Don't go sentimental on me, General," he said, releasing her. "I was watching out for my own ass. And I thought you were above a fit of maidenly vapors."

"I am!" Stung by his mockery, she straightened her spine, her soft expression vanishing in a glare of exasperation.

"Come on, then. Your grandfather needs you, and the

others can load the coaches. Taffy and I have some work to do before our friends here recover themselves.''

Reminded of her duties, Genevieve hurried to Everett's side, and moments later began shooting orders to restore their possessions and get everyone back into the coaches. With the drivers' and Taffy's help, Bryce saw their assailants securely tied and left to lick their wounds under a sprawling oak until a magistrate from the next town might be sent to retrieve them, but while this was carried out, old habits of suspicion gnawed at him like rats at a cheese rind.

Usually a robbery of this nature was a quick hit, snatch the purses and then be gone. Why had these thieves risked discovery and ultimate failure to search the baggage? Bryce's questions to the sullen, vanquished highwaymen met with only grunts or curses.

''You say no one put you up to this?'' he demanded of the leader, whose resentful face was still pasty gray in the faint glimmer of dawn.

''Nobody.''

Bryce hunkered down on his haunches beside the man, idly turning the thief's own dagger over and over in his hands. His voice was companionable, almost friendly. ''Really? You made a mistake searching the baggage, didn't you? What were you looking for?''

''Usual booty.''

''And you're a bad liar, friend.''

''Go to hell,'' the would-be thief snarled.

Bryce's smile was chilly. ''I've already been there. But I'll be glad to hurry you on your way if you don't tell me the truth.''

''So what?'' Defiance and resignation mingled in the leader's black eyes. ''Just as soon die now as at the end of a noose later.''

There was a note of desperation and despair in those words that echoed along Bryce's memory. He'd been to that well and drunk the same bitter draft himself. He changed his tack. ''Been to the war, have you?''

"Aye. Same as you."

"And the others?"

"Them, too. Never thought them days fightin' Boney would look so good."

Bryce rose to his feet. "You made a mistake tonight."

"Maybe the last one."

"Maybe not."

Removing a sovereign from his pocket, Bryce impaled it on the bole of the tree with the point of the dagger. "From one old campaigner to another. To pay for a physician—or an undertaker."

Turning, Bryce walked back toward the coaches. Taffy fell in step with him.

"You givin' those cutthroats a chance?"

"If they work at it, they may escape before the magistrates arrive."

"Why?"

"They're amateurs, Taffy. Not like you and me." Something dark moved across Bryce's face, then vanished at the appearance of wry half grin. "Hanging for a first offense—especially a botched one—is rather drastic, don't you think? Maybe this experience will make them seek a new line of work."

Taffy squinted against the growing brightness, his brown eyes amazed. "Cor, Captain! You ain't going soft at this late date, are ye?"

Bryce's gaze swept to Genevieve waiting beside the coach with her grandfather. When she caught his eye, a delicate peachy blush shaded her cheeks. She gave him a tentative smile.

Soft? Bryce wondered.

There hadn't been an ounce of softness in his life for longer than he could remember. Maybe that's why he found Genevieve's tender mouth so tempting—it represented things he'd never had or deserved. And now she thought he was some sort of hero. Damn. If he had any decency at all, he'd tell her the truth. That would put her back up, ignite the fire in her eyes again, maybe give her some protection from his blackguard inclinations. *So noble!* sneered that inner voice again. Who was he saving—her or himself? He was a fool, dithering over whether to charge or retreat.

Bryce saw Genevieve's smile fade and her even white teeth tug uncertainly at the fullness of her lower lip. As he imagined himself doing the same, a peculiar weightlessness burned low in his belly. What the hell. Despite well-meaning pressure from both his father and his half sister, he'd made no promises to Clorinda North yet, and he had reason to explore Genevieve's talents—in more ways than one. What matter if he played this minor farce through? He'd long ago learned to take advantage of every situation.

"No, Sergeant," Bryce said slowly, "I haven't gone soft. The truth is, I've been past redemption for a very long time."

Weary, but still overexcited by their narrow brush with danger, the Maples Company broke their journey at mid-afternoon to take dinner at a tiny inn located in the quaint village of Wayside. Though they were still hours from Sadler's Wells, the rest of the journey could be accomplished on the well-trafficked main roads. Genevieve meant to arrive that evening, however late, so that they might get settled before their scheduled performance the following night. But even dauntless actors needed to rest and eat.

They dined on roasted beef, brown bread, and ale, with apple tart to finish. While waiting for fresh horses, they wandered in drowsy groups down the grassy banks behind the inn to the edge of a picturesque stream. Everett and Maebella found seats on a sunny, rustic bench, and soon Mike brought forth a flute and Audrey gave them a gay tune.

There was a renewed sense of camaraderie among the company for their having shared a dangerous adventure, and a certain deference on everyone's part for the skill and courage of their newest member. With crossed arms and a faint smile on his handsome face, Darcy listened to the song and then to Arthur's and Winfred's hair-raising tales of similar incidents. Whatever reservations still lingered in Genevieve's mind appeared totally insubstantial in the face of such overwhelming acceptance.

Finding her gaze too often on the object of her thoughts, Genevieve slipped away to a stand of willows farther down the bank. With the ribbons of her bonnet looped over her elbow, she indulged in an unaccustomed moment of solitude and contemplated the morass of emotional turmoil that had once been her sensible brain. Though Darcy had ridden his own mount after leaving the scene of the holdup, she had been as aware of his presence as if he still sat beside her in the coach. He had to be the most thoroughly exasperating man she'd ever known—and also the most fascinating.

Steady on, she cautioned herself. A trio of fat white ducks floated across the stream's sparkling surface, and she reached into her pocket for a crust of bread she'd saved. She tossed crumbs to the quacking threesome, automatically stooping to retrieve several molted feathers to add to her trove of useful rubbish just like the magpie Maebella accused her of emulating. Absently stroking the feathers across her cheek, she gave herself a stern lecture.

Just because Darcy had acted courageously, coming to her rescue like a Lancelot, it didn't mean she felt more than gratitude toward him. And his simply stealing a kiss didn't indicate anything, either, other than that he was an unconscionable flirt. Nothing changed the fact that he was as much a rootless wanderer as she was, and even though he might be a valuable replacement for Claude, he could offer her nothing she really needed on a personal level. As pleasurable as a flirtation with such a man might be, it was dangerous to wager one's heart on a scoundrel's smile. Yes, Genevieve decided, a woman simply had to be practical about these matters.

A sudden sneeze brought on by a feathery tickle caught her by surprise. Smiling slightly at herself, she ran the feathers between her fingers, enjoying their softness. By nature she was a tactile person with a well-developed sense of touch, and sometimes she wondered at the almost sinful pleasure she took from the feel of things—the delicacy of a flower petal, the lushness of the heavy velvet in one of her costumes, the whisper of a warm afternoon breeze against her moist skin. But there was a practical side to her inclination, for even limp feathers might be trimmed and dyed to grace a bonnet or a savage's headdress, combining frugality and imagination in her couturiere's art. With a quiet laugh for her own idiosyncrasy, she tucked the feathers into her pocket, then strolled beneath the faintly clacking shower of willow fronds to lean against the tree's mottled trunk and watch the water.

"Do you wish for company, or should I leave you to your solitude?"

Genevieve looked over her shoulder at Darcy. "You know, I've almost become accustomed to your creeping up on me like that."

He grinned. "Miss Maples, I do not creep."

"On the contrary, you creep very well for a man of your size, rather like one of those African lions one sees in the zoological exhibit at the Tower of London. Although I was thankful for your talent this morning, it's extremely disconcerting in polite company."

"I'll make an effort to stumble over my feet whenever I approach you from now on."

She turned her face back toward the water, attempting a cool façade to mask the sudden erratic tendencies of her heart. "I'd appreciate the warning."

He moved to her side, surveying the little stream and the dappling of light and shadow under the willows. "A pretty scene."

"Mmm. I'd like to sketch it. But I'd add a boat there." She pointed. "And maybe a little boy with a fishing pole just on that stone."

"Ah. Someone to ride in the boat."

"Certainly not!" Her smile turned impish, and she shot

him a sideways glance. "My little boy is much too young for boating. But he may take his string of trout home to his proud mother. Perhaps I'll even draw her, waiting on that hill over there."

"And where is the father of this fortunate lad?" asked Darcy, playing her game.

"Working hard in the fields, thinking about his family and a fish dinner!" she said with a laugh.

"Are you artist enough to bring such a delightful fantasy to life?"

"Would that I were so fortunate," she murmured obliquely. Shaking off the phantasm, she steered away from personal revelations by taking up business concerns. "In all the confusion, you haven't had a chance to learn our lines."

"I thought you meant me to audition for your grandfather."

"After what you did this morning? Grandpapa is totally besotted by your bravery and heroism. You may spout Lord Byron's new poetry instead of your part for all he cares. However, *I* expect you to know your lines. Now, while we've a moment, let me explain the story . . ."

For the next few minutes, behind the screen of willows, Genevieve explained the melodrama's plot, Darcy's action and stage cues, and had him repeat the few lines required of him. To her dismay, his declamation was wooden and inept, his actions awkward, even comical. For a man with as much innate self-assurance as Darcy, she found this turn of events astonishing.

"Not very good, is it?" Darcy asked after a particularly ear-wrenching rendition of his final line. "You'd better concentrate on finding someone else for King Harold."

"No, no. Maybe comedy is your strength, but I'm sure you can do this," Genevieve hastened to reassure him. Groaning to herself, she knew she'd never find another replacement in time. She simply had to work with the King Harold she had. "You're just tense, that's all. Maybe if you moved around some . . . Here, let's review the sword fight."

Reaching up into the tree, she snapped off a willow branch and passed it to him. "Use this as the sword. Now, here's what you do . . ."

But Darcy seemed even more awkward than ever, slicing the air with his branch and jumping about like an overgrown bullfrog.

"No, not like that!" Genevieve snapped at last. "How came a soldier to know so little of swordsmanship?"

"I served in the calvary. Ask me to ride a horse."

"Never mind! Do it as I showed you, Darcy."

Slipping off his coat, he tossed in onto a handy branch. Blotting his perspiring face on the sleeve of his openthroated shirt, he grinned apologetically. "I'm trying, Little General. If you could show me once more . . . ?"

Genevieve set aside her bonnet, then positioned herself at his side, showing him the footwork, stretching out her arm along his much longer, brawnier one, using her body as a shadow of his to keep him on track. With her back to his front, arm outstretched, she was entirely too conscious of the rocklike solidity of his physique, the crisp sprinkling of dark chest hair revealed by the vee of his shirt, and the musky scent of virile male sweat. She tried to concentrate on his movements, but it seemed that she could feel the heat of his body straight through her muslin gown and petticoats. And still he did not improve.

"You're making this much harder than it has to be," she insisted.

"That, my dear Genny, is a matter of opinion," he said in a strangled voice.

Puzzled, Genevieve took a moment to realize the full impact of his innuendo. With an affronted gasp, she whirled in his arms, her face ablaze. "You vulgar, uncouth—"

He kept her from jerking away by placing a hand on her waist and curling his sword arm around her back. "I'll remind you that I'm not the one who started pressing herself against me like a cat in heat in full view of the countryside.''

She blinked in realization. "You—you merely pretended to be so clumsy, didn't you? I'll give you credit. You're a much better actor than I thought.''

He inclined his head in gracious acceptance of her accolade. "I owe everything to my teacher.''

"I was merely trying to help you!" she spluttered.

"And I wouldn't be much of a man if I didn't enjoy it, would I, Genny?'' He growled, wicked amusement lighting the fire in his blue eyes.

"Unhand me immediately, you lout!" Mortified, she would not dignify this conversation by struggling. "I'm no ha'penny harlot for you to insult as you will.''

"Why is it insulting to know that I find you desirable? What greater compliment can a man pay a woman?''

Her color went from rose to crimson at his frankness. "This isn't seemly," she croaked. "Let me go. Someone will see.''

He sighed but obediently loosened his hold, letting one hand slip under the chestnut curls piled at her nape. Her involuntarily wince made him swear.

"By God, the bastard did hurt you!" He pushed her hair back to reveal a line of purplish bruises, then lightly traced the welts with a fingertip, cursing under his breath all the while.

"They're not bad," Genevieve said, shaken by the savagery of his expression and by the pleasure-pain of his brief caress on her tender skin. The hairs on her arms quivered. "Darcy? It's all right. I'll heal.''

His thumb came up under her chin, lifting her face so that he could see himself reflected in the forest-colored depths of her eyes. "Forgiveness for the enemy, is that it, General, but none for me?''

"We're not enemies," she answered, breathless and dizzy.

"I hope to hell not. If we weren't standing out in the

middle of a public field, I'd kiss you until you believed it, too.''

"Why did you kiss me before?" she whispered.

"What man in his right mind wouldn't?"

"What?"

He shook his head, his lips twisting in a wry, self-deprecating smile. "You have no idea what your mouth does to a man, do you? It makes promises without ever saying a word. That's why I kissed you, to see what those promises taste like. You're addictive, Genny. One taste, and a man may never be able to get enough. You'd have been safer if you'd slapped me silly and yelled for help.''

Bemused by his speech, she answered with guileless honesty. "I didn't want to.''

He sucked in a breath, and the thumb that had been stroking her throat went completely still. "It's dangerous for you to say things like that to me.''

"I have a feeling we're both very dangerous people," she murmured.

"Are you willing to find out?"

Genevieve smiled to herself. Ah, he was good! Seducing her with words and the heat in his beautiful blue eyes. But beyond that, there was a loneliness in him that called to something kindred in her. Could she believe in that promise? Or was she merely pretending, drawing another pretty fantasy out of thin air because all of a sudden her life seemed so empty? It was crazy and unreasonable, this sudden infatuation with a stranger, yet perhaps they'd have time to get to know each other if he stayed with the company. They could take it slow . . . if it wasn't already too late for that.

Smiling, she took his hand from her throat, then folded her slender fingers around his lean, brown ones. "Perhaps we should try being friends first, Darcy.''

"So cautious!" he teased.

"Just practical. No doubt you've used your charming ways to woo many an unwary lady to your bed. I could ill afford to make such a mistake.''

Laughter rumbled deep in his chest. "Mistake, is it? Now you insult me! But once in my bed you'll find how wrong you are."

"Rogue! You assume too much."

"Do I, Genny?" he asked quietly, his gaze suddenly intense.

The jade depths of her eyes grew dark and turbulent with confusion. There was much she dared not ask. What if the magic she felt was all one-sided? Yes, she wanted to fall in love, have a family, a home—but could Darcy give her those things? Would he even want to? Or was she simply another conquest to be won, now that the war was over? Common sense urged caution, while the thumping excitement in her heart ordered her to throw that mundane virtue to the four winds. But she had responsibilities.

She dropped her gaze to study the tips of her kidskin slippers. "Yes, you do assume too much. For now."

"A ray of hope! You are not so cruel as I feared."

"I swear, you are the most infuriating man . . ." She laughed at him, her smile pure and dazzling. "Stay with us, Darcy. Woo me if you will, and if your interest is genuine *and* your intentions upright, perhaps I'll encourage Grandpapa to give you leave to pay your addresses."

A flicker of a frown narrowed his brow. "Genevieve, I must tell you some—"

"Hey, you two, come on!" Young Mike waved his knitted cap at them from the top of the slope. "The coaches are ready. Everybody's waitin'!"

"Oh, my goodness! Hurry, Darcy!" Genevieve urged, dragging him by the hand. He hung back long enough to scoop up his coat and her bonnet, then raced her up the hill. Laughing and breathless, they hurried toward the waiting coaches.

"You'll ride inside this time?" Genevieve cajoled sweetly, her eyes sparkling. "After all, with Grandpapa and me both working on you, you're certain to know all your lines by the time we reach Sadler's Wells!"

There was nothing he could do but agree. The remainder of the journey passed in a pleasant haze for Genevieve. There was a good deal of hilarity as Everett tutored Darcy in elocution, going off on vague tangents at times but being turned back to the subject by Genevieve's skillful manipulation of the conversation. Darcy put himself out to be charming, pointing out various sights from the coach window and recounting humorous anecdotes and bits of gossip about Napoleon Bonaparte, old King George's lunacy, and the scandalous behavior of the prince regent.

Sitting on the leather seat next to Darcy, excitement dancing along her nerves, Genevieve felt happier than she had all the summer season. They were headed for London, the troupe had work, Grandpapa seemed content for the moment, and an exciting man flattered her with his interest. Who knew what wonders the future would bring?

When they finally made the turn at King's Cross onto City Road it was dusk, and their tired teams had to fight the busy London traffic the last half mile to Sadler's Wells. There were no performances scheduled for this night, and the proprietor, Mr. Driggers, hurried out to meet them as they pulled to a stop before the impressive white stone building rising from an aboreal setting a stone's throw from the banks of the New River.

"Hope he reserved us better rooms this time," Maebella grumbled, gathering up her ridicule.

"I'm sure we could all do with a wash, some supper, and a good night's sleep," Genevieve agreed as the coachman opened the door. She gave Darcy a quick smile of thanks for the supporting hand he placed on her elbow, then stepped out of the coach.

"I'd just as soon have a tot of good brandy," Everett said under his breath and followed her. Giving a hearty stretch, he advanced on the stout proprietor with his hand extended and a jovial smile. "Mr. Driggers, sir! How good it is to meet you again."

Driggers shook hands and bowed. "Mr. Maples, it is always my pleasure to accommodate your company. And Miss Maples, welcome. I trust you had a good journey?"

"Hmmph! Fell upon by ruffians, we were, sir!" Everett announced. With a dramatic flourish, he pointed to the ebony-haired individual just climbing from the coach behind Maebella. "Why, if it hadn't been for this young man here, there'd be no telling what dire calamities might have befallen us!"

Driggers gave a muffled exclamation, and his button eyes brightened with calculation. Tugging at his waistcoat, he hurried past Everett, bowing and scraping. "Well done, sir! My congratulations. A valiant deed, coming to the aid of a brother artist. Driggers is the name, sir, proprietor of Sadler's Wells Theater. It's a great honor to have you here."

Reluctantly, it seemed to Genevieve, Darcy shook hands with the officious little man. "Mr. Driggers. I remember you well."

"If I might say so, Mr. Cormick, sir, your performance in *Richard* was brilliant. Absolutely inspired."

"Thank you. Now, if you'll excuse me—"

"Let me offer you some hospitality," Driggers said. "After all, it isn't every day I can have the best of both the young and the old generations at my table. And perhaps my longtime associate, Mr. Maples, may be prevailed upon to recommend my playhouse for one of your productions."

Genevieve frowned in confusion. Was the man addled? Darcy was no— The thought shattered and she gasped. *Cormick?*

"Here now, Driggers," Everett interrupted. "What the devil are you blathering on about? My granddaughter just hired this man."

"To work with you? Here?" Driggers radiated delight. "The finest actor in London on *my* stage?"

Everett preened. "Really, Driggers. My modesty . . ."

Driggers shot Everett an irritated look. "Not you. *Him.* This is incredible! Miss Maples, my compliments!"

"I'm afraid there's been a misunderstanding," the object of the discussion began.

"There certainly has!" Genevieve's voice shook. She grabbed Driggers by the arm and pointed at Darcy. "Who is this man?"

Befuddled, Driggers tugged at this stock. "You mean you don't know?"

Eyes hard as green marbles, Genevieve shook her head. "Evidently not."

"Why, that's B. D. Cormick, drama's newest rising star!"

"Darcy?" Everett's voice registered his confusion.

"Bryce Darcy Cormick, sir," Bryce drawled, his attitude bored. "And really, Driggers. My modesty—"

Livid with rage, Genevieve stepped in front of Bryce. *"Now* I want to do this."

Then she slapped him silly.

Chapter 3

"I do *not* want to speak to that man."

Safely ensconced at a cluttered desk in yet another set of dreary rented rooms the evening of their arrival at Sadler's Wells, Genevieve moved her pen over a poorly executed drawing of a fairy's gown and fed her fury.

"I'd say you made that abundantly clear," Bryce Cormick replied from the doorway, his tone dry. "Nevertheless, I insist."

The nib of her pen snapped, blotching the drawing. Genevieve whirled in her chair with an enraged hiss. "Who let you in?"

"I tried to stop him," Maebella said, bobbing ineffectually behind Bryce in the grimy hallway that smelled of stale cabbage.

"Don't blame Miss Smythe. I doubt a legion of dragoons could stop me."

Genevieve carefully placed her ruined pen in her sketchbook, closed the cover, and set it on the desk beside three white feathers. "If you've come for an apology, very well. I apologize for striking you. It was unladylike, and I'm sorry. Now go away."

"Dammit, Genevieve!" Bryce shoved his black hair off his forehead and dragged a hand down his beard-shadowed jaw in exasperation.

"I don't recall giving you leave to address me in such a familiar fashion." Her words were icy with contempt. "Now that you've had your fun with us, I'd like you to go."

"By God, you're a stubborn woman," Bryce said, striding into the room. He still wore his same soiled blue coat, and she was struck anew by his military bearing. "Aren't you the least bit interested in why I came looking for you?" he demanded.

Genevieve rose, as regal as a queen in her fresh lilac gown, her attitude one of quiet defiance. "No, I'm not. Maebella, please fetch my grandfather so he can show this person out."

"Miss Smythe, stay where you are!"

Maebella studied the two angry faces glaring so fiercely at each other. Since she knew for a fact Everett Maples was presently snoring in his rented bed, she decided discretion was in order. Her retreat went virtually unnoticed.

Bryce gave a small, annoyed snort. "I know that you're angry, but it was a very small deception, hardly worth all this fuss."

Angry? Genevieve knew that scarcely covered the gamut of emotions she'd experienced today. Furious, hurt, mortified—these words did not even begin to describe her humiliation, her rage at her own gullibility. She'd been charmed, enchanted, mesmerized by this . . . this fraud, and no doubt he'd laughed uproariously at her naiveté. Standing before her was the consummate actor of all time, and at this moment she hated him so much she wanted to scratch out his beautiful eyes.

"You played a dishonest game with me from the very first," she said, endeavoring to keep her voice even. "I find that unforgivable."

"I've often traveled incognito." He shrugged negligently. "I'd have told you if I'd had the opportunity."

"When? You deliberately let me believe I'd hired Claude's replacement. Now, I'll be lucky to find anyone to play King Harold before tomorrow night."

"You merely assumed I'd agreed, organizing me along with everything else in your path, Little General. And, admit it, good fortune was on your side, otherwise those highwaymen might have gotten away with more than your purse."

"I suppose you'd like me to feel grateful that you did the decent thing on at least one occasion."

"Keep your gratitude. But I do have a business proposition for you."

She went pale, and then scarlet with outrage. "*I'll just bet you have!* But you have nothing that interests me, Mr. Cormick. Contrary to what you seem to believe, I'm not one of your easily bought cyprians. You may take your 'proposition' and go straight to—"

Bryce's deep laughter interrupted her passionate soliloquy. "Hold on, General! You've got the wrong idea entirely. It's not your virtue I want, it's your talent as a costumer."

Genevieve blinked foolishly, losing steam like a tea kettle snatched from its hob. She had not known that it was possible for her to feel any worse than she already did. Now she understood the meaning of the phrase "adding insult to injury."

"What about my costumes?" she managed finally.

"Why else do you think I came looking for you in that backwater playhouse? I'd been told the Maples Company always sported the best costumes of any touring group. But when I found that their creator was so young, I thought it prudent to get to know you better and to see your work up close. So I tagged along in order to decide if you could handle my assignment."

"What assignment?"

"I've purchased the Athena Theater on Long Acre with the intention of mounting a new version of *Othello* as its first production. I'm sure you could design the costumes I want. Will you do it?"

"Work with you?" she wheezed.

"Of course. I guarantee the wages will please you."

Genevieve gaped at him, then slowly shook her head. "You must think I am the world's greatest fool."

"You'd be a fool not to jump at this opportunity. It could be a chance to make your name in this business. Unless you like traveling with a second-rate company and an aging star."

"At least they don't lie to me," she said in a scathing tone. "No, thank you, Mr. Cormick. Since I now know exactly what kind of 'gentleman' you are, there's nothing on earth that could induce me to work for you."

He took a step closer. "Genevieve, be reasonable. I explained why I kept you in the dark. A small thing, surely?"

To her shame, she retreated behind her chair. "Reasonable! Sweet heaven, you have the utter gall to ask this of me after all that's happened? Mr. Cormick, the unvarnished truth is that I don't trust you."

His dark brows drew together in a foreboding line. "I didn't lie about everything, you know."

"Is that so?" Her disbelief was palpable. "Is that why after only a few hours' acquaintance you had the effrontery to insult me with unwanted attentions? Oh, yes, it was very clear you tried to worm your way into my good graces with risqué speech and daring actions no true gentleman would ever condone. But it didn't work, Dar—Mr. Cormick. I was aware of your insincerity from the first, and only played along to see how far you'd go and to what purpose. Well, I know now, don't I? So take your so-called offer and go. I have no time for worthless, contemptible creatures like you."

Bryce's countenance had grown darker and darker during her tirade. "Very well, if that's your final decision."

Genevieve lifted her chin. "It is."

"Then I hope you don't have cause to regret it, Miss Maples. I'll see myself out."

Maebella popped out from where she'd been eavesdropping behind the door facing. "This way, sir."

"Thank you, Miss Smythe." He sent a final glance toward Genevieve, but she stared implacably through the fly-specked window, refusing to look at him again. He hesitated, then reached into his pocket and presented Maebella with a small white card. "In case the little general changes her mind."

Maebella escorted him out through the hall, but only after the front door slammed behind him did Genevieve's ramrod posture relax. She sank unsteadily into her chair as Maebella bustled back into the room clutching the card to her ample bosom.

"Such foolishness!" Maebella said. "That two grown people should act like babes!"

Genevieve buried her face in her hands. "Oh, Maebella, not now," she pleaded.

"You've grown so high and mighty you can afford to turn a handsome offer down flat?" Maebella propped one hand on her round hip and shook a finger in Genevieve's downcast face. "And such an offer! Work you've been pining to do since you were a wee thing. Girl, you're cutting off your nose to spite your face!"

"Maybe so," Genevieve flared, "but I'd sooner walk across hot coals as help that . . . that mountebank!"

"So he flirted a bit with you, did he? And what's the harm in that, says I? You're a lovely girl."

Genevieve heaved a tired sigh. "You don't understand, Maebella."

"I understand you haven't had a chance to meet many young gentlemen, as unsettled as we've always been. So perhaps you were hoping for a bit too much from this one? Well, he isn't the shiftless soldier you thought he was. He's well respected and successful at his chosen field. Isn't that reason to be glad? Isn't that reason to give the lad a chance?"

"He isn't . . . an honorable man, Maebella. I'm not going to change my mind."

"Suit yourself, then," Maebella snapped, tossing the card into Genevieve's lap. "I'm going to bed."

Maebella's footsteps died away down the hall, and Genevieve hesitated, then picked up Bryce's card, intent on destroying the hateful name engraved on it. But when she touched it, the thin piece of cardboard still seemed to carry the warmth of his body. With a stifled groan, she pressed the card against her heart. In the space of less than a day, to have had her most secret hopes raised and then dashed to the earth by a handsome, conscienceless rogue was too cruel indeed.

"It's not fair," Genevieve whispered to the empty room, then laid her head on the cluttered desk and wept.

If he'd been a man given to melancholy, Bryce Cormick thought, he'd have just cause to weep.

Sprawled naked on the large bed in his fashionable St. James town house, Bryce cast a scowl at his ink-smeared fingers, then locked his hands behind his head and contemplated the bars of morning sunshine stippling the upholstered velvet bed canopy. The smell of freshly brewed coffee and lemon oil permeated the air, but the luxury of the room made as little impression on Bryce in his present state of mind as a soldier's bivouac.

Never mind the fact that his excursion to Dunstable as a favor to his former mentor had been an exercise in futility, he'd welcomed the opportunity the assignment had given him to track down a certain lady costumer of growing repute. It was rare, however, that he misjudged a situation—or a woman—so completely. He would have to start his search for a costumer all over again because he'd botched everything from start to finish with Genevieve Maples.

Every single aspect of the Athena's successful debut was important to him. After all, it was time his life had some purpose, some focus. He had the memory of his free-spirited French-born mother to thank for his knowledge of the theater, and it had been a place to start, a career to replace his soldier's art, something with which to fight the creeping malaise of the soul and the stultifying ennui that was his wartime legacy. His near-overnight success had surprised him as much as the critics, but it had also given him the wherewithal to undertake an ambitious project like rejuvenating the slummy Athena into London's premier theater, never mind that Covent Garden and Drury Lane owned the monopoly on legitimate drama.

That's why he felt so disgruntled, he told himself; not because he'd been counting on an enjoyable liaison with a red-haired witch, but because her uncommon stubbornness was interfering with his plans. If he could convince her to change her mind . . .

The thought was interrupted by a brisk rapping at the door and the appearance of a wiry, nattily dressed man of middle years.

"What? Still abed? My God, man! You'll get as fat as Prinny."

Bryce scowled down at himself, knowing he was lean to the point of spareness from years in the saddle. But Hugh Skerry, the Earl of Huxford, had a way of putting a man on the defensive—if one let him.

"You've got a hell of a nerve, Hugh, invading my bed-chamber unannounced," Bryce drawled. "What if I'd had company?"

"Then I'd have begged an introduction," Huxford said with an amiability belied by the flat gray of his eyes. Throwing himself into a nearby chair, he propped his highly polished Hessians on the foot of the bed. "Had a good trip, I hope? How is Sir Theodore?"

"My father is quite well, thank you."

"And that delightful sister of yours?"

"You're perfectly aware that Allegra is my half sister," Bryce replied with growing irritation.

Rolling from the bed with the deceptively powerful grace of a campaign-hardened veteran, he tugged on a silk paisley robe, casually tucked the evidence of his midnight scribblings into a desk drawer, then poked at the breakfast tray Taffy had delivered earlier in his usual efficient manner. "Allegra is fine, too," he continued, rattling cutlery. "She and Clorinda North ride my father's thoroughbreds daily, when they're not plotting their assault on London town.''

"North? Not Calhoun's sister?''

An old pain flickered across Bryce's face. "Yes.''

"Heavens, is that whey-faced chit old enough to come out?''

"So it seems. And she's grown into a pretty little thing, very ethereal. I promised Cal I'd watch out for her.''

"Keep the fortune hunters away and all that?'' Chuckling, Huxford scratched his temple, where a distinguishing flash of silver peppered his brown locks. "With you as watchguard, it seems rather like locking the fox in with the hatchlings!''

"Cal was my best friend,'' Bryce said in a stony voice. "I wouldn't dishonor his sister.''

"Lord, I know that! Damned shame, his dying in that ambush. He was a good soldier.''

"So were we all . . . once.''

Memory tightened Bryce's lips. They'd been a bit drunk that night, off-duty in a Spanish tavern, never expecting a traitor's trap. When the smoke cleared, his best friend was dead, the stalwart, smiling, every-steady companion of Bryce's turbulent boyhood. Thrusting aside the painful vision, Bryce set the coffee carafe back on the tray with a clatter, facing Huxford again with his cup in hand.

"At any rate, you now know everyone in Suffolk— Clorinda, Allegra, my father—is fine. I daresay the whole bloody world is fine. Now that you've had the news report, you can find your own way out.''

"Nasty temper you're in,'' Huxford commented. "I take it you had no luck with that other—er, matter?''

"No more than you expected. One look and I could have told you the Maples Company was hardly the den of thieves you'd led me to believe. An eccentric old man and a handful of Haymarket players trying to scrape out a living.''

Huxford shrugged. "So my sources were less than reliable this time. It wouldn't be the first occasion a traveling

band found itself trafficking in contraband or worse, and
these are still precarious times. However, I've learned to
trust your instincts, so if you say they're harmless . . .''

"Harmless as fleas."

"That's the end of it, then. Hand me that toast if you're
not going to eat it?"

Bryce passed the laden plate. "Doesn't that countess of
yours feed you?"

"With all the gala celebrations, Celia rarely rises before
noon these days, except when Robbie and Arthur sneak
into her room." Huxford's tone, muffled by a mouthful of
toast, was fond. "I tell you, Bryce, there's nothing like
having sons to make a man's life worthwhile. You ought
to try it."

"Thank you very much for the advice, my lord," Bryce
returned sourly.

Settling in another chair, he nursed his coffee cup.
Sweet, timid Clorinda, the mother of his sons? The notion, which had seemed so fitting when subtly presented
by a loving sister and concerned father in the homey atmosphere of the Cormick country holdings, jangled his
system now like a too-hot swallow of the bitter brew. He
was groping in the dark, trying to find a key that would
open the door to a normal life. The Athena, Clorinda—
both were attempts to fill the emptiness. But if truth be
told, he felt more passionately about the theater than he
did about Clorinda. Was it guilt that prompted him? An
old debt to Cal? Neither was a very admirable motive for
matrimony, and both were unfair to Clorinda, especially
since he'd lost no time lusting after another woman.

Genevieve's visage filled his mind and stirred his sex.
Damn! There hadn't been a woman that disturbed him this
much in years. His irritation overflowed, landing on the
handiest target, who was munching toast and expounding
the genius of the two youngest Skerrys.

"I'm sure the little monsters are delightful," Bryce interrupted rudely, "but I know this isn't a social visit, so
why don't you get the hell to the point?"

Huxford swallowed a last bite of toast, then slowly set aside the plate. "All right. I need the Griffin."

Bryce went very still. "No."

"Look, Bryce, I wouldn't ask—"

"No, my lord. The war's over."

"And Bonaparte is merely a caged eagle, ready to fly from Elba at the first opportunity." Huxford's amiable expression vanished, revealing the face of a man accustomed to giving life-or-death orders and having them carried out to the letter. Hiding behind a nominal appointment to the war ministry, Lord Huxford had in fact been the head of an intelligence service renowned for both its resources and its ruthlessness. "You're still my best man. No one has your experience or your unique background."

Bryce shook his head. "I'm finished, sucked dry. I only agreed to poke around in Dunstable for you because it suited my own plans. So don't get any other ideas. The Griffin's in permanent retirement."

"I know that last assignment in Lyons was a nasty bit of business, Bryce." The earl ignored the thunderous expression that suddenly clouded Bryce's face. "But there's something else. The Abbot's back."

Bryce's blue eyes turned icy. "How do you know?"

"The usual signs. The Abbot's at work again within the ministry all right, but this time the bastard's got a problem."

"Let me guess. It's something only the Griffin can handle."

"Perceptive as always, my friend."

"Go to hell, Hugh."

Huxford cocked an inquisitive eyebrow at Bryce. "You surprise me. I thought bringing the Abbot to justice at last would interest you. After all, his network of French spies and sympathizers almost cost us the war at one point. And still there's sensitive information leaking out of the ministry!"

Bryce rose and began to pace. "Goddammit. You never

let up, do you? Have you forgotten I took a knife in the back in Lyons that should have killed me?''

"Certainly not. And I'm grateful that French assassin wasn't as skilled as his reputation led us to believe," the earl said dryly.

Bryce winced. The bitter memory of his failure and what it had cost not only him, but also his friends, made his stomach twist with nausea. He'd always been careful, but by Lyons he'd been so tired, so soul-sick of all the things he'd had to do in the war, he'd let down his guard, taken the comfort he'd so sorely needed—and suffered indescribable consequences. Grimly, he buried the memories again in the deepest, darkest crevice of his mind, the only way he was able to survive these days, and glared at the earl.

"Can't you understand how sick I am of all this? What more do you want?''

"The Abbot's Seal."

Bryce froze. *The Abbot's Seal.* Rumor hailed the ancient and mystical talisman, a rose-colored gemstone of magnificent proportions, reputed to have been carved with the imperial eagle of Rome at the time of Christ, and thereafter secreted in the Styrian Mountains by a succession of abbots of a holy order of monks. Whosoever possessed the Abbot's Seal, legend had it, could command fate, and so for centuries men had coveted it, killed for it, won and lost kingdoms in search of it.

In this century, somehow the seal had come into the hands of the man who'd been a thorn in Huxford's side, the man who'd taken his *nom de guerre* from the antiquity, styling himself another Abbot and directing his minions under the sign of the eagle's talon in the French emperor's cause. With Bonaparte's defeat and exile, however, it seemed the luck of the Abbot's Seal had failed at last. But now Bryce wasn't so sure.

Watching Bryce carefully, Huxford leaned forward, forearms braced on his knees, his palms up and open. "Damnation, Bryce! I nearly had it. I was so close I could almost taste it!''

"What happened?"

"We believe the Abbot intended to send the seal to Elba."

Bryce lifted one dark eyebrow in inquiry. "To Bonaparte?"

"Exactly. Perhaps it was meant to signal the emperor that a renewed conspiracy to reinstate him is ready to move. But apparently not everyone is interested in the possibility of the emperor's return to France. Or perhaps greed took over. At any rate, the Abbot's courier was set to board a smuggler at Maldon from the Essex coast to the Continent when he decided to sell the seal instead."

Nodding, Bryce moved restlessly to the heavily draped window and stared out at the pleasant, tree-lined street below. "At which point you caught the scent of the thing, I take it? You must have been fairly drooling over the possibility, Hugh, since the Abbot uses the seal to send orders to his conspirators."

"Indeed. But the damned fool of a courier hadn't the sense to come direct to me for amnesty and clear passage to the Americas. Instead, he sold the seal to some petty thief, and then promptly got his throat slit when the Abbot's men caught up with him before I could!"

"So the Abbot got his property back?"

Huxford's flat gray eyes narrowed slyly. "Ah, there's the crux of the matter. They were too late, it appears. So the courier's dead, the fence he sold the seal to has long since vanished, and the prize has passed into the robbers' network to surface again wherever it may."

"So that's why you sent me to Dunstable after a ring of petty thieves?"

" 'Twas worth a try, especially since the route was more or less on a direct line from Chelmsford, where the Abbot's courier was killed. You know as well as I that anything of value stolen in the provinces, whether taken by highwaymen, burglars of gentlemen's country estates, or smugglers, passes from hand to hand through the countryside by way of the underground thieves' network until it finds its way to London for resale at the receiver's bureaus.

"A piece like the Abbot's Seal is rare, and highly traceable. It *will* surface again eventually. Our only problem is to find it before the Abbot can. But he's got men infiltrating all levels of society, including the brotherhood of thieves. That's why I need the Griffin's expertise. Between you and Taffy, I can count on covering every gin mill and dive in the East End, every thieves' kitchen, every brothel."

"My true element," Bryce commented sourly.

"Think, man!" Huxford's words were imperative. "Think what we could accomplish if we find the seal before the Abbot has a chance to change his methods of communicating with his people both here and abroad!"

"You like the idea of the mischief you could cause, don't you, Hugh?"

"Payback time, my friend. I intend to unmask the Abbot and see his head on a pike over London Bridge. Whoever he is, he's a traitor, Bryce, and you have reason to hate traitors as much as I do. Say you'll help."

Hell, how could he refuse? Bryce thought. A traitor still ran unchecked within the ministry, and it had been a traitor that had been responsible for Cal's death. But Cal had not gone unavenged. In a single-minded obsession to find his friend's murderer, Bryce had tracked down and destroyed an enemy who'd long eluded more experienced men, thus calling the earl's attention to his skills in the process. That act of retribution had set Bryce's feet on the path that made him into Huxford's Griffin, a deadly, invisible, relentless weapon against Napoleon's tyranny—all in the name of God and country.

Jesus, how he needed to put that sinister part of his past behind him! There were things even Huxford didn't know. He wanted to think about building a theater and wooing chestnut-haired women, not about gore and thunder and death. But here stood Huxford with that damned expectant light in his merciless gray eyes, and duty—that bloody bitch—beckoned him yet again.

"All right, I'll help," Bryce agreed. "But this is the last damned time I go to hell for you. Understood?"

With a slight smile, the earl relaxed again in his chair. "You wouldn't by any chance have a spot of jam to go with the rest of that toast, would you?"

"Miss Maples! Oh, I say—Miss Maples!"

"Oh, Lord, not again," Maebella moaned. She tugged insistently on Genevieve's arm. "Don't answer him. We're almost home. No, don't turn around—keep walking!"

"I couldn't be so discourteous," Genevieve protested, pausing on the unevenly paved sidewalk before their lodgings.

She furled the parasol that matched her heather-green walking gown and struck what she thought a *ton*-ish miss might call an attitude to show off the fine lines of her and Maebella's latest creation. Being well dressed was the best advertisement for their skills, and one never knew when someone might demand the name of one's couturiere. She summoned up a pleasant smile. "Why, Mr. Chesterson, how nice to see you again."

The slender young man hurrying toward them with a hopeful look in his caramel-colored eyes bore an enormous bouquet of lilies-of-the-valley and the eye-shocking garb of a dandy. Yellow gaiter inexpressibles, a plumped and padded purple tailcoat, and a black-and-white-checked vest hinted at his commitment to fashion, as did the intricate knotting of his neckcloth and the eye-threatening height of his collar points. Sweeping his top hat off corn-yellow locks curled *á là* Titus, he bowed deeply.

"So good of you, Miss Maples," he said, rather out of breath, Genevieve suspected, because of the tightness of his stays. He thrust the bouquet at her. "Please accept this token of my admiration."

"Mr. Chesterson, you're too generous," Genevieve protested, accepting the fragrant, tissue-wrapped bundle.

She couldn't resist stroking the satiny petals "Really, sir, your floral offerings have made my room into a veritable garden!"

"A fitting tribute for one so lovely," he said gallantly. Maebella gave an audible sniff, but he forged on. "And please, you agreed to call me Jules, remember? I wanted to say your performance last evening was inspired."

"You attended again?" Genevieve's soft laugh was thoroughly amused. In the ten days of the Maples Company's run at Sadler's Wells, it appeared her admirer hadn't missed a performance! "Mr. Ches— Jules, I'm flattered. Though what pleasure you receive from seeing me tromp around under King Harold's heavy disguise and flowing beard, I can't imagine."

"That's what makes it so delicious, my dear Miss Maples, seeing the wondrous transformation!" Jules's fine brown eyes shone with youthful enthusiasm and a galloping case of calf love. "You're incredible."

"And you're no drama critic," Maebella mumbled under her breath.

"Alas, I wish that everyone's opinion was as kind as yours," Genevieve said quickly. "I confess, with my other duties, I'm finding King Harold's role rather trying."

"You're working much too hard for a lady of your delicacy," Jules said. "Please, let me offer you some entertainment. I have my curricle, it's a fine day, and I'd be most honored if you'd allow me to drive you through the park."

Genevieve, unwilling to crush the young man's feelings, but also unwilling to encourage his obvious infatuation, cast around for an excuse. "I'm so sorry, Jules, but I can't accept your kind offer. My grandfather has been feeling poorly, and I promised I'd do my bit of shopping and hurry right back."

Crestfallen, Jules let his shoulders slump. "You're certain? Well, another time, perhaps."

"Yes, another time. Thank you for understanding,"

Genevieve said warmly, briefly touching his arm. "And thank you again for the flowers. They're lovely."

Glowing again, Jules bowed, watching raptly as the two ladies entered the boardinghouse.

"Pest!" Maebella grunted. Her round hips shook and her straw bonnet bobbed as she mounted the steps ahead of Genevieve. "How can you abide that fawning peacock? Everywhere you turn, there he is again. He's even worse now than the last time we played in London."

"I think Mr. Chesterson's devotion is rather sweet," Genevieve replied with a sympathetic laugh.

"If your grandfather knew what a nuisance he's making of himself, he'd take his cane to the insolent puppy! You ought to cut him dead and put an end to this nonsense."

"I see no need to hurt the boy's tender feelings, Maebella." Genevieve shrugged and buried her nose in the bouquet to hide an unexpected pang. Though it had been over a week since her final interview with Bryce Cormick, her pride still bore the marks of his thoughtless bruising. While Jules's foppery scarcely competed with Bryce's masculine magnetism, Genevieve could be compassionate toward Jules's position.

Maebella dug her key from her ridicule with a disdainful snort. "Your Jules may be young, but he's got a man's ideas, especially about you."

"If I continue to offer nothing but friendship, no doubt he'll outgrow his infatuation in due course." Genevieve followed the older woman into the apartment. "Besides, Mr. Chesterson is evidently both well off and very good *ton*. You never know when a wealthy patron might come in handy."

"Perhaps you have a point. *Now* would be a perfect time, for instance." Maebella stripped off her gloves with unwarranted vehemence. "Are you going to tell your grandfather that Driggers cut our percentage of the gate again?"

Frowning, Genevieve removed her hat, newly trimmed with the very feathers she'd found on the riverbank with

Bryce. Clearing a place on the desktop among the growing clutter of minor treasures that was beginning to turn this dreary room into more of a home—a cologne bottle with a tiny posy of violets, a lacy sachet, a bird's nest containing half a spotted blue eggshell—she set aside her hat and ridicule, then turned back to Maebella.

"I suppose I must, though I hate to upset him with more bad news. We're barely making enough now to meet the players' salaries and pay expenses. Claude's absence is hurting our performances, which in turn keeps down the attendance. I'm making a mishmash of King Harold, but where am I going to find the money to hire a replacement now?"

"You could have taken Mr. Cormick's offer," Maebella pointed out with alacrity.

Genevieve pulled a face. "Put myself at the mercy of that blackguard? No, thank you!"

"Well, what *are* you going to do?"

"As badly as I hate it," Genevieve said, chewing her lip, "I suppose I'll have to ask Grandpapa to tap into our savings."

"Genny, no!"

"Just a small loan to hire another actor," Genevieve hastened to explain. "I'm certain our work will improve, and then so will the attendance and our profits."

"But that money's for a house!"

"Yes, I know, but this is an emergency, and the more I think about it, the more I'm sure it's the best way." Genevieve nodded decisively. "It's almost time to wake Grandpapa to go to the theater anyway. I'll explain the situation, and we'll see the banker tomorrow."

But moments later, Genevieve looked aghast at her grandfather's guilty, haggard face. "Gone? What do you mean, it's gone?"

Everett sat in his nightshirt in a creaking rocker beside his narrow bed. Silver stubble glittered on his jaw, and he looked suddenly frail and ancient.

"I tried to tell you, Genny-girl." His usually strong voice trembled. "I—I lost it all, months ago."

"Lost?" The air squeezed from Genevieve's lungs with such force she had to sit down on the lumpy mattress. "Everything we'd saved? How? Where?"

"At the faro tables."

"Gambling?" In her mind, Genevieve saw her dream cottage collapse like a house of cards. "Oh, Grandpapa, how could you?"

"It was for you, Genny."

"Me?" She jumped to her feet, hands clenched at her side. "How dare you say such a thing?"

Everett's hazel eyes filmed with moisture. "I'm going mad, Genny."

"What?" Alarm raced along Genevieve's overstretched nerves. "No, of course you're not!"

"Just like King Lear. I know it, Genny-girl. I've known it for a long time. But I wanted to see you well settled, feather our nest a bit before . . . before . . ." He held his iron-gray head between his hands, swaying back and forth, moaning softly. "So I went to the gambling hells with Samson Baggart."

"Mr. Baggart, the impresario? But you know that for all his airs, he's cheated many an actor out of honest wages! How could you trust *him*?"

"I thought he was merely being sociable, and I did win at first. But then I began to lose, and I had to keep playing to win it back again, because you trusted me to keep you safe, didn't you? And now there's nothing left at all."

His voice cracked, and he buried his face in his hands.

"Oh, Grandpapa." Kneeling beside the rocker, Genevieve threw her arms around his heaving shoulders, trying to keep the dismay out of her voice. "Shhh, don't take on so. You should have told me. Don't worry, everything will be all right."

But Everett would have none of her comfort. Tears streaking his lined cheeks, he pushed her away. "Foolish girl! You are too forgiving. You don't realize what I've done. I've gambled away your legacy and sold myself to the devil in the process!''

"You're imagining things again," she said, suddenly afraid his distress was causing delusions.

"Am I?" Everett laughed shrilly. "Ask Samson Baggart. He holds my markers. He pipes the tune, and I dance like a trained bear."

"Markers?" Genevieve whispered, feeling the blackness of the nightmare closing around her. "You owe Baggart money? How much?"

"More than we could pay in a hundred years," Everett said heavily. "But it isn't the money he wants, it's my soul."

Infuriated and frightened, Genevieve lost her temper. "Stop it! Stop blathering on as if you were Faust and this merely a bad play! Is this the truth or some trick of your mind? It's all too unbelievable!"

Everett leaped from the rocking chair with sudden, hectic energy.

"Believe this, then, if you will, my fine miss!" He slammed open the lid of his traveling trunk and grabbed up the fractured chest of props, rummaging frantically, shoving item after glittering item into Genevieve's paralyzed hands. "Believe this and this! *Now* do you see?"

Bewildered, her hands full, Genevieve stared at her grandfather, wondering if he'd truly lost his mind at last. "Grandpapa," she choked, "never mind. You don't have to do this."

"Look at it, Genny-girl! Don't you recognize stolen booty when you see it? Baggart's turned me into his packhorse. A regular mule, I am."

She gasped, looking down at her hands in horror as if instead of jeweled chains and pins she held a writhing mass of poisonous snakes. "You mean . . . these are *real*?"

Everett laid a finger aside his nose, grinned slyly, and nodded. "You've got the ticket now. What better place to hide a robber's cache than under one's nose? And how easy for a traveling band of players to transport boodle, my dear.''

Genevieve began to see what he was driving at, and it sickened her. "Why, Grandpapa?''

"Because Baggart is a thief.'' Everett scraped the jewelry from her nerveless hands with desperate, frenetic haste, shoving everything back into the casket.

"But why are you helping him?'' she cried.

"Weren't you listening?'' Everett demanded, suddenly petulant. "The markers! He'll call in the markers unless I deliver his damned packages.''

"But that's ridiculous!'' Genevieve's fury erupted. "He can't make you an accomplice! I'll . . . I'll go to the magistrates and explain—''

"No. No!'' He clutched the little chest to his middle, and there was a wild light behind his hazel eyes. "I daren't. There's no proof. I can't!''

"Yes, you can, and you will,'' Genevieve said firmly. "We'll show them these things—''

"You can't have it.'' Whimpering, his jaw slack, Everett backed into the corner of the room and sank down in a self-protective ball. His eyes darted this way and that with animal-like furtiveness. "Go away. I must give it to Samson.''

"Grandpapa, please.'' She reached for him.

"No! Get away, I said!'' He shied away, scuttling out of her reach with his aged shanks showing beneath his flapping nightshirt. Genevieve's throat constricted with the threat of tears.

"But why? We can put an end to this Baggart, if only you'll let me help you. Why won't you let me help?'' she begged.

"Because they put debtors in Fleet Prison, my dear, but they put madmen in St. Luke's Hospital.''

"What?'' Genevieve's voice was faint with shock.

"He'll do it, too. He's promised, and he's a man of his word.'' Everett laughed horribly, pitifully, his face white and bloodless. "Honor among thieves, you know.''

"Grandpapa—"

"Don't, Genny-girl. Don't help him send me to St. Luke's." Everett gasped for breath. "I shall go mad soon enough."

His eyes rolled upward beneath his eyelids, and he slid into a curled-up position on the floor, muttering gibberish.

"Oh, dear God!" Genevieve was beside him, calling his name, frantically searching for a pulse. She screamed. "Maebella!"

Maebella appeared in an instant. "Whatever—"

"A doctor, quickly!"

Maebella took one look, then ran.

An anxious time later, Genevieve stood beside her grandfather's bed, listening to Dr. Pinchley's quiet instructions while Everett muttered fretfully in his sleep.

"The laudanum will ease his nerves if he should become overexcited again, Miss Maples," the doctor was saying. "It's often the same in cases of dementia; even the slightest shock will bring on violent outbursts. I'm afraid it's something you must become accustomed to, for the frequency of such episodes often increases as the disease progresses."

"I understand." Though her voice was calm, Genevieve felt chilled to the bone.

The physician touched her shoulder kindly. "Take heart, miss. From what you've told me, your grandfather is still able to function well, for the most part. He may even return to the stage tomorrow if he feels up to it. There will come a time, of course, when it will become impossible for him, but until then there is no need to curtail his normal activities. I would caution you to avoid upsetting him if possible, of course."

"You've been very kind, Dr. Pinchley," Genevieve murmured.

The doctor picked up his bag and hat. "Call on me any time, my dear, even if only to talk. The care of these patients can be trying."

"I'll remember, thank you."

When the doctor had left, Genevieve sat down on the side of Everett's bed and picked up the old man's hand. *Dementia,* she thought helplessly.

"Genny-girl?"

"I'm here, Grandpapa," Genevieve said in a soft voice.

"I'm late. The theater . . ."

"I canceled the performance tonight. Everyone needed a rest."

"No damned good, am I?"

Genevieve kissed the veined hand she held between her own, and love for her grandfather filled her heart near to bursting. "Everything's going to be all right. You're just tired."

Drowsy from the drug, he still attempted to sit up. "Baggart's booty?"

"Safe." She eased him back down, plumping his pillow and smoothing the shabby coverlet. "Don't worry. I'll help you deliver everything to Baggart just as he wants one last time. Then you're quitting."

"The money . . . St. Luke's!" Everett's heavy eyelids fluttered.

"No one's sending you to St. Luke's, that you can be sure of. We'll get Baggart his money somehow."

"But how?"

Genevieve leaned over and pressed another kiss to his brow. "I'll think of something. Now you go back to sleep."

Everett murmured sleepily and surrendered again to the laudanum-induced slumber. Genevieve wished she could lose her cares as easily, but round and round inside her head a dilemma chased its tail.

She had no one to turn to, no resources to call on to come to her rescue. Briefly she thought of young Jules Chesterson, then dismissed the notion. Though he might be willing to make her a loan, no doubt he'd expect more than a handshake in return. No, as badly as she hated to admit it, there was only one way to earn at least a portion of the money she needed to free Grandpapa from Baggart's blackmail and the threat of the insane asylum. She could swallow her pride and go to work for the detestable Bryce Cormick.

Trembling trepidation clutched her middle, but she had no other alternative. At least this time she would be invulnerable to his so-called charm. Yes, she'd snap her fingers in his face and dare him to try his tricks again!

Watching her grandfather sleep, Genevieve bit the lower lip that had so pleased Bryce and hoped he hadn't given the job to someone else.

Please God, she prayed, *let him still want me!*

Chapter 4

❦❦❦

"**F**or goodness sake, Arthur, don't let Driggers's crackbrained scene shifter drop the flats on you this time!"

Genevieve Maples's imperious command drifted across the empty seats of Sadler's Wells Theater and into the shadowy area under the balconies where Bryce Cormick stood with Taffy McKee. Bryce's smile grew wider as he listened and admired the slim figure in a biscuit-colored gown directing an afternoon rehearsal of the Maples Company.

"Cor, Cap!" Taffy grumbled at his elbow. "The way ye're grinnin', you'd think we found gold in Spitalfields instead of nothin' but trouble."

"Depends on what you mean by trouble," Bryce drawled. Since a carefully worded missive from Miss Genevieve Maples rested this very moment in the pocket of his pearl-gray waistcoat, he could afford a smidgen of masculine smugness.

"Haunting every flash ken and gin spinner's from Seven Dials to Westminster for a fortnight and earning nothing but a topper for your efforts is what I mean," Taffy retorted, sneaking a hand beneath his low-brimmed hat to gingerly rub a tender lump.

Bryce listened to the Welshman's grumbling with only half an ear, his attention focused on the flurry of entrances and exits Genevieve marshaled on the stage below. Sadler's Wells relied on a mixed bill of fare, from trained dogs to precocious children's recitations to sensational aquatic spectacles such as *The Siege of Gibraltar*. Bryce suppressed a shudder of distaste as the Maples Company's *Tragedy of King Harold* melodrama unfolded before his eyes, fervently promising himself that no financial pressure would necessitate such low, though undoubtedly popular, offerings at his Athena.

Taffy continued to grouse under his breath. "Ramblin' about like a pair of dunces! But it ain't me what's got to answer to his lordship, anyways."

"I can handle Huxford, you rag-mannered old alley cat," Bryce replied easily, sparing his friend a wry glance. "Complain all you like, but I know you've taken up with a new lightskirt every night—and gotten the best of it by the looks of you."

Taffy's pug countenance widened into a sheepish grin. "Can I help it if the ladies adore my appealin' qualities? 'Tis their surprise when they find I've more curls under my linen than on my dome!"

"Would that I had such a secret talent to sweeten a lady." Bryce grinned ruefully and patted the pocket holding Genevieve's note. " 'Tis rather a disadvantage following the vixen to her own den, still—"

He broke off as a disturbance erupted onstage. Mike, the youngest member of the Maples Company, scurried from stage rear, his orange freckles standing out in stark contrast to his white face. "Miss Genny! I still can't find him anywheres!"

His instincts for trouble prickling, Bryce moved in his usual soundless fashion toward the woman standing in the orchestra pit.

"Calm down, Michael," Genevieve ordered the boy. "Did you check the King George? What about Whistler's?"

"Yes, miss." Mike hopped from foot to foot at center stage. "Nobody's seen 'im."

"But that's impossible—" Genevieve began.

"Is there trouble?" Bryce asked at her side.

Genevieve whirled with a startled gasp, and a wave of rich apricot color washed over her cheeks, then as quickly receded. Bryce scowled. Damn if she wasn't as jumpy as a green-eyed cat!

"Darcy! Ah, Mr. Cormick—"

Genevieve stifled a silent groan of pure dismay. Her normal equanimity was shattered not only by Bryce Cormick's sudden materialization out of thin air, but also by his well-turned-out attire, a handsomely tailored blue coat that made his shoulders appear twice as broad as she remembered and close-fitting leather riding breeches. "This is most unexpected . . ."

"In my eagerness to discover what miracle had so changed your opinion of me, I found I could not wait on courtesy," he murmured, his blue eyes intent, assessing. "What's amiss?"

"It's the old master, sir," Mike interjected miserably. "Gone off hours ago, he did."

"Why this concern over Everett?" Bryce inquired. "He's a man full grown and well used to the world. Is he in some sort of trouble?"

If you only knew! Genevieve frantically squelched a hysterical urge to laugh. While Everett had suffered periods of vagueness over the last days, he'd been generally calm, performing with all of his old aplomb, and making a lie of Dr. Pinchley's diagnosis—at least until this morning when Samson Baggart's man had delivered an invitation from the impresario himself. Only they knew the summons to meet the successful broker of actors and plays at his office tomorrow afternoon was nothing less than a demand for obedience.

She'd been on edge since then, waiting for something dire to happen—and now Grandpapa had disappeared! And why did she have to deal with Bryce Cormick now, too? She'd had her petitions carefully rehearsed—suitably penitent, yet businesslike; professional, but cool and proud so there'd be no getting the wrong idea—and now every syllable had flown completely out of her head.

Bryce's gaze narrowed on Genevieve's pale countenance. "By God, you're really frightened, aren't you?"

"No, of course not." She shook her head, knowing that was a lie. In fact, she was terrified—of Baggart's menacing summons, of Everett's inexplicable behavior, of Bryce Cormick with his uncanny perception . . . and of her own susceptibility. Still, she denied it all. "It's not like Grandpapa to miss rehearsal. He hasn't been well, and he gets . . . confused."

Knowing the cast was avidly watching these proceedings, she dismissed them, then glanced helplessly at Bryce. As badly as she needed the chance of employment he represented, she had no choice but to risk annoying him. "I'm sorry, Mr. Cormick. I do wish to discuss your—er, proposition, but I must locate Grandpapa, and he—"

"—can't have gone far. Taffy and I will help you."

"That's not necessary," she protested, embarrassed. "I'm sure we can manage."

"Little General." His voice was gentle, but his smile was laden with self-mockery. "I'm very good at this kind of thing. Besides, with two more, the search will go faster."

Concern overpowered pride. Biting her lower lip, she nodded. "Of course, you're right."

A punch in the midsection would have done less damage to Bryce's equilibrium than the sight of her white teeth worrying her soft lip. Swallowing hard, Bryce succumbed to the urgent need to touch her by grazing her cheek with his knuckle, and smiled in encouragement. "Don't worry. We'll find him."

But several anxious hours later, the hunt had spread farther and farther afield into the city night with no success, and Genevieve's anxiety had metamorphosed into something akin to sheer panic.

Wringing her gloves, she peered out the window of the hired hackney at the narrow, squalid back lane lined with rickety tenements. Cadaverous dogs rooted in the filthy gutters in direct competition with gin-soaked drunkards while hard-worn drabs plied their trade under the torchlit signposts of a succession of disreputable coffeehouses and gin mills. What dire mischief might befall Grandpapa in such a place? Had he wandered here in a mental haze, or, even worse, had he received additional word from Baggart and come to deal with the villain by himself?

"This area is too rough for a lady," Bryce told her, leaning through the coach's door. "I'm sending you back to your lodgings."

"No! You don't understand. Grandpapa has suffered— ah, nervous episodes lately, and I'm the only one who can calm him." Impulsively, Genevieve placed her hand on Bryce's arm, tilting her head to look at him from under the fluted brim of her bonnet. "Please. He needs me."

"A most fortunate man, indeed," Bryce muttered, snared by the softness of her eyes.

Nonplussed, Genevieve withdrew her hand, her cheeks coloring, then jerked at Taffy McKee's shrill whistle.

"Hey, Cap!" The wiry Welshman stood halfway up the lane, gesticulating vigorously. "I found the old master. Come, double-time!"

"Wait here." Bryce set off in a ground-eating lope, but Genevieve scrambled out of the hackney after him.

"No, I'm coming, too!"

Exasperation tightened Bryce's jaw, but he led her around the worst of the filth, protecting her with his presence from the ribald comments and leering glances of the street's male inhabitants.

"If your tender sensibilities are offended by the sights, sounds, and stench in this place," he said, "it's no more than you deserve, for I can't abide disobedience in a female, Miss Maples."

"Then we're well matched, Mr. Cormick"—she gasped, indignant and breathless with the effort it took to keep up with him—"for I abhor high-handed men!"

Bryce's muffled snort could have been a laugh, but the

next moment they ducked through a leaning doorway into a smoky, noisy, ill-lit den reeking of cheap spirits and unwashed flesh. Men and women of every shape and description crowded around the sticky, scarred tables and the long wooden bar, drowning their miseries in the false comfort of Blue Ruin and thin beer. Genevieve had never imagined such a mass of writhing, howling, sweating, spitting, cursing, drunken humanity, and looked aghast at what appeared to her inexperienced eyes to be a pitched battle.

Unconsciously, she edged closer to Bryce's protection, then drew a strangled breath. "Grandpapa!"

Everett stood atop a wobbly table in the middle of a boisterous group, lifting his tankard as he led a cater-wauling rendition of "Old David's Sow." His hair stood up in silver spikes, his cravat was missing, and his waistcoat hung drunkenly from a single button.

"Why, the oldster was just after a bit of diversion," Bryce said. Both amusement and relief made him give Genevieve a mischievous wink. "No doubt he needed a respite from his granddaughter's organizing hand."

"Your humor does not amuse, sir!" With a fulminating glance at Bryce, she pushed her way through the sodden revelers. "Grandpapa! Come down at once. It's time to go home."

"What's that you say, girl?" Everett peered down myopically into his granddaughter's stern face. "You'll bring another pitcher of porter? Excellent idea! Hey, nonny-nonny!"

At her heels, Bryce grinned. "Why begrudge his fun?"

"Fun!" she exclaimed. "Grandpapa, come away at once. 'Tis undignified in a man of your years."

" 'That he is old, more the pity, his white hairs do witness it,' " quoted Everett.

"Oi, leave him be," a snaggled costermonger interjected. "We've had a right fine time listening to the old cove, we have."

"Aye," agreed another red-nosed celebrant. "Do the merchant again, mate!"

"No, Caesar!" wailed a tipsy washerwoman.

Her companion cuffed her on the ear. "Shaddup, d'you hear? We want that Shylock fellow again, and dance another jig while ye're at it!"

Horrified at her grandfather's apparently disintegrating decorum, Genevieve ignored the squabbling chorus and reached up to tug desperately at the knee of Everett's pantaloons. "Grandpapa, please! You're acting the fool."

Everett shook her off with a sly grin and quoted from one of his favorite roles. "Hsst, girl! 'God help the wicked! If to be old and merry be a sin, then many an old host that I know is damned.' "

Genevieve sent a harried glance toward Bryce. With a grin, he answered her unspoken appeal, addressing Everett with a similar jocularity.

"Why, upon my word, if it's not old Jack Falstaff himself! 'Tis a fine night for revelry, is it not, sir?"

"Well said, lad!" Beaming, Everett took Bryce's outstretched hand and made an unsteady descent from the tabletop. Catching sight of Genevieve's glowering expression, he chucked her under the chin, asking Bryce, " 'And is not my hostess of the tavern a most sweet wench?' "

" 'As the honey of Hybla.' " Bryce's gaze sought Genevieve's meaningfully, and his blue eyes gleamed at her heightened color.

Everett squinted and frowned, a timorous warble undermining the basso of his voice. "I know you, don't I, boy?"

"Aye, sir," Bryce answered kindly, "I think you do."

"By Gad, it's Prince Hal!" Everett's countenance transformed with delight, and he caught Bryce in an exuberant bear hug. Suddenly his voice choked with emotion, and he buried his lined brow against Bryce's shoulder. "How I've missed you, lad."

"He must be in his cups," Genevieve said, unnerved

by the gleam of moisture trickling down Everett's seamed cheeks.

"Hal!" Everett grasped Bryce's lapels, his gnarled fingers strong with desperation. "Banish not old Jack Falstaff from thy company."

"Rest easy, old friend, thy Harry dotes on thee." Bryce skillfully turned Everett toward the door while Taffy opened a passage before them through the crowd. "Come, let's find a quieter place to plan our mischief."

Obediently, the old man quieted, docile once again. Genevieve marveled in openmouthed amazement at the way Bryce handled her grandfather's delusion. Then Bryce reached back and dragged her impatiently after him.

"March, General. Before we have to send a rescue party after *you*."

Minutes later, the hackney carried them toward their lodgings. Everett kept up a constant tipsy stream of garrulous conversation, still affecting the persona of Shakespeare's Falstaff. Bryce parried every verbal sortie with a dry witticism or acid comment of his own, apparently enjoying himself, and Genevieve was overwhelmed with gratitude at his compassion and gentleness with a comparative stranger.

At the same time, she was still deeply disturbed by the episode. Everett's affectation of Falstaff's character seemed almost too real. Was he seeking escape from their imminent meeting with Baggart by retreating into fantasy? What would she do if he wasn't able to meet Baggart at all?

By the time Bryce and Taffy helped Everett up the steep stairs to their shabby rooms, the alcohol and nervous excitement had taken their toll on the older man. He was already snoring when they removed his boots and rolled him onto the sagging lodginghouse bed.

"I'll sit with him." Maebella spread a coverlet over Everett's oblivious form, then took her sewing basket to the nearby rocker. Genevieve nodded, then quietly closed the door behind her and joined the men in the hall.

"The old gen'men'll be fit as a fiddle come morning,

miss," Taffy said cheerfully. " 'Tis a shame he worried ye, but the gents will have their fun."

"Thank you for your help, Mr. McKee," Genevieve answered. There was a weary quiver to her smile. "You've been very kind."

Taffy ducked his bald head and blushed. " 'Tweren't nothing, miss." He glanced at Bryce. "I'd best go after our mounts now, Cap, or the hostler may sell 'em out from under us."

Bryce nodded. "I'll be down after I have a word with Miss Maples, Sergeant."

"Aye, sir."

As Taffy clattered down the staircase, Genevieve led Bryce into the sitting room, fighting an unaccountable wave of shyness. The strain of the last hours, coupled now with overwhelming relief, made her overly sensitive to his presence. Though she longed for a few moments of solitude to collect her scattered resources, she was determined to express her gratitude. In front of her unlit hearth, she turned to face him.

"I want to thank you for everything you did tonight, Mr. Cormick." Her smile was too bright, her laugh brittle. " 'Tis quite a habit you have, rescuing damsels in distress. I shudder to think what might have become of Grandpapa without your help."

During this discourse Bryce removed his hat and idly examined the trinkets littering the desktop next to her battered leather sketchbook. Touching the delicate network of a bird's nest, he realized he liked the way she made the place her own, filling it with flowers and little mementos, creating a homey illusion in an otherwise dreary room. Even the peeling mantelpiece sported a collection of inexpensive books, a china candlestick, and what appeared to be a worn-out flue brush. She finished her stilted speech, so he abandoned his examination of the nest to give her a faintly mocking smile.

"Prettily said, my dear. Now why do I receive the impression you'd just as soon see me go to the devil?"

Her jaw dropped, and again she damned his unerring perception. "Why . . . I . . ."

He stepped closer, cupping her cheek in his warm palm. "Forgive me, I'm a wretch to tease you when you've been through so much. Has your grandfather been like this for long?"

"Like what?" Ignoring the unnerving sensation of Bryce's fingers lightly caressing her cheek, she pulled back slightly and forced a brilliant smile that did not match the worry in her eyes. "Grandpapa's so imaginative, he's sometimes carried away, that's all. And, of course, the drink makes him forgetful. No doubt he'll feel no lasting ill effects of this night's revelry come the morrow. Now, I believe you came to discuss my letter. May I offer you some refreshment? I could make some tea, or I believe there's some brandy . . ."

Bryce caught her shoulders. "Don't try to organize me off the subject, General. You're not going to trust me, are you?"

"I don't know what you mean." She refused to meet his piercing gaze, unwilling to confess Everett's awful illness, somehow secretly ashamed of the stigma.

He heaved a regretful sigh. "I don't suppose I've given you cause to trust me, at that."

"There's nothing you need be concerned about."

"Everett's more than just merely forgetful, isn't he?" he probed.

She swallowed. "Y-yes. And I fear he's getting worse."

"I know it's painful for you to see him changing like this."

At the sympathy in his tone, she felt the hot sting of tears prickle behind her lids. "Stop it," she said, her voice husky. "Don't be kind."

"Is that what this is?" His voice was warmly amused, yet compassionate, and therefore dangerous to her equanimity. Gently, he enfolded her in the circle of his arms, easing her stiff form against the broad protection of his chest. "I confess I'm so rarely kind that I scarcely recognized such a tender emotion."

"Don't mock me," she pleaded, her cheek pressed against his lapel. It was deceptive, she knew, a mere illusion of the senses, the comfort she drew from their shared closeness, but for just a moment she basked in the overwhelming luxury of his strength. What would it be like to have it always?

"I would never mock so valiant a warrior," Bryce replied, smoothing circles across her back. "Is Everett's mental deterioration the reason why you're willing to reconsider my offer?"

She hesitated, then nodded. Let him think that was all it was. Beneath her cheek she heard a chuckle rumble.

"I'm absolutely crushed, my dear. While I thought my charm had won you over, it was only your infernal pragmatism."

Genevieve leaned back in his arms and, despite herself, smiled at his foolery. "You are truly an incorrigible rogue, Mr. Cormick, and quite full of yourself, too, I might add. Now release me, if you please."

"It hardly pleases me." He grinned. "You're quite delectable, you know."

She blushed to the roots of her chestnut curls. "Is confusing me at every opportunity your greatest delight?"

"No." Though his tone was deceptively mild, mischief danced like a blue flame in his eyes. "But this is."

Dipping his dark head, he kissed her, expertly fitting his mouth against the softness of hers . . . and was instantly lost.

What he'd thought to keep lighthearted changed subtly, surely, when he felt her lips quiver, and he tasted the sweetness of her sigh. He captured her nape in one hand, holding her still until lack of breath forced him to lift his head again. Where his thumb rested, her pulse pounded an unsteady rhythm, and there was an answering cadence within him. Her lashes fluttered, and he was drowning in the mysterious and misty gray-green pools of her dazed eyes, in the softness that was so compellingly feminine, and so utterly missing in his life. With a groan of need, he caught her close, and kissed her . . .

. . . *again*. Oh, God, Bryce was kissing her again, Genevieve thought helplessly. Involuntarily, her hands crept up to twine around his neck as her senses exploded in a wealth of sensory impressions. The black silk of his hair whispering against her fingers, the firm pressure of his lips, the delicious rasp of beard-shadowed skin against her tender cheek. How could she endure the floodtide that was sweeping along her bloodstream, filling her with fire and brilliance? And how could she survive if he stopped?

With a deft stroke of his tongue, Bryce breached her defenses, plunging past the trembling barrier of her lips to deepen the kiss intimately. He introduced her to countless wonders with wicked expertise, then surrendered himself when her response washed over him in a scalding waterfall that swept them both under and away from all realization of time and place and sense.

The edge of the mantelpiece pressing into Genevieve's back finally demanded notice, the minor pain a reminder of a world and a situation that jerked her back from the precipice of passion with cruel authority. Breathless, she pushed at the rocklike muscles beneath the blue coat.

"Darcy." She shuddered as he trailed a path of fiery kisses down her neck and his palm unerringly cupped the fullness of her breast. "Oh, stop this. We must stop!"

"Sweet Genny," he muttered, his voice thick. "Say my name again."

Realizing her slip, she cringed inwardly at her weakness, at the terrible, bittersweet longing for a captivating soldier, the vision that for a moment in time on a secluded riverbank, he had been *her* Darcy. But this was Bryce Cormick, the famous actor, a proven deceiver. She struggled in earnest.

"Mr. *Cormick,* we can't . . ." His mouth dammed her protest against her lips in another drugging kiss. With a strength dredged from an unknown source, Genevieve broke free, hastily putting the width of the desk between them. "Desist, you—you rake!"

Bryce blinked, shook his head as if to clear it, then burst out laughing. Guffawing, he threw himself into a sprawl on the threadbare settee.

"Good God, Genevieve!" he hooted. "Do my ears deceive me, or did that sound like the seduction scene of an excruciatingly bad melodrama?"

Genevieve's knees felt as weak as watered milk, and she grasped the edge of the desk for support, shaken more than she was willing to admit and now incensed at Bryce's frivolity. She took a deep breath with the intention of giving him a good tongue-lashing, then choked when her eyes fell on the clearly discernible evidence of his passion straining against the leather fall of his breeches. She covered her flaming face in both hands and turned her back, breathing deeply and praying for composure.

"Lud, child," Bryce drawled, inspecting the slump of her slender back, "don't take on so. This kind of thing is bound to happen from time to time."

"Not to me!" Whirling, Genevieve glared at him, the fire in her eyes replaced with Arctic-green ice. "And especially not with you!"

Mockery lifted one dark eyebrow. "Indeed? Do you find my attentions so repulsive, then?"

How could she answer that? Truthfully, she'd never felt so wanton yet so wonderful as when in his arms, and it was clear that he knew the powerful, tempting effect his lovemaking produced in her.

"Since your intentions are not honorable, and I have no intention of becoming any man's doxy, whether there is an . . . attraction between us is not the issue."

"On the contrary, Genevieve," he said, "it is exactly the issue at the moment."

"As you said, you've given me no reason to trust you, sir, and I must see to my own cares. You must accept that, if we've any hope of working together."

He gave her a lazy look from beneath hooded lids. "You wouldn't consider combining business with pleasure?"

"No!"

"Now there's a pity." The corner of his shapely mouth twisted. "A waste, too. Especially considering the sparks we rub off each other, General."

"I—I was at a low ebb, and you took unconscionable advantage of me!" she spluttered. "Sir, you are a cad."

He laughed again. "And you, miss, are given to such a vainglorious turn of phrase that I give thanks that your talents lie in areas other than playwriting!"

"My point exactly," she said in her severest tone. "So if it's my talent you want, pray take leave of these attacks on my virtue, for only under that condition will I agree to work for you."

"Ah, but is your talent worth such a great sacrifice?" he goaded.

Incensed, she picked up her sketchbook and fairly hurled it at his head, along with her challenge. "Judge for yourself!"

For the next little while, silence reigned in the room, except for the occasional rustle of a page being turned. Genevieve stood at the hearth, struggling to keep her countenance free of all expression. She licked her dry lips, then groaned inwardly at the taste of Bryce that lingered on her own skin.

No matter what her traitorous body told her, she knew to her sorrow that Bryce Cormick was nothing more than a charming scoundrel. Furthermore, she already had enough problems without adding a dangerous dalliance with an unscrupulous rogue. But would Bryce abide by her edicts? Or had she spoiled her only chance to redeem Everett's markers with her hasty ultimatum?

Bryce shut the sketchbook with a snap that made Genevieve jump. She watched him warily, saying nothing.

"I assume you're as skilled with a needle as you are with a pen?" he asked abruptly. "And you've had experience directing other seamstresses?"

She nodded uncertainly.

"I've let workrooms in Long Acre near the Athena, including quarters for my costumer. I open in *Othello* the tenth of September with Darlena Letchfield as Desdemona. Can you meet such a deadline?"

Her head spinning at the name of London's most revered actress, Genevieve tried to calculate approximate yardage, working hours, numbers—and gave up. No matter how difficult, she'd make it—Grandpapa's future depended on it. She swallowed convulsively and nodded once more.

"Good. I'll expect you to begin immediately."

"You—you mean you like what I've done?" she finally managed.

Bryce grinned wryly and indicated her sketchbook. "I know genius when it hits me over the head. You've evoked the antiquarian element I want for *Othello* with an originality and a thought to character I find astonishing. You're most definitely hired to direct my troops for me, General, if you'll have me as a field marshal. I may be a cad, but I assure you my money's still good."

The generous salary he named shocked and elated Genevieve. It would make a substantial reduction in Everett's debt. But there was still another matter.

"And . . ." She colored. "And the other?"

A look of regret carved hollows in his lean cheeks. "*Damme*, woman, you do call for the hard choices, don't you? Ah, well, we're in agreement, then. I'll curb my lustful tendencies if you will."

"Sir!"

He raised his hand to stay her heated rejoinder. "Nay, my dear, no need to rebuke me, for I'm the one caught on the horns of this dilemma. However, I'll sacrifice even so sweet a prize as you to ensure the success of my Athena."

Relief as well as a mystifying and somewhat shameful stab of disappointment flooded Genevieve, but her smile was genuine. "A gallant speech, Mr. Cormick, and I assure you that you'll not regret this decision."

"Impossible, sweet Genny," Bryce said, the warmth of his glance lingering on her mouth. "Cad that I am, I already do."

"Are you certain you brought it?" Genevieve asked the following afternoon.

"You needn't keep asking over and over, gel! I may be forgetful, but I'm no fool." In his green kerseymere coat and tall beaver hat, eyes bloodshot from the previous night's excesses, Everett Maples resembled a belligerent bullfrog. He scowled at a pudgy pair of marble cherubs perched atop a scalloped Roman pedestal in the carved and gilded anteroom of Samson Baggart's Regent Street offices, then patted his jacket pocket. "All his booty is here in my pouch."

"I'm sorry, Grandpapa. I'm just nervous." Genevieve slipped her hand through the crook of his elbow and shivered beneath her stylish chintz walking costume. Although Everett seemed to have suffered no permanent ill effects of last night's outing, Genevieve's nerves screamed with tension.

Fighting for calm, she forced herself to study Baggart's rather eclectic tastes in decoration. Belgian tapestries, furniture á là Egypte, and ancient artifacts ranging from the fat cherubs to crumbling Mesopotamian pottery warred for precedence with ornately framed playbills of Baggart's current stage offerings and past triumphs. Why would a man of such obvious success stoop to thievery and blackmail? She set aside her curiosity with a silent exclamation. Nothing mattered except putting this nasty business behind them as quickly as possible. Then Baggart could go to Hades!

"We're agreed, aren't we, Grandpapa?" she asked, as much to reassure herself as to reinforce Everett's memory. "We'll hand over the . . . the package, and I'll explain about my commission from Mr. Cormick. The promise of payment must surely appease Mr. Baggart."

"I like it not," Everett huffed. "A young lady on her own—"

"Now, don't fret. We've been over and over this. Time is tight, so I must accept Mr. Cormick's offer of lodgings nearer the Athena."

The magnitude of the task before her and the knowledge that she would be working closely with her very disturbing employer evoked a flurry of butterflies under Genevieve's heart, but thanks to Bryce Cormick she had the wherewithal to negotiate with Samson Baggart on Everett's behalf. Nevertheless, it had taken quite a bit of effort to convince her grandfather of the necessity of the plan. She reminded him of their agreement.

"Maebella will look out for you until the run ends at Sadler's, then you can join me. That way we'll both be doing our parts," she said reasonably. "And no more— ah, excursions, either. I'm depending on your discretion while I'm gone, Grandpapa."

"Yes, yes." He waved an impatient hand. "But I've lived too long to see my own flesh and blood slaving away for a stranger because of me. You'd be better off if I wore my shroud."

"What absolute stuff and nonsense!" she said fiercely. "Where would I be but for you? And I know you were only trying to do your best out of love for me."

"A feather for your nest, yes, that was it," he mused, his expression going a bit vague.

"Grandpapa." Genevieve tugged his sleeve to revive his wandering attention. "We've come through worse together, so no more about it, all right?"

Everett's distinguished features quivered with almost maudlin affection. "My darling gel! What would I do without you?"

Reassured, Genevieve smiled and squeezed his arm. A pair of paneled doors swung open at that moment, and an obsequious secretary intoned, "Monsieur will see you now."

"The damned rascal," Everett muttered under his

breath. "Let's give him a good show, gel." Lifting his leonine head, Everett swept into Samson Baggart's opulent office with all of his old vigor and verve, booming a greeting. "Good morrow to you, Mr. Baggart!"

A slender figure rose from behind a massive mahogany desk. "My dear Everett. How good of you to come."

The impresario was a man of middle years with a long thin face and bountiful, curly salt-and-pepper side whiskers. Taken separately, his features were regular and his garments were of the finest quality, yet as a whole, the picture he presented was slightly off-balance, lacking a certain polish. His small, red-brown ferret eyes flicked to Genevieve, evoking a sensation of insects crawling over her skin, then his aquiline face split into a smile of marked insincerity.

"And the lovely Miss Maples! My dear, what a pleasure to meet you again. But someone so young has no interest in two fusty old relics conducting business. I'm to organize the Royal Victory Gala, you know. So much to plan, and other . . . business to discuss. Boring stuff. But my garden is charming and I'll ask Jean-Claude to have some tea brought to the sitting room—"

"I think not," Genevieve interrupted, unable to stomach Samson Baggart's pleasantries another instant. She retrieved a purse from her ridicule and placed it on the desk. "Here's partial payment of the sum my grandfather owes you, sir. I've taken a position at a theater in Long Acre. If you will but be patient, we'll have another installment shortly."

"You're a hoity-toity miss, I must say," Baggart responded mildly. After a single contemptuous glance he ignored the purse, its slight weight so obvious he wouldn't even deign to pick it up, much less examine the contents—nearly all the funds Bryce had advanced to Genevieve. "I'll wager she rules your household with a velvet hand, eh, Everett?"

"Oh, aye, she likes her way, she does," Everett said, chuckling. Distracted, he shook his gray head and winked conspiratorially, as if Samson Baggart were an intimate member of the family.

Twin spots of color rouged Genevieve's cheeks, but she refused to be dismissed like a child. "Grandpapa! Must I remind you why we're here?"

"What?" Everett looked blank, then flushed as recollection dawned. He cleared his throat uncomfortably. "Of course not, gel. What do you take me for?"

"Then give it to him, Grandpapa, so that we may conclude this matter." Obediently, Everett retrieved the pouch from his pocket, jangled it once with a childlike look of regret, then passed it to Baggart. Though he had been unmoved by Genevieve's purse, Baggart's eyes now took on an avaricious gleam, and he immediately delved into the contents of the pouch, scratching and poking among the stolen items.

Genevieve released a silent breath of relief. Thank God! Everything was going to be all right.

"You'll have what you're owed, sir, but now that I know the truth of the matter, my grandfather will no longer be an unwilling accomplice in whatever unlawful schemes you're perpetrating. Come along now, Grandpapa," she said, catching Everett's arm, overwhelmed by an urge to breathe fresh air. "We're done here."

"Stand where you are, you thievin' doxy!" Rage stripped Baggart of his cultivated accent, but it was the tiny silver pistol that appeared in his hand that froze Genevieve in her tracks. With his face screwed into murderous lines, Baggart poked the muzzle at her chin. "All right, hand it over. I'll have the rest of it!"

Genevieve gulped and clutched at Everett's arm. "I—I don't know what you mean."

"You know, don't you, old man?" Baggart snapped, pointing the weapon at Everett. "Where is it?"

"No trouble, no trouble," Everett muttered, staring in horror at the menacing pistol.

"Don't try to play the innocent with me," Baggart warned icily. "I've already paid well for the trinket, and 'twas to be delivered with my usual shipment of goods. With half the city looking for it, don't think you'll snatch the prize from me!''

"Something's missing? But what?" Genevieve demanded desperately. "Perhaps if I understood—"

"A bit of antiquity, Miss Maples, of great rarity and of a . . . religious nature, taken by treachery from an associate of mine. But the Abbot was careless with his treasure, and now the prize belongs to me. My future and my fortune will be assured when I offer this antiquity to the former emperor of France himself!''

She gaped at him. "Bonaparte?"

"Even in exile, he has interest in . . . collectibles. I deal in artifacts of great value and beauty, and the piece I seek is purported to have mystical powers that can tempt even the Conqueror of the World.''

"You mean you have others take the risk of transporting your booty while you—" She was so incensed at his greed and ruthlessness, she couldn't finish the sentence.

Baggart merely shrugged his narrow shoulders. "If I found a use for traveling players beyond the usual, and they were not adverse to an extra bit of income, what's the harm?''

"You undoubtedly swindled my grandfather and then used him to suit your ends!" she cried. "We have no 'antiquity' and if we did, we'd gladly hand it over just to be finished with this sordid business. Isn't that right, Grandpapa?''

"Nasty things," Everett mumbled. "Never did like 'em, nasty loud things, too much smoke and noise. Nigh to deafen a fellow.''

Baggart scowled. "What mummery is this?''

"Genny-girl, hurry now, we'll be late to the theater.'' Everett's expression grew even hazier until his gaze lit on Baggart, and he brightened. "I say, old friend! Would you care to hear my latest ditty? Quite wicked it is, a real crowd-pleaser!''

"Later, Grandpapa." Genevieve tried to soothe him,

then winced as Everett spread his arms and launched into "Old David's Sow," serenading the plaster gargoyles peeking over the ceiling moldings at the top of his lungs.

"Cease your screeching, you fool!" Baggart ordered. Receiving no response from the older man, he gave Everett a shove. "Didn't you hear what I said?"

Everett looked blank, then smiled beatifically and launched into another chorus.

Exasperated, Baggart glared at Genevieve. "Damn! It's a poor time for one of his spells!"

"He's not well, can't you see?" she cried. "All your threats have made him worse. At times he hardly knows his name."

Baggart grimaced in disgust, lowered the pistol, and hid it away again on his person. "Aye, I've seen the addle-pated old cove like that at the gaming tables."

"And taken gross advantage of his illness," Genevieve replied with heat. "Well, he can't help you anymore."

"Then *you* will, for it's too late to change my plans to visit the Continent, and I will not be thwarted," Baggart retorted coldly. "Evidently there's been a delay. There's no help for it. You'll have to take the next delivery from Old Blind Jacob in your grandfather's place, Miss Maples, and hold it for me until I return from my business abroad." He dug quickly in the desk drawer. "Take these passes to the gala. I will return no later than that night, and you may bring me Blind Jacob's delivery then."

Genevieve recoiled in panic from the proffered passes, shaking her head vehemently. "You're mad! We won't be your pawns any longer."

"On the contrary, my dear, I think you will," Baggart said, his reddish eyes piercing her. "Remember, I've got Everett's markers. How easily I can ruin him or take his freedom. All it would require is a word in certain high places as an old a valued colleague, a concerned friend who states that Everett Maples is no longer competent, and a danger to his family and society."

Her throat constricted with fear. "Is this antiquity so precious that you must torment an old man so?"

"To his death if need be." Baggart's voice was coldly ruthless. " 'Tis more precious than you can know, girl. Some would do anything to get their hands on it."

"Anything?" Realization struck Genevieve full force, and she blanched. "Dear God! Is that why we were attacked on the highway? Other thieves are looking for this thing, too!"

Baggart cursed obscenely and rounded his desk. "Did they get anything?"

"N-no. Help came in time."

"You must be extremely circumspect. There is a man— a very dangerous man—who seeks this prize in order to harm me and my old master. The Griffin would destroy us all if he could."

"Oh, no." Genevieve felt physically ill with horror, her stomach cramping and her extremities numb. What other unknown dangers threatened them because of Baggart's greed? In the background, Everett's booming song stretched to a high note that finally snapped her tenuous control. Whirling, she shouted at the old man. "For goodness sake, Grandpapa! Be *quiet!*"

With a hurt look, he subsided, except for a quietly defiant humming. Desperately, Genevieve turned back to Baggart. "You can't put innocent people in danger! If you persist in your threats, I—I'll go to the magistrates."

Samson Baggart relaxed, laughing at her pitiful defiance. He gestured at Everett. "Look at him! How long do you think he'd last in a place like St. Luke's?"

Genevieve's eyes jerked to her grandfather. He sat crosslegged on the edge of Baggart's desk like an ancient Pan, idly picking lint from his pantaloons and whistling cheerfully into his hat. She shuddered uncontrollably. Dared she take Baggart's threats seriously? How could she not? Flinging Everett into Fleet Street Prison for debt would be intolerable to a man in his precarious state of mind. He would not survive in St. Luke's. She swallowed hard, weighing the choices.

"If—if I do what you want this once, will you leave us in peace?"

"Absolutely."

Genevieve licked dry lips and forced herself to meet Baggart's merciless red-brown eyes. "What is it you want me to do?"

Baggart smiled benignly and offered her the gala passes. "First, Miss Maples, I'd like you to be my guest . . ."

Chapter 5

Genevieve tucked her brown paper-wrapped package more securely under her arm and scurried down the busy Long Acre thoroughfare, barely casting a glance at the industrious hive of activity at the Athena Theater. Damp wisps of fog tugged at the green duck feathers in her pert hat and the hem of her topaz sarcenet pelisse, signaling an end to August's heat. Despite the overcast sky, carpenters, roofers, journeymen, and laborers of all descriptions swarmed the network of scaffolds lacing the Athena, unceasing in their efforts to restore the shabby playhouse to her true glory by opening night.

Oblivious to the activity, Genevieve clutched her prize even tighter, her thoughts churning as she turned the corner into the next lane. The ramshackle building dominating the teeming business section had been in its day a bank, a bookseller's, and a stay maker's, and now housed the scene-painting studio, sewing rooms, carpenter's workshops, and lodgings that Genevieve had occupied for over a week in her new capacity of costumer for Bryce Cormick.

Mounting the steps, she automatically looked for the upper windowsill marked by a pot of golden asters, the only concession she'd made toward making the rooms her own. She should have been enjoying the unaccustomed freedom and privacy the arrangement afforded, but pressures from all fronts kept her in a constant state of anxiety. Would she be able to completely costume an entire production on time? Was Grandpapa behaving properly at Sadler's? Her fingers twisted convulsively on the brown paper bundle. And as for Samson Baggart's chore . . .

Her thoughts racing in a thousand directions at once, she reached the entrance only to run headlong into a flamboyant figure.

"Miss Maples! There you are!" Jules Chesterson swept his curly-brimmed beaver off his yellow locks and beamed his delight. Attired in mauve pantaloons, an emerald-green waistcoat, and a striped crimson jacket, he was the pink of fashion. He plucked her package out of her grasp. "Oh, do allow me!"

To her dismay, Genevieve lost the brief tug-of-war while fighting to keep a straight face. "Mr. Chesterson," she choked, "how do you do? You're looking very . . . well."

"Thank you, but I'm afraid my valet is hopeless in achieving the proper mathematical," he said, pointing ruefully to the intricate knotting of his neckcloth. He swept her costume with a practiced and admiring eye. "You, on the other hand, are always so well turned out, and today is no exception. Could I recommend your dressmaker to my sister? Has abominable taste, you know. Needs all the help she can get."

Genevieve hesitated only momentarily. "Then you may give her my direction, for Miss Smythe and I are responsible for all my gowns, and we have a mind to open an establishment of our own just as soon as we can secure a suitable location. We wish to be very exclusive, you understand."

"Oh, completely. But you must allow me to assist you. I have many associates with properties. I could make inquiries for you," he said eagerly.

She beamed with pleasure at his offer. "Thank you, Jules. How kind you are!"

"And how entirely admirable you are—a woman with

ambition! But I must confess I was floored when I heard you'd taken up new employment as a costumer.''

Juggling her bundle and his ebony cane in one hand, Jules held open the door. With an anxious look at her package, Genevieve preceded him into a lobby illuminated by a pair of long windows and cluttered with all sorts of theatrical paraphernalia. Women's voices drifted from the sewing rooms to the right, punctuated by hammering from the cellars, while the pungent smells of raw lumber and paint assaulted their noses. They paused before the narrow staircase leading to the upper levels and her apartment.

''And I'm amazed at how closely you follow my progress,'' Genevieve responded dryly.

''My dearest Miss Maples, you know I hold you in the highest esteem.'' Jules's youthful face was earnest. ''Imagine my dismay when I returned from rusticating in the countryside to find my favorite King Harold has been replaced by a freckle-faced boy under that hoary beard!''

''Our young Mike deserved the promotion,'' she explained. ''And not before time, wouldn't you say?''

''Oh, no, I adore seeing you in any guise,'' Jules protested. ''I'm devastated, truly. Won't you be performing again?''

''One never knows in the theater,'' Genevieve said vaguely, reaching for the elusive package. ''I'm only comfortable behind enough makeup to give me stage courage, you know. Despite my upbringing, I've no illusions about my dramatic ability.''

''Oh, no, you're wonderful,'' Jules contradicted, gallantly, sweeping another bow and ignoring her efforts to retrieve her belongings.

She squelched her irritation behind a pointed smile. ''And you are too kind to my meager talents. I confess I'm quite elated at my new employment. That package you're holding represents a full morning's work.''

''Whatever could it be?'' Jules asked playfully. He shook and squeezed the bundle, crackling the stiff paper like a child with a Christmas gift. ''Jewels? Treasure?''

Genevieve stiffened. The dandy's teasing words struck nerves rubbed raw by her morning's frightening excursion into the seedy precincts of Field Lane and the memory of Blind Jacob's milky eyes—blind with age, yet somehow still able to peer into her guilty soul. Blind Jacob's tiny, ill-lit shop had been crammed full of musty bolts of age-rotted calico snugged beside the finest contraband French silk, trunks of rags and boxes of finery from bygone ages, dusty hats and broken shoes. And at her mention of Baggart's name the humped, ancient fence had pressed into her trembling palms the finest piece of brocade she'd ever seen, rolled around a small, incriminating package that was the key to freeing Everett from Samson Baggart's blackmail. Now both rested in Jules's foppish grasp.

"Something even more precious," she said lightly, trying to smile. "I've been in every draper's shop and rag-picker's from Bond Street to Holborn to find a bolt of French brocade for Desdemona's gown that is certain to meet even Mrs. Letchfield's demanding specifications."

"She is without parallel, is she not?" Jules asked eagerly, his toffee-brown eyes lighting up. "I try never to miss one of her performances."

Genevieve paused, struck by a sudden inspiration. She looked at Jules's guileless face and cursed Samson Baggart for what he was about to make her do.

"Ah, Jules," she said, licking lips gone suddenly dry, "as it happens, a friend"—she nearly choked on that—"has given me tickets for the upcoming Victory Gala at Covent Garden. I believe Mrs. Letchfield is scheduled to perform. You've been so generous to me in the past, and I'd like to return your gestures of friendship. Would it be too forward of me to ask you to accompany me to the event as my escort?"

The young dandy was thunderstruck with delighted amazement. He caught her hand and pressed it reverently to his lips. "Genevieve, you've made me the happiest man in London town! You know I could never refuse you the least request. Can you not tell that my heart is yours?"

Somewhat alarmed, Genevieve tried to extricate her fingers from his ardent grasp. "Mr. Chesterson—Jules, you do me a great honor, but please understand that this invitation is made only in friendship. If you cannot accept it on those terms, then I must withdraw it."

"Why? Is there another?"

Genevieve laughed unsteadily, taken unawares for a giddy instant by a vision of devilish blue eyes. She pushed the image aside and reclaimed her hand. "Really, Jules, such impertinence!"

"Forgive me, but desperation makes me bold."

Despite the comical nature of his attire, there was an earnestness about Jules that made Genevieve pause, one foot on the first step of the staircase. The guilty knowledge that this day she'd become Baggart's accomplice, however unwillingly, and now made use of Jules's affections to further Baggart's plans, made her feel very much older than the dandy, though he could only be a year or two her junior.

"Now, you must listen to me," she said gently. "I shouldn't want to hurt you by encouraging feelings that I can't return."

"But there's no one else?"

"Well, no," she hedged. "That is—"

"Then I'll settle for your friendship for now, and hope someday to have my affections returned."

"Jules, that's not fair to you," she protested. "You should be meeting young ladies of your own status."

"Hen-witted ninnies, all of 'em!" he dismissed with a disdainful snort. "Can't abide the way Mama parades me through that marriage mart, either."

"I can see how that could be quite daunting," Genevieve agreed solemnly. "But I meant what I said about my invitation. Perhaps it would be better if we didn't change the foundations of our friendship in this way."

"You could not be so cruel as to withdraw your invitation now! I understand your conditions fully," he said with the eagerness of a puppy begging forgiveness. "I promise not to make a nuisance of myself. Best behavior at all times.''

Genevieve couldn't suppress a smile. "Really, Jules! But I'm still not certain this is wise . . .''

Slyly, he added the coup de grace. "I'm certain my sister will be there, as well as scores of her friends. Appear in some riveting creation of your own, and with a few choice words of praise from yours truly, I'm certain they'll all be beating a path to the door of your salon.''

Despite herself, the image of a swatch of antique tapestry she'd seen that very morning and immediately coveted jumped straight into her head, and with it a full-blown design for a evening gown of surpassing elegance. Of course, she'd have to locate the finest of iridescent tissue in a subtle blue-green . . .

Genevieve drew her speeding thoughts to an abrupt halt, then wryly promised herself not to underestimate Jules again. Indeed, even though her presence at the gala would be at Samson Baggart's command, she could ill afford to miss the opportunity he presented so adroitly, not only for the sake of her future career but also for the chance of earning even more to help reduce Everett's debt. She smiled up into the young man's anxious face.

"Then we're agreed, sir. I'm sure we'll have a delightful evening together—as friends.''

"Really?'' Jules's caramel eyes shone with his elation. "Splendid! Oh, jolly good!'' He bowed, backing toward the door, and bowed again. "I'll call for you that night, shall I? Lovely!''

"Jules!''

Instantly, he was back at her side. "Yes, my dear?''

"My package.''

He looked with comical surprise at the brown paper bundle he still grasped, then hastily set it down on top of the broad newel post at her side. "So sorry. Silly of me. Well, good day.''

With a tip of his hat, he sailed out the door, and Genevieve was hard-pressed to know if his boots ever touched the ground. Bemused, she shook her head, indulgent humor lighting her eyes, her anxieties momentarily forgotten for the first time in days.

"Don't tell me that overdressed coxcomb is an admirer of yours?"

Genevieve jumped, startled by the acid comment. Bryce Cormick's broad-shouldered silhouette filled the doorway of the carpenter's workroom. He'd evidently just lent his hand to some heavy task, for as he advanced, he rolled down his cuffs and slung his coat over one brawny arm.

"Good day, Mr. Cormick." Embarrassed annoyance made her tone tart. "Is it so inconceivable that I should evoke admiration in a gentleman?"

Bryce's lip twisted. "I merely thought you had better taste."

"Mr. Chesterson has long been a fan of the Maples Company."

"It's the Athena that demands your attention now. I must complain when your social commitments interfere with your commission."

Genevieve's breath caught in indignation. "Your charge is totally unfounded! Why, I've only just now met Jules by chance. Anyway, I set the ladies to stitching the servants' costumes before I went to find *something* to please your precious Mrs. Letchfield!"

"Darlena's giving you fits, is she?" Bryce asked, suddenly amused. "I'll admit she can be a bit difficult."

"Perhaps she's had lessons from you!" Genevieve snapped. "Excuse me, I have work to—"

"Stop! Halt, ye thievin' whoreson!" bellowed a male voice.

A ragged, soot-smeared urchin careened at top speed into the lobby, followed closely by a red-faced carpenter swinging a hammer and shouting at the top of his lungs. The boy's face was pinched with panic, and his black eyes widened at the sight of the man and woman in the lobby.

"Grab 'im, sir!" gasped the carpenter. "Little bastard's filched a gob from the toolbox!"

With a burst of desperate speed, the boy agilely ducked past Bryce and rounded the banister toward the freedom of the front entrance. Almost as an afterthought, he scooped up Genevieve's package under one rail-thin arm as he went by.

Baggart's precious bundle! Disaster loomed for Genevieve and her grandfather. She leaped forward with a strangled yelp. "My brocade!"

The boy jerked open the door, but Bryce lunged, catching hold of his collar. In the next instant, Bryce held only a handful of rotten fabric as the youngster tore free with such force he sailed head over heels down the front steps. He hit the brick pavement at the bottom with a sickening thud and lay still.

Bryce cursed and vaulted down the steps, Genevieve and the carpenter on his heels.

"Oh, my God," Genevieve breathed, her eyes widening at the smear of red on the bricks under the urchin's matted head. "Is he . . . ?"

Bryce bent over the small, still form, his large hands taking careful examination of the child's bony limbs. "Just stunned, I think."

"Dear heaven! Look," she murmured, pushing aside a ragged, filthy sleeve to reveal a painfully red, smut-crusted carbuncle covering the boy's elbow.

Bryce's mouth went grim at the brutal evidence of a chimney-sweeper's lot. "A climbing boy."

"Run away from his master, no doubt." The red-faced carpenter snorted, then reached in the child's waistband to retrieve several chisels. "And a wretched little thief, lootin' my tools. A spell in Newgate'll teach 'im!"

"He's just a child, and half starved at that!" Genevieve protested. She scooped up the disputed package and fixed Bryce with a look of appeal. "Bring him inside."

"And just what do you intend to do, General?"

"I don't know, but we can't just leave him here."

The carpenter gaped at Bryce in amazement. "Blimey,

sir. Why take the trouble? Let the Charlies transport the bugger.''

"Go back to work, Ellis,'' Bryce ordered, and carefully lifted the child.

Moments later, Genevieve ushered Bryce through her small sitting room to one of a pair of sparsely furnished bedrooms. While Bryce laid the child on the narrow bed, she hastily put away the silently condemning package, stripped off her pelisse and hat, then brought towels and a pitcher of water from an ancient dresser. "Do you think he's hurt badly?''

"No, but he'll have quite a knot on his skull,'' Bryce replied, stepping back to give her room.

"Poor thing, he's been terribly abused,'' Genevieve murmured.

Too many hungry, homeless children lived and died in the poorer neighborhoods of the city, their plight a national disgrace. While outraged by the injustice, now Genevieve was moved to pity by the reality of one child's wretched existence. She wiped the boy's face and hands, then turned her attention to the lump on the side of his head and shot Bryce an anxious glance. "What's to become of him?''

"Think I'm such a monster I'd hand him over to the magistrates?'' Bryce's mouth twisted, and there was a flicker of something bleak behind his eyes. "Believe it or not, Miss Maples, I feel a kinship with our erstwhile thief. Most of my own boyhood was spent in much the same battle for survival on the docks of Marseilles.''

Her smoky green eyes grew wide with confusion. "Truly? But . . . that is, you spoke of your father, and I thought—''

"That I'd been born and reared in the verdant bosom of England?'' Bryce's short laugh was humorless. "Hardly. I was conceived during one of those lulls in the hostilities that induces wealthy young English gentlemen on a Grand Tour to sow their seed among the continental maidens. But growing up in French dance halls and theaters where my mother worked made me quite . . . independent at an early age, just like our small friend here.''

Genevieve's heart constricted with compassion at the painful image Bryce's words evoked. Still sponging the insensible child, she tried to keep her tone even, knowing instinctively that Bryce would resent any show of sympathy.

''You've come far then. But I still don't understand how you came to be an Englishman.''

Bryce leaned an elbow on the plain wooden headboard and gave her a mocking smile. ''Curious, are you, General?''

Her chin came up a fraction at his tone. ''As I would be with any enigma.''

''Am I so mysterious, then?''

''You're not an easy man to know,'' she said carefully. Wringing out the towel again, she laid it on the boy's brow, then straightened and met Bryce's gaze directly. ''I wager you hide your secret self beneath that facile charm.''

''Quite an indictment.''

''Yes,'' she answered seriously, ''for that barrier rarely allows anyone close enough to discover who you really are.''

''Perhaps my exact intention.''

''And your loss, sir,'' she answered softly.

Stung, he hardened his jaw. ''What I am would chill your heart, my dear Genny. Better you should keep your illusions.''

''I'm not so fainthearted. What could you possibly confess that I've not already guessed?''

Genevieve's naiveté made Bryce angry. Visions of horror and death, blood and deceit, and his own part in the carnage threatened to overrun him like the evil spirits released from Pandora's box. He'd seen too much, lived too much, and even telling himself he'd only done a soldier's duty was feeble comfort. How dared she taunt him, even from her innocence?

''Trying guessing at the kind of life where a boy of ten

might witness his mother murdered at her enraged lover's hand," he said in a hard voice. Ignoring Genevieve's gasp, he continued relentlessly. "Could you imagine even in a hundred lifetimes how a boy might take up a knife and seek revenge on such a man?"

"Did . . ." Genevieve swallowed. "Did you kill him?"

"Unfortunately, no. But the man was powerful and my mother only an actress of questionable virtue, so for my efforts I spent five months in a Marseilles dungeon."

"Prison?" The word was barely a whisper from Genevieve's constricted throat.

He nodded. "That's where my father found me."

"I don't understand."

Bryce stared out the window at the gray sky. "He'd had no idea of my existence, you see, not until the old hag who'd worked the crib decided there might be a coin or two in the knowledge and sent him word."

"Your father must be a very good man."

"Sir Theodore Cormick is that, I'll grant you, and one who knows his duty," Bryce said with revealing bitterness. "No matter that one consequence of a youthful indiscretion turned out to be a foulmouthed guttersnipe with blood on his hands."

"It must have been terribly hard for both of you, coming together as strangers like that. Yet you're certainly a son to make any father proud, and you carry his name."

"Aye, he gave that to me, for his wife was dead, and he had only my half sister Allegra to carry on the Cormick name. He educated me and taught me to love this country as my own, but as for familial ties . . ." Bryce made a dismissive gesture. "Let us just say we've had our differences."

"Why do I think you're much too hard on yourself?" she asked.

Bryce's lips twisted. "Because, despite everything, you persist in clinging to your illusions. But don't be deceived, sweetheart, or life will knock you flat."

"You are very much a cynic, aren't you?"

Smiling slightly, he made a mock bow. " 'Tis my greatest calling."

A soft moan from the child on the bed stayed Genevieve's retort. Instead, she hastily dipped the towel in the cool water again and reapplied herself to her ministrations. The boy opened his black eyes. Then, with the feral instincts of a wild creature, he came instantly aware of his situation, and struggled to rise.

"Stay now, you're safe," Genevieve soothed, pressing him back. "That was quite a blow you took, young man."

Panic and suspicion etched the boy's expression with a wariness beyond his years. "Lemme up. I didn't mean nothin' by it. 'Tweren't my fault!"

"That lump seems to have loosened his tongue," Bryce said. He helped the boy to a sitting position on the edge of the bed, but kept a steadying hand clamped to his bony shoulder. "Rest easy, lad, I haven't sent for the magistrates—yet. Give a good accounting of yourself, and we might avoid further unpleasantness. Now, tell me your name."

Seeing there was no escape, the boy reluctantly complied. "My mates call me Jack. Jack Potts."

"Any family, Jack?"

The boy shrugged and shook his head.

"How old are you?"

"Thirteen."

Bryce frowned. "You can't be more than six, lad."

"I'll be ten come Christmastide, and that's a fact," Jack said indignantly, then looked instantly chagrined at his revelation.

"Apprenticed to a sweep, are you, Jack?"

Jack's black eyes widened in real alarm. "No! I ain't going back there! The master puts hot coals to my feet to make me climb up the flues. I ain't never going back."

"So you're on your own? Well, Jack Potts, what were you doing on my premises?"

With a look of transparent calculation, the boy decided to brazen it out. "Nothin', sir, I swear," he said stoutly.

"I wouldn't try to gull a swell cove like ye, sir, that I wouldn't."

"I see. Thief and a liar, too," Bryce said, his mouth twitching. "A man after my own heart."

"Don't torment him," Genevieve scolded. "He's frightened enough already."

"Oh, yes, missus, ye're right," Jack agreed ingenuously. "Fair thought I'd swallow me tongue when I fell. 'Course some'd say if a body were *pushed* that's a different thing altogether. Murdering poor innocents being an un-Christian act and all."

"Blackmail, too." Bryce laughed. "Wonderful!"

Jack Potts gave Bryce a highly indignant look, then broke into a sheepish grin that transformed his gaunt face. "Can't blame a body for trying, can you, guv?"

"Absolutely not," Bryce agreed. "But such will surely get you transported in due course. Is that what you want?"

Jack hung his matted head. "Nay, sir."

"He . . . he could stay here," Genevieve offered impulsively.

"That's as complete a bit of fudge as I've ever heard!" Bryce snorted.

Genevieve persisted. "There's always errands to run, and pins to find, and threads to pick. It would be a help to have another pair of hands, especially considering how pressed for time we are."

Annoyance darkened Bryce's face. "From what I've seen, you can barely take care of yourself, General."

"Well, we just can't turn him out again," she protested.

"I can look after meself, I can," Jack Potts muttered, squirming under Bryce's grasp.

"Bloody hell!" Bryce ground his teeth. "I'm surrounded by imbeciles. All right, then, I'll take him with me."

"I ain't goin' to no orphan home!" Jack broke for freedom, only to be caught up short again as Bryce clamped a hand in his waistband.

"Hold, you half-pint busman!" Bryce dangled Jack in

midair, reducing the effectiveness of the lad's flailing fists. "It happens I have need of a boy in my establishment. For a loyal worker, it could be a comfortable station, plenty of victuals, a warm safe place to sleep, wages for spending."

Jack's black eyes grew round, and he ceased his struggles.

"Would you consider such a position with Mr. Cormick, Jack?" Genevieve said gently.

"Well . . ." The boy's mouth trembled, but he bit down hard to still the betraying tremor. "I don't take charity."

"And I don't give it," Bryce retorted, setting the boy to his feet. "Strictly a business arrangement, man to man. And you're out on your ear if I catch you thieving again."

Jack's features twitched with a mixture of innate pride and wary eagerness. "I might give it a go—for a while."

"Then give me your hand on it, lad," Bryce said.

As they shook hands to seal the bargain, Genevieve's heart gave a dangerous lurch. For all his show of reluctance, Bryce had known instinctively how to appeal to the boy, had reached out in generosity to the waif, revealing more of himself than he knew. Tender admiration softened her gaze and her defenses.

Bryce glanced up in time to be utterly snared by her gentle scrutiny. *Fraud,* she silently accused, and her smile made a mockery of his pretenses. He had the disturbing sensation that she'd peeked into a secret place inside him without his knowing, and he reacted instinctively to shore up those startling cracks in his emotional bulwarks, withdrawing abruptly.

"Come, young man, you've taken up enough of Miss Maples's valuable time." Bryce guided the boy through the sitting room toward the door, leaving Genevieve to trail after them. "You need a good feed up and a few days' rest to make certain there are no lasting ill effects of that tumble."

"I'm fit, sir, I am!" Jack said, worried his golden opportunity might turn into dross.

"We'll take no chances, is that clear, Mr. Potts?" Bryce asked. He flicked a glance in Genevieve's direction. "Bid *adieu* to Miss Maples, and let's be off."

"Yes, sir." Jack looked shyly at Genevieve. "Thankee, miss."

"I hope you'll prove Mr. Cormick's faith in you is justified, Jack," she said.

The boy's dark head bobbed vigorously. "Aye, miss. Jack Potts is a man of his word."

"I'll view your progress on the costumes another time, General," Bryce said. He gave a curt nod, then herded the boy down the stairs. "I'm going to introduce you to my old sergeant, Jack. He'll set you right."

"Aye, sir!"

A bit dismayed at the rapidity of Bryce's decision and abrupt departure, Genevieve stood at the top of the staircase listening to their voices echo up the stairwell, grappling with a wealth of conflicting emotions. What she'd learned about Bryce's past moved her deeply, and his kindness to a child proved he was not as hard as he'd have her believe. Yet to care for the man was dangerous, another complication in an already complicated situation, compounded as it was by her guilt and dishonesty.

From its hideaway, Baggart's package taunted her. She could not indulge in any further emotional entanglements until that nasty business was done. Perhaps it was just as well for her own peace of mind that she had Jules as a buffer and a defense against any foolish romantic inclinations. Firmly, she disciplined all her unnamed longings, locking them away so they could not betray her.

A small boy's indignant wail reverberated up the staircase.

"Take a *what*, sir?"

Bryce's deep voice rumbled an answer, and, heedless of her heart, Genevieve laughed out loud at Jack's reply.

"Oh, sir! Anything but that! Anything but a *bath*!"

* * *

"Ouch! Dammit, General! Watch what you're doing," Bryce yelped several afternoons later. "Are you trying to impale me on that thing?"

"I'm sorry, but if you'd kindly be still, I'll be done in a moment," Genevieve mumbled around a mouthful of pins. She made deft readjustments to the drape of the military tunic she was fitting on Bryce and began to pin. "You want this costume to be perfect, don't you?"

"Not at the expense of my hide!"

"It's no concern of mine if you wish to carouse the night through, but I'd appreciate it if you'd refrain from taking your ill temper out on me," she said with some asperity.

"Since carousing implies some degree of pleasure, I wouldn't call what I did last evening anything remotely related," he answered with a sour grimace.

Another useless round of drinking and information seeking for Huxford had earned him nothing but a headache. Only the knowledge that, if the Abbot's Seal came on the market, every house cracker and receiver would now know that a certain Mr. Griffin D'Arcy would top any offer made for it gave him any satisfaction.

"Would you like Jack to fetch you some black coffee?" she asked.

Jack Potts looked up from the pile of fabric scraps he'd been sorting. "I'll be glad to pop right down to the chop shop, sir!"

A thorough scrubbing, abundant food, and medicinal salves had transformed the boy, bringing a bloom to his cheeks and a sparkle to his eyes in scarcely a week's time. Bett, Lucy, and Agnes, the middle-aged seamstresses employed to assist Genevieve, had immediately made him the pet of the workroom, Lucy even taking on the task of teaching him his letters. Now he scrambled up from the worktable located under a bank of long windows and looked eagerly at his benefactor.

"It'd be no trouble at all, sir!"

"I don't want any damned coffee," Bryce said, then

relented at the boy's crestfallen face. "Thanks anyway, lad."

Genevieve stepped back and laid a comforting hand on Jack's shoulder. Almost absently, she took a scrap of fabric and deftly twisted and knotted it into a clever Punch puppet that brought the gleam back to Jack's black eyes.

"Perhaps some comfits or bonbons from the confectioner's might sweeten his disposition." Handing Jack the puppet, Genevieve gave him a wink that evoked an answering grin, while the seamstresses tittered behind their thimbles. "I know we'd all enjoy such a delightful change."

"Just get on with it." Unamused, Bryce glared at her through bleary eyes, wondering if her snappish mood had anything to do with the feverish pace they'd been setting over the last days.

Indeed, there was an air of strain on Genevieve's delicate features and faint plum shadows of worry under her eyes. But then, the Athena's opening was drawing near, and everyone was under considerable strain, himself included, with what the headaches of rehearsals at the Athena and Covent Garden, dealing with the carpenters, and Huxford's damnable prodding for results. All that, coupled with his growing obsession for this testy siren, was certainly enough to put a man into the blackest of moods.

Genevieve opened her mouth to make another retort, but a glance at Bryce's scowl made her think better of it. "Jack, why don't you go for the post instead?" she suggested.

"Yes, miss!" Jack disappeared out the door in a flash.

"Now, Mr. Cormick, stand up straight, if you please," Genevieve said, restocking her mouth with the lethal pins.

Bryce stoically submitted to her tender mercies and watched her work. Over the golden-hued gown that matched the asters blooming in her apartment window, she wore an apron whose pockets were stuffed with scissors, measuring tapes, and pincushions. Occasionally she referred to the watercolor rendering of her sketch for

Othello's tunic that was tacked up on one wall among all the rest of her designs for the production. He had a chance to admire not only her efficiency but also the generous curve of her breasts, and for the thousandth time he cursed the promise he'd made not to woo her.

Why was forbidden fruit the sweetest? Bryce wondered. Since he and Genevieve had made their pact, he'd been hard-pressed to keep his end of it, all thought of Clorinda and the possibility of marriage banished by the soft green depths of this chestnut-haired witch's eyes, the memory of her mouth under his, and the unsettling way she seemed so often to see right through him. He'd tasted the fire beneath her composed façade, and if searching for the Abbot's Seal made his head hurt, then being in a perpetual state of unrelenting lust definitely made him surly.

If he had any sense at all, he'd be home sleeping off his late night instead of trying to come up with another excuse to keep her company. He'd already given her the grand tour of the Athena and taken her to the musicians' rehearsal on the pretext of designing matching coats for the orchestra. He was using the time-honored tactic of adding a musical score to *Othello* during the spectacle scenes to circumvent the Licensing Act that gave only Covent Garden and Drury Lane the right to produce "legitimate" drama. She'd been attentive but wary during it all, as if she sensed that his motives in having her along were suspect.

She had the right idea about his character, he admitted with a groan as her sweet floral fragrance rose about him in heady, intoxicating waves. His inclinations were certainly not the best, not even on a par with that pompous fop, Chesterson, who'd made a damned nuisance of himself by hanging around. Not that he was jealous of Chesterson, Bryce assured himself, just because he found himself longing to throttle the young pup every time he saw him making calf's eyes at Genevieve.

A frown marring his dark brow, he stared at the top of Genevieve's head as she neatly basted a sleeve in place.

Surely she had better sense than to involve herself with a society buck who'd use her for his pleasure, then discard her like yesterday's soiled neckcloth. But wasn't seduction exactly what was in his own mind? Bryce recited a silent list of obscenities.

Genevieve caught sight of Bryce's glowering expression. "I'm almost done."

Bending close, she bit off the thread, giving him such a sensation of homey intimacy that he had to grit his teeth and clench his fists to keep from reaching for her right there in front of everyone. She looked up, startled by the ferocious tension in his face. "Is anything wrong?"

His voice grated harshly. "Can I get out of this damned thing now?"

"Yes, of course." She helped him slip the tunic over his head. "Careful of the pins."

Freed at last from the restraints of the garment, Bryce found that he was sweating. While Genevieve and Lucy positioned the tunic on a nearby tailor's dummy, he reached for his coat, surreptitiously blotting his damp brow.

Damn if this wasn't getting out of hand! He wanted her, that was clear, but she wasn't the kind to indulge in a quick grope and tumble in the stage wings with the likes of him. The work of costuming the production was well started, and he had to admit that Genevieve was competent, needing none of his trumped-up supervision. No, there was nothing else to do but keep his distance from her from now on, as much for his own peace of mind as for hers. He turned to take his leave just as Jack dashed back in, clutching a letter.

"Here's another one for ye, miss," the boy said.

Love letters? Bryce wondered. From Chesterson? Knowing he had no claim, he could not suppress a sense that something threatened what belonged to him. The primitive and possessive anger made him crazy.

Genevieve caught Bryce's baleful eye upon her. "From

Maebella. She's been letting me know how Grandpapa goes on," she explained.

"Everything all right?" he asked, relaxing again.

"He's very calm," she replied. Bryce's concern eased her edginess. Tucking the note into her apron pocket, Genevieve gave him a tentative smile, crying truce for the moment. She gestured to a table at the far end of the room. "Would you like to see how the rest of the garments are coming?"

She looked so hopeful, he didn't have the heart to refuse, despite the fact that he was still sweating. So he endured the bittersweet torture of her nearness while she pointed out the finer details of a serving woman's coif and a duke's raiment, leading him past several tailor's dummies wearing half-constructed coats and untrimmed hats, chatting animatedly all the while. He had to admit that the execution of her designs was even more breathtaking and dramatic than he could have hoped. He paused to admire the particularly striking ivory brocade that Desdemona would wear, then his eye caught on a smaller model tucked back in the corner behind the rest.

"What's this one?" he asked, pointing. "I don't recall anything like this in your sketches."

To his surprise, she flushed.

"Ah, it's something I'm working on for myself. Wouldn't you like to examine the soldier's tunics?"

He ignored her, fingering the unusual multicolored tapestry of the square-cut bodice, imagining Genevieve wearing this delectable creation, imagining the man lucky enough to be her companion running his finger across the top of that bodice, touching the creamy flesh swelling—

He jerked his hand away as if burned, silently cursing all bargains and promises. Scowling, he vented his frustration on her. "I'd rather imagined you had no time for anything but my costumes, but I see young Chesterson's attentions have given you reason to cater to your vanity."

"Do you see any signs of my neglecting my work, sir?" she demanded, eyes flashing. "No, nor will you! What I do on my own time is my concern. Besides, what better way for a couturiere to advertise than to be seen in her own designs? When this commission is finished, Maebella and I might be able to open our own salon.''

''And give up the theater?''

She shot him a suspicious look, but seeing no mockery began to fuss with the bits and pieces of yet another costume laid out on the table. ''Sometimes you make choices out of necessity. Grandpapa needs stability, and I—well, I have no objection to having a permanent home. Since each gown I design is a step toward that goal, you may be sure I take every care. It's as important to me as making a go of the Athena is to you, wouldn't you say?''

''Since I've sunk every farthing of my military bonus into it, yes.''

''It's more than that for you,'' she said, watching him closely. ''Don't try to deny it.''

He stirred, restless at her probing. ''I suppose . . . it's a new beginning.''

''After serving in the war, you mean. Most men desire to relive their exploits over and over, yet you never speak of them.''

''I have no fond memories.''

Sympathy softened her expression. ''Was it so very awful?'' she asked quietly.

An icy bleakness clouded his features. ''It made hell look like a country holiday.''

''Yet you must feel some satisfaction that your efforts helped reap an English victory?''

Crossing his arms over his chest, Bryce leaned a hip against the edge of the table where she arranged and rearranged pattern pieces in an endless puzzle. ''You think I took pride in making war on the country of my birth? In using the heritage of my youth as a weapon against my mother's race?''

Startled, Genevieve stared at him. ''A bitter choice.''

''At times only the surety that Bonaparte's defeat would heal the wounds of both nations kept me sane.'' His mouth twisted with a humorless grimace. "I believe Richelieu once said that treason is a matter of timing. Under the right circumstances, I could have been hanged by either country."

"Don't be maudlin," she snapped, her impatience at his self-indictment clearly written on her countenance. "Obviously, you're no traitor."

"So sure, are you?"

"Be serious, sir! It is inappropriate to make light of such a subject." Exasperated, she swept her pattern pieces into a pile and glared at the mess she'd made.

"Oh, I'm deadly serious, my sweet, for I have a personal interest in the topic."

"What does that mean?"

"A traitor's deceit cost my best friend his life. Cal's death taught me to hate every form of the villainy, even that within myself." With an effort, Bryce pulled away from the dark inward tug of memory. Smiling wryly, he caught her hand and rubbed his thumb back and forth across the delicate hills and valleys of her knuckles. "Be warned, General; war makes men into things that aren't quite human."

"But the time has come to put all of that behind you," she protested.

"You're right." He lifted her hand, brushing the back of it with his lips, and his vivid gaze fell across her features, heating her skin with its intensity. "Fortunately, more pleasant matters command my attention now."

Sudden tension throbbed in the air between them, making them forget the murmur of conversation from Jack and the seamstresses at the other end of the long room. There were only the two of them, caught in a blue-green web of temptation.

Abruptly, Genevieve looked away, breaking the connection, but her reply was breathless. "That was not our agreement."

"Are you always so duty bound?"

"When circumstances warrant."

"And if circumstances were different?"

A flicker of the deepest longing and regret shimmered behind her suddenly lowered lashes, and the candor of her soft reply took him by surprise.

"Then, sir, in such event, we might both discover that some promises are made to be broken."

Chapter 6

❝Look, there he is! And the duke's with him!"
Jules Chesterson's excited voice rose over the expectant hum of the audience packing the Covent Garden Theater on Victory Gala night. As he craned forward in the private box he occupied with Genevieve, a smattering of applause broke out, then grew into a thunderous ovation. From the royal box, the portly figure of the prince regent waved and bowed to his subjects while a tall man with a striking profile and a soldier's carriage stood erect at his side.

"Prinny takes the homage that is Wellington's due." As Jules sat back again, his caramel-brown eyes reflected his amusement and his admiration for his lovely companion. Genevieve had the air of a medieval princess in her tapestry gown with its flowing sea-colored sleeves and skirts. Her soft gray-green eyes sparkled and her chestnut ringlets, caught up in a faux-pearl aigrette, shone with the light of hundreds of candles burning in the lusters hanging above their heads. More than a few casual glances lingered on their box, and for once it was not Jules's finery that caught the eye.

"His Majesty surely knows a hero's worth, and that adds value to his own popularity," Genevieve replied. "Did he not elevate Wellington to the dukedom with all haste?"

"Only to have his opposition accuse him of stinginess and promptly double the duke's living!" Jules chuckled. "You know His Grace leaves shortly for Paris as ambassador to Louis's court."

"Quite a change from soldier to diplomat." She leaned forward to examine the crowd. "Who else is that with them?"

"The chancellor, I believe, and the Earl of Huxford. And there's Heinrich von Throder. I introduced you to the baron as we were coming in, didn't I?"

Genevieve nodded. The roly-poly Prussian diplomat with the Father Christmas face was evidently an avid fan of the theater, for he had immediately recognized her name and connected it with her grandfather.

"Had the pleasure of seeing Everett Maples perform just last week at Sadler's," the baron had said, his pale blue eyes beaming. Catching Genevieve's fingers in his stubby hands, he'd bowed with old-fashioned courtliness and kissed her knuckles. "Splendid performance."

"Thank you, sir. You're very kind," Genevieve replied, quite charmed, and a good deal relieved that Grandpapa was getting on well despite her absence.

"No, my dear, I've merely been a lover of talent since I was a youth in the seminary. Thankfully, diplomacy suited me more than holy orders, so I can indulge my taste for entertainments such as your illustrious grandfather has provided me on so many occasions. Will he be performing tonight?"

"Regretfully, no." She made a vague gesture. "His health . . ."

The baron smiled kindly. "Age will tell on us all, unfortunately."

The crush in the saloon at that point had begun to separate them, so the baron bade Genevieve send Everett his compliments, and then she and Jules had continued to their seats, but not without many pauses as he introduced her to his numerous aristocratic friends.

Genevieve watched Jules in amusement now as he waved and nodded to people he recognized from their box.

"Do you know everyone?"

Jules's grin was boyishly endearing. "No, only the most fashionable. Would it amuse you to hear me recite while we wait for the entertainment to begin, my dear Miss Maples?"

Genevieve's laugh tinkled brightly. "Please."

Jules launched into an amusing discourse, pointing out famous and infamous personages and giving the latest gossip with wicked editorial asides that had Genevieve giggling behind her fan.

"And of course, there's Lord Eldon, whose intrigues within the war department are notorious, and that exceedingly fat man beside him is Lord Birmingham. The poor man has the misfortune of having two of the most horse-faced daughters I ever met!"

"Jules, you are incorrigible!" she mocked-scolded, smiling despite herself.

"Just trying to keep my lady entertained. But you grow weary of gossip. Shall I obtain a playbill so that we can learn what offerings the illustrious Mr. Baggart has prepared for us?" he asked.

Jules's innocent mention of the impresario jolted Genevieve from her fool's haven and made her heart buck. In the young man's entertaining company, for a brief moment she'd almost forgotten the noxious package weighing down her ridicule and the true reason she was present at the gala: now she, too, was one of Baggart's pack mules. Only the knowledge that the ordeal would soon be over and her grandfather's predicament solved kept her from bolting from her seat.

Fighting for calm, she nodded her assent to Jules. "Yes, that would be helpful."

With many assurances that he'd only be a moment, Jules left the box and returned shortly, clutching a sheaf of inky foolscap sheets and accompanied by a trio of tittering, badly dressed young ladies. As Jules introduced her to his sister, Deirdre, and her friends, Lady Elizabeth Mont-chance and Miss Lorna Poole, Genevieve hoped that none of the mixture of dread and elation she felt showed in her expression.

Dutifully, Jules remarked on the beauty of Genevieve's gown, and soon they were all clamoring for the name of her dressmaker. In a moment of inspiration, Genevieve feigned reluctance, whetting their appetites even more, finally explaining that "Madame Bella" was so exclusive that *she* interviewed her potential clients. Nothing would do then but for Genevieve to take the ladies' cards and promise that she would ask madame to call on each of them.

"You wretch," Jules whispered as the orchestra struck up the opening number and the three ladies departed for their own seats. "Now we'll have a string of Deirdre's envious friends parading through here for the rest of the evening!"

"What else could I do?" Genevieve asked with a twinkle of mischief. "I couldn't tell them to call at the Athena's workrooms, and, besides, this way I may hazard a guess at potential business while I continue to look for a suitable establishment. My commission for Mr. Cormick and my grandfather's run at Sadler's Wells will end soon, so we'll need a place by then."

"I'm sorry none of the locations I've scouted so far has been acceptable," Jules said, "but I'll keep trying."

"You've been of invaluable help. It's quite a challenge to find an elegant address when my purse strings are so tight!"

Jules pouted. "If you'd only agree to accept my help—"

"We've already discussed that," she reminded him firmly.

"But I'd consider it an investment."

"And I'd consider it an imposition on our friendship. No, you've done more than enough already by introducing me to your sister and her friends."

"A tremendous sacrifice, I assure you," Jules said, only partly teasing, "since I wanted you all to myself. And what a crush we've had!"

Genevieve laughed at his disgruntled expression while accepting the playbill from him. "It's been my experience that most of the *ton* comes to the theater to socialize and rarely to watch the performances anyway."

"Unfortunately, yes," Jules grumbled. "And though my bubble-brained friends usually come late, once they've seen you—"

He broke off with a "see what I mean" look as a pair of beaming young men in a Macaroni's finest attire barged into the box, thumping Jules heartily on the back and demanding that he introduce them to this "exquisite creature."

Jules's gloomy prediction held true. The performance was well into the third musical selection before the stream of visitors, both male and female, slackened and Genevieve had a chance to examine the inky playbill soiling her kid gloves.

"I believe Mrs. Letchfield comes next," she murmured for Jules's benefit. "There's a comic pantomime for the finale, too, and—oh!"

Fortunately, Jules was tapping his highly polished toes to the rousing chorus taking place on the stage below them and didn't hear her soft gasp. She traced the name printed in bold black letters: B. D. Cormick.

Though she'd had occasion to see her employer several times over the past days in connection with the progress of the costumes, he'd mentioned nothing about the gala. How like the inscrutable Bryce Cormick to keep so closed-mouthed about this honor! Was it privacy or modesty or sheer indifference that had kept him from volunteering the information that he'd be among the distinguished program of actors tonight? Annoyance and curiosity and a tingling anticipation held her impatient all through Darlena Letchfield's interpretation of Joan of Arc and the crowd's enthusiastic response.

Finally the green velvet curtain opened again, revealing, to Genevieve's surprise, a tableau from Sheridan's *School for Scandal*. Bryce and Mrs. Letchfield performed a scene from the comedy, the fast-paced action and witty repartee proving very much a crowd-pleaser. Bemused, Genevieve observed Bryce's impeccable timing and inherent grace on the boards, and was forced to admit she'd rarely seen a livelier performance. Laughing with the audience, she applauded his skill, marveling that he continued to surprise her with his versatility and talent.

"Letchfield is certainly the epitome of elegance," Jules said as the curtain drew closed, "but your employer stole the show. No wonder the critics are so enamored of him."

"Really?" Genevieve folded the playbill, keeping her tone casual. " 'Tis the first time I've seen him perform."

"And what did you think?"

"Quite nice."

Jules chuckled. "You damn Mr. Cormick with faint praise!"

"I fear I approach anything to do with Mr. Cormick with a jaundiced attitude because his demands for perfection with his own upcoming venture have kept me most occupied of late."

Boldly, Jules took her hand. "I'm well aware of that, my dear, and it grieves me sorely. You must promise me more of your time when this project is happily concluded."

"That, sir, will depend on a number of things," Genevieve responded, "including whether or not you allow me to retrieve my hand." She laughed softly as Jules hastily released her, then called his attention back to the playbill. "Look, it appears we will have another performance by Mr. Cormick."

Indeed, at that moment, the curtain parted again, but this time without its usual orchestral fanfare. Bryce stood at center stage, surrounded by a covey of weary, battle-scarred infantrymen. Dressed in leather buckler of an earlier day, he was instantly recognizable to all in the role of

King Henry V, dominating the stage with his very stillness and the penetrating blue fire of his steely gaze. His oration before the battle of Agincourt began low, rumbling deeply from his chest, and the audience quickly settled, every ear attentive to the majestic tones tripping from the tongue of the man who looked more like a prince than the true monarch watching from the royal box.

The patriotic message of the speech was not lost on the audience, not at an event celebrating another English victory, not before a duke whose heroism and leadership had been likened to King Henry's himself. As Bryce's deep, melodious voice rose like thunder in the hall, mesmerizing his listeners, Genevieve shivered with the irony. Perhaps of all those present, only she understood the division that plundered Bryce Cormick's soul, his half-French soul, the part of him that despised war and what it had cost him.

But she was no more immune to the magic he wrought than anyone else. For a brief time, he *was* Henry, as bright and shining as the blade he raised to exhort his men in the bard's immortal words:

And gentlemen in England now a-bed
Shall think themselves accurs'd they were not here,
And hold their manhoods cheap whiles any speaks
That fought with us upon Saint Crispin's day.

There was a long moment of silence, then the spell broke with waves and waves of tumultuous applause, bringing the prince regent himself to his feet to add his accolades to the ovation. Beside her, Jules stood, stomping and whistling his approval along with the others, but Genevieve, touched to her core, too moved even to weep, could only stare at the man taking a gracious bow on stage.

In the last second before the closing curtain whisked Bryce out of sight, he lifted his head and captured her with his piercing blue gaze, pinning her motionless with only a look across the space that separated them.

Jules he assessed and dismissed in that brief instant, and Genevieve understood that Bryce had known she was there all along, and that something special in his performance had been just for her, something to respond to and challenge the admission that had surprised her as much as it had him on their last meeting. The partly defiant, partly triumphant half smile on his handsome face spun into her dazed brain, careened down to perform amazing feats on her heart, then lodged low in her being to leave her breathless and trembling, stunned and wanting.

Jules dropped back down on the bench beside her. "Absolutely magnificent, wasn't it?"

Her throat and heart full, Genevieve could only nod.

Fortunately, a new tide of visitors deluged them at that moment, and she was granted a moment's reprieve to collect her scattered senses. But she wasn't really aware of anything after that. Though she made polite conversation, took innumerable ladies' cards to pass on to Madame Bella, and watched with apparent pleasure the various spectacles and farces that made up the balance of the long program, her thoughts were focused on the time when she would be alone to think about the brilliance of Bryce's performance and exactly what he'd intended to convey with that blatant, challenging look.

When a page brought Jules a summons from an acquaintance, she was hardly aware that he excused himself, leaving her alone in the box just as the comic Harlequin pantomime began. Moments later a rustle of clothing and a tight voice jerked her from her reverie.

"You have something of mine?"

Genevieve nearly strangled on her gasp. Baggart! How could she have forgotten? His hand clamped painfully on her shoulder when she would have turned.

"No, stay as you are," he ordered in a sibilant whisper, keeping to the shadows in the rear of the box.

While the antic Harlequin on stage cavorted hilariously, Genevieve's low reply was strained. "I trust your visit to the Continent was pleasant, sir?"

"Pleasant and successful, Miss Maples," Samson Baggart said with a dry chuckle. "And your trip to Holborn?"

For answer, she passed him her ridicule, making the utmost endeavor to control her shaking hands. "I hope this concludes our association, Mr. Baggart."

Again, his dry chuckle rattled, along with the brown paper wrapping of Blind Jacob's package. "You are an audacious female, my dear. I—"

He broke off with a violent expletive that made Genevieve swivel in her seat. Then a delicious malice spread through her at his obvious disappointment.

"No antiquity again, sir?" she taunted softly, amazed and pleased at her own temerity.

"This is intolerable! My sources have never failed me before." Dully elegant in evening dress, Baggart glared his frustration at her.

"Perhaps it is true that there is no honor among thieves."

"But there is revenge for betrayal." His gaze was a red, feral glitter in the shadows of the theater box. "They found the man who stole my former associate's prize minus his eyes, his tongue, and his liver."

Genevieve shuddered at the grisly image, thinking that the Mr. Abbot the impresario had mentioned must be an even more vicious and dangerous villain than Baggart himself. But even though Baggart's warning was all too clear, she refused to cower, lifting her chin in haughty defiance. "Then you risk much to cheat your associate out of his possession due to your own greed."

"You'd best hope this is merely another delay. If the Griffin has stolen this treasure from me, I'll have his heart on a stake—and yours and your grandfather's, too."

"I know nothing of this prize, not even what it looks like, so how could I take it?"

"Men covet it for the beauty of its rare rose stone . . . and its power over other men."

"That could mean anything," she accused in an angry undertone that contrasted sharply with the audience's rising laughter. "How do I know you're not just trying to dupe us again? For all I know, you've had this prize you seek all along!"

"Don't be a fool!" Baggart crumpled the paper wrapping viciously in one boney fist. "The mark of the eagle's talon is what I need to assure my future. With kingdoms at stake, I don't play deadly games with puling chits!"

"I brought you the package just as Blind Jacob gave it to me, I swear."

"I believe you, Miss Maples. You wouldn't try anything imbecilic." His voice was razor-sharp with barely leashed ruthlessness. "Should you dare, I have a commitment form signed by King George's personal physicians, waiting in my office for you and your grandfather. John and Robert Willis have had considerable experience with patients who suffer from nervous excitement."

Genevieve swallowed convulsively. "What are you saying?"

"You must go back to Jacob's."

The Harlequin performed a series of acrobatics, and laughter erupted from the audience, but Genevieve was as still as death. "No. I can't. Not again."

"I find you're too handy to release just yet, Miss Maples," Baggart said with an oily smile. "If you intend to keep Everett out of St. Luke's, you'll do as I say."

A murderous red haze replaced Genevieve's shock, and a desire for violence burned through her bloodstream like an all-consuming fire. If she could have put her hand to a knife at that moment, she would have joyfully buried it in Baggart's black heart.

"No." Surging to her feet, she glared at the impresario with hate flaring behind her eyes. "I swear I'll go to the magistrates, no matter what the consequences."

"Sit down, Miss Maples," Baggart ordered sharply, unmoved. "Why so squeamish now? For your actions you've already done more than enough to earn yourself a hempen necklace."

Genevieve's knees gave way. She sank into her chair

again as her pent-up breath leaked from her lungs in a
disbelieving sigh. "That—that's insane."

"The law would see only your complicity in a felony."

"But you know differently. Besides, you don't need
me," she said in desperation. "You can go to Blind Jacob's yourself."

"You'd be surprised what eyes follow my movements.
No, a lovely young lady, someone who's above suspicion,
who wants to save her own neck as well as her grandfather's, makes a valuable conspirator. The Griffin cannot
find the fire because you are the smoke in his eyes. No,
my dear, you're much too valuable a tool for me to give
up just yet."

"I could go to the authorities . . ."

"Turn me in, girl," he said, "and I'll swear both you
and your grandfather worked for me from the start. We'll
all go to the gallows together, if my former associate's
men don't finish us first."

Her green eyes were harried. "Don't you understand?
It was all I could do to bring you this."

"Come, come, Miss Maples. What's so difficult? A visit
to the rag seller's shop, then another pleasant appointment
somewhere. For your dear grandfather's sake."

Genevieve swallowed hard on the dryness clogging her
throat. "This . . . this is the last time I can help, no matter
what."

"I give you my solemn promise."

A thief's promise. Genevieve already knew how much
that was worth, but what else could she do? Confusion,
fear, and an overwhelming feeling of impotency kept her
mute.

Samson Baggart smiled, satisfied, then stepped back into
the shadows as the music rose to a boisterous finale. "I
knew I could count on you to be sensible, my dear. Now,
you must go back to Jacob's on the usual day . . ."

Within moments after Baggart's departure, Jules burst
back into the box with profuse apologies over his delay
and several curses for the dim-witted page who'd led him

on a fool's errand. He broke off suddenly in consternation, taken aback by the one sight guaranteed to render any male helpless.

"Genevieve! My dear, whatever's wrong?"

Boisterous applause exploded from the audience at the Harlequin's comical finale, but silent, incongruous tears streamed down Genevieve's stricken face.

"Pay no attention to me, Jules," she said in a voice thick with misery. "I'm always moved by a great performance."

Genevieve found the dim confines of the backstage area of the Athena Theater familiar and strangely comforting. The network of ropes and pulleys and flies and stacks of canvas scenery panels evoked recollections from her childhood, of time when things had been simple and magic possible.

She was a long way from innocence now, Genevieve thought as she packed up her sewing basket following a long afternoon of final fittings. In the three days since the Victory Gala, she'd tried without success to think of some way out of the coil of Baggart's treachery.

Now, alone with her pins and tape measures, the merino flounces of her tobacco-brown spencer jacket and skirt dusty, her knees aching from hours of kneeling and pinning and adjusting hems and sleeves, she was forced to admit there seemed only one logical solution. No matter that it would mean sacrificing the potential success of Madame Bella, she had to take Maebella and Grandpapa far away—to Ireland, Italy, or even America—to be out of the reach of Baggart's manipulations and threats. And she had to do it soon.

Unfortunately, since she'd given that detestable individual most of her money on her grandfather's debts, she lacked the funds to get farther than Westminster. With a sound of disgust, she put away the last soldier's tunic and closed the dressing room door behind her.

Crossing the lofty, echoing backstage area, she acknowledged what she'd known all along. Though she'd pushed both herself and her workers, there was only a slim chance that she would have the costumes finished before she was forced to visit Blind Jacob again in just a few day's time. And even if by some quirk of fate Bryce decided to pay her beforehand, she had so much of herself invested in the project—and, yes, felt too much loyalty to Bryce for giving her the chance in the first place—to abandon it unfinished. Even so, she'd been working like a woman driven. She knew better than to trust Samson Baggart now.

With a decisive nod, she made her plans. As soon as she completed her commission, she'd use her wages to purchase passage by ship to the most distant port she could afford. In fact, Genevieve resolved, she'd make inquiries at the shipping offices tomorrow. She assured herself the twinge she felt at the thought of saying goodbye to a certain ebony-haired actor was nothing more than a sense of relief that she'd be free of such a rake's dangerous attraction.

The sound of voices drew her past the greenroom where actors would await their turn on stage and through a complicated maze of props waiting in readiness for opening night—flags and standards, tables and chests for the duke's council chamber, and even the richly draped poster bed where Mrs. Letchfield would meet her fate each night as Desdemona. In the stage wings, Genevieve met a pair of carpenters preparing to leave for the day.

"Good evenin', miss," one said, tipping his hat respectfully.

"Is everyone gone, then?" she asked.

"Near enough."

She followed them toward the stairway, then hesitated and turned back, drawn almost irresistibly onto the stage herself. "I think I'll have a look around before I go."

"Sure, miss. I'll throw the bolt so no one'll disturb ye. G'night." Tools in hand, the carpenters headed for the exit.

Almost hesitantly, Genevieve wandered toward the open stage. Things had changed considerably inside the Athena since her last visit. Scaffolds had come down, and although the dimness was pierced by only a couple of oil lanterns, Genevieve could see enough to know that the Athena's glorious resurrection was almost a reality. And such a reality! It took her breath away.

Though much smaller in capacity than either Drury Lane or Covent Garden, the Athena had been transformed into an intimate showplace of elegance and style that clearly showed Bryce Cormick's talented hand. Intricate moldings of pristine white accented with gilt circled the galleries and box seating and framed a sky-blue ceiling. Graceful plaster medallions crowned gigantic crystal chandeliers that glittered like diamonds overhead.

The stage itself, though still lacking its velvet curtain, was wide and spacious and graced with the most modern of traps, grooves, and devices, including the newest innovation, gas footlights. Standing center stage, looking out over the empty pit, Genevieve knew it would truly be a pleasure to perform in such surroundings.

She bit her lip, regretting deeply for the first time in her life that her acting talent was either too meager or too undeveloped to meet the challenge represented by the Athena. What a triumph it would be to play Ophelia or Juliet on such a stage! A shameful envy that Bryce should be so close to accomplishing his dream while her life lay in tatters and shambles stabbed at her. But no, that was unworthy. He deserved his success, needed it in ways she could only guess at, and she would not begrudge him that, here in the heart of his dream turned reality.

"Genevieve."

She turned slowly at the sound of the deep voice, her brown skirts foaming gently about her ankles. How long he'd stood watching her from the wings, she couldn't be certain. His dark suit blended with the shadows, only the white of his shirt and the brilliant, predatory flare of his eyes visible as she strained to make him out. A shiver of awareness coursed through her, making her voice strangely husky.

"Yes, Mr. Cormick?"

With the lean and hungry grace that was so much a part of him, Bryce crossed the stage, revealing an expression so ferocious that Genevieve took an involuntary step back. For a panicked second she thought he knew all her secrets, all her shame and condemned her for her crimes. But no, how could he? She struggled for composure.

"I hope you don't mind. I couldn't resist taking a look." She gestured toward the empty theater. "It's truly wonderful, a remarkable accomplishment."

"If it's so damned wonderful, why the hell are you leaving?"

Guilt leeched the color from her cheeks. How had Bryce guessed her plans when they were only just now formed in her own head? She looked away. "I was going to tell you."

"How very charitable," he said.

"I'll fulfill all obligations first, so you've no reason to be annoyed."

"My God, I've never met a woman with your gall!"

"I see no reason why I should be insulted over a personal decision," she responded with growing heat. "Excuse me, I'm going home."

"With him?" Teeth bared, Bryce grabbed her arm, looming over her like a dark, avenging angel. "Damn you, answer me!"

Genevieve glared back at him. "I haven't any notion of what you mean."

"Such pretty protestations! You deserve a standing ovation for your performance, General. You know damned well I mean you and Chesterson."

"Jules? What's he got to do with anything? You're not making sense." Confusion mingled with anger and stretched her overwrought system to the breaking point. She tugged at her captured arm. "Let go, you're hurting me."

"I'd like to hurt you," he said, tightening his grip. There was something dangerous in his eyes, something wild and untamed, barely held in check by the trappings of civilization. "How can you lie to my face when I know full well he's secured a house for you?"

"A house?" Her expression softened with amazed delight at the prospect of realizing an old dream, however remote it might be now. "Really? How do you know?"

"Then you don't deny it?"

"No." She frowned, puzzled. "Why should I?"

Bryce's eyes blazed. "Damn you and your cursed agreement, woman! I could strangle you for putting me through this hell of wanting you. That soft-as-butter mouth and those witchy tits have been driving me crazy, and all the while you've been bedding that fop. Or did he have to provide an establishment first before you became his mistress?"

"Mistress?" Stunned, Genevieve stared at Bryce until the full impact of his accusation hit her. White-faced with fury, she jerked out of his grasp. "You . . . bastard!"

Ignoring the epithet, he stalked her across the stage and into the wings, his lean face chiseled with an ominous determination. "I'm that and more, as you shall see."

"Threats now? How charming." Icy disdain frosted her words, even though her teeth chattered with shock. Like a wounded creature, she had but one thought—escape. Turning, she fled toward the exit, only to be caught up short by the iron-hard length of Bryce's arm around her waist, crushing her against him.

"Don't touch me!"

"By God, I intend to do more than that!" Scooping her up high in his arms, ignoring her futile struggles, he looked around the cluttered area. In the next instant he flung her onto Desdemona's bed and pinned her beneath his body, one knee insinuated aggressively between her thighs. Twin spots of high color dotted his cheekbones, and his voice was an angry rasp. "Why shouldn't I sample what you're giving Chesterson?"

"I gave him nothing!" she cried, pushing ineffectually against his shoulders.

"Holding out on him, too?" Deftly, he untied the ribbons at the neck of her jacket. "The war is over, General. You'll surrender to me."

Burying his fingers in her hair, he kissed her, demanding entrance, then sweeping the cavern of her mouth with his rapacious tongue. Genevieve felt consumed, devoured by a passion loosed from all control. Releasing her mouth at last, he lightly raked her neck with his teeth, his hands now busy on the buttons of her gown.

"You great lunkhead! Listen to me!" Genevieve gasped and groaned as his skillful fingers breached the boundaries of her clothing and slipped beneath her chemise to caress her naked nipple. Frantic, she curled her fingers into the black silk of his hair, pushing him back, forcing him to look at her. "I've no arrangement with Jules. I don't care for him that way."

"Since when did a *poule* consider love a prerequisite?" he taunted, doing wicked things to her flesh with his fingers and smiling as he felt the response she could not conceal.

"Even a harlot usually has a choice," she retorted, giving his earlobe a vicious twist.

"Ow! You know how I felt! I made it clear, more than once—"

"You never made me a single offer, you buffoon!"

Taken aback, Bryce scowled down at her. "Is this a bidding war, then?"

"I'd like to know how much you think I'm worth."

"Hell, Genny! Can't we strike a bargain after—"

"How much, Mr. Cormick?" She gave him a seductive pout, and cupped her own breasts suggestively with her hands. "Or don't you know the going rate for 'witchy tits'?"

With a growl of disgust, Bryce released her and rolled to a sitting position, raking his hands through his hair. "Damn, I had no idea you had such a mercenary streak."

Watching him cautiously, she sat up and began adjusting her clothing, sensing the ebb of his unfounded rage, yet infuriated enough to seek her own revenge.

"Am I supposed to live on love?" she asked lightly.

Bryce grinned suddenly and reached for her again. "Shall we find out?"

But she was too quick for him, dancing away just out of his reach, then swaying provocatively and smoothing her garments in a manner meant to display her feminine charms.

"How badly do you want me, Mr. Cormick?" she purred. "Am I worth a house? A carriage and four? A living of five hundred pounds a year?"

"You know I've got practically everything I own tied up in all this." His gesture indicated the theater. "But yes, damn you. In the state you've gotten me in, you're worth all that and more."

She sniffed. "Not enough."

His pride affronted, Bryce glowered at her. "Well, what the hell will it take to induce you to share my bed?"

"I'll blush if I say it aloud, so . . ." She leaned forward as though to whisper in his ear, then shouted instead: "A wedding ring, you ninnyhammer!"

With that, she went for the stage door. Bryce caught up with her there, swinging her around into his arms before she could release the bolt.

"You've livid," he guessed.

Her eyes flashed with a rare gleam of emerald ire. "And you're jealous!"

"I'm not the marrying kind."

"You jackass! I wouldn't have you on a silver platter!"

"That conniving Jezebel farce was all an act, then?" Bryce's cheek creased with reluctant admiration. "Either I'm in such a state of frustration my brain has turned to sauce, or you're a better actress than anyone gives you credit."

"Thank you very much, I'm sure!"

"And Jules—"

"He's a *boy*! What do you take me for?"

Bryce looked up to heaven and groaned. "A maddening female who's driving me out of my mind! All I could think of since the night of the gala was you in that damned seductive dress and that coxcomb's hands all over you. So when I went by the workrooms and found the message Chesterson had left about the house, I thought you and he . . . oh, hell!"

"So you decided to take what you want? Is this what you learned in the war?"

That barb struck home. He looked at her—really looked—and the angry hurt he saw lurking behind her bravura made him swallow hard and swear. "Genny, I'm sorry . . ."

"Jules is helping me find a property where I can open my salon. Working for you was only a temporary commission, after all. You knew I'd leave sometime."

"I see. I do apologize. Genny? I suppose I've really mucked it up now." With a sigh, he brushed a kiss over the curls tumbled on her forehead.

"Don't." Standing in his embrace, she quivered like a reed in the wind. "You know nothing can come of it."

"It could if you would let it happen," he murmured in her ear. "How can you ignore what we do to each other?"

"It's not enough." She tried to shrug off the whispery caresses he laid against her temple. "Stop it. I can't think when you do that."

Tempting laughter rumbled from his chest. "So don't think."

"It's not that simple! I have . . . responsibilities, and it's so terribly hard—"

Gently, he caught her averted chin and lifted her face so that he could see into her eyes. "What is?"

Her voice was the barest whisper, but rawly honest. "To say no to you."

"Sweet Jesus!" he breathed. "You're not exactly appealing to my better nature when you say something like that, you know."

"I'm depending on it."

"Even though we both know I could take you back to that bed and *make* you want me?"

"Even so."

A muscle twitched in Bryce's jaw, and there was a startled silence, as if no one had ever before believed in the possibility of his goodness. Even after facing the full force of his blackest, most primitive anger, she still trusted him to have the forbearance not to force her down a path that would ultimately hurt her. She'd thought him a hero the first time they'd met. As he let his hands fall away from her shoulders, he only hoped she realized the depth of his heroism now.

"Then I suppose," he said, "I must uphold your confidence in me."

"I expected no less."

Stymied, he allowed an involuntary appeal to burst from his throat. "Genny, can't we—"

"No, Mr. Cormick. We just don't want the same things, you see." Her lower lip trembled. "It will be best for us both if I complete my commission and leave your premises as soon as possible."

His expression heavy with regret, Bryce had to accept that. Though he ached with the frustration of wanting what he could not have, he admitted to himself that he was too fond of his little general to hurt her by continuing his pursuit. Though she'd proven resourceful in staving off a rake's advances, she did not have a demirep's experience to withstand a prolonged campaign.

"Perhaps that would be best," he said at last.

Without another word, she turned and walked to the stage door.

Bryce's voice echoed behind her through the wings. "You'd be better off with Jules anyway."

She paused, but did not look back. "I know."

Then she disappeared through the door, leaving behind her a man utterly baffled by the wound he'd just dealt himself.

* * *

Five days before the opening night of *Othello* at Bryce Cormick's Athena, Genevieve attached the last spangle to the last gown and stepped back to admire her handiwork.

"Oh, mum!" Bett, the seamstress breathed, "They're lovely, every blessed one of 'em!" Her co-workers, Agnes and Lucy, nodded in solemn agreement as a cold evening rain spattered fretfully against the windowpanes.

Displayed on wall hooks, laid out on the long tables, draping half a score of tailor's dummies, the finished costumes for *Othello* filled every nook and corner with a blaze of color, from resplendent noble's robes to the lowliest servant's, the richness of each according to their station, yet every one constructed with such detail, workmanship, and intuition, one could hazard a guess at the personality of the character who'd wear each garment before a single player appeared to don the costumes.

"Mr. Cormick will be pleased, I'm sure," Agnes commented, sticking her needle into a fat red pincushion, her cheeks rosy with satisfaction and the warmth of the cozy fire crackling inside the workroom stove.

"I couldn't have done it without all of you," Genevieve said, proud and sad at once, gratified to have completed her finest project, but knowing now her departure from both Bryce Cormick's employ and her homeland was imminent and imperative.

In just five days, her commitment to this project would be complete. With wages in hand, she could collect Grandpapa and Maebella from Sadler's and spirit them all out of Baggart's malevolent reach. Unfortunately, Genevieve could not savor this moment, for she was due to visit Blind Jacob in Holborn again on the morrow, and she dared not give Samson Baggart any cause for suspicion by defying his instructions. She hoped they would be well away before she was summoned to meet Baggart again with this latest detestable package.

Mingled anxiety and hope strummed along her nerves, and a secret dejection she was loath to admit even to herself at the thought of leaving her fractured relationship with Bryce Cormick in such an unfinished, unsatisfying state. Hoping her companions would assume her distraction was simply a result of overwork, she tried to shake off her manic melancholy and turned to black-eyed Jack Potts.

"I'd say this calls for a celebration, wouldn't you, Jack?"

"Yes, miss!"

"Then run down to the shops for me. There's money to spare in Mr. Cormick's coffers, and we all deserve a treat!"

Shortly thereafter, a jolly group circled the glowing stove, munching buttered scones and roasted chestnuts, plum jellies and potato cakes, washing the victuals down with quantities of ale and tea, while exchanging ditties and proposing toasts to all the prestigious names they could think of. Grabbing up her sketchbook, Genevieve drew quick caricatures of each new honoree, evoking howls of mirth at her renderings of the prince regent, Lady Jersey, and the Duke of Wellington, who, from all reports, was doing an outstanding job keeping the Frenchies in line in Paris while King Louis formed his court in accordance with the new regime.

"Another toast!" Lucy cried, warm and slightly tipsy with the abundance of ale. "To Miss Maples!"

"You're too, too kind," Genevieve said, mimicking a top-lofty *ton*-ish miss. "But just see what all this work has done to me!"

Determined to enjoy this impromptu party despite her inner turmoil, she held up a not-so-flattering self-portrait of herself as Macbeth's witch. With curls flying in every direction and bags of fatigue under her eyes, the cartoon Genevieve waved a magic wand to direct armies of scissors and needles in a military assault on a new project.

The sketch drew appreciative applause and whoops, and an "Oh, you're much prettier than that, miss!" from a smitten Jack Potts.

"Mr. Cormick never expected us to finish so quickly," Genevieve said, turning the sketchbook back over. She sniffed in disdain, her pen flying as she made additions to the picture. "Much that overbearing individual knows! We've shown him!"

With mischievous triumph, she revealed the sketch again, only now the legions of sewing implements at her command had neatly stitched a very worried, very long-nosed Bryce Cormick into a sack, trussing him up like a Christmas goose.

Shrieks of laughter applauded her talent. Jack turned a back flip to show his appreciation, and Lucy threw her apron over her head and fell right off her stool, giggling helplessly in a heap at Genevieve's feet while everyone else howled until tears rolled down their cheeks.

"What the devil's going on here?"

The question thundered across the workroom, stunning the revelers into guilty silence. Bryce Cormick stood in the open doorway, shaking the rain from his many-caped wool coat, his face sporting the blackest of ill-tempered scowls. Blue eyes fierce, he raised one black eyebrow at Genevieve.

"Well, Miss Maples? Would you care to explain why my money's being spent on high living and riots?"

"Riots!"

Astounded, Genevieve looked at the evidence of their bacchanal—littered nut shells, half-full teacups, jelly-smeared plates—and burst out laughing.

With her eyes shining and her cheeks rosy, she looked very young and carefree to Bryce, everything delightful and desirous that he coveted but had so royally proven he did not deserve. In fact, after his hellacious day with Hux-ford, everything from her bright curls to the elegant lines of her forest-green gown was altogether too appealing to him—and that made him scowl all the more.

"Look about you, sir," Genevieve managed at last, "and tell me if there is not reason for celebration?"

Halfway out of coat and hat, Bryce went still, his eyes

flicking over the room, taking in everything. "You're finished."

"Every last stitch, sir!" Agnes helped Lucy to her feet and gestured at the assembled costumes. "And ain't they beauties?"

Bemused, Bryce rotated in place, taking in the splendor of the finished garments, finally coming back to Genevieve's expectant face. "Beautiful."

She flushed, rising out of her chair, nervously clutching her sketchbook. "Would you care to inspect them now?"

"And spoil the party?" He shrugged out of his outer garments, handing them to Jack to lay aside.

While heartened at the completion of the costumes, he felt a sinking sensation in the pit of his stomach at the thought of what it meant. God, he couldn't let Genevieve leave now! Not when the memory of her perfect mouth and the peace in her soft green eyes had been the only thing that had kept him going these last brutal days. A ring of expectant faces recalled him from his dark reflections. Smiling slightly, he bowed.

"My congratulations to you all. Perhaps you'll ignore my abominable manners and allow me to join you?"

"We'd be right honored, sir!" Lucy piped up, leaning against Agnes in tipsy affection. "Bett, fetch ale to warm the master. For certain, it's cold as a witch's heart outside."

"That it is, madame." Bryce stepped closer to the glowing stove to warm his hands, and his gaze latched on to the pages Genevieve held. "Regarding witches, what have you there?"

"Nothing!" She shoved the damning sketches behind her back as a wave of bright color stained her cheeks. "Just foolishness."

"May I?" Without waiting for permission, he retrieved the sketchbook, flipping through the drawings until he reached the caricature of himself. While the group held its collective breath, Bryce studied the rendering. At last his mouth twitched, and a reluctant chuckle rumbled deep in his chest.

Genevieve breathed a sigh of relief, echoed by the others. Grinning over the drawing, Bryce caught Genevieve's eye.

"You are quite a wit, Miss Maples."

Genevieve blushed again as Bett shyly handed Bryce a foamy tankard. "Here, sir, won't you have a dram? And come take your ease here by the fire. Faith, ye look all in."

"That I am, madame," Bryce admitted.

His eyes were grainy and his nerves were raw, for he'd spent the last days following a new lead of Huxford's, rumors that the Abbot himself, tired of his minions' failures, had joined the search for the Abbot's Seal. More important that the seal itself was the possibility that its lure would reveal the Abbot's identity, and Huxford's excitement brooked no opposition. Thus, Bryce and Taffy had again taken to the streets, following false rumor after lie after inaccuracy, returning to Huxford with only the most gossamer and frustratingly fine threads of truth. Bryce only hoped that with his spider's ways Huxford could weave out of those bits and pieces a web strong enough to catch a spy.

Now, gratefully, he tasted the brew Brett handed him and nodded his approval. "Thank you."

Bett tittered and took her own place again, giggling behind her hands with Agnes and Lucy.

"Come sit here," Genevieve offered softly, indicating her vacated chair. "I believe Bett is correct in her assessment of your condition."

"Do I appear so haggard?" he asked with a wry laugh. Seating himself, he set the tankard on the floor and tapped the sketchbook with one long finger. "In truth, I confess your pen has pricked my ego no little amount."

"Surely you aren't so sensitive," she scoffed, reaching for the offending drawings. He held the book out of her reach, grinning.

"I assure you I am, but I wish to keep this likeness so that I'll never grow above myself. I have only to gaze on that nose to be made completely humble."

Genevieve shifted uncomfortably. "I meant no offense. Surely a man as handsome as you can abide a bit of harmless fun?"

He laughed again, his pleasure at her compliment revealed in a flash of white teeth. "How cleverly you couch praise and insult in the same blow!"

"Mr. Cormick." Exasperated, she glared at him. "You are most absurd."

" 'Tis been an absurd day for me. I daresay I am a bit daffy with fatigue," he confessed with a tired shake of his dark head. He caught her hand and squeezed it. "But I'm not so weary I can't see what a magnificent job you've done, and quite before time, too. *Othello* will be the best costumed play in a generation because of your efforts. I thank you."

"It's been a labor of love for me." She drew a deep breath, and her fingers quivered beneath his. "I'm glad you're pleased."

"Indeed, I am. I'll send men over to transfer the lot directly to the Athena. In the meantime, we'll have to consider another assignment for you."

Startled, Genevieve glanced up from their clasped hands. "Another? But that won't be possible . . ."

"I'll want a comedy for the spring," he mused aloud, ignoring her garbled protests. "A pageant or panorama, something light with fairies and goblins to please the crowds. If I'm lucky, there's a chance I may be able to entice Grimaldi himself to perform as clown in the main piece. Would you consider it? 'Twould certainly be a prime opportunity to show your versatility as couturiere to your new clients."

Nervous consternation chased across her countenance, a mixture of longing and . . . guilt? he wondered. She was tempted, and not just by his offer of more work; he was arrogantly male enough to feel certain. When she licked her lips before answering, he nearly groaned aloud.

"I'll have to . . . to think about it," she said unsteadily. "I don't know what to say."

Neither did Bryce exactly, for the idea had popped into his head and out of his mouth without volition. But despite their last encounter, and the tacit agreement they'd reached to part company at the end of this venture, keeping Genevieve near was a deep, imperative need in him that he could not deny. And how better to accomplish that than by ruthlessly tempting her with the one thing he thought she could not resist—advancement toward her chosen career and a permanent home base?

"We'll discuss it later, shall we?" he suggested, all charm. He drew Genevieve around to perch on the edge of the chair with him. "It seems we're to have some entertainment."

She nodded, grateful to drop the subject as Jack bowed to the assembled company, then launched into a sprightly Welsh ditty that Bryce instantly recognized as one of Taffy's old favorites. The rendition was enthusiastically applauded by the admittedly biased audience, and that was all the encouragement it took to convince Jack of the merits of an encore.

Smiling at the boy, Bryce inhaled the sweetness of Genevieve's scent, enjoying the brush of her shoulder against his, and felt the tension of the past days begin to melt away. Warmed by the fire and the intangible, unspoken acceptance of the little group, he felt a simple peace creep into his soul, momentarily banishing the demons that had haunted him since Lyons. And God, he needed that.

He needed the shy honesty he found in the softness of Genevieve's eyes, the pure and unsullied sweetness of her being that made him feel, just for a moment, less defiled by war and violence and the hateful center of himself that made him Huxford's excellent weapon. Out of necessity, he'd had to harden himself from boyhood and through the bloody days of the war, and sometimes his yearning for the quietude of feminine comfort was more than he could bear. And because his need was so great, and because in his heart Bryce knew he was the lowest of cads, he would avail himself of Genevieve's goodness by any device he could conjure up—for as long as she and what was left of his conscience would let him.

Chapter 7

Located in a marginal area behind Drury Lane, the Four Queens was a club where, for a price, a gentleman could find a game of cards, an excellent meal, convivial company, and a vast array of diversions, perverse and otherwise.

"Heard you was a great success at the Victory Gala, Mr. Cormick."

"Thank you, Smasher." Bryce pressed a wad of currency into the proprietor's meaty fist, a feature that had seen him in good stead in an earlier career as a pugilist. "For your trouble. Dinner was excellent. Keep your ears open, will you?"

"Aye, sir, that I will."

Since Smasher's childhood ties to the rookeries of Cheapside and Spitalfields remained unsevered, Bryce had often taken advantage of the fact that the former boxer was privy to a variety of information, everything from racing tips to the names of men with no compunctions against murder. Now the boxer-turned-club-owner examined the plush room reserved for his most honored visitors, particularly those with a special need for privacy, and nodded his satisfaction.

"And I'll send another bottle. Hope you enjoy the rest of your evening."

"I'm certain we will." Bryce shut the door behind him,

reseated himself at the littered supper table, then blandly met his companion's frustrated glare.

"Dammit, Bryce!" the Earl of Huxford complained. "We're running out of time."

Bryce made a sour grimace. Unfortunately, Smasher's inquiries had produced no new clues, and Huxford was simmering with frustration—which he had no compunctions against taking out on Bryce.

"Your repetition on the theme is exceedingly tedious, Hugh. Smasher has the ear of every dimber damber in the city. If even he hasn't learned anything by now, I say to hell with it!"

"You needn't snarl at me," Huxford said, foraging among the serving plates for an overlooked morsel. "All I suggested was that a few days beyond the pale might uncover something. If we locate the seal, then we're bound to find the Abbot himself, and I want the bastard! Sooner or later, every piece of stolen property passes through one of the receivers in Field Lane. Now, if you were to spend a day or two there . . ."

Bryce scowled. "You know the Athena opens this week. I've got too much at stake to don the Griffin's wings again. You'll recall none of this was my idea anyway."

Hugh popped a grilled mushroom into his mouth and eyed Bryce consideringly. "Lord, this assignment has made you ill-tempered! If I didn't know better, I'd say your foul mood was woman-related."

Bryce laughed shortly. "You're such an expert?"

"It's against nature for a man to live like a monk." Huxford jabbed a forgotten potato with his fork and pointed it at Bryce. "You, sir, clearly have need of a woman."

Bryce sipped the remains of his wine, letting the fruity bite of the beverage coat his palate and fill his head with its pungent fumes. Huxford's assessment was too astute. He did need a woman—a truth testified to by the unrelieved heaviness in his loins—but not just any woman.

While he could have his choice of any number of luscious representatives of the demimondaine, and Darlena Letchfield had made her interest plain, his need focused on a certain green-eyed costumer with the softest mouth in creation. What was equally clear was that Genevieve was the last woman he had any business pursuing. Not that that had any bearing on his actions, Bryce thought in acid self-contempt.

It was baffling, this hungry obsession that mingled desire with an unaccustomed protectiveness. Even while he schemed to keep her near until he could find a way through her defenses, he cursed his selfishness. She wanted more than he could give, and he refused to put a name to a need that tied him in knots. For to need with such intensity was to be a slave, and his freedom was the only thing he'd ever really owned.

Bryce's mouth compressed in disgust. Maybe he ought to take Hugh's suggestion. A few days of living on nerve alone in the city's most dangerous warrens would certainly cure this malaise. But before he could make such an offer, there was a soft knock, followed by the giggling entrance of a pair of buxom, thinly clad "hostesses," one fair, one dark, bearing the promised bottle of wine.

"Ah, here's something to lift our spirits!" The earl winked and pulled the brunette onto his lap. "Among other things."

"Oh, m'lord, how you do go on!" The whore leaned over to whisper in Huxford's ear, showing a daring bit of cleavage and dusky nipple.

Meanwhile, the blond batted her soot-darkened eyelashes at Bryce and ran inquisitive fingers across his broad shoulder. "La, you're a big one, aren't you, luvie? Being extra obligin' to such fine gentlemen won't be no trouble at all, will it, Sal?"

Though both women were comely and appeared clean enough, Bryce wasn't tempted. Rising, he captured the blond's limp hand and brought it to his lips in a gallant gesture.

"Regretfully, my dear, I have a pressing engagement."

"You're sure, Bryce?" Huxford asked, his gray eyes ever analyzing, ever mocking. "I guarantee 'twould do you no end of good."

Bryce met his friend's gaze. He would trust Huxford with his life; indeed, had done just that on more than one occasion, yet the fact that the earl would dally with a light-skirt was oddly disturbing. Many among the nobility and society thought nothing of discreet unfaithfulness for both partners, especially after heirs had been assured. It was a practical solution in an age of arranged matches. Hadn't he contemplated just such a passionless union with Clorinda? No doubt if he followed through with that plan, someday he'd find himself much in Huxford's position, with a family and an outwardly sound marriage hiding an empty relationship.

The sterile image depressed him. Bryce knew suddenly that it wouldn't be enough. To voluntarily leg-shackle himself, to sacrifice his freedom, the inducement would have to be great indeed.

The softest mouth in creation . . .

Bryce shook his head, denying the unbidden thought, but in that moment he put aside all notion of wedding Clorinda North. Cal would understand, would probably thank him for sparing his sister the humiliation of a straying husband. He'd take Cal's place as mentor when she and his tomboy sister made their assault on the city, but he'd spare them both a marriage that, knowing himself, he was sure must ultimately fail—just like Huxford's.

Bryce bowed to the earl. "It appears I have an appointment in Field Lane, my lord. But don't let my departure interfere with the—er, entertainment."

"Perhaps I'll linger a bit, then," Huxford agreed easily.

Bryce bestowed his most dazzling smile on the disappointed blond. "Another time, *chérie*."

"Cor, luv," she purred. "For you, any time. Just ask for Dorie." But in the manner of all true businesswomen, Dorie was competing with Sal for the earl's attention before Bryce was through the door.

* * *

By late the following afternoon, after prowling the seamy boroughs of Holborn all night and most of the day, Bryce was no closer to solving either his professional or his personal concerns. Field Lane had long been associated with receiver's bureaus, those establishments run by individuals who were more than willing to accept a pickpocket's takings or a cracksman's booty. These businessmen paid the risk-taking thieves but a pittance for their ill-gotten gains, then turned around and sold the items at nearly their full price, often to the original owners.

Dressed in the rough garb of a hostler, a day's stubble shadowing his lean cheeks, Bryce made the rounds of the bureaus, ostensibly to find the best price for a set of sterling spoons he'd purloined from his own breakfast table. In the process, he made discreet inquiries about the whereabouts of a certain seal—a small item, used for marking the wax of official letters, inscribed with the claw of a bird.

Frustratingly, by late afternoon, he'd had no better luck than any of his compatriots before him, though he'd been up and down Holborn from Saffron Hill to Shoe Lane. Slouching against a leaning storefront between a rag and glass shop and a handkerchief seller's, his cloth hat tugged low about his ears and his ragged collar turned up against the damp wind, he jotted a few scraps of information and impressions in a small leather journal. The stubby pencil moved almost automatically, a habit he'd acquired on the Peninsula.

Cal had chaffed him unmercifully about the way he'd scribbled, oblivious to time and place—while being shelled, or by feel alone in the pitch blackness of night, or when everyone else was busy seeking an hour's entertainment in the arms of some buxom senorita. But it was a way of keeping his perspective, even his sanity, in times of tension, and some of those entries had even found their way into another project of late.

Bryce stuck the notebook into his breast pocket and

turned his attention to the fascinating bustle of working-class pedestrians—dock workers, dairy maids, dustmen, pickpockets, and thieves—milling through the narrow lanes in pursuit of a dubious living. More at home in this milieu than ever in his father's fashionable drawing rooms, he experienced the familiar scents and sounds and all the intimate details of life on the lowest rungs of humanity with a sense of homecoming. Here, everyone was accepted just as he was. In fact, before he returned to the Athena's business, he was of a mood to seek out some jocular company in the nearest gin mill and have some fun—

Bryce froze in absolute astonishment as Genevieve Maples hurried past him without a glance. Immobilized with incredulity, he stared after her as she threaded her way past vegetable carts and flower booths lining the curb.

What the devil was she doing in this disreputable neighborhood? And unescorted, too! Her high-crowned bonnet and modish tobacco-brown spencer stood out like a beacon in this rough section, marking her as easy prey. Cursing feminine stupidity, Bryce melted into the crowd after her.

She moved quickly, purposefully, casting furtive glances to each side and to the rear, clutching a small string-tied package to her breast. As she paused at a filthy gutter, she shot another anxious glance over her shoulder, and her eyes widened with alarm. Lifting her skirts, she darted across the lane between a drayman's wagon and a coal peddler's barrow, narrowly missing being run down. A flurry of curses from the wagoner followed her as she fled down another squalid sewer of an alley where the sun never reached and only the meanest life forms survived.

"Damn!" Ducking through the traffic, Bryce increased his pace, his annoyance mingling with suspicion. What was she up to?

Practically running now, Genevieve took a winding path past beggars and prostitutes, heading deeper and deeper into the gloomy warren of hovels. Cold fury narrowed

Bryce's expression. Any crime imaginable might occur in these environs. Had she no idea of her foolhardiness?

To cut her off, he made a sharp turn into another even narrower passageway, silent as a big jungle cat, twisting, turning—then stepped directly into her headlong path. With her attention focused behind her, she didn't see him until it was too late, and she skidded directly into his arms with a startled shriek.

"Stop it!" Growling imprecations under his breath, he dragged her into a chute between two crumbling tenements.

In her furious struggles, her package flew in one direction, her bonnet in another. Screaming again, she kicked out and caught him squarely on the shin with her foot. Bryce grunted in pain, then jerked her flat against his massive chest.

"Goddammit, Genny! What the hell's the matter with you?"

Her struggles ceased instantly, but her shallow, ragged breathing was evidence of her terror. With eyes dilated by fear, she stared up at his grim visage, peering past the slouchy hat and day-old stubble into vivid blue eyes she'd recognize beneath any guise. "Bryce!"

Her relief was so intense she went light-headed, swaying suddenly and collapsing against his chest. Bryce supported her quaking form with an arm around her waist.

"You chucklehead! I ought to throttle you! Who'd you think it was?"

"I—I—" She couldn't get an answer past the burning in her lungs.

"Bugger man after you, eh? Serve you right."

"I didn't know . . . the way you're dressed . . . I thought . . ." She shuddered.

"I can guess. But you're damned lucky 'twas only me and not some drunken jailbird out to ease the ache between his legs on the nearest female. I ought to—"

Genevieve's small fist caught him just under the breastbone, producing a sudden exhalation and effectively end-ing his tirade. Her voice shook with a furious, white-hot indignation.

"You scoundrel! How dare you call *me* chuckleheaded? You frightened me near to death!"

"Let that be a lesson to you," he snapped, unsympathetic. She drew back to pound him again, but he closed his hand around her wrist, twisting it behind her. "Cease, you hellcat!"

"Spalpeen! Poltroon!" she cried. "Let me go!"

"Not a chance. Not until you give me some answers."

Bryce surreptitiously rubbed the spot she'd hit, secretly amused and impressed by the strength she'd placed behind that blow. But she had to understand how foolhardy her very presence here was, in a place where life was cheap and the unlucky or unwary disappeared every day. Mouth set in a stern line, he continued to berate her.

"Don't you realize you're as out of place here as a butterfly in a snowstorm? What the deuce were you doing in Holborn alone anyway?"

Genevieve blinked, searching for an explanation, fighting a hysterical urge to giggle. She'd certainly wipe the ferocious look off Bryce's face if she told him she'd been to Old Blind Jacob's to pick up Samson Baggart's latest shipment of stolen articles! Stricken, she gasped, "My package!"

"What?" Bryce's eyebrows cranked up his forehead in mystification.

"Ah—rags!" Genevieve improvised. Wriggling out of Bryce's grasp, she frantically searched the muddy, littered ground. "I went to the rag seller's for more costume materials. And I wasn't alone. I hired a hackney, only it didn't wait as I instructed, and I lost my way looking for another, and then you chased me . . ."

"Is this what you're looking for?" Bryce offered the string-bound bundle in one hand, her bonnet in the other.

"Yes!" She pounced on the package as if it were salvation itself, as indeed it was—salvation and freedom for her and her grandfather, once the dratted antiquity was safely delivered. At Bryce's astonished look, she gave a shaky, sheepish smile. "After all this trouble, I certainly don't want to lose it now."

"Are you stark mad, woman?" Bryce bellowed. "Risking your neck for a bunch of *rags*?"

"I—I needed more threadbare worsted for the rustic's robes. The others didn't turn out to my satisfaction, so I'm going to remake them," she gabbled, snatching her bonnet and jamming it on. "*You* said, get whatever I wanted. *You* said, keep it authentic. *You* said, time was running out—"

"I know damned well what I said!" Bryce jerked off his hat and threaded his fingers through his black hair in exasperation. "But I never meant for you to act like a crackbrained ninny!"

"Me!" she exploded. "I'm not the one masquerading as a ruffian! Going incognito again, Mr. *Darcy*? What mischief are you up to now? What tales are you telling some other gullible maid?"

Bryce scowled as her jibe stuck a nerve of truth. "Call it a study in character or merely the way I relax after a trying day of rehearsals."

"Oh, so now that you've played before the prince regent, you don the airs of a temperamental artist!" she accused. "How very convenient. Had Mrs. Letchfield no congratulations to offer on your stellar performance?"

"Darlena made her felicitations in her own manner, but 'tis no concern of yours, at any rate."

"At least we agree on that!" she snapped. "I must say working for you has been an education. I can't wait until opening night when my 'chuckleheaded' presence will no longer be the object of your scorn!"

"You mean you'll miss shrilling at me like a fishwife at every opportunity."

Genevieve realized their shouting match had drawn the attention of several of the alley's lowly occupants, and she flushed hotly. Fishwife, indeed! Damn Bryce Cormick for bringing out the worst in her! Damn him for confusing her with the way his hot gaze scorched her and made her very much aware of her woman's body. Damn him for not being the kind of man who could offer her the simple, sedate life she wanted, and double-damn him for making her want him anyway!

Chin lifted haughtily, she gathered up her skirts to leave, her voice icy. "Kindly point the way back to the main highway, sir. I've much work yet to accomplish."

"Hell!" He grabbed her arm and hustled her back down the twisting path they'd come. "You're mad if you think I'm letting you out of my sight. I knew I should have chosen a man for this job—women are always trouble!"

Genevieve's breath hissed between her teeth. "You insufferable—"

"Careful, General," Bryce warned, a muscle twitching in his jaw. He flagged down a hack with a whistle and an imperious wave. "Remember, I'm still your employer, and I probably saved you from the proverbial 'fate worse than death'—again."

"—beastly"—she gritted her teeth, entering the coach with a flounce of peevish temper and overstrained nerves as Bryce barked out their destination to the driver—"odious—"

"Genevieve." Seated beside her, he rapped the roof of the compartment, setting the hack in motion. His expression was ominous, annoyed, his entire bearing faintly menacing and sinister. "I'm warning you—"

"—vile, obnoxious—"

With a long-suffering sigh, Bryce jerked her across his lap, bent his head, and kissed her, thoroughly and for a long time. She was limp, dazed, and light-headed again when he finally released her, thrusting her into the opposite corner as if he didn't trust himself to have her within arm's reach.

"Mankind's only effective weapon against a nagging female," he quipped, his deep voice not quite steady for once.

Heat scalded her cheeks, and she sucked in an outraged breath.

"Don't," he warned, his gaze locked on the tremulous, passion-stung softness of her lower lip. "For once, General, just hold your tongue, before I do something we'll both regret."

Words of castigation burned on her lips, but something in the cobalt depths of his eyes stopped her. Something warned her that the next time he kissed her like that, there'd be no stopping, no turning back—for either of them.

Quivering, Genevieve forced herself to look away. Her fingers clenched on the paper-wrapped package, recalling her to her duty and her guilt. She would deliver Baggart's damned shipment if necessary, but as soon after opening night as she could fetch Grandpapa and Maebella, they were leaving London, and it wasn't just Baggart she'd be running from. Torn by her impossible attraction for this intriguing, infuriating man, she had to remove herself as soon as possible from Bryce's unsettling proximity—before *she* did something they'd both regret.

They rode the rest of the way in silence. It was well past dusk when the hackney drew up before the workrooms, now silent and deserted since all the work had come to an end. Bryce handed her down, then took her keys and went before her carrying the torch left by the link boys through the foyer to her door.

"Thank you for escorting me home," Genevieve said, her words prim. "It was good of you."

"You'll never know how good, General," Bryce replied dryly.

He took a candlestick from a table by her door and lit it. Over the flickering flame, their eyes met and melded in a heightened awareness that was as much confusion and regret as latent passion. He handed her the taper, unlocked the door, and gently pushed her through the opening. "Good night, Genny."

Inside, she leaned for a moment against the door, then caught the tips of her gloves between her teeth and tugged them off, preoccupied with the knowledge that Bryce would have met with little resistance should he have desired to come in and wondering why he hadn't pressed her. Inscrutable, incomprehensible man—he was determined to keep her permanently off balance! With an annoyed huff, she lifted the candle, then gasped aloud—the room had been ransacked!

Before she could move, hard hands grabbed her, covered her mouth, and the package, ridicule, and candle went flying, plunging the room again into darkness.

"Where is it?" grated a guttural voice. "Nary a peep, hear? Just tell me what I want to know, and there won't be no trouble."

Shocked and terrified, Genevieve jerked her head in a nod, nearly gagging on the salt-sweaty taste of the foul-smelling thug's hand against her lips. Encouraged, the ruffian loosened his grip.

"So where is it, eh?"

Genevieve opened her mouth—and screamed the one word that meant deliverance. "Bryce!"

Snarling, the burglar cuffed her across the mouth. She fell to the floor, scrambling away, shrieking, but he grabbed at her skirts, hauling her in hand over hand. The front door rattled under a heavy assault, then exploded inward, the lock pulverized by a savage kick. Bryce burst into the room, took one look, then leaped at the man's throat with a roar of rage.

Hand pressed to her bloody lip, Genevieve dragged herself up while they grappled in the darkness, Bryce landing body blows that produced grunts of pain from her assailant. In the next instant, the thug picked up her pot of asters and slammed it into the side of Bryce's head, stunning him momentarily. It was just long enough to permit the burglar a panicky retreat, and he clattered down the dark stairs as though the devil himself were after him.

Bryce shook his head, focused on Genevieve long enough to see she was not seriously harmed, then went after the culprit. Shuddering, Genevieve raced through the doorway after them. But it wasn't the villain who frightened her now; it was Bryce, for his face had been a cold, unrecognizable mask. A killer's face, vicious and determined and . . . not quite human.

She reached the top of the landing as Bryce launched himself over the banister in a flying leap that brought down the fleeing man from behind. They tumbled and rolled, knocking down stacked lumber and canvas scenery panels. Bright steel flashed in the dimness, and the burglar lunged at Bryce with a knife.

Genevieve choked back a scream, her hands locked on the rounded rail of the banister, but Bryce dodged, then whirled and kicked out, sending the lethal weapon flying from the man's numbed fingers. With a faint squeak, the burglar fled again, disappearing into the dark confines of the carpenter's workshop with Bryce at his heels.

"Bryce! Stop!" Genevieve raced down the stairs and across the foyer, her breath sobbing in her chest. "For the love of God—let him go!"

She paused uncertainly at the darkened doorway, straining her eyes, listening to the bang of boxes and boards and breaking glass. There came a great final crash, cursing, the sound of running feet, then quiet.

"Bryce?"

A groan. "In here."

As her eyes adjusted, Genevieve could see a form struggling to his hands and knees. With a faint cry, she hastened through the rubble to his side. "Sweet heavens above! What happened? Are you all right?"

Bryce staggered to his feet, cursing virulently. "Damnation," he muttered, "I'm getting too old for this waggery when I can't handle a couple of rusty clodpates like those!"

"Someone hit you from behind?" Shoving her shoulder under his arm, she helped him pick his way across the shattered room. Her fingers encountered something warm and sticky, and she gasped. "You're bleeding!"

"Easy, General. I'll survive."

"Eh, sir? Ye're all right in there?" The hackney driver, followed by an ancient constable, timidly poked his nose through the open front door. "We 'eard the ruckus, an' . . ."

Roiling emotions made Genevieve indignant. "Constable, we've been accosted and burglarized! Two men fled out the back way. Hurry and you may still catch them!"

Bryce waved his hand tiredly. "Never mind, gentlemen. Wouldn't be any use. Our friends are miles away by now."

"You can't just mean to let them go!" Genevieve cried.

The withered watchman was eyeing Bryce gratefully. "If ye're certain there's nothing to be done, sir . . ."

"No, nothing that a sticking plaster won't fix."

Mumbling about the state of the world, the driver and the old Charlie withdrew, but Genevieve was still incensed by their lack of enthusiasm.

"The very idea!" she fumed. "What's a law-abiding citizen to do? Come along, Bryce. We must see to that hurt."

Mounting the stairs, Bryce shook his aching head. "What I want to know is what the devil the fellow was doing in your rooms."

"I—I have no idea."

To her chagrin, Genevieve found that she was shaking badly, perhaps from reaction, perhaps from the lie she'd just told. The burglar had wanted "it." No great act of deduction was needed to discern the only "it" worth having was Blind Jacob's cache of stolen property. Someone besides Samson Baggart had an interest in the elusive antiquity. Was it the mysterious Griffin he'd mentioned? Whoever it was, now *she* was caught in the middle between them!

Bryce put a tentative hand to his temple and winced. "I must say, General, our acquaintance has been fraught with peril. First highwaymen, now house crackers! I—"

He stopped so abruptly that Genevieve nearly lost her balance on the staircase. "What on earth!"

"Did you get a good look at that first fellow?" Bryce demanded roughly.

"N-no. It all happened so fast . . . Why?"

"Nothing, I suppose." He shook his head. "But there was something about him that reminded me of one of those highwaymen . . . No, too impossible a coincidence. Or have you persistent enemies I know nothing about?"

Genevieve quivered inwardly. For a desperate instant she was tempted to blurt out the whole ugly, sordid truth about her predicament to Bryce. But no; though he'd been kind, he might not take to the notion that his employee was involved, albeit unwillingly, in such an illegal morass. Besides, the Maples clan had always been self-sufficient. She'd deal with this problem herself by taking her grandfather out of Baggart's way immediately—or just as soon as *Othello* opened and Bryce paid her off. Setting her chin, she glared at him.

"Of course not! That blow must have addled your brains."

Kicking shut the shattered door of her apartment, Bryce examined his temple gingerly. "It certainly feels like it. The fellow did you no harm?"

"Not really. He didn't have a chance, thanks to you."

With swift movements, she relit the candle, only to hesitate as the guttering light revealed the extent of the destruction. Even her newest finds, a spruce cone, assorted buttons, and a ten-penny nail, had been swept from their place on the windowsill. Steeling herself to ignore the violation of her strewn clothing and ripped books, she scooped up her ridicule and Blind Jacob's package and hurriedly put them away, then examined Bryce's bloody countenance.

She swallowed hard, and her whispered confession was brutally honest. "I—I'm not certain who frightened me more."

Bryce grimaced and looked away, muttering. "Unfortunately, my darker nature still has its uses."

"Come sit down," she ordered, chilled by what she'd seen him become and by the caustic self-recrimination in his words. Removing her spencer, she pulled him down in the straight wooden chair before the tiny hearth, then hastily lit the kindling and set the water kettle to heat. "Let me see what that blackguard did to you."

She fussed over him for several minutes, requiring him to strip off his bloodstained neckcloth, then washing the cut over his temple and the trails of drying scarlet that marked the side of his face and his corded neck. Bryce bore her ministrations meekly, but Genevieve was not so unaffected.

His hair was black silk under her fingers, the tautness of his jaw and the whisper of dark stubble decorating it a feast of sensual experience. She lingered over her mission, inundating Bryce with her warmth and scent until he was wound tight as a coiled spring.

Finally, she drew back, examining her handiwork critically. "There. I think you'll do."

"You missed a spot," Bryce said huskily.

"Where?"

"Here."

Before she could react, he pulled her onto his lap, took the cloth from her nerveless hands, and dabbed gently at the small dot of blood crusting her lower lip. His azure gaze was so intense Genevieve could not breathe, could not protest when he bent closer to lave the tiny slit with his tongue. At his raspy touch, an almost inaudible moan escaped her, and her hard-won control slipped and shattered. With a cry, she flung her arms around his neck, clinging to him as her eyes filled.

"Oh, Bryce, I was so frightened!" The emotion clogging her throat made her voice husky. "So afraid for you!"

"Me?" He chuckled. "I'm indestructible, didn't you know? So far beyond salvation even the devil won't take me."

"If anything happened to you, I couldn't bear it."

"Genny, don't cry. It's all over."

He sipped the tears from her lashes, the curve of her cheek, the corner of her mouth, then plundered her sweetness gently, yet with a thoroughness that demanded a response. Genevieve was helpless to withhold it, melting against him as sensation exploded deep within her center, arousal flowing like molten honey through her veins. He was so very male and vital, and his strength beckoned her like a moth to a flame. When his tongue twined sinuously around hers, she quit breathing altogether, electing only to *feel*.

With tentative movements, she drew her fingers across his angular jaw, down the strong column of his neck into the vee of his collarbone, reveling in the crisp texture of the chest hairs curling there. She was awash with sensation: the rock-hard wall of his chest, the persuasive firmness of his mouth, the musky scent of his battle-warmed skin. An incredible urge to explore him, to touch him—everywhere—surged through her. Shyly, she slipped her fingers between the buttons of his rough workman's shirt, surveying the hard map of chest muscle with feather touches that made him quake and shudder.

Groping blindly, Bryce tugged the pins from her chignon, spilling her hair about her shoulders. He buried his fists in the red-brown mass, luxuriating in the vibrant quality of her curls, holding her still while he took undisciplined advantage of her pliancy. At last, he released her mouth to bury his face in the fragrant hollow between her neck and shoulder.

"God! You must truly be a witch to have such power over me," he murmured roughly. "I could have killed that bastard for touching you."

Her breath caught at the ferocity she sensed behind his words. She touched his face. "You came, and that's enough."

His arms tightened around her. "Sweet Genny, how little you know."

"I know what's important."

She shuddered uncontrollably. He might have been badly hurt, even killed, all because of her. Life was precious, and love was even more rare. That was the truth, perhaps the only kind that really mattered. How could she deny

what was in her heart a moment longer? With a courage
she had not known she possessed, she whispered, "I know
I love you."

Bryce stiffened, and as he drew back to stare down at
her, something savage flared behind his eyes. "Don't love
me, Genevieve. I'm not worth it."

How that pierced her heart! Only in her guilty soul, she
knew she was the unworthy one, for she needed him desperately to fend off the demons that threatened her, at least
for a while. But the very strength that drew her had been
forged by the tribulations of war and the hardships of his
youth, things totally outside her experience. On a deep
interior level he was as untamed as an eagle, as fascinating, and as dangerous. Was she foolish to hope she might
be the one to gentle the predator within him? To offer him
some solace from the dark places in his soul while she
took her own comfort? Foolish or not, she knew the choice
was no longer hers to make.

"Don't say that!" she ordered fiercely. "Don't ever say
that again."

"You think that will change anything?" He laughed
harshly. "My God, you are an innocent!"

"So you say." Daringly, she brushed her lips against
his.

Bryce gave a start of surprise and something more. With
a jolt of feminine triumph, Genevieve felt the way his
hands trembled, saw desire flicker in the depths of his
eyes. An answering need sluiced through her, reducing all
uncertainties into a single pivotal question.

What if she never fully experienced the promise of
Bryce's passion? If he knew about Baggart, he'd surely
despise her, and she would miss forever the chance to
show him he was indeed worthy, estimable, and lovable
in her eyes. She would never have a claim on him, for his
freedom meant too much to him, but how could she leave
him, how could she *survive* without knowing his most intimate touch, without having him for her own, just once?

Then, whatever came, she'd have that much to cherish forever.

Recklessly, deliberately, her heart pounding at her boldness, she kissed him again, then gasped as he bent her over the crook of one arm, cupping the fullness of her breast in bold possession. A groan vibrated deep in his chest.

"Stop it, Genevieve, or you'll rue this day forever."

"Impossible." Genevieve shivered, wanting yet afraid. His thumb flicked the tip of her nipple through her gown, and she gasped, excitement and need mingling in equal portions. "Darcy, please . . ."

He nibbled the tender cords of her neck, convulsing her with shivers. "When you call me that, I'm yours to command, *mon general*. So use your head and tell me to go."

"No. I can't."

"You don't know what you're saying, Genny." Hunger warred with conscience. "Don't do this to me."

"My Darcy." With a tender smile, she cupped his face between her palms and pulled his head down. "Please. Let me do this—for *us*."

Chapter 8

❦

There was no restraint in him then.

With a groan of absolute need, Bryce loosed the bonds of self-control and plunged into the sweet abyss of passion, taking Genevieve's soft mouth to test the texture of her yielding. The tender, tentative flicker of her tongue against his in response changed her surrender to victory, taking his breath, what remained of his honor, and all of his sanity.

Coming to his feet, he pulled her closer with feverish hands, crushing the womanly softness of her breasts against his chest. In answer, she wrapped her arms around his neck, arching, pressing, seeking even more closeness while tongues danced in a primitive mating that sent fire surging to Bryce's loins. To his intense pleasure and surprise, he found her need burned with as much desperation as his own.

"Genny." His hoarse mutter was a pagan hymn against the velvety skin of her jaw. Nosing her curls aside, he explored the tender hollow behind her ear, and inhaled the flowery, intoxicating fragrance of madness.

"Yes." Shuddering, she moved her hands over his nape, caressing, stroking the tense cords of his neck, then fumbled with the buttons of his shirt. He obligingly stripped out of his shirt and coat, his gaze never leaving her flushed face.

Her breathing became even more labored at the sight of his naked chest, all hard planes and angles in the flickering firelight. With a look of intense absorption, she reached out, tracing the taut, hair-dusted muscles with her fingers, learning him by touch. With a growl, Bryce gathered her up and carried her through the wreckage of the apartment to her bedroom and laid her gently on the cot.

Toeing off his boots, he slid down beside her, catching her lips in another drugging kiss, his fingers trembling and eager on the fastening of her gown. With the air of a man who'd just received a long-awaited gift, he loosed her bodice, drawing back slightly to smile down at her. Eyes glittering wickedly, he trailed the tip of one finger beneath the lace edge of her chemise and stays, over the uppermost curve of her bosom, tantalizing and tormenting them both.

"Your skin . . ." he whispered, brushing his lips over her collarbone. "It's so soft. And your mouth . . . God, I love your mouth."

She moaned, plucking at her garments fretfully. "Help me . . ."

With a thousand kisses and caresses, Bryce happily obeyed, helping her to remove her gown, stays, and petticoat. He made a full production of rolling down her stockings and removing her slippers, then slid his warm hands back up over the slender curve of calf and thigh, covered only by the thinnest of lawn drawers, examined her neat waist, then rolled his palms over the aching centers of her breasts.

Genevieve made a little ragged sound of excitement and reached for him, pulling him down beside her. "Bryce. I want to touch you."

He shuddered, and his lids drooped. "Oh, Lord, yes."

At first with hesitation, then with growing assurance, she ran her hands over his massive shoulders, exploring the contours of his flesh, the play of bone and sinew beneath the taut muscle, then moved over the tanned skin of hard biceps and washboard ribcage. Bryce held himself still for her investigation, amazed at the flare of pleasure such simple touching wrought. Blood surged, hardening his throbbing sex with each liberty she took until he thought he'd explode. When her thumb brushed the pebbled coin of his nipple buried under its nest of crisp dark curls, he jerked uncontrollably. But when she moved to draw her hand away in fright, he caught her wrist and pressed her palm against him again.

"No, don't," he said, his voice thick. "It's perfect."

"I don't know how . . ." she wailed softly.

"Yes, you do." To prove it to her, he pulled her hand down even further, catching her startled gasp in his mouth, letting her feel the hard length of his desire through the fabric of his trousers. She whimpered deep in her throat, but did not resist the intimacy, relishing the feel of him instead, measuring and stroking until Bryce broke the kiss with a groan and jerked her hand away.

"Witch! You push me too far, too fast." He straddled her, pinning her wrists at her sides. "I want to savor you."

Bending his head, he nuzzled her neck, then moved lower to suckle the cockled tips of her breasts through the thin chemise. Her hands clenched spasmodically on his thighs, sending rivers of incandescent sensation cascading through Bryce. Eagerly, he released her hands and whipped off the chemise, devouring the dimly revealed peach and honey tones of her rounded flesh with his hungry gaze. He tasted the velvety underside of her breasts, then made her cry out and bury her fingers in his hair when he bathed each nipple with his tongue.

Panting, she strained against him, shifting her legs restlessly, then jerking when his agile fingers found the slit in her drawers. With expert skill and infinite care, he caressed and probed the sensitive, dewy folds of her womanhood. That she was slick and hot and ready for him nearly undid Bryce completely. With a low growl, he snapped the drawstring of the garment and tugged it down her slender legs, exposing the chestnut-brown curls at the apex of her thighs.

Revealed, vulnerable, she was totally feminine, delicate

. . . beautiful. Swallowing, Bryce raised his eyes. In the dim confines of their trysting place, her tremulous gaze was rife with naked need . . . and a challenge he could appreciate. They'd come too far to turn back now, but the act they were on the verge of consummating would force irrevocable changes, perhaps move them in paths neither was ready for. Bryce only knew he couldn't deny himself this woman even if his life depended on it.

He shucked out of his trousers and knelt over her, nudging her legs apart with a knee, his face etched with tension, his eyes smoky with need. Bending, he sipped one honey-flavored nipple, smiling to himself at her gasp of pleasure. He claimed her mouth again in a deep, lingering kiss while her hands moved over his back and down to the base of his spine in fleeting butterfly caresses that threatened his tenuous control.

Cupping her buttocks in his large hands, he lifted her slightly, probing the silky wetness between her legs, dying bit by bit as he slid into her softness. She trembled beneath him, then tensed as his entrance met resistance. Wrestling for the last of his control, Bryce pulled his mouth free and buried his face in the tender hollow behind her ear. Elated, humbled, he was filled with a sense of primitive possession and tenderness at the evidence of her gift to him.

"Hold on to me," he whispered, his tone raw with regret. "I'm sorry, *chérie.*"

With a single powerful thrust, he plunged past the frail barrier of her virginity. He held her until her quivering subsided, whispering praise and love words until she was pliant and relaxed again, stroking her breasts and thighs until the heat within her built anew and he could at last begin to move as his body so urgently demanded.

Thrusting slowly, drawing out this first time with Genevieve, savoring the way she sheathed him in her warmth and softness, Bryce knew he'd never experienced anything so good. Though he could not return her avowal of love, an overwhelming tenderness flooded him. Sliding deeper and deeper within her, losing himself in her sweetness, he was bathed by a sense of rightness, of acceptance, of homecoming that filled his heart to bursting.

Bracing himself on his arms, he looked into Genevieve's flushed face, gauging the growing tension in her expression, determined to give her a gift as precious as the one she'd bestowed on him. Suddenly, she shattered before his eyes, dissolving in an exquisite climax that made her gasp and arch in an ecstatic female release. Bryce had never seen anything so beautiful.

Milked by her tiny interior contractions, Bryce buried himself within her softness one last time, hurtling toward his own completion. With a primeval grown of pleasure, he poured his seed into her in hot, liquid pulsations, exulting in the glorious power of the act they shared.

Genevieve floated in the quietude that followed, every nerve tingling with aftershocks. She felt as if her senses had expanded to heretofore unknown reaches. Still joined to Bryce, she welcomed the weight of his sweat-slickened body, listened to the music of his ragged breathing, inhaled the musky male scent of his skin. She understood then that she'd been starving all her life, and now Bryce had brought her to a feast of the senses and of the heart. Emotion roiled up within her on a powerful wave, and she caught her breath on the crest of a sob.

Instantly, Bryce shifted, sliding his weight from her, but dragging her with him so they lay together on their sides, his arm crooked beneath her head. His voice, lazy with lassitude, was at the same time husky with concern.

"Genny, sweet, don't cry. Did I hurt you?"

"No." Her breath shuddered, and she reached out for him, burying her nose in the vee of his collarbone. "It's not that."

"You're a brave soldier," Bryce murmured into her hair. "It's not always good for a woman, especially the first time."

Remembering her wanton abandonment, Genevieve blushed. "It was good. I never knew . . . It was good," she repeated lamely.

His pleased chuckle tickled her ear. "And can only get better with practice, my sweet. You'll see."

"I—I will?" she asked faintly.

"Assuredly. Now that you're mine, I intend to take good care of you from now on . . . in every way."

His arrogant assumption took her breath away, and she closed her eyes against the pain that stabbed her heart. It was only reasonable that Bryce would assume she'd be content to be his mistress now. That he'd been considerate and masterful only made her love him more. But she knew she could never settle for being only a part of his life, for never having the home and stability that only a true commitment could bring. In an ironic way she blessed the situation with Baggart and her plan to take Grandpapa away, for it took the decision out of her hands. When she left, she had only to remind herself that she'd wanted this, and if she had regrets, she had only herself to blame.

But not yet . . .

Swallowing harshly, she closed her eyes and snuggled even closer, loath to destroy so soon the fantasy encompassed by his embrace. Her inquisitive fingers discovered a ridge of scar tissue transversing Bryce's back and side, and she caught her breath. "Sweet saints above! What—?"

Raising up on one elbow, Bryce caught her questing hand, his face suddenly hard. " 'Tis nothing. And old injury, long healed and best forgotten."

"Secrets, Bryce?" she asked then grimaced at the mockery of her own words. Her own secrets were damning.

He shrugged off her question. He didn't want to think about Lyons, about the failure that had cost a woman's life, about a killer with strange slanted eyes who haunted his dreams. "A memento of a time I'd rather not recall. Nothing to concern you."

Having a door slammed in her face so effectively made her flush with anger. "Don't think you can bed me and then expect me not to care, Bryce. Everything about you concerns me, whether you wish it or not."

Frowning, he tucked a stray strand of hair behind her ear. "I have no desire to recall that dark time. Why taint what we share with my old horrors?"

His effort to compartmentalize her, to diffuse the power of a love that might be the means to free him from past hurts, made her knit her brow in frustration. "But—"

"Don't argue, Genevieve." His tone was implacable, and his hands tightened on her inexorably. "Some secrets deserve to be kept."

"Perhaps you're right," she murmured, reaching up to smooth the grim line of his upper lip with the tip of her finger. He caught the pad of her finger lightly between his teeth, sending an erotic shock through her system.

"Forget the past," he ordered hoarsely. "This is what matters now."

He silenced further protest with a sense-rocking kiss. Dizzy, lost again in Bryce's magic, Genevieve clung to him, her head spinning. When Bryce drew back to gaze down into her uptilted face, whatever he saw there made his eyes—his oh-so-beautiful blue eyes!—ignite. His lean cheek creased, and he smiled, a smile so full of tenderness and promise, Genevieve knew she was lost even before his mouth moved to cover hers again.

Quite a long time later, Genevieve bolted upright in the rumpled bed, roused by an impatient "Halloo" and an imperative knocking from the entrance below. Bryce grumbled drowsily in protest and reached for her, but she threw his bare leg off her own and scrambled up in a panic, dragging the sheets around her naked form in an agony of pure consternation. The voice rising from the darkened street was one she knew all too well!

"Oh, dear Lord! Grandpapa!"

"What—?" Bryce rolled over, his heart drumming as his mind swam with remnants of an old nightmare. He forced back the miasma as new alarms went off inside his head at the sight of Genevieve's appalled features. *"Chérie . . . ?"*

"Oh, God! What's he doing here now?" Genevieve

cried, her fists pressed against her mouth. She looked at
the nude man in her bed in absolute horror as the cacoph-
ony below increased in volume. How in the world would
she explain this to Grandpapa? She reached for her discarded gown and pitched Bryce's trousers toward the bed.
"Quick! Get dressed!"

Tugging her wrinkled gown up over her shoulders, she
flew to the window, brushing down her skirts and trying
to ignore the high color that heated her cheeks. Throwing
open the glass, she leaned over the sill, breathing in the
cool rush of night air in grateful gusts. Below her, Everett
Maples raised his cane again to rap on the door as Maebella paid off a hackney driver just setting their battered
luggage to the pavement.

"Grandpapa! Maebella!" Geneveive called and waved
to get their attention. "What are you doing here?"

Everett Maples raised his leonine head and roared.
"Sacked! Booted! The utter nerve! Don't just stand there
chittering, gel—open up and let us in!"

Genevieve's gaze darted to Maebella. The older woman's face was lined with weariness, her shoulders stooped
with resignation.

"I'm coming!" Genevieve shouted in alarm, turned,
and plowed straight into Bryce, who had donned pants and
boots but held his shirt in one hand. He caught her shoulders to steady her, but she shrugged him off impatiently.
"Let go. Something's happened!"

"You're damned right," he growled. "We both discovered a bit of paradise tonight! Don't tell me you're ashamed
of that?"

Confusion clouded her eyes, and her succulent lower lip
trembled. "That's between us. Grandpapa . . . he wouldn't
understand. Please, Bryce!"

He rubbed the pleat between his strongly marked brows,
disturbed by the agonized appeal in her gray-green eyes.
Her lack of sophistication had been part of her appeal, after
all. He could not fault her for lacking the brazenness of a
practiced courtesan in this situation.

"All right, we'll let it go—for now. I'll go let them in, but I suggest you take the opportunity to right the place as best you can so the oldster won't be unduly alarmed."

Her gaze moved askance over the ransacked rooms, surveying the wreckage accurately for the first time. Indeed, it looked as if Bonaparte's legions had marched through it—and recently. Baggart's booty must be precious indeed to warrant such a search. And like a dumb pack animal, she carried it without question!

"Yes, I'll do what I can," she said. A muscle in the side of Bryce's jaw flexed, but when he would have reached for her, Everett took up his pounding again. Without another word, Bryce turned on his heel and left the apartment.

Genevieve gazed after him a fleeting second, the darted into action, fastening her gown with shaky fingers and shoving her feet into her slippers. Throwing her tangled hair over her shoulders, she straightened what she could of the rooms, sweeping everything else into piles and shoving them into the drawers of an old cupboard. She'd cleaned up just enough that a first glance wouldn't prove too shocking when Bryce, arms laden with baggage, escorted Maebella and Everett through the door. Genevieve flew to her grandfather's side.

"Grandpapa, whatever's happened? You're supposed to be at Sadler's Wells!"

"Sadler's—bah!" Everett flung down his hat and cane, his face florid with agitation. "What does that damned fool Driggers know? He can't sack me! I'm Everett Maples, known from Dublin to Paris! Bah!"

Dumbfounded, Genevieve swung her gaze to Maebella, who was removing her bonnet and listening to Bryce's quiet explanations about the burglary attempt. Maebella's sharply inquisitive coffee-brown eyes darted back and forth between the two of them, assessing Bryce's presence and Genevieve's flushed cheeks. Genevieve urged her grandfather into the chair at the hearth, then gave Maebella a quick hug and a look that begged for explanations.

" 'Tweren't no good, dear." The plump wardrobe mistress's fading butter-colored curls quivered as she shook her head. "Disaster after disaster, night after night. And then this evening . . ."

"What happened?"

"Oh, Genny! There he was, saying his piece same as always, all the while disrobing right in front of the entire audience! Stockings, waistcoat, shirt—it was like he'd lost his mind. He'd have gone right down to bare skin if Arthur and Mike hadn't carried him off! Driggers had no choice."

"Oh, no." Genevieve blanched. "What about the others?"

"Gone their own ways, the lot of 'em."

"So the Maples Company. . . ?"

"It doesn't exist anymore, I'm afraid." Maebella's face was sorrowful.

"Oh, no. If only I'd been there—"

"You couldn't have done anything to save it. He's worse, Genevieve."

Their gazes swung to Everett, who was busy venting his outrage to Bryce.

"I told my son nothing would come of this engagement, but would he listen? No! Why, when I was a young man— eh, what's this?" Everett glanced around distractedly. "Where's the host of this establishment? Why can't a man get a dram when he needs it?"

"You must be tired, Grandpapa," Genevieve soothed automatically, conscious of Bryce's watchful gaze. More than a little bewildered, embarrassed, and confused, she latched on to the comforting routine of a mundane chore to ease the awkwardness of the moment. "Let me make something hot to drink. A strong cup of tea will set us all right."

"I want to go to my room." Everett's voice went plaintive, and he seemed to shrink in the chair, looking suddenly feeble.

Genevieve's mind reeled with the lightninglike changes

in her once-robust grandfather. "There's a bed made up in the second bedroom, Grandpapa."

"Here, I'll help you, Mr. Maples, sir," Maebella said, gliding to his side to take his hand.

Everett looked up into her gentle, smiling countenance with an air of surprise. "Ah, Bella. It's good to see you."

"Come, sir, a bit of a lie-down will do you no end of good." Maebella took his arm and guided him toward the smaller bed cubicle with the ease of old friendship.

Genevieve stared after them in dismay, then felt Bryce's gaze on her and flushed hotly. "I—I'll get that tea."

"Hellfire!" Raking a hand through his hair, Bryce followed her over the hearth. He watched her deal with the kettle and tin canister of fragrant leaves as if she were indeed one of *Macbeth*'s witches concocting some sinister potion. "Tea, my dear Genevieve, is hardly what's on my mind."

The spoon she wielded clattered to the floor, but she made no move to pick it up, staring at him with eyes filled with uncertainty. "Would you shame me in front of my family?"

His chin grew stubborn. "They'll know eventually."

"Know what? That I gave my heart unwisely?" She drew a shaky breath and looked away. "Perhaps you are accustomed to liaisons of a romantic nature, but despite society's opinion about actresses, I cannot pretend to such worldliness."

Her disquiet pricked his conscience. "I won't hurt you, Genny."

"Then don't press me now!" She wrung her hands in agitation. "Can't you see? Not now . . ."

Gently, he drew her into his arms, his mouth twisting with remorse. "I can see that I'm a selfish bastard. Forgive me, *chérie*. 'Tis only I am loath to leave you for fear this will all prove only a dream."

She stared at him for a long moment, then reached up to stroke his jaw in wonderment. "I feel the same," she confessed, "but you must go. Grandpapa and Maebella are both tired and upset. Mayhap in the morning . . ."

He heaved a sigh of resignation. "I understand. All right, General. I'll be on my way. But nothing's settled."

"I know." Troubled shadows darkened her eyes.

"I'll call for you after rehearsal tomorrow. We can dine at my house and . . . discuss matters."

"Not tomorrow! With Grandpapa here, I can't possibly—"

"All right. Then the day after that."

"But that's dress rehearsal! Wouldn't it be better—"

"No. I'll be half crazed by then anyway. Promise me."

She couldn't deny the demand in his expression or her own need. "Yes."

Bryce smiled and kissed her fiercely. "Don't worry. We'll be together, and that's all that matters."

"I pray you're right."

"You'll see."

Maebella came quietly back into the sitting room then, and Bryce reluctantly released Genevieve.

"I was unwilling to leave Genevieve alone after our brush with her intruder," he said to Maebella, "but since you and Everett are come to keep her company I don't think there will be any further trouble, so I'll bid you *bonsoir.*"

"But your tea," Genevieve protested, holding up a steaming cup.

Bryce's lids dropped, hooding his expression. He bent to kiss Genevieve's hand in a most courtly manner. "The throbbing in my cracked pate . . . and elsewhere . . . demands something stronger, I'm afraid."

Smiling at her mortified expression, he picked up his coat and went to the door. "Good night, General. Miss Symthe."

Maebella nodded, her gaze all too knowing. "Sir."

As the door shut behind him, he smiled as he heard Maebella's insistent demand. "Genny, you must tell me everything!"

Walking down the torchlit cobbles moments later, Bryce was astonished to find he was actually whistling.

He shook his head in amazement. God, how far the Griffin had come! And it was all due to sweet Genevieve with her soft mouth and softer body. She had no idea how good they were together, but he was determined to show her, over and over again. Just as soon as *Othello* opened, and he reported his latest lack of success to Huxford, he'd concentrate on nothing else. Genevieve was so different from any woman he'd ever known—

Bryce's self-absorbed bubble of well-being popped on a sudden realization, and he came up short in the darkness of a deserted street corner.

She *was* different. Honest with her feelings as he'd never learned to be. Innocent and untouched—at least until he'd taken that from her. The sudden memory of the hurt confusion in her eyes gnawed at him. Genevieve certainly wasn't like the demireps he was accustomed to bedding and then forgetting. And she wasn't the type of woman to adapt easily to the role of mistress, no matter how deeply her feelings were involved. Hadn't he known almost from the beginning of their acquaintance that she longed for a traditional home and family? And if he couldn't provide that, sooner or later she'd become so unhappy that he'd lose her. Dammit, no! Life without Genevieve's blessed softness—he couldn't let that happen!

"My God." He spoke his astonishment aloud to the empty street. "I'll have to marry her to keep her."

A slow, surprised smile curled his mouth, and once more he began to saunter down the street . . . whistling.

Unable to sleep, her thoughts spinning like a dervish, Genevieve listened to Maebella snoring softly in the bed next to her. So much had happened in so short a period, she was at a loss to come to grips with it all.

Bryce. Her body throbbed in every secret, sensitive place, longing for him, even while her conscience prodded her for her sins. She was hopelessly compromised now.

Without knowing how, she'd become no more than one of the cyprians she'd held in such contempt. Sweet Jesus! What had she done? *The only thing she could,* her heart whispered. She loved Bryce and could not regret the physical magic they'd shared. But how could she bear to leave him now?

She'd put Maebella's questions off with the news about the opportunities for Madame Bella and an overlong description of Bryce's encounter with the burglar. When the older woman was nodding with fatigue, Genevieve suggested they conclude their discussion in the morning and both turn in for the night.

But now Baggart and his threats loomed like specters in the darkened bedroom, and poor Everett slept on the other side of the wall in a state of childish dependency. If only there was some way to know if she was doing the right thing!

With a start, Genevieve realized there was one thing she'd overlooked. She eased out of the bed so as not to disturb Maebella, threw her shawl across her shoulders of her linen night rail, and padded silently into the sitting room. Pearly gray predawn light filtered through the shutters along with the distant chants and calls of the street vendors. Heart thumping in her chest, she retrieved Blind Jacob's package from its hiding place, hesitated, then grimly tore into the paper wrapping.

"Catherine, is that you?"

Genevieve swung around with a startled gasp. Tugging on his dressing gown, Everett shuffled out of his bedroom, yawning and rubbing his silver-stubbled jowls. With a sinking heart, Genevieve realized he'd called her by the name of her long-dead grandmother.

"It's me, Grandpapa."

Everett blinked and stretched. "Genny-girl. Ah, I must have been dreamin' of your grandmama. What are ye doing up so early?"

"Grandpapa?" Amazed, Genevieve stared at him, for he seemed clear-eyed and lucid, his old normal self.

Grateful for this miracle, however momentary, she grabbed his arm and urged him to a chair at the rickety table, then sat down beside him. "Grandpapa, we must talk. Everything's a mess! Baggart—"

"Calm down, gel! Ye're chattering too fast for my old head. Have ye any tea and bread? I'm right peckish. Say, is that a bit of cheese in that paper?"

"That's what I'm trying to tell you, Grandpapa! It's Baggart's. He wasn't content with one delivery as he promised. He's looking for something, and he'll not release us until he finds it. I only hope to heaven it's in here!"

She ripped into the package, then spread its glittering contents on the table. It was a motley collection of several fine pieces—a seed pearl tiara, a silver chain, a garnet and gold bracelet—mixed with pieces of less value or obvious fakes. She sifted through the lot frantically, but when she lifted her head again, her eyes glittered with tears of frustration.

"Damnation and hellfire! Baggart's blasted antiquity still isn't here!"

"Watch your tongue, gel. Such language isn't fitting for a young lady."

"Grandpapa, you don't understand. Baggart won't be satisfied with this, either. And unless I agree to remain his pack mule, he'll try to put you in St. Luke's!" She dropped her face into her hands, shuddering. "I can't do it again. We must go where Baggart's threats can't reach us. France, maybe, or America. As soon as Bryce pays me, we'll have enough money to make some plans."

"Is your garret empty, gel?" Everett's leonine countenance registered his adamancy. "I'm an Englishman! I'm not going to run away. I intend to die on English soil."

"Very well for you, perhaps, but I don't want to go to the gallows as part of Baggart's ring of thieves!" Rising, she paced back and forth, automatically setting the kettle to the hob and poking up the fire in the grate. "Consider, Grandpapa! Because that's how it will be unless he gets his eagle's talon. You know his love of antiquities. He's obsessed with this thing, says it has powers or some such superstitious nonsense.''

Everett's spiky silver brows drew together in a formidable line, and his forehead creased with thought. ''That's peculiar.''

Genevieve brought a loaf and pots of jam and butter to the table, then began slicing the bread with vicious jabs. ''I can't stand it anymore! All the hiding and deceit and lies! I'm going to tell Bryce everything and damn the consequences. Maybe he'll help.''

''Hold on now, gel!'' Everett interrupted. ''What's Cormick got to do with us?''

Genevieve's spate of nervous energy deserted her suddenly, and she wilted. ''I—I'm in love with him, Grandpapa.''

''My dear gel!'' Everett's rheumy eyes softened with concern. ''And does the gentleman return your sentiments?''

''No . . . yes . . . I'm not sure, but''—her voice dropped miserably—''he won't marry me, so it's just as well if we go away. Please, Grandpapa! Just for a time. As soon as I can find passage money—'' She broke off with an incredulous cry.

''What is it?'' Everett demanded.

''I'm such an addlebrain!'' Her soft laughter bubbled like the kettle on the hearth. She dropped the knife and plucked the silver chain from the pile. ''We have the means to get away right here. Now, today! Why should I take these things to Baggart when he'll only use them against me?''

''Why indeed?'' Everett replied, and his expression became sly. Reaching into the depths of his dressing gown, he dragged out an object hanging around his neck on a tarnished chain and wagged it in her face. ''We're of one mind, gel. Best feather the nest while the weather's fair, eh?''

The back of Genevieve's neck prickled with a horrible

premonition. She pounced on the bell-shaped, egg-sized article, turned it bottom upward, and—

"The mark of the eagle's talon!" The fine ancient etching winked up at her from the surface of the rosy gem, tantalizing, mystifying. " 'Tis beautiful . . ."

"Aye, a magnificent stone, the stuff of legends—that's it!" Everett slapped his knee in delight. "I saw a picture of it in a book on talismans and mystical symbols I borrowed from the lending library at Bath. Some sort of seal, I seem to recall now. No wonder it caught my eye."

"So you've had it all the time! Oh, Grandpapa, what have you done?"

"Outfoxed a ferret, that's what," Everett said gleefully. "Fair exchange for being swindled out of our money, I'd say. I've kept it on my person since those damned cutthroats tried to take it on the highway at Dunstable."

"You're only partly right. Someone called the Griffin tried to steal it again yestere'en! We're caught betwixt two villains." She groaned. "You could have spared me much if you'd only given it to Baggart in the first place. Then he could have returned it to Mr. Abbot and we'd—"

"Abbot!" Everett hissed, grabbing her wrist in a surprisingly forceful grip. "What do you know of that traitor?"

"Why, n-nothing," she faltered. "Just something Baggart said made me believe this belonged to him. Who—"

"Higgledly-piggledy! What a kettle of sow's mash this is!"

Genevieve drew back, tugging at her wrist, alarmed that Everett's period of lucidity was fading. "Grandpapa?"

"The Abbot!" He nodded his head vigorously, then released her to rub feverishly at his temples. "Yes, yes, I recollect it all. Heard the talk at one of those gaming hells Samson was so fond of. Thought I was out of my head with drink, no doubt, but I was thinking, sure enough. As Hamlet said, 'I know a hawk from a handsaw.' The Abbot's a master plotter, a purveyor of information and schemes *against the crown.*''

It took a moment for Genevieve to absorb that, and then she paled, going white as alabaster with shock. "Baggart said he wanted this . . . this seal to send to Bonaparte!''

"The Abbot's Seal." Everett's lined face grew haggard and gray. Slowly, he lifted off the chain and placed it on the table between them.

"Grandpapa, what are we involved in?" she whispered in horror.

"A great wickedness, I fear, Genny-girl, and it's all my fault.''

She snatched up the seal. "Then we must get rid of this immediately! I'll take it to Baggart right now.''

"Stop and think, gel," Everett said heavily. "If this is truly a treasonous coil, would Baggart be eager to let either of us live, once he has what he wants?''

Treason. The word hung on the air between them. Paralyzed, Genevieve watched the tarnished chain slip out of her nerveless fingers. The Abbot's Seal fell and lay gleaming like a giant's tear on the brick hearth.

But her desolation was too profound for tears. Although innocent of any precalculation, by her involvement in this she would be branded a traitor—the very thing the man she loved hated above all else. *He must never know,* she vowed in silent anguish. If Bryce knew the truth, he'd hate her forever, and that she could endure even less than never seeing him again.

"We must leave here as I planned," she croaked at last.

"No.''

"Grandpapa!''

"I'll not make you an eternal wanderer, an exile from your homeland because of my foolishness.''

"I don't care! We'll be safe—''

"Only until Baggart finds us. There's no guarantee.''

"Then what. . . ?" she began.

"I'll undo what I've done. We have something this Abbot wants, do we not? Then, for a price, we'll give it to him.''

''What price?'' Genevieve asked warily, not liking the shrewd, calculating light gleaming in the old man's eyes.

''Getting Samson Baggart to leave us in peace—permanently.''

She swallowed. ''How, Grandpapa?''

Everett grinned, an aged but still mischievous Puck. ''I have a plan.''

Braving the dubious pleasures of a sojourn to Holborn once was an adventure for any soul. Having to endure it twice more in the space of twenty-four hours was almost more than Genevieve's overstretched nerves could bear.

''I came as soon as I received your message,'' she said to Blind Jacob. ''We were here only yesterday. Is there a response already?''

''Could be.'' The old man's milky eyes looked somewhere over Genevieve's shoulder, as if examining the inventory lining the dusty shelves of his tiny shop. ''Ye like my brocade, do ye, miss? Just feel how fine a piece this is!''

Genevieve suppressed a shudder as the old man's gnarled fingers guided hers across a bolt of midnight-blue fabric, but she could not subdue the nervous fluttering of her heart. Again she questioned the wisdom of Everett's plan to contact the Abbot through Blind Jacob and the thieves' brotherhood, but it was too late now. The two of them had set the wheels in motion only the day before, and already they were threatening to run out of control. The excitement had taken a serious toll on Everett, forcing him to his bed while Genevieve answered Blind Jacob's summons alone.

Everett was confident Blind Jacob could contact the Abbot, and that the Abbot would order his associate Baggart to leave them in peace in exchange for the seal, but Genevieve had her doubts. She'd begged her grandfather to take the cursed emblem to the nearest magistrate and plead

innocence of all treasonable implications, but he'd refused. Nor would Everett consider fleeing the country, for
he was adamant in insisting that he would see this business
through. To further increase her anxiety, she had promised
to meet Bryce tonight after the final rehearsal of *Othello*.
But with her conscience in shambles, how could she bear
to see him at all? Perhaps she should plead her woman's
courses as an excuse . . .

Pitching her voice low, though she and Jacob were the
only ones in the cluttered shop, she demanded, "I must
know what's happened. Answer me!"

"The old cove you was wif before said your business
with the Abbot was urgent," the old man hedged.

"Yes. Yes, it is." She pulled her hand away. "Quite
urgent."

"Aye, and that got me thinking." Jacob lovingly stroked
the fabric as though it were a woman's skin. "Why wait
to turn a doubtful gain when an upright businessman like
myself can guarantee you a sure profit right now?"

"What?" Genevieve's voice went faint.

"That's right, miss. I'm willing to take your—er, article, off your hands for a fair price. What would be simpler? Then a lady like yourself won't have to make any
more trips to Field Lane for Mr. Baggart or anyone else."

"That's not what we agreed!" she said angrily. "If
profit was our aim, we'd have sold you the seal yesterday."

"Think on it, miss. Dangerous man is the Abbot. Se-
cretive, mysterious, deals in things not fittin' for a delicate
lady to know."

"I'm well aware of that," she said through gritted teeth.
" 'Tis the services we can exchange with this Abbot fellow that interest me and my grandfather, and we'll deal
with no one else, is that clear?"

Blind Jacob ducked his head in submissive assent. "As
you say, miss. No need to fret yourself."

Afraid that the entire plan was unraveling because of
the shopkeeper's greed, Genevieve continued furiously.

"We gave you a garnet bracelet to pass on our message. Either do so or return the bracelet immediately."

"Now, no need to be hasty. If the Abbot is interested, you'll hear soon enough."

"But time is short, and the imprint we made of the object is proof of our sincerity," she said, her voice rising on a note of desperation.

"I'm a poor man, crippled by my infirmity," Jacob whined. "I can only noise the word about among my cronies on the streets. What comes of it . . ." He lifted his shoulders, denying responsibility.

Genevieve's mouth curled in unnatural cynicism as she finally realized the subtlety of Blind Jacob's tactics. Drawing the silver chain from her ridicule, she pressed it into his hand. "Would this help to ensure that our message reaches the proper ears in all due haste?"

Instantly, the chain disappeared into the voluminous folds of the old man's stained smock, the same way the garnet bracelet had done the day before. "Your generosity will be well rewarded," he murmured, "but my offer is an honorable one. Won't you reconsider?"

"Just see that our message is delivered!" Genevieve snapped, apprehension getting the better of her. Raising her voice as though the shop were filled with customers, she took her leave. "I don't believe this brocade is what I wanted after all. Good day."

"I've another dimber piece back o' the storeroom, miss," Blind Jacob offered hopefully to her retreating back, but the swish of her skirts and the tinkle of the bell over the shop door as she left were her only response.

Jacob gathered up the bolt and carried it unerringly through the dusty burlap curtain that separated the shop from the storage area, then slid it into its place on a cluttered shelf. "She wouldn't budge an inch. Ye heard it yourself, Mr. D'Arcy."

"I heard plenty, Jacob."

Bryce Cormick pressed his back against the storeroom wall and struggled to suck air into his tortured lungs. He wore the rough guise of Griffin D'Arcy, a receiver with a bankroll large enough to tempt even Old Blind Jacob, who'd heard the whispers that Mr. D'Arcy would pay well for a certain seal. Once Jacob's sensitive and avaricious fingers had discerned the shape of a talon in the wax imprint of Miss Maples's offering, and he'd realized he had the makings of a gold mine within his grasp, it had been a simple matter to bring the two interested parties together. Mr. D'Arcy's wish to remain undiscovered while negotiations began was only standard practice in a business where caution was the watchword.

Now the old man cocked his grizzled head, listening to Bryce's rapid, angry breathing. "Something the matter, sir? I tried my best, I swear, sir. You might have come out to bargain with the lady yourself if you wasn't pleased with my dickering."

" 'Tis clear she'll deal only with the Abbot," Bryce replied.

His fists clenched with shock; only many years of discipline kept him from howling his rage and disillusionment like a mad dog. God, Huxford's guess about the Maples Company had been right from the start! What a fool he'd been. What an oblivious, lovesick blockhead! It was hard to conceive of sweet Genevieve as that cool bit of mercenary, traitorous baggage he had just observed, but she'd played him so well that he never suspected, never guessed. It was clear from everything he'd seen and overheard that she knew exactly what she was doing and what kind of treasonous filth she was involved in. And she was in cahoots with Samson Baggart, too, whose infamous practices were notorious among those who knew such things. Damn her! She had acted the innocent so perfectly, she had almost had him believing in himself again . . .

Shaking his hoary locks in disagreement, Jacob interrupted Bryce's racing thoughts. "Nay, sir. She'll come around, ye'll see. She and the old cove will never know I ain't passed their word on yet. They'll get tired of waitin' and will sell me the trinket you want, mark my word."

"You'd sell your own mother to the devil for a profit, wouldn't you, Jacob?"

"A blind man's got to eat, same as one who sees."

Jacob wasn't the only one who'd been blind, Bryce thought bitterly. Anger and wounded pride, white-hot and scalding, bubbled through his veins like lava. He'd make her pay. He could easily catch up with her now, find a secluded alley where justice could be meted out with one's hands around a lying bitch's throat . . .

But no. There were better ways, and Huxford knew all of them. They'd always been after larger game, anyway, and now the perfect bait lay ready to be set in the perfect trap. Damn Genevieve for the lying, deceiving whore she was, but she'd lead them to the Abbot, and then they'd have them both!

Forcing himself to unclench his fists, Bryce straightened. "I've changed my mind, Jacob. There's more profit in dealing with larger fish. I want you to pass the lady's message on."

Jacob's milky orbs widened involuntarily. "But—but, sir!"

"Here," Bryce said tightly, passing a purse heavy with coin into the blind man's hands. "To make it worth your while."

"Ah." Jacob tested the weight of the purse as his seamed face crinkled with understanding and reluctant admiration. "Scheming to outwit 'em both, ain't ye, sir? Now there's a man after my own heart!"

Bryce's mouth thinned into a grim, determined line of vengeful anticipation. "Just do it."

Chapter 9

"It didn't go well?"

"An unmitigated disaster!"

"Congratulations, then, Cap!" Taffy McKee said with a grin as he accepted Bryce's many-caped greatcoat, then turned to help Genevieve with her wrap.

Bryce snorted and stomped through the marble-tiled foyer of his town house into the elegantly appointed drawing room and straight to the well-stocked sideboard. Taffy shot a puzzled glance at Genevieve. "Bad dress rehearsal usually means a certain success, don't it, miss?"

Nodding, Genevieve adjusted the surplice bodice of her cream broche silk gown and handed the former sergeant her gloves and sewing bag. "That's the superstition, Mr. McKee. But knowing that doesn't offer much comfort sometimes."

Crystal clinked as decanter met glass, and Bryce saluted them from the other room. "Hell! It was the worst excuse for a play I ever saw. I ought to fire the cast and cancel the whole thing! And that includes that prima donna bitch, Darlena Letchfield!"

"He's very upset," Genevieve murmured to Taffy. "Mrs. Letchfield was . . . difficult."

Indeed, Bryce had been so infuriated by the shambles of a rehearsal that he'd dragged Genevieve away from the Athena without giving her a chance to beg off tonight's engagement. In his precarious mood, she'd been disinclined to test his temper until he'd had a moment to cool off, even though she herself was strung tight with tension that was a mixture of physical awareness, apprehension, guilt, and despair.

How could she possibly pretend things were just the same between them, knowing she was involved in something Bryce would condemn as utterly abhorrent? And how could she present a calm front when this morning's conversation with Blind Jacob had already borne fruit?

She shivered and rubbed her arms at the thought of the message that had been delivered just before she'd left for this evening's rehearsal. The Abbot agreed to meet Everett for discussion of business. Surprisingly, the appointed place was the Athena; the time, following tomorrow night's opening performance.

Genevieve supposed it was a logical place—neutral ground with plenty of comings and goings, not far for an old man to walk, and with easy access since as company costumer she held a key to a rear door. But knowing that Grandpapa's plans were really unfolding filled her with such dread she feared her hard-won composure would crack at any time. It was even harder to act naturally knowing that this was likely to be her last time with Bryce.

Even if this mysterious Abbot solved their problem with Baggart, they couldn't risk remaining within either villain's reach, and Everett had finally succumbed to her pleadings to go as far as the Emerald Isle. Without asking for explanations, loyal Maebella had agreed to go also. Bryce had paid his cast and employees during this evening's rehearsal, and tomorrow Maebella would take Genevieve's wages and the remainder of Blind Jacob's booty and go to the docks to purchase their passages on the next available ship. Since Genevieve had no idea what she could say to Bryce that would make any sense, she'd decided not to say anything at all. When the time came, she'd simply leave, make a clean break.

It was all arranged. It was necessary. Even so, to Genevieve this time together with Bryce was excruciatingly difficult, for in her heart, it was farewell.

Taffy urged her in the direction of the drawing room, where a table for two was laid with gleaming silver and translucent china. "There's a nice bit of a cold supper cook laid on. Maybe that'll help ease the Cap's nerves a bit."

Genevieve took a hesitant step toward the man who stood with one lean pantaloon-clad leg propped on the brass fireplace fender, scowling down into his cut-crystal tumbler. She hovered at the door, then caught a flicker of movement from the staircase.

"Why, Jack Potts! My dear, what are doing up so late?"

"Hello, Miss Genny." The former climbing boy stifled a yawn. "Helpin' Taffy, is all."

Genevieve bent over the boy. "Are you well? I've missed you."

Lord, what an actress! Bryce thought, gulping another swallow of his brandy as Genevieve spoke softly with Jack. She gave the boy one of her spine-melting smiles, and his black eyes sparkled. Even at such a tender age, no man was immune to the traitorous witch's magic. One would think she genuinely liked the lad, but Bryce knew there wasn't a genuine bone in that lovely, treacherous body. Huxford didn't know what he'd asked when he ordered Bryce to continue as if nothing had changed while they placed Genevieve and her grandfather under surveillance and waited for the Abbot to make his move. "Business as usual," was Huxford's instruction. It was the hardest damned assignment the Griffin had ever had, but by God! he'd play the part as coolly as she did or die in the attempt.

Bryce slammed the tumbler down on the mantelpiece and stalked to the door. "Off to bed with you now, Jack."

"Yes, sir." Jack folded his arms across his middle and made a leg that would have been well received in the most elegant assemblies. "Good night, Miss Genny."

She murmured her farewells to the boy as Bryce gripped her arm and herded her into the drawing room, nodding to Taffy to close the double doors. "Sergeant, I won't be needing you again this evening."

"Aye, sir."

When they were alone, Genevieve shot Bryce an uneasy glance from beneath her lashes. "I mustn't stay long. Grandpapa isn't well."

"Nothing serious, I hope?"

She fidgeted under Bryce's watchful examination, caught between the desire for truth and the need for caution. "He appears to be somewhat improved in his mental faculties since the stress of performing has been removed, but he does have a cough, and at his age one can't take chances."

"I'm sure Miss Smythe can stand to duty in your absence, at least long enough for you to join me in cook's excellent repast. Please. I have need of company tonight."

It was a bittersweet choice, but one she couldn't resist. He seated her at the highly polished mahogany table, poured a Burgundy wine into their goblets, and then took the seat beside her with a self-deprecating half smile curving his lips.

"My ability to be a pleasant companion may be lacking, but I am an excellent footman. Shall I serve?"

Genevieve nodded, but then could only pick at her plate of delicate pastries, slices of cold beef, and marinated vegetables while Bryce ate. In mild alarm, she watched the way he refilled his wineglass over and over while rehashing the botched scenes and missed cues of the evening's calamitous rehearsal, and lamenting the fact that his father and sister were already en route from Suffolk and could not be warned off from attending what would surely be the laughingstock of the London theater season.

"You are too critical," Genevieve chided gently. "Your production is the finest I've ever seen, and all the city will turn out for tomorrow night's inauguration of such an elegant playhouse. The tickets are sold out, are they not?"

"Scarcely reassuring at this point, my dear," he said morosely. "After Darlena's hysterics, I only hope she shows up at all."

"I'm sure Mrs. Letchfield was having as trying a case of nervous excitement as everyone else," she commented. "When she lunged, your grip on the dressing gown nearly ripped it asunder. I'll have an hour's work putting it to rights. I can't think why she screamed like that."

"Can't you?"

Bryce rose, goblet in hand, and stood behind Genevieve's chair. He touched her ear briefly and flicked a stray tendril of chestnut hair with his fingertips, then drained the glass and set it aside. She could feel the heat of his body radiating into hers, and her breath subtly increased its pace.

"As an actress you should understand that things can become very . . . intense on stage," he said in a low tone. "Perhaps her fear in the death scene was too realistic. Mayhap I was more in tune with Othello's murderous impulses than I knew. Tell me, how would you feel if I placed my hands around your slender throat, thusly?"

Genevieve jumped as his large, masculine hands closed around her neck. Bending, Bryce laughed softly in her ear.

"Not nervous of me, are you, my love?"

Her swallow was automatic and revealing, and she shivered as he stroked the tenseness from her neck. "I—I've never seen you like this," she said.

"Opening night is a little like going into battle." His fingers continued to do wondrous things to her skin, sliding lower and lower until they brushed the vee-shaped neckline of her bodice. His whisper was a hot wind blowing through her mind. "The heart pounds, and the blood rushes, and you think about life and death. Can you imagine that, Genevieve?"

"Yes." It was increasingly difficult to draw breath, and her breasts felt swollen and achy.

"There's a fire in your belly that won't be quenched, and nothing in your brain but the desperate need for some action that will relieve the tension that just keeps building and building . . ."

Genevieve's heart raced and her chest heaved with the

effort to obtain enough oxygen. He reached ever further beneath her neckline, slipping under her shift and running callused fingertips over the velvety swell of her breasts, flicking the puckered aureoles with a deftness that released a liquid rush between her legs. Then, with a movement so sudden her vision swam, he let her go, reaching for his wineglass and refilling it with studied nonchalance.

"But you did not come here to speak of war, did you? Forgive me, *chérie*." He threw himself down in his chair again, loosening the high folds of his neckcloth and drinking deep while twin spots of dusky color stained his cheekbones.

Genevieve reached for her own goblet, sipping the fortifying liquor to gain strength and to hide the fact that she was totally unnerved. The leashed violence she sensed in his mood was both frightening and arousing. It was almost as if he knew . . .

He can't know, she thought, reason winning out over instinct. She was overwrought, she decided, torn between her love for Bryce and her loyalty to her grandfather.

"You are too quiet, Genevieve," Bryce said abruptly. "Something is weighing on your mind, and I know what it is."

A trill of fear spiraled into her stomach. Fighting down the automatic reaction, she sought to keep her voice even, but it came out husky, her simple words fraught with ironic overtones. "Do you?"

"All lovers face the same fears and worries. Do I please my beloved? How long will we be together? Will she betray me? Will another take my place?" Bryce's blue gaze was intent, assessing each question as though it were an arrow hitting a target. "We are certainly no different."

A flush of peachy color rose from Genevieve's throat to her temples. "You will have to be the judge of that, sir. As you know, I have no experience in these matters."

"What a useful tool that is."

"What?"

"Your virginity. You could wield it like a bludgeon if you desired. Why did you give yourself to me?"

Disconcerted, she looked away. "You know why."

"Love? Another weapon."

The look she flashed at him was brimming with hurt. "I do not understand your point."

He swirled the remains of his wine around the sides of his goblet, lifted it in a silent toast, then swallowed the bitter dregs and set the glass aside. His look was bland. "I had thought to take you to wife."

The blood drained from Genevieve's face, and her life's breath seeped between her lips in a whisper of disbelief. "What?"

"Indeed, matrimony has been much on my mind of late. But then it occurred to me that a woman with such a promising career ahead of her would have no use for such ties."

"Bryce. I—you—" No sensible words formed within her stupefied brain.

"Calm yourself, *chérie*. I will not force my half-baked notions on you. On further reflection, I realize we're so much better off as lovers, as equals, not as dull spouses. When propriety demands, I can wed Cal's sister as my father urges, but as my mistress, you will always be so much more exciting—"

She came to her feet with a strangled cry. How dare he taunt her this way, trampling her dreams, degrading what she felt for him! She turned to flee, but he was there, blocking her path, pushing her with his lean body against the edge of the table.

"Do my plans not meet with your approval?" he asked, catching her upper arms.

"You blackguard!" she hissed, struggling against his hold. "Let me go! I'm leaving."

He controlled her easily, smiling at her frustration. "But we have so much more to . . . discuss."

"You'd take what little I have to give and throw it in

my teeth. I'll not stand here and be insulted, nor will I let you make me your doxy!''

His eyes gleamed with a wicked light. ''Isn't it already too late for that?''

She lunged at him with an angry cry, fists raised, but he foiled her attack effortlessly. Pulling her against his chest, he ground his mouth against hers, then jerked back, cursing. ''You hellion—you bit me!''

Half blinded by tears of outrage and hurt, Genevieve strained away from him, bumping into the table, rattling the cutlery and overturning the wineglasses. ''What are you doing? This is all wrong.''

Growling, he clamped one arm around her waist and grabbed a fistful of her hair, forcing her face upward, ravishing her mouth so forcefully that she had to submit or suffocate. When he raised his head again, his blue eyes were narrow slits, and air rasped harshly through his bared teeth. ''There! Does that feel *wrong*, my dear?''

Her soft mouth was swollen and tremulous. ''Why are you punishing me?''

At her question, the red haze began to lift from Bryce's brain, and he was achingly aware of her body pressed between the edge of the table and the cradle of his thighs.

''Maybe it's not you,'' he muttered.

For it was exquisite punishment to feel her so close, to have the taste of her mouth on his tongue, and it was hell itself to want her still, knowing she was false and treacherous. Was he punishing Genevieve for her perfidy? Or himself for his blind stupidity and unrelenting need?

''You want me.'' Genevieve's eyes widened with accusation. ''But it's dangerous to want too much, isn't it, Bryce? You're trying to destroy what I feel for you because you feel something, too—only you aren't man enough to admit it!''

''*This* is all I feel,'' he snarled, rolling his hips against her so that she could not mistake his meaning. Gasping, she arched, pressing against his arousal in response. Her eyes narrowed in challenge, and her hand stole around the back of his neck. Surprised, he resisted her insistent tugging.

"Coward!" she taunted softly, both Eve and Delilah, watching him from behind her lowered lashes, her lower body making seductive circles against his swollen manhood. "Are you afraid of me?"

His control snapped. With a maddened swipe of his arm, he hurled the dishes from the table, then pushed her down on the shiny surface while the remnants of their meal smashed onto the floor unregarded. Straddling her hips, he held her down, claiming her lips over and over again, his tongue taking wild, undisciplined liberties within the sweet cavern of her mouth, nibbling and nipping with insatiable hunger.

Whimpering, Genevieve pulled him closer, her hunger flaring just as wildly. She met him kiss for kiss, digging her fingers into his black hair, arching and groaning as he pushed her gown from her shoulders and feasted on the delicate flesh of her breasts, licking and teasing her nipples into puckered buds.

Liquid fire poured through Genevieve, lodging low in her center, and she shuddered, moving urgently beneath Bryce's massive frame. Breathing heavily, he lifted his head, staring into her eyes with a primitive and pagan need that would not be denied etched into his features. Holding her gaze, he shrugged out of his coat and reached for her skirts, dragging handfuls of fabric to bunch at her waist, then fumbling with the buttons of his trousers. Shoving her hips to the edge of the table, he opened her knees, cupping her mound with his palm, kneading and massaging her through the slit in her drawers until she had no breath left at all, and she was dazed with pleasure.

He entered her then, sliding into her moist depths with a power that made her cry out. Lifting her stocking-covered legs, he guided them about his hips, bending over her to consume her mouth, his tongue probing as deeply as the velvety steel of his sex within her secret depths. His thrusts were deep and powerful, a primal, masculine staking of possession that evoked everything feminine within Genevieve. She met each stroke freely, gladly, demanding more and more of him in an uninhibited coupling that stole his reason. Aggressive, selfish, they took and took from each other, trying to meld their flesh into one being, and when they reached the instant of achievement, they climaxed in a simultaneous explosion of the senses.

Spent, quivering with delicious aftershocks, they lay panting against the tabletop in sweaty, half-clothed disarray. As the fog lifted from his brain, Bryce was overcome by a creeping horror. Like some sort of rutting animal, he'd used Genevieve's slender body to cleanse his anger. No matter what she'd done, he had no right to render such punishment, and shame claimed him. But when he made a motion to lift himself free of her softness, her legs tightened on his thighs.

"Don't," she murmured. Like a debauchee's wildest dream, she lay drowsy, half naked and pliant on top of the gleaming wood.

"Genevieve." Remorse choked him.

"You decadent rake." She opened her eyes and, unaccountably, began to laugh. "I had no idea tables were so useful!"

Nonplussed, Bryce drew back, awkwardly adjusting his clothing as her laughter continued to bubble forth, and he wondered if she were hysterical. "That was unforgivable of me. I beg your pardon."

"Well, you shan't have it!" She whipped down her skirts and slid off the table, darting through the rubbish of their meal to perch provocatively on the nearby damask lounge. "Not until you've shown me another use for a sofa as well!"

"What!"

She sent him a look from under her lashes that was pure woman. Draping one arm over the back of the lounge so that her rosy breasts pouted over the remnants of her bodice, she then lifted a dainty foot onto the cushion to reveal a hoydenish length of well-turned leg. "I'm waiting. Wouldn't you like to beg my pardon over here?"

"Jesus Christ, woman!" Thunderstruck, he stalked to the sofa, intent on putting an end to this idiocy, but when he touched her he somehow found that she'd pulled him down on top of her, and then there was nothing left to do but kiss her again. And the flames of passion licked at him, igniting his senses like dry tinder while Genevieve's laughter rang in his bemused head.

Just before he lost his reason yet again, she took his face between her small palms and met his eyes. All humor was gone from her expression now, replaced by naked need and a poignant satisfaction. "You *do* care."

Bryce shuddered, because he knew it was the truth. And he knew it didn't—couldn't—matter in the least.

"Damn you." As he sank beneath the waves, it was the final defiant cry of a lost soul. "Ah, Genny, damn you!"

The *Theatrical Inquisitor* would later report that never had the London stage been graced with such outstanding performances as B. D. Cormick's and Darlena Letchfield's on the opening night of *Othello*. The forepiece, a short play called *The Weathercock*, was a delightful burletta, or drama with music, but it was the tragedy that made the night. Waxing poetic, the reporter proclaimed the majesty of the spectacle scenes, the power of the score, the stunning beauty of the costumes, and the elegance of the Athena Theater itself, with its innovative gas footlights and unusual series of traps and grooves. The report also noted the unprecedented opening night attendance by such dignitaries as Princess Charlotte and her royal aunts and a significant representation from the *ton* and both houses of Parliament. Genevieve had also seen the chubby-cheeked face of Baron von Throder beaming from a prime box seat, evidently delighted with the opening night performance as only a true drama connoisseur could be.

But as Genevieve watched the cast take yet another curtain call before the tumultuous audience, she could only think of how precious it was to her to see the man she loved in his moment of triumph. And she could only hope that when he learned that she had left England, someday he'd find it in his heart to forgive her.

Fighting a prickle of tears, Genevieve scurried through the crowded wings past stagehands and extras all flushed with success. Maebella was already waiting with their packed trunks at a commercial wharf, and within a few hours Genevieve and Everett would join her there to take passage aboard the *Richland* to Dublin. The passionate, perplexing tryst she'd shared with Bryce the night before had only convinced her more firmly of the intolerable nature of her dishonesty to him and the wisdom of leaving the country now, just as soon as their business with the Abbot was complete.

In the dressing rooms, she retrieved her cloak and the bouquet of late roses that Jules Chesterson had sent by way of congratulations, then looked around for a suitable place to leave the letter she had written to Bryce. She knew the note was an inadequate explanation for her abrupt departure, but since she couldn't bring herself to tell him face to face, she felt it was the least she could do.

Smoothing the heavy parchment between her fingers, she prayed Bryce would understand what she'd written. While she hadn't been able to bring herself to confess her involvement with the Abbot, unable to abide the thought of Bryce viewing her with complete contempt, she had explained somewhat about Samson Baggart's threats against Everett over gaming debts and the necessity of putting a safe distance between them and the blackmail attempts. She'd written of her grandpapa's precarious health, and her own weakness when it came to Bryce. While she loved him desperately, she hoped he would accept that she couldn't remain as his mistress. Wishing him only happiness, she knew she'd never forget him, and hoped that sometimes he would think fondly of her.

Placing a final poignant kiss on the letter, Genevieve spied Bryce's many-caped greatcoat on a hook by the door.

With trembling hands, inhaling the masculine odors of tobacco, wool, and the faint, lingering scent of Bryce's skin, she slipped the letter into an inside pocket. As an afterthought, she added a single sweetly fragrant rosebud from Jules's bouquet, then, blinking back tears, slipped through the rear stage doors, away from the thunderous applause still booming from yet another curtain call, and into the cool September night.

A few minutes' walk brought her to her workroom apartments, and she hurried up the stairs, tense with both expectation and dread. In just a short while Everett would go back to the Athena alone to meet the Abbot as instructed, and she had to make certain her grandfather did not miss this momentous appointment. Their association with the accursed seal, and, she hoped, Samson Baggart's blackmail, was finally coming to an end.

"Grandpapa?" She burst into the sitting room, now stripped of all their personal belongings, her arms full of roses. "Are you ready? It's almost time to—"

". . . and then he crooned, old David's sow, nonny-nonny nay—"

"Grandpapa!"

"Eh?" Clad in nightshirt and boots, Everett sat before the fire pouring brandy and cracking nuts with the Abbot's Seal. He looked up into his granddaughter's horrified face without recognition, his hazel eyes glazed and vacant. "I can't find my shoes. Where the bloody hell are my shoes?"

Genevieve choked, and roses showered to the floor. "You're wearing them."

Mystified, he looked at his feet, then giggled. "Well, so I am! Old David's sow, she went to town—"

"Stop it!" Terrified, infuriated, Genevieve wrested the brandy glass out of his hand and smashed it into the hearth. She grabbed his nightshirt in her fists and shook him. "What have you done? For the love of heaven! Grandpapa, you've got to meet the Abbot. Don't you remember?"

Everett flinched away in fear, cowering. "Don't strike me! I'm just an old man! I don't know what you want!"

Conscience-stricken, Genevieve instantly released him. "I'm sorry, Grandpapa. I'm so sorry . . ."

Everett beamed at her. "Here now, no harm done. Have some walnuts. You have the look of a gel I met just the other day, Catherine by name. What do you call yourself?"

"Genny." Hands pressed over her mouth, she fought for calm, her mind racing furiously.

"Go on, then, Genny-girl. Have some." Everett pushed a handful of nuts and the Abbot's Seal into her hands. "Now if I could just remember the chorus . . . Old David's sow, nonny-nonny, nay."

Surrounded by the brown nutshells in her palms, the rosy gem Genevieve cradled winked with soft sunset lights. She shuddered in abhorrence at its deceptive beauty, and knew she could not abide its presence any longer. Even without Everett's help, somehow, tonight, she had to free them from the yoke of this traitorous possession. She placed the chain around her neck, and the seal dangled between her breasts like a millstone.

Lovingly, she rubbed the old man's shoulders. "Will you promise to stay by the fire awhile, Grandpapa? I—I have to go out again."

". . . nonny-nonny, hey!"

"Have you seen Miss Maples?" Bryce asked a passing stagehand.

"No, sir. I believe she left already. Just about everyone's gone."

Mouth tightening, Bryce used a towel to wipe away the last trace of makeup and dismissed the stagehand with a wave. "Right."

A moment later, the Earl of Huxford became the last dignitary to offer his congratulations at the star's dressing room door. "Well done, Bryce. I see your aptitude for dissembling has not been wasted."

"Thank you, my lord, I'm sure," Bryce said, his tone bitter. "Genevieve's gone, by the way. I hope that your minions are doing their work."

"My men are meticulous. They won't let her out of their sight a moment. Every movement she makes is being noted. I might add that the time she spent at your abode last evening was of considerable interest and speculation."

"You're a real bastard, Hugh."

The earl smiled. "That's why we work so well together, my friend. But if you have any doubts about the efficiency of my surveillance, I suggest we go now to get a report. Then, if you're satisfied, I'll let you buy me supper at the Four Queens. I've a taste for some of Smasher's confections."

Bryce shrugged out of Othello's tunic and hung it up, finding to his disgust that his hands lingered on the garment crafted with such care by Genevieve. The spirited, yet strangely untouched woman who had fascinated him was no more than a fantasy, something he'd undoubtedly conjured up out of a weakness in his own character. But he knew what a ruthless adversary she was, sacrificing her own body to put him off the track, then wielding his weakness against him. He flushed to think of the way she'd forced him to confront his need for her. But it was the fantasy he cared for, he reminded himself viciously, not the female traitor who'd probably been working for the Abbot all during the war. What enraged him most was the fact that he was a victim of his own illusions.

Overly warm from the weight of the tunic and his thoughts, Bryce pulled on a linen shirt, then opted against a neckcloth. He threw his frock coat over his arm, and leaving his greatcoat hanging next to the door, ushered Huxford out.

Half an hour later, they were parked on a deserted street corner in Huxford's elegant coach not far from the workrooms, waiting for one of the earl's observers to make an appearance. The wiry man scratched on the door, then scrambled inside, doffing his wool cap.

"What news, Terney?" Huxford asked.

"The older lady left early on, yer lordship, along with

a parcel of trunks and baggage. Went to the docks, she did, but the partic'lar lady you was interested in arrived from the theater a while back and ain't come out agin.''

"Well done, Terney. You'll keep me posted?''

"Aye, yer lordship.''

Huxford relaxed back against the tufted velvet seats. "I think we can safely head for Smasher's. Isn't likely much will happen at this late hour.''

"There's been no other activity?'' Bryce asked Terney.

"Nothin' but a couple of cats and a raggedy man makin' his rounds, sir.''

"Not the old gentleman?'' Huxford asked sharply.

"Nay, sir, just a queer-lookin' old cove, all bent and wif a great beard.''

"Beard, you said?'' Something niggled at the edge of Bryce's consciousness. Frowning, he met Huxford's expectant gaze, then suddenly swore. "King Harold! Oh, *hell*!''

Moments later, Bryce took the stairs two at a time up to Genevieve's rooms with Huxford on his heels. He pounded briefly on the door, then tried the handle. The door swung inward with no resistance, revealing Everett Maples hopping on one foot, trying to pull his trousers on over his boots.

"Everett!'' Bryce gripped the old man's arm. "Where is she?''

"Tetched fey creature! What was she thinking?'' Everett moaned, hopping and tugging, trying to worm his boot through the narrow opening of the trousers leg. With a loud rip, he finally pushed it through and hiked his pants up around his paunchy middle. "It's all my fault, poor gel! I can't think, can't think!''

Briefly wondering why the room smelled of roses, Bryce caught the old man's shoulders. "Genevieve—where did she go?''

Everett frowned, beetling his brow as he stared at Bryce, fighting for recognition. "It's you, then. My gel loves you. You've got to help her. She can't handle those fiends by herself. Addled lass took my dueling pistol—hasn't been fired in twenty years! What's a man to do with a woman like that?''

"Everett, think!" Bryce growled in frustration.

"Did she take it with her?" Huxford demanded. "Has she got the Abbot's Seal?"

"Seal, you say?" Everett shook his silver pate. "It's important, isn't it? God blast my eyes! Why does the fog come now? Little Genny—yes! She has the trinket. Trade it, we will, free us from Samson's trap. Dangerous business, lad. No place for a woman.''

"Then let me help her!" Chilled by Everett's babbling, Bryce wanted to shout at the old man. "Where did she take it? Think, Everett! Where?"

Everett looked on the verge of tears. "I can't remember . . . someplace . . .''

"A house?" Huxford suggested. "A street?"

Bryce added to the list of alternatives. "Inn, tavern, garden—"

"Maybe Sadler's?" Everett said hopefully.

Bryce and Huxford turned toward the door.

"Or was it Drury Lane?" Everett asked himself.

Bryce groaned aloud. "Everett!"

The old man looked rattled, then hopeful. "Something . . . Greek? Yes, that's it!" he announced with a beatific smile. "The Athena!"

Sweat trickled between Genevieve's shoulder blades beneath her heavy, padded coat, and Everett's unwieldy dueling pistol, primed and loaded, pressed painfully against her leg. To make matters worse, King Harold's long false beard tickled her in a thousand places.

Despite these discomforts, she sat absolutely still and silent on a seat in the first stage-level box of the Athena as per Everett's communication with the Abbot. The box actually lay on the apron of the stage itself, and if she'd been of a mind to do so, she could have reached out and stroked the rich burgundy velvet curtain. Instead, she perched immovable as a statue, praying the Abbot would take one old man the same as another in the almost pitch-blackness of the theater, so they could conduct their business before her nerve gave out entirely.

But the waiting seemed interminable. Her ears buzzed, and phantoms skittered on the periphery of her vision. She jumped at every creak and moan of stone and wood in the building, and she knew if he didn't come soon—

Lantern light blossomed just beyond the half wall separating box and stage, illuminating a grimacing death's head. Genevieve squeaked in terror, her mind frantically trying to make some sense of what she saw. Then the lantern shifted and the upward rays of illumination changed, revealing a sight even more terrifying: The phantom was not the mysterious Abbot, but Samson Baggart!

She sprang for freedom, away from the light toward the dark rear exit of the box, but a stocky shadow, muffled in a hat and scarf, blocked her way, grabbed her roughly, and shoved her back to the front of the box.

"Ah, Everett, my old friend . . ." Baggart's silky words broke off with an oath. "What frippery is this? Who—?"

With Baggart's henchman at her back, Genevieve's only hope was that Baggart wouldn't recognize her. " 'Ere now, guv!" she said in her best gruff cockney. "Leave a body be!"

For an instant, Baggart's ferret-red eyes flickered in consternation. Then he reached across the retaining wall and ripped the false beard free. Genevieve gasped in shock, her cheeks stinging from the abrupt removal of the adhesive she'd used to attach the disguise.

"Bring her across," Baggart growled, stepping back. Immediately, the thug holding her half slung, half carried her across the little wall and stepped across himself. Holding the small, cylindrical stage light higher, Baggart regarded her with intense dislike. "Just full of tricks, aren't you, my dear?"

Fighting the urge to swoon at his feet, she gulped and demanded, "What do you want?"

His slap caught her full across the mouth. Her old-fashioned tircorne and wig flew off, and she fell backward into the thug's arms.

"Don't play games. I know you have the Abbot's Seal. I knew the minute I intercepted your puny message in the thieves' channel. Thought you'd go over my head with it, did you?"

"Yes!" Defiance hissed from between her bloodied lips. "Anything to get free of you!"

"You'll learn not to double-cross me the same way Jacob did."

Genevieve gulped. "J-Jacob?"

"Always trying to play both sides against the middle for his own profit, even after all the good I'd done him, the disloyal wretch! But his greed got the best of him on this occasion. It wasn't hard to trace an interest in the Abbot back to Jacob, and thence to you and Everett. 'Twas an even easier matter to set up this meeting by tempting you with the Abbot's name." Baggart's smile was chilling. "Poor Jacob. He won't be causing me any more trouble."

"Dear God," she whispered.

"Yes, pray, my dear. Did you really think to outwit me? Not even the Abbot truly appreciated my expertise. My former associate will come to regret his shortsightedness."

"So you're a traitor, too," she accused in a shaky voice.

Baggart gave a disdainful snort. "What do I care of politics? But wealth, power, influence—all will be mine once I have the mystical antiquity in my grasp. Now hand over the seal!"

Genevieve struggled for breath, feeling the weight of the seal bump between her breasts and the tug of the loaded dueling pistol in her pocket. Dared she risk it? She had no other choice.

"All right," she mumbled, moving her hand toward the deep pocket slit of the padded coat.

"Hurry up," Baggart ordered impatiently, "and perhaps I'll spare you the death you deserve for playing the traitor to me.''

Behind Genevieve, a deep chuckle rumbled from the henchman's throat, and a silver-handled pistol appeared in his stubby hand. ''There will be no such reprieve for you, Samson.''

The pistol discharged. Genevieve shrieked, and a bright crimson blossom appeared on the front of Baggart's white shirt. In the instant before he fell, lantern and all, into the footlights, Genevieve thought she saw a glimmer of hor-rified recognition, then terror surged through her system in a chilling wave. She knew she was going to die, too.

The gruff voice was strangely courteous. ''You sent for the Abbot, mademoiselle? *Voilà*, I am here.''

''What was that?'' Everett demanded.

Bryce stopped Huxford and the old man at the Athena's rear stage door with an abrupt movement. ''A shot.''

''What!'' Everett squawked. ''But my darling Genny's in there!''

''Stay here,'' Bryce ordered, his mouth flattened into a grim line. ''Do you understand? Don't move! Hugh, bring the men.''

With that, Bryce disappeared into the dark interior of the cavernous backstage. Stone-faced, Huxford nodded to Everett, then loped off around the perimeter of the build-ing with a soft but piercing whistle.

''Feckless cowards!'' Everett shouted. ''What about my gel?''

He paced, muttering to himself, whipping his cane back and forth like a sword.

''That's long enough!'' he announced to the world at large. ''No one left but old Jack Falstaff to rescue the damsel. By Gad! The villains! They've *me* to reckon with now!''

And he followed Bryce into the theater.

Chapter 10

❦❦❦

"**T**ake it," Genevieve choked.

She grappled at the throat of her shirt for the chain attached to the seal. The Abbot loomed over her in the near darkness, his hand clamped to her arm, his features indiscernible behind his thick scarf except for the pale, reptilian glitter of his eyes. She drew the object free of her collar, then nearly wept as the chain snagged in her tumbled locks. Shaking in every sinew, she wrestled frantically with the links. "We never wanted it."

"You'll be well rewarded." His words were muffled behind the scarf, gruff and oddly cadenced.

"No, no! All we wanted was to be free of Mr. B-Baggart."

"You have your wish."

Genevieve shuddered uncontrollably and tried not to look at the body sprawled in the footlight ditch, illuminated by ghostly flickers of burning oil seeping from the smashed lantern. Nausea clogged her throat and made her voice thick. "Murder was not our object."

"Samson was too greedy for his own good, and stupid, too, not to see past my disguise. You see, you are not the only one to use such a ruse, mademoiselle. But my purpose was to witness his betrayal and mete out justice accordingly. Now the seal, if you please."

With a final desperate tug that ripped strands of hair out

by their roots, she wrenched the chain and seal over her head, thrusting it at him. "Here! Take the cursed—"

"Unhand my granddaughter, ye whoreson!" Like an apparition from hell, Everett Maples rose out of a trap in the stage floor behind them, brandishing his cane and roaring in challenge.

Genevieve gasped in horror. "Grandpapa!"

"Give it here, gel!" With a flourish, Everett grabbed for the seal in her hand, but in his fumbling they both lost their grip on the gem, and it bounced across the stage and into the shadows.

The Abbot snarled a curse and shoved Genevieve toward Everett, pointing with the double barrel of his sliver pistol. "Get it!"

"Ah, so you see the folly of defying me, sir!" Everett chortled, backing away.

"Grandpapa, help me find it!" Genevieve pleaded, frantic, scrambling on hands and knees after the elusive seal.

Puzzled, Everett looked around his feet, then bent to retrieve the object just as sounds of a disturbance broke out from the entrance of the theater, muffled blows and scuffling and yelps of pain. As Genevieve regained her feet, they froze, listening.

"Quickly!" the Abbot ordered, but it was already too late.

In the blink of an eye, a figure slid down a dangling scenery rope, pistol trained on the three of them. "Don't move!"

"Bryce!" Genevieve's cry was both glad and appalled.

Behind the Abbot's concealing scarf, his pale eyes glittered, concluding the worst: a trap! He raised his pistol to punish the one responsible.

"*Cocotte!*" he snarled at Genevieve, and fired.

Deafened, blinded, she felt a blow and wondered if this was how it was to die. Then her sight cleared, and she realized that someone had pushed her to safety. She turned just as Everett crumpled.

"Grandpapa!" He'd stepped into the path of the bullet meant for her!

Bryce's pistol fired, but the Abbot's shadowy figure leaped feet first into the open trap door, rolled the sliding door shut, and shot the bolt home, cutting off pursuit. With a curse, Bryce charged into the wings. Half a dozen armed men, including the Earl of Huxford, converged on the stage. Oblivious, Genevieve crouched over Everett, who vaguely touched his chest, the chain of the Abbot's Seal still wrapped around his fingers.

"Oh God, no!" Genevieve breathed. She tore off her cravat and pressed it to the steadily expanding circle of crimson. "Grandpapa, why?"

"Better this way, gel," he gasped. His gaze was clear and lucid at last, and vastly regretful. "Best I could do for you. So sorry for everything . . ."

"Don't talk, Grandpapa," she begged. "You'll be all right. A doctor—"

"Can't fix what's wrong with me." Pink spittle foamed his lips. "Didn't want to die an idiot anyway. Rather this than St. Luke's."

"No, no! Don't say that! I need you, Grandpapa!"

Everett's lids fluttered, and something rattled wetly in his throat. "Forgive me, Genny-girl. I just wanted to feather your nest . . ."

Frantic, Genevieve touched his face, his hands, but no breath whispered, no life remained, and already his skin was growing cool. Choking, she called him one last time, "Grandpapa . . ."

A man hunkered down on his heels beside the fallen actor, and Genevieve looked up in wordless appeal at the Earl of Huxford. Emotionlessly, he lifted an eyelid and checked for a pulse.

"He's gone," Huxford said, then unwrapped the blood-ied chain from Everett's lifeless fingers and claimed the Abbot's Seal. Anguished, Genevieve tenderly stroked Everett's silver hair. Huxford rose again as Bryce stormed back onto the stage.

"Any success?" the earl asked.

"Vanished. Not a sign, damn all the luck! Could have gone in any direction!"

"Blast! Slippery as an eel, that one," Huxford said.

Grim-faced, Bryce looked at the two still figures sprawled on his stage. "These . . . ?"

"Both dead. There'll be no help there." Huxford's thwarted expression changed slightly, taking on an element of gloating. With fingers bearing the stain of Everett's blood, he held up the seal. "But we haven't come away empty-handed. We'll get him yet. I knew when I set the Griffin to this task, I wouldn't be totally disappointed."

"The Griffin—you?" Genevieve's incredulous cry brought all eyes to her.

"Only the crown's finest agent would do for such a sensitive operation," the earl said.

She struggled to her feet, a slim form in a ludicrous padded coat and trousers, her hair wild and her eyes frenzied with grief and the dawning of a terrible realization. She pointed to the seal in Huxford's grasp as though it were the single most obscene thing in the universe. "You bastards! You *used* us to get what you wanted, and look what it cost!"

"Traitors have no rights," Bryce said coldly.

Agonized, she stared at the man she'd loved, the man she'd thought she'd known. It was lies, all of it. She was wrapped up in lies and betrayal, and because of Bryce Cormick, Everett's body lay cooling on the stage. Something deeply primitive within her unleashed itself. Icily calm, she dragged Everett's dueling pistol out of her pocket and aimed it at Bryce, intent on murder.

Everyone froze. Arms aching with the weight of the heavy weapon, Genevieve swayed unsteadily, hate roiling through her, searing her soul with bitterness and pain. Bryce's blue eyes glittered like the blue-orange flickers of oil burning in the footlight trough behind him.

"Do it, General," he taunted softly. "Do it and put us both out of our misery."

She curled her finger around the trigger—and couldn't. With an enraged cry at her craven frailty, she turned the pistol aside and fired.

Her shot shattered a footlight globe, smashed a valve, and with a *whoosh,* the escaping gas caught the flames still licking at the oil from Baggart's broken lantern. Faster than thought, the row of footlights exploded with a series of pops, coalescing into a single geyser of fire that licked across the wooden stage planks and scampered up the velvet curtains and swags in the blink of an eye. Immediate pandemonium claimed the consternated onlookers.

Heat radiating into her startled face, Genevieve began to laugh, a crazed, half-mad sound. Her cowardice was paying off with unexpected results, and with an unholy glee, she relished the crackling sounds of paint blistering and fabric combusting. Men ripped at the flaming curtains, shouted orders and curses, and still she laughed, hysteria bubbling from her throat as she fell again on her grandfather's body.

"We did it, Grandpapa," she whispered. "We'll make him pay with the only thing he loves."

A hand clamped down on her shoulder, pulling her away.

"Get up!" Bryce ordered, his mouth set and grim. "You've got to get out of here."

"Leave us alone!" She shook him off furiously. "Haven't you done enough?"

"You stupid bitch! The whole place could go up, thanks to your idiocy!"

"I won't leave Grandpapa."

Bryce called to a couple of men battling the flames to come help him with the bodies. "Satisfied?" he demanded of Genevieve. "Now come on!"

"I have nothing to live for." The icy bleakness and defiance in her eyes contrasted with the fiery inferno leaping up on all sides. "You've shown me hell, and I want to stay."

"By God, you won't cheat your fate as easily as that!" he cried, dragging her toward the wings.

She screeched her fury, kicking and clawing for freedom. "You gutter spawn! Base, double-dealing, French Judas! Are you too cowardly to die with me?"

Cursing, he fought her off, but she was maddened, unreachable, driven by hate. She never saw the fist that grazed her chin, only the spangles that exploded behind her eyes and then the blessed darkness of oblivion.

Flinging Genevieve's limp form over his shoulder, Bryce carried her from the burning theater with the sure knowledge that all his dreams had just gone up in flames.

Huddled under her dirty, bloodstained jacket, Genevieve laced her fingers through the wild bramble of her disheveled curls and tried to stop shaking. It was an unnerving experience to awaken in a prison cell with a throbbing jaw and no idea how long you'd been there—other than the knot of hunger in your stomach that bespoke at least a day's meals missed—or how long those in control expected you to stay. It was even worse when your beloved grandfather was dead, and the man you thought you loved was a false, blackhearted scoundrel who happened to have the crown's approval for his perfidies.

Furnished with only a thin cotton mattress and a slop jar, the tiny room stank of mildew and despair. The walls were dank stone, and the only light came from a dingy lantern in the corridor. Curled into a corner, Genevieve stared into the nothingness that was the ruins of her life. For there was truly nothing left. No family, no career, no freedom, no love, and in time, no life.

Everett was dead, and for his loss she grieved, dry-eyed, her mourning too deep for mere tears. For her part in the Abbot's plot, she'd surely face the gallows for treason, brought to "justice" by the man she'd given everything, body and soul. She was a gullible fool, and Bryce

Cormick was the world's most accomplished liar, but even now Genevieve wondered how she could have been so deceived. Had all the tenderness, all the passion, been merely a sham, a ruse to force her into paths whose purpose was known only to the Griffin and his master, that odious Huxford?

She had to accept the raw truth for what it was. Bryce had come to her not for love, not even for her costumes, but at the behest of Huxford to retrieve the Abbot's Seal, and he had used her without mercy. The importance of the gem was evidently even more crucial than she and Everett had feared, but she still could not hazard a guess as to its true purpose, even if it had cost two men their lives.

Staring at the dripping stone walls, Genevieve allowed the worst pain, the pain she'd managed to hold at bay until now, to claim her fully. Betrayed by Bryce's lies and her own heart, her falsehoods to save Everett gone all for naught, she was just as culpable for this tragedy as Bryce, and she knew that she could never forgive him—or herself. Bowing her head, she prayed for the release of death.

A key grated in the lock, and the heavy iron door swung inward with a screech of protest.

"Miss Maples, at last. Those incompetents! I had no idea they'd bring you *here*."

Genevieve lifted her head, staring without expression at the Earl of Huxford's genial face. Nattily dressed, he eased carefully past the wet walls to spare his tailored coat. He was followed by Bryce Cormick.

Genevieve hugged her knees and looked away, but not before she noted Bryce's smoke-reddened eyes and the small burn angling above one dark eyebrow. She wondered absently how much damage her lucky shot had done the Athena, then buried the twinge of guilt as deeply as she'd buried all the emotions she'd once felt for Bryce, save one—her hate.

"My dear, I do apologize for the accommodations," the earl continued in a cordial tone that grated on Gene-

vieve's nerves. "In all the confusion since last night's encounter . . . Well, this has been an ordeal for us all. With
the Athena in ashes—"

"What?" Genevieve blanched, and the raspy texture of
her own voice sounded unnatural in her ears. That she'd
caused destruction on such a scale floored her.

"You didn't know?" the earl asked kindly. "Quite gone,
my dear. Invested heavily, didn't you, Bryce?"

Bryce stood silent, arms folded, his mouth an immovable line. From his implacable expression, it seemed evident her letter had burned along with everything in the
Athena. Genevieve was suddenly fiercely glad he hadn't
had the opportunity to read her explanations or her
avowals of love, and grimly joyous that in the havoc her
actions had wrought, she'd deprived him of further ammu-
nition with which to wound her. She owed him *nothing*.

She asked Huxford the question that had been weighing
on her most heavily. "What about my grandfather's remains?"

The earl had the grace to look uncomfortable. "Under
the—er, circumstances, a simple interment this morning
in Potter's Field seemed advisable. The theater community
is devastated at the loss of two of its most illustrious personages. I believe a memorial is planned."

"I—I see." Although her face was stony, Genevieve's
heart twisted with anguish. She couldn't even secure her
cherished grandfather a decent resting place. Instead, he'd
lie for eternity with paupers and criminals. It was too much
to bear.

"But it's the living we're concerned with now," Huxford continued. "There's much to sort out."

Genevieve rose stiffly from her crouched position, using
the damp wall for support. "When am I to hang?" she
demanded.

Huxford blinked, then chuckled. "What an absurd child!
Whatever gave you such an idea?"

" 'Tis customary to hang traitors, is it not?" Her eyes

were wide, mossy-green and fathomless. "I should rather it be sooner than later, my lord."

"My dear, you're far too valuable to hang. This is no incarceration, merely a . . . a temporary stop while I consulted with my superiors regarding the best course of action for your future." He gestured to his companion. "Bryce, reason with her."

"Miss Maples will take little credence in anything I might add," Bryce replied woodenly.

"Play no more games with me." She faced Huxford squarely, a fragile creature in man's clothing with a purple and yellow bruise flowering on her delicate jawbone. "I know what I've done."

The earl was sympathetic. "I'll admit there is the unfortunate matter of certain charges—transporting stolen goods, aiding an enemy of the crown, conspiracy to commit treason . . ."

Genevieve had grown paler with each crime he listed, so that now the lips she keep firmly clamped over her chattering teeth took on a blue tinge.

As the earl continued, his gaze strayed to Bryce's rocklike countenance. "Although there are those who condemn your actions, I, myself, am of the opinion you were innocently duped, for the most part."

Genevieve's lashes fluttered in surprise, and her heart began to pound with this first glimmer of hope. Then she shook her head.

"I knew what I was doing." Her eyes flashed with defiance. "And I'd do it again."

"You money-grubbing serpent," Bryce muttered in disgust. "The welfare of your country means nothing to you, does it? The Abbot and his ilk would see Britain's defeat at a foreign monarch's hand, but you wouldn't lift a finger to stop them."

"I care nothing for this silent war of yours except that it's cost me my grandfather!" Pain and indignation made her voice crack while angry color splotched her pale countenance.

"If that's all you lost, you're one of the fortunate ones," Bryce said in disdain, and deliberately turned his back.

"There's nothing but a prison sentence to be gained with such rash talk," Huxford chided Genevieve. "I'd hoped you might welcome the opportunity to clear yourself of the most serious charges."

Genevieve pressed closer against the rock wall, her look suspicious. "How?"

"You are one of a select few who have ever seen the Abbot."

She shook her head. "It was dark. Everything happened so fast. I might be able to sketch my impressions, but that's all."

"I was thinking of something a bit more daring." Thoughtfully, the earl rubbed his lower lip with his thumb. "Perhaps a trap to ensnare the Abbot."

"Your last trap cost two men's lives," she returned bitterly, then shrugged. "Since that's all I have left, I suppose you want mine, too."

"Your value to the enterprise I have in mind is considerable, my dear. Cooperate, and in return I'll guarantee that none of these charges I mentioned need ever be brought into court."

She shook her head, confused. "I don't understand."

"These things must be carefully orchestrated," the earl explained with the patience of a parent instructing a small child. "Various messages marked with the Abbot's Seal are even now being dispatched at home and abroad. We'll need time to evaluate the response before making our move to snare the Abbot."

"By using me as bait."

"Not entirely. But the possibility cannot be overlooked. That's why I've concluded the only reasonable thing for me to do is place you in Mr. Cormick's custody and care for the duration."

Genevieve couldn't have been more astounded or more appalled if the earth had opened and Lucifer himself had stepped forth. Looking at Bryce fully, she saw the blue venom shining in his eyes and shuddered.

"You're mad. You're *both* insane!"

"You misunderstand my intent," Huxford said smoothly. "You certainly can't stay here, but you can't possibly go about on your own for fear of the Abbot's reprisal. By placing you beneath the Griffin's protective wings, I guarantee your safety and your participation in our enterprise. I'm sure you'll be comfortable in Bryce's home for a few weeks."

"No." Her voice was a cracked whisper. "Find another way."

Huxford's brow lowered ominously. "Perhaps you do not understand the seriousness of your situation. Your involvement with the Abbot is damning if taken by itself. Only your complete cooperation will suffice to eradicate the blot on your name."

"But surely this isn't necessary," Genevieve protested. "I'll do whatever you want. You're afraid I'll run away or something. Well, I won't."

"I know you won't," Huxford agreed, and his certainty chilled Genevieve to the bone.

Nausea clenched her stomach at the earl's ruthlessness. The Abbot had tried to kill her once, and now Huxford wanted to make her a target again. But as frightening as that was, being under Bryce's total control was even more terrifying, for she knew to her sorrow that Huxford's ruthlessness was nothing compared to the Griffin's. "I can't."

Bryce turned on his heel with a growl. "By God, you will! Otherwise, none of your story holds water. Your woeful tale may ring true for some, but you've proven a skillful liar. I think you may yet be in the Abbot's employ."

Genevieve gasped. "That's not true!"

"Then prove it," Bryce challenged.

"You don't really wish to go to prison do you, my dear?" Huxford asked. "Things could be quite . . . unpleasant."

Cornered, Genevieve weighed the alternatives. Huxford's threat didn't move her, for what more could they take from her? But she couldn't ignore a chance to clear her name and her grandfather's. It was little enough to do for Everett after the way she'd failed him. But she harbored no illusions about Bryce's involvement in the scheme. It was clear he viewed her forced acceptance of Huxford's plan not only as a way to smoke the Abbot out of hiding, but also as an opportunity to mete out the punishment he thought she deserved.

Hate simmered in Genevieve's soul. Perhaps she could surprise them both, the bastards! She might be coerced into cooperation, but it didn't have to be a pleasant experience. She was glad the beautiful Athena lay in ruins, she told herself. Served Bryce Cormick right! There should be other ways she could repay him for all the misery and turmoil he'd caused, especially in his own home, and she intended to find and use them without mercy. Thought he was an expert on making her suffer, did he? Well, just wait!

"I—I don't suppose it would make much sense to oppose this," she said at last, hiding her expression behind lowered lashes.

"None at all," Huxford replied kindly. "And you'll be doing your country a service by helping to bring a deadly criminal to justice."

Resolutely, Genevieve lifted her chin. "Then could we go now? I'd like a bath."

"Excellent!" The earl beamed. "I'm sure that can be arranged."

"And Maebella. Can I have her with me?"

Bryce's face darkened, and his tone turned nasty. "You won't need a chaperone to protect you from my attentions, I assure you."

Humiliated, Genevieve choked on her ire. As if she would entertain resuming intimacies with this man under any condition! Hateful, despicable, arrogant ape! It was the most difficult thing in the world to respond mildly, but she did it. "As you wish."

"The fewer at risk, the better," Huxford said, "though Miss Symthe may certainly visit if you swear to keep what has transpired today to yourself."

"Yes, I understand. Thank you."

Huxford smiled again. "Don't worry, Miss Maples. All will be well. The Griffin has never yet failed to complete an assignment, so rest easy. The crown's most excellent servant will be watching over you."

Genevieve shuddered. *That's just what I'm afraid of.*

"You *should* fear me," Bryce said some minutes later.

They'd been led through the tortuous underground maze of prison corridors to a waiting coach and now rode through the bustling London streets toward St. James Square.

Genevieve reluctantly dragged her avid gaze away from the sunny city scene. With a grimy hand, she brushed a knotted strand of hair out of her face and looked at him with tired disinterest. "I don't."

That her defiance was intact despite her sojourn in the bowels of the jail infuriated Bryce. "You will if you don't follow all instructions to the letter. Like it or not, I'm responsible for you. You'll come or stay at my command, and no questions asked."

"Perhaps I misunderstood. This holiday visit to purgatory wasn't your idea?"

"Hardly!" His bark of laughter was harsh. Playing nursemaid to a traitoress? The woman responsible for burning down his theater and turning him overnight into a pauper? But for Huxford's support, he would already have creditors breathing down his neck. And all of it was wound up with the Abbot. Now Bryce had a personal as well as a patriotic reason to bring the bastard down!

From the opposite seat, Genevieve ridiculed him, her lip curling into a sneer. "So we play out this farce because his lordship browbeat us both?"

"I'm a soldier still, thanks to you. I follow orders."

"How very commendable." She made the words an insult.

"Until this is over and the Abbot is behind bars or dead, we'll both do as we're instructed." His voice lowered ominously. "Or I'll make you heartily regret it."

Scornful, she shook her head. "I already have regrets aplenty. What can you take from me that I haven't already lost?"

Reaching across the space that separated them, he caught her chin and lifted her smudged face. "General, you don't want to know."

She glared at him, and her breath hissed between her teeth. "I despise and detest you."

"Quite an about-face from your earlier protestations, *chérie*." Bryce released her with a contemptuous laugh.

"What I felt was for someone who never existed. For . . . Darcy." Pain flickered across her face, then she looked at him with eyes that burned bright with hate. "Never you. Never!"

"A blessing indeed."

"Just leave me alone!" She turned her shoulder into the corner, retreating behind an invisible wall of loathing. In her stained, mannish attire, she still managed to look vulnerable and very feminine. With a silent oath, Bryce tore his gaze away, wondering how he could possibly be moved to pity by a deceitful witch.

Genevieve was reeling with fatigue by the time they reached Bryce's town house, but wouldn't let him so much as take her elbow to help her up the steps. She walked into the black-and-white-tiled foyer with all the reluctance of a convicted felon approaching the gallows.

"Where the devil is everyone?" Bryce said, taking out his annoyance on his hapless servants. He indicated the drawing room. "Wait in there while I roust someone to see to your room."

In a near-stupor of weariness, both physical and mental, Genevieve complied, only vaguely aware that Bryce van-

ished into the nether regions of the house shouting for
Taffy. A small apple wood fire crackled in the hearth, and
she migrated toward its warmth instinctively. Halfway
across the room, she faltered, overcome by a resurgence
of memories.

Gulping, her cheeks hot with humiliation, she remembered the passion that had flared in this room. Every article of furnishing sat in silent, accusatory judgment of her
wantonness. Sweat popped out on her brow, and she
shrugged out of her suddenly suffocating coat, blotting her
forehead on the soiled cuff of her shirt. She hated Bryce
for what had occurred here, but her self-loathing ate at her
gut like a thing alive. How could she endure living in this
house with him under any circumstances?

She swung around at a disturbance in the foyer. Two
young women in stylish bonnets and ruffled pelisses and
a tall older gentleman appeared in the arched doorway,
accompanied by Taffy McKee. Taffy said something jovial
that evoked a ripple of subdued laughter, then, to Genevieve's horror, he pointed toward the drawing room and
disappeared. Genevieve took an involuntary step backward, nonplussed. As the group enter the room, they
caught sight of the disheveled figure frozen before the fireplace, and the trio's desultory conversation came to an
abrupt halt.

In that instant of paralyzed astonishment, Genevieve was
able to examine the visitors. She recognized them immediately. The older man, though hazel-eyed and fair with
silver among his sandy locks, was a slightly less rugged
edition of Bryce, and could only be Sir Theodore Cormick. That meant the taller of the women with her sedate
coil of shiny blond hair and violet eyes was undoubtedly
Bryce's half sister, Allegra. The other visitor was a girl
still in her teens, her angel-fine brown hair frizzed attrac-
tively around a heart-shaped face. Could this chit be Clorinda North, the one Bryce thought eventually to take to
wife?

The trio staring back at Genevieve couldn't have looked

more shocked if they'd found serpents in their teacups. Genevieve's eyes narrowed, and her back stiffened with resolve. She could not let a faint heart deprive her of such a ready-made opportunity for revenge.

"Come in, then. Mustn't stand there with your potato traps hanging open like you was uncivilized or sumpin' queer."

Genevieve's words were flavored with the rough dialect of the East End. Feverishly, she racked her brain for every bit of street talk and thieves' jargon she'd ever heard. "It's a bob ken, all right, but the nob what owns the place don't mind sharing a bit of hospitality. Cormicks, ain't ye?"

"Well, yes," Sir Theodore began, then cleared his throat and began again. "See here, young woman—"

"I warn you, he's got a case of the blinkin' blue devils today. 'Course, it ain't surprising, considerin' the Athena burned to the ground. It's enough to make you cast up your accounts, I must say!"

"Are you here to see my brother?" Allegra asked incredulously.

Slender and statuesque, Bryce's sister wore with absolute indifference an unflattering, highly flounced gown that was probably her rural mantua maker's proudest creation. At her side, doll-like Clorinda North was wide-eyed with fascination, horrified yet intrigued by Genevieve's use of the cant of thieves and rogues, a thing no true lady would ever dream of doing.

"Oh, Bryce lets me run tame around the house, God love 'im! I was sayin' to me mates at the spouting club that the brothers of the buskin depend on each other, y'know." Genevieve grinned brightly and caught the legs of her baggy trousers to show off her attire. "I'm a great one for breeches parts, I am."

"Really!" Allegra nodded as though she was beginning to understand. Her movements as she crossed the room were athletic, too bold for strict drawing room society, as if she had no patience with the usual restrictions of skirts.

"Aye, he's full of heart, that one," Genevieve replied,

then snapped her fingers. "What's say we all have a tipple?"

She walked with easy familiarity to the sideboard and made a production of checking several empty decanters. "Nothin' but dead men here. Ah, here 'tis!"

Pouring a generous dram of brandy into a tumbler, Genevieve made certain to slosh the liquor over the sideboard so that the room soon reeked of spirits. Raising the glass in a salute, she tossed the contents to the back of her throat and swallowed it. Instantly, fire rushed to her brain and down her gullet. She choked, coughing, and her eyes watered.

"Lud, what a bolt!" she gasped, sniffing loudly as the fumes filtering through her sinuses made her nose run. "Ain't got a specked wiper I could borry, do you, sir?"

Sir Theodore, trained gentleman that he was, reached automatically for his handkerchief, then caught himself. "Absolutely not!"

"Busman got it, eh? Bad luck." Gamely, Genevieve tugged her filthy shirt out of her waistband, mopped her eyes and blew her nose on the ragged hem, then grinned innocently at the stunned observers. "Think I'll have another. Sure you won't join me?"

"No, we won't!" Sir Theodore exploded. "Now kindly explain what the devil you're doing in my son's home."

Genevieve feigned a hurt demeanor. "It's not what ye're thinking, guv'nor. I had a bit of a dust-up with the Charlies, is all. Bryce dawbed the turnkey with a goldfinch to spring me."

"What!" Sir Theodore's expression turned thunderous. "Allegra, you and Clorinda had better leave the room until I clear this up."

Allegra was too intrigued to be so easily dismissed. "But Father—"

"Yer brother's a true genl'man, miss," Genevieve said. "Why, some I know'd expect to get into a woman's commodity for turning 'is blunt to such a job, but not 'im! And 'im so devilish pretty, too."

"Allegra!" Sir Theodore roared. "I'll not have you exposed to this outrage. Leave us at once!"

" 'Ere now!" Genevieve huffed, taking highly indignant offense. "I ain't no Covent Garden nun! I'm as respectable as the next 'un. And you're dicked in the nob if you think I'll take insults off such a lumping great clodpate as you!"

Clorinda giggled inanely, then clamped a hand over her mouth. Allegra hustled her friend toward the door, her lips twitching slightly at the sight of her country gentleman father made totally speechless by a slender termagant in boy's breeches. Sir Theodore's outdoorsman's complexion flushed brick-red with vexation.

"You insolent hussy!" he growled, thoroughly irate. "You're going out on your ear for that! Who the devil do you think you are?"

"On my ear, eh? Just you try it!" A slow, satisfied smile curled Genevieve's mouth. "For your information, Bryce don't stand for anyone laying hands on his *wife* but him!"

To Genevieve's delight, *that* set them back on their heels. Clorinda whimpered and sank into a swoon. Allegra gasped and stared, never seeing the younger girl slump to the floor. Sir Theodore's face darkened to a shade of scarlet that threatened apoplexy.

From the doorway came an enraged roar. "Genevieve!"

She clasped her hands demurely and dipped her head. "Oh, dear," she said in a small voice, "have I made a fox's paw?"

"Bryce, what the devil's the meaning of this?" Sir Theodore choked.

"Sir, I can explain—"

Genevieve nimbly skipped to Bryce's side, clinging to his arm adoringly. "Yes, do tell them, dearie! Insulting your bride indeed! I might have had second thoughts about the wedding if I'd guessed this was the kind of reception I'd receive."

"Enough of your mischief!" Bryce snapped, his face hard and unloverlike.

Genevieve threw her hair out of her eyes and pouted. "Don't be vexed, sweetheart. I can't help it if your addle-brained sire and hen-witted sister have the conumdrums. Why don't you explain?"

"Yes, why don't you?" demanded Sir Theodore.

Bryce visibly ground his teeth. "It's a matter of some difficulty, sir."

"Don't try to gamon the old cull, dearie!" Genevieve cried gaily. "Came to my flash panney, he did, and fair swept me off my feet! One snooze with a mort like me, and nothing would do but to carry me off to the parson's!"

"Unbelievable!" Sir Theodore muttered, shocked to his core.

Genevieve smiled archly. "Well, it was past time he made good on all those court promises he'd made to get 'twixt my—"

"That's enough!" Bryce shouted.

"Oh, stubble it yerself, ye great thumping lump!"

With a snarl of absolute fury, Bryce grabbed her and hauled her toward the door. "Shut up, Genevieve, or by God I'll throttle you!"

Looking back over her shoulder, she cast a witchy smile at the room's stupefied occupants, lifting her chin so that they had a clear view of the bruise on her jaw.

"He always likes to knock me about a bit . . . before," she explained with a conspiratorial wink. "Not to worry, though. I've rather gotten to like it!"

Chapter 11

❧◦◦❧

"**G**enny, wake up."

Genevieve started slightly, rippling the tepid water of her bath. She rolled her neck languidly on the curled edge of the tin slipper tub, luxuriating in the touch of the silky, scented liquid on her well-scrubbed skin. The cloud of her hair hung over the side of the tub to dry while a small fire blazed in the bedroom hearth.

"Genevieve."

"Hmmm?" Drowsy, bemused by the images of freedom still soaring behind her lids, she raised her lashes to gaze into eyes as blue as the open sky. "I was dreaming of mountains," she murmured, regretful. "And there were eagles . . ."

"Your water is cold. Get out before you drown."

Awareness burst her golden bubble of euphoria, and she struggled upright in the rub, splashing, then as quickly realized her situation and sank back into the soap-filmed water, glaring and hissing at Bryce like a scalded cat.

"Get out! Can't you leave me in peace for even a moment?"

In his dark coat, Bryce loomed over her like a vengeful archangel, and righteous fury sharpened his tone. "If peace is what you wanted, why the sterling performance for my family as a ha'penny trollop?"

Genevieve reached for the sponge floating beside her

220

knee and shrugged, causing the water to lap tantalizingly around her breasts. Though the power of Bryce's masculinity within the dainty bedchamber nearly overwhelmed her, she'd die before she let it show. Instead, she smiled with a bravura she was far from feeling and casually sponged water over her shoulders.

"I rather relish the role of strumpet."

Bryce scowled. "Do you? Well, it's the role of wife you've bought yourself with your outrageous behavior."

"Wife?" Startled, she frowned, then laughed. "They didn't believe that pack of lies, did they?"

"They will when you make your apologies to them and corroborate the tale I had to concoct about eloping to Gretna Green to fulfill a promise I'd made to Everett to look after you."

"That ridiculous!" she spluttered. "You don't mean to pretend we're married?"

"Unfortunately, you began this charade. Now you'll have to live with the consequences," he growled. "I won't have my family humiliated over the situation when a little playacting will smooth the deception. It works as well as any other subterfuge to explain your presence here. At least your reputation remains intact."

"As if that matters!" Crossing her arms over her breasts, she sank lower in the tub, glowering at him. "I won't do it. Besides, you'd hardly wed a street creature like the one I played. They'd never accept that."

"No, but they readily accepted that you were out of your head with grief over your grandfather's death and couldn't be held accountable. Damned if you haven't backed us both in a corner with your nonsense this time, General."

"Good! Wiggle out of it the best you can, for I won't have any part of it! Now get out. I want to dress."

Bryce swore furiously at her show of defiance and took a menacing step forward. "You'll do as I say."

Her sopping sponge smacked the middle of his well-dressed chest. "The hell I will!"

She was halfway out of the tub before he caught her, but the slippery wetness of her skin gave her an advantage. She nearly wrestled free, but with an oath he lifted her bodily and threw her down on the damask spread covering the billowy feather bed. He pinned her flailing legs with one of his own, then shackled her wrists with his hands. Her nudity contrasted erotically with his fully clothed state, so that every contact was like an electric shock, and just as alarming. Breathing hard, Genevieve called him every vile name she could think of.

"Odious, slime-eating toad! Get off me!"

His smile was wicked. "Why? I'm enjoying this."

"Arrgh!" With a cry of rage, she tried to bite him.

His hands tightened, and he jerked her flat. "Cease, you hellcat! I'll have that apology. And from now on you'll be as demure and quiet in my family's presence as my lady wife should be. Is that clear?"

"I don't care what they think!"

"Well, I have to. And you'd better learn to, if you know what's good for you."

His searing glance raked her flushed cheeks and damp skin, then followed a drop of moisture from the hollow of her throat down between the valley of her breasts. His gaze was as palpable as a touch, and to her utter humiliation, her nipples puckered invitingly.

A groan tore from Bryce's chest. "Damn you, woman! I know what you are. Why do I still want to taste you?"

He buried his face in the hollow between her neck and shoulder, sipping the moisture from her skin like a connoisseur.

"G-get your hands off me." Her agonized whisper held a tremulous wobble. Gooseflesh broke out all over her, and deep within her body, a shaming dew collected. It was either capitulate or die of utter chagrin and humiliation when he discovered her involuntary response. "All right," she said, gasping, "I'll play your damned wife. I'll even apologize. Just let me up."

He released her and rose in one movement, then tossed

her his own paisley dressing gown, the only thing Taffy could find on such short notice.

"Cover yourself," he ordered brusquely, turning his back. He took up a rigid stance before the mantel as if the sight of her disgusted him.

Humiliated beyond belief, hating him with every atom of her being, Genevieve shrugged into the oversized garment. Perching uneasily on the foot of the bed, she tugged the robe's satin lapels closer about her throat as if to ward off a chill that made her lips tremble.

Her mouth firmed into a stubborn, resolute line. *He won't make me cry.* Bryce might have won this battle, but the war was far from over.

"For how long do I have to play the dutiful wife?"

Bryce shot her a narrowed look over his shoulder. "Until the Abbot is brought to justice and I'm done with you. While you're under my protection, you'll remain quiet and housebound here, in mourning for Everett. Everyone will understand if you are subdued."

"So I've merely exchanged one prison for another," she said bitterly. "I wonder if I've made a bad bargain."

Turning, Bryce pierced her with a warning glance. "This unrepentant attitude will only make things harder."

"Should I be abject? Cringing?" Resentment burned through every pore, and her smile was brittle. "Perhaps you'd prefer me to play the adoring, besotted bride for the benefit of that chit downstairs."

"Leave Clorinda out of this."

"Poor Bryce!" She laughed. "Huxford and I have made it awkward for you to continue to court the child, haven't we? What will you do to explain the awkwardness of an unwanted wife when all this is finally over?"

"Something will be arranged. In the meantime, I expect you to be cordial to my family and their guest. They've engaged rooms at the Excelsior to enjoy the season's social life, but I'm sure we won't be able to avoid a certain amount of interchange, especially knowing Allegra's curiosity."

Bryce's expression was almost fond, and Genevieve heard the genuine affection in his voice as he spoke of his half sister. It was another soft spot in Bryce Cormick's armor to be noted and taken advantage of later.

Bryce came to stand in front of Genevieve. "Will you behave yourself, or must I confine you to this room until Huxford has need of you?"

"Again, I find I have little choice," she muttered. Weariness pressed down on her, and she did not have to feign a giant yawn of boredom. "Is that all? I'd like to rest now."

Bryce had to be satisfied with her less than positive answer. "All right. I'll have Jack bring a tray later. Are you up to seeing Miss Smythe?"

Genevieve's drooping posture straightened. "Maebella? Is she here?"

"Downstairs."

She scowled in annoyance. "Why didn't you tell me!"

Bryce caught her chin between his fingers, and his stare was hard. "Mind what you say, General."

Unnerved by his touch, she swallowed, but her mouth remained sulky. "You needn't keep reminding me."

His face darkened, and he stroked her neck, trailing his fingers down to the notch in her collarbone where her pulse was making erratic forays into her throat. "I can make you sorely regret anything you're planning, Genevieve. Don't make me prove it."

When Maebella knocked on the door some minutes later, Genevieve's heart was still pounding with the aftereffects of Bryce's softly spoken promise. She fell into the stout little woman's comforting embrace with an intensity that wrecked Maebella's composure completely.

"There, there, don't weep. Your grandfather wouldn't want it," Maebella said, sniffling copiously.

"Maebella, I miss him so much," Genevieve whispered, hugging the older woman's plump shoulders. She closed her eyes against a wave of pain, but no cleansing tears came. When the sharpest edge had passed, she pulled

Maebella to a seat beside her on the edge of the bed. "Are you all right?"

"Mercy, yes, but I was so worried about you! Thank the Lord you were in Mr. Cormick's safe hands all the time," Maebella said, dabbing at her eyes with her handkerchief. "Who could have thought his fancy gas footlights would cause such an accident? So tragic to lose both your grandfather and Mr. Baggart that way. I still can't believe it."

"Nor can I."

"You poor lamb! You're still in shock, I'm sure. Mr. Cormick told me how you came to wed. Though rushed, it's so romantical! I know your Grandpapa would approve, considering the tragic circumstances and all. You need someone strong to take care of you now that Mr. Everett is . . ."

She couldn't finish, choked, and buried her face in her sodden handkerchief. Genevieve patted her shoulder, wondering what Maebella's reaction would be if she knew that Bryce was her curse, not her salvation. And who knew how long Bryce and Huxford would demand the farce go on? What would happen to her life in the meantime? Perhaps she was helpless now, but that did not mean she could not plan for the future.

"Maebella, do you still have all our belongings?" she asked abruptly.

"Of course." Wiping her eyes, Maebella nodded. "I've been staying at the Wayfarer's Inn, but when I got word from Mr. Cormick today, I brought your things, knowing you'd need them. Oh, dear," she said, struck by a thought. "We'll need to begin on your mourning clothes . . ."

"Yes, but there's something more important." Genevieve took Maebella's hands. "We must get you comfortably settled. Redeem our passages and take the money to Mr. Chesterson to engage the house he found."

"Whatever for? I don't need a big place—"

"No, but Madame Bella does. Then you must take those cards from Miss Chesterson and her friends, put on your

best costume—the cherry worsted with the military braid,
I think—and go call on them. Though my . . . situation is
changed, there's no reason we cannot continue with our
plans, for you need the employment and I must have
something to do or I'll go crazy here!''

Maebella's expression was astounded. ''My lands,
Genevieve! I couldn't do a thing like that! What do I know
about society?''

''It doesn't matter. All you have to do is bully these
young misses a bit, and they'll think you're marvelous.
And we both know you've had years of practice bullying
me.''

''And you're a sassy miss!'' Maebella considered, her
brow puckering. ''I confess, I have been concerned about
my future, though I suppose I could always find work as
a seamstress, but if you're certain Mr. Cormick won't object . . .''

''Why would he object to my designing a few gowns?
Please, Maebella. So many other dreams have faded. Let's
try to make this one a reality.''

''You're right, of course. Your grandpapa would expect
us to go on, wouldn't he?''

''Yes. Thank you.'' Genevieve hugged Maebella again,
overwhelmed by a sense of relief. It was comforting to
know that when all of this was over, she'd have a place to
go. Whether it would be a home or a hiding place remained to be seen.

A very tense week passed before Genevieve found herself seated in the drawing room making good her promise
to Bryce. Looking very much different from the breeches-
clad guttersnipe of her first encounter with his family, she
made a demure picture in a somber vandyked mourning
gown of her own design. The black bombazet fabric set
off her delicate coloring like a star against the night sky,
making her peachy skin glow and her hair shimmer with
red-gold lights.

Since her most arduous task over the last days had been

ignoring Bryce's rare appearances and fighting her fidgets with lessons for Jack Potts and innumerable sketches for Madame Bella's salon, she'd had plenty of opportunity to rehearse her apology. Now she made her speech in her most polished syllables, and begged Allegra's and Sir Theodore's pardons with a nicety that had the older gentleman exchanging his wary expression for one of complete sympathy.

"We'll say no more about it," Sir Theodore said gruffly, self-consciously tugging at his leather waistcoat, and looking as though he wished he were back in Suffolk with a morning's shoot ahead of him instead of a round of social calls.

"I thank you for your understanding. I was not myself, sir," Genevieve returned quietly.

Clorinda and Allegra, dressed in patterned Jaconet walking dresses that made Clorinda appear dainty and feminine and Allegra overdressed and cloddish, watched from across the laden tea table, quite amazed at the transformation. Bryce stood at the arm of the sofa in apparent support of his new "wife," but Genevieve knew that he would pounce on her like a jungle beast if she showed any signs of recalcitrance. Shrewdly, she knew a more effective method of annoying her jailer. Reaching out, she slipped her hand into his and looked up at him with an adoring expression.

"If not for Bryce's love and attention these past difficult days, I'm sure I wouldn't have survived. He is so good to me."

Bryce squeezed her hand in warning, nearly grinding her bones, but her besotted smile never wavered even though she knew that across the room Clorinda's expression was stricken.

Genevieve hardened her heart. Where once she might have felt guilty for inflicting such a hurt on an innocent, now hate made her cold-blooded. So what if the twit had a *tendre* for Bryce? Genevieve was actually doing the girl a favor by keeping an ogre like Bryce away from such a tender bit. No doubt his passion would frighten the child senseless, she thought sourly, if he could even work himself up to bedding such a milky babe.

Bryce seemed to follow the direction of her thoughts. Bending in an affectionate show, he brushed his lips against her cheek, murmuring. "Cool your ardency, General, or mayhap we'll *show* them how useful a sofa can be."

Genevieve blushed fiery red, and Sir Theodore hid a knowing, but entirely misguided, smile behind a great deal of loud throat clearing. "Perhaps the ladies will excuse us now, Bryce. I'd like to speak to you privately."

"Of course." Satisfied that Genevieve was sufficiently chastened, Bryce rose. Despite the cordiality, there was a certain awkwardness between father and son that was immediately noticeable. "We'll use my office."

"Might I invite Genevieve to promenade with us in the park in the morning?" Allegra called after them. "The autumn weather has been so extremely fine—"

Flicking a cautionary look at Genevieve, Bryce put his sister off with an excuse. "I'm afraid Genevieve isn't strong enough yet for an outing."

"What a harebrained notion," Allegra protested, clumsily juggling cup and saucer. With an annoyed moue, she set it aside. "She'll become as pale as milk without air and exercise! Do say she may come."

"As much as I hate to disappoint you, Allegra, you must let me be the judge of what's best for Genevieve. Excuse us now."

"Stubborn bullheaded man!" Allegra sat back in her chair with an irritated flounce, batting down the layers of ruffles on her hems as if putting out a brushfire. She tilted her head sideways to consider her new sister-in-law. "No doubt you've run broadside of some of Bryce's more obdurate qualities already."

"You could say that," Genevieve agreed cautiously. By making Allegra an ally, she might be able in a small way to defy Bryce's edicts, perhaps even cause dissension within the family. Crushing all twinges of conscience, determined to forge ahead with anything that might make Bryce regret his part in this charade, she made her smile one of feminine complicity. "But don't worry about Bryce, Allegra. I'm certain I can persuade him with a few sweet words, and I would very much enjoy an airing. Might I meet you in St. James Park at eleven tomorrow?"

"Of course!" Allegra's violet eyes sparkled with amusement and admiration. "I can see that my brother has found his match in you. But I should warn you that he is likely to be in a temper after speaking with Father."

"Why is that?"

"Father intends to offer financial help to make good the loss of the Athena. I told him it wouldn't help and would only infuriate Bryce, prideful male that he is. He'll never accept anything that remotely smacks of charity, even from those who care for him, even if he has to work himself to death in the meantime to repay his creditors. This part he's taken at Drury Lane—well, I'm sure you know all about it."

Genevieve reached for a teacup with studied nonchalance. "No, he's mentioned nothing . . ."

"A Haymarket player's role, hardly befitting an actor of my brother's caliber, but Bryce said the salary was too tempting—" Allegra broke off with an exclamation of dismay as Genevieve's disinterested expression wavered. "Forgive me, Genevieve. My father says I can be blunt to a fault. I'm sure Bryce didn't say anything merely to spare you further worry, and now I've spoiled the broth."

"No need." Genevieve studied the liquid in her cup. "I realize that our hasty—er, marriage has taken everyone by surprise, including us. In many ways I don't know Bryce at all." That, at least, was the truth!

"I can tell you he can be quite stiff-necked. He's always been like that, hasn't he, Clorinda?"

"I've known Bryce since I was a child," Clorinda said, her blue-gray eyes shining with pride that she could make such a boast, "and he's always been the most considerate, kind, and thoughtful gentleman."

"And you've always been half in love with him," Allegra scoffed, "ever since he and Calhoun let you trail after them like a puppy."

"As if you never did!" Clorinda countered indignantly.

"Oh, I was always more like one of the other boys," Allegra admitted cheerfully. "At any rate, you've always been blind to Bryce's faults. Fortunately, you'll be spared the worst of them, now that he's taken a wife."

"Of course, I wish you every happiness, Mrs. Cormick," Clorinda said in a stiff little voice.

"Thank you, Miss North." Genevieve nearly choked on the words.

"I'm delighted for you and Bryce, too," Allegra added. "I've long urged him to marry. And please don't take anything amiss when I tease Clorinda about her infatuation. She's more like a little sister to Bryce, even though there was some thought of a match—"

"Allegra, please!" Clorinda's expression was mortified.

"I simply want my new sister to know that she is most welcome in our family. I hope that we'll become good friends."

"You're very kind," Genevieve murmured. Allegra's natural warmth made her ashamed of the lie she and Bryce were living. Determinedly, she thrust such weakness aside. It was clear there was much about Bryce even his own family did not know, and sooner or later he would have to deal with the consequences of his deceit.

"Perhaps now Clorinda will pay more attention to the eligible young men she meets at the assemblies," Allegra said with a humorous gleam. "They flock about her like geese, you know."

"Allegra, please. I've had enough of your teasing for one day," the younger girl said, blushing.

"Are you enjoying your stay in London, Miss North?" Genevieve asked.

"Oh, yes!" Clorinda showed a pair of delightful dimples. "However, the bachelors I've met do not hold a candle to . . . to your husband. Perhaps I shall take a page out of Allegra's book and refuse all offers.''

Genevieve turned a quizzical look at Allegra. ''Have you been unlucky in love, then?''

Though the blond's eyes darkened momentarily, she shook her head and smiled. ''You must not pay any attention to Clorinda. My come-out was a miserable failure because I'm too straightforward and prefer my books and horses to society, whereas Clorinda is so clever and winsome, I'm certain she will be the toast of the town!''

Clorinda colored prettily and made suitable demurrals. While Genevieve had to admit the girl was quite lovely to fashionable eyes, she found Allegra, with her down-to-earth manner, much more attractive. For an instant Genevieve imagined the blond in a more elegantly styled gown that would show off her splendid carriage and coloring, not hide her assets under layers of unsuitable lace and ruffles. Her reverie was interrupted by Taffy's appearance at the door of the drawing room.

''Beggin' your pardon, missus,'' he said, rubbing the back of his balding pate in irritation. ''The Cap left strict orders that you wasn't to be disturbed, but there's a gent here what insists on seeing you.''

Genevieve spotted a flamboyant figure loitering in the foyer and came instantly to her feet. How dare Bryce try to cut her off from all friendly contact! ''Jules! Taffy, of course you must show Mr. Chesterson in.''

''But the Cap said—''

Genevieve put on a forlorn countenance. ''Surely I'm to be allowed to receive the condolences of my friends in my time of grief?''

Taffy's shiny bald head turned beet-red with remorse, and he shuffled his feet uncomfortably. ''O' course, missus. I was forgettin'.''

''Genevieve!'' Jules rushed into the drawing room a moment later and caught her hands ardently, oblivious to two pairs of watchful eyes. ''My dear, I'm quite overcome with despair!''

"Jules. How good of you to come. Please meet my guests." Genevieve drew the dandy into the room and made introductions.

While Allegra responded cordially, it was clear that Clorinda was dazzled by the brilliance of Jules's costume. He wore canary inexpressibles, a shocking blue waistcoat, and a black-and-white-striped coat with puffed sleeves and saucer-sized buttons. His collar points were so high they stabbed into his cheekbones each time he bowed.

"Ladies, it is my pleasure," he said, his gaze straying back to Genevieve. Allegra astutely engaged Clorinda in conversation on the far side of the table, leaving Genevieve to have a private word with her visitor as they sat on the sofa together.

"My dear, I can't tell you how distressed I am," Jules said under his breath. "My deepest sympathies over your grandfather's passing."

"Thank you, dear Jules." Genevieve pressed his hand warmly. "And thank you for your assistance with Maebella's new house. She informs me she is quite delighted with its venue."

"You know that I'm always glad to help in any way." Jules's caramel-colored eyes held the hurt appeal of a lost puppy. "Could you not have come to me in your time of trouble, rather than rush into this precipitous marriage? My heart cracked in twain the moment Miss Smythe told me. In faith, I may have to hie myself off to the Continent to wallow in my despondency like the poets."

Still simmering over Bryce's presumptive actions and determined to flaunt his authority at every turn, Genevieve responded recklessly. "Do not take on so, dear friend. 'Tis but a marriage made expedient by circumstances. My heart is not engaged, and neither is Mr. Cormick's."

"A marriage of convenience?" Jules said, dumb-founded, his jaw hanging open. "Then you mean—" He broke off, dusky color rising at his own lack of sophistication.

"I am to have my own life and so is Bryce," Genevieve

said with airy unconcern. Inwardly, she gloated, thinking of Bryce's chagrin when he found this bit of gossip making the rounds, as it surely would now that Jules was privy to it. She squeezed the dandy's hand again. "You will be discreet, won't you?"

"Yes, of course. That is, no, not a word," he gabbled, renewed hope lighting up his eyes. "Might I see you again soon?"

Her lashes drifted down, veiling her expression. "I'd enjoy it immensely."

Genevieve marveled at the way her ordeal was revealing the ruthless tendencies within her own personality. Now, as cold-bloodedly as the Abbot or the Earl of Huxford had ever connived, she was planning to use a friend to take her vengeance on Bryce. She'd make it up to Jules later, she promised herself, but for now, in order to act on her hate, she was desperate enough to use any means that came to hand, be it Jules, Bryce's sister, or even his almost-fiancée. She smiled her most charming smile for the besotted young man.

"There are ways to meet most innocently, Jules, and we must find them."

Their heads were bent together making plans when Bryce reentered the drawing room. A thunderous scowl darkened his face at the sight of the brilliant coxcomb fawning over his "wife." Added to his annoyance was the altercation he'd just had with his father over money. Sir Theodore was again trying to do his "duty" by his bastard, and this grated on Bryce fiercely. Barely holding on to the frayed edges of his temper, he stalked to Genevieve's side. Jules stood, his guilty color high.

"Sir, allow me to extend my congratulations on your nuptials."

Bryce gave a curt nod. "Make your excuses, Genevieve," he ordered abruptly. "I don't want you to become overtired."

"You are ever considerate of my welfare," Genevieve murmured, her gray-green eyes wide and guileless. "But surely we can stay a moment? Jules has promised to wrangle vouchers for Almack's for Clorinda and Allegra, and we would not want them to miss such a treat.''

"Almack's?" Clorinda breathed in awe. "Truly?"

Jules bowed. "It would be my pleasure to arrange it all, Miss North, Miss Cormick. My mother is close friends with one of the patronesses.''

"Why, thank you, Mr. Chesterson," Allegra said, surprised and pleased. "I know Clorinda would enjoy attending the famed assembly rooms.''

Bryce frowned, unwilling to be beholden to Jules, yet reluctant to deprive the ladies of their pleasure. And while still suspicious of Genevieve's motives in calling up favors from Jules, he had to admit that perhaps she'd decided it was politic to appease him with this kindness toward his sister and Clorinda, in at least an outward display of wifely devotion.

At last, he nodded. "It's good of you to take the trouble, Chesterson.''

"What say you now, sir?" Genevieve smiled innocently at Bryce. "Is not a wife a handy thing to have?''

While the ladies turned their total attention to Jules's proposals, Bryce wondered if Genevieve's innocuous question was in truth a poisoned barb. In the troubled fortnight that followed, he had more than ample opportunity to decide.

While charming both his father and Allegra, Genevieve managed to flaunt nearly every order Bryce gave and made him appear the tyrant and herself the helpless victim. Whether it was unauthorized walks in St. James Park or unsupervised excursions to Madame Bella's new salon with Allegra and Clorinda to select gowns for their evening at Almack's, Genevieve always managed to make his grievances look petty in front of his family. Forgetting their initial encounter with the chestnut-haired hellion, they'd taken her completely to their bosoms and now championed her against Bryce. Even Sir Theodore suggested to Bryce that he was being too hard on his new wife, little realizing that in doing so he played right into the scheming traitor's dainty hands.

And then there was that fool, Chesterson, always hanging about, sending posies to Clorinda and Allegra and bouquets the size of bushel baskets to Genevieve, and bringing around countless equally brainless friends to fawn and coo over the two single ladies while eating him out of house and home. Any complaint Bryce made earned him a sharp rebuke from Allegra, who demanded that he not begrudge Clorinda the opportunity to meet eligible young men, especially since Bryce had taken a wife so unexpectedly and dashed the girl's hopes.

Later, when he took Genevieve to task for ignoring his safety precautions, she was invariably as icy as a Norwegian princess, pointing out that Taffy and Jack were always in attendance and berating both him and Huxford for the undue length of time the entire affair was taking. Bryce found he could not entirely disagree with that complaint. When he met with Huxford at lunch one day to voice his own protests over the delay, the enigmatic earl merely munched his apple tart, commended Bryce for his ingenuity in concocting an elopement as a cover story, and counseled patience.

Patience, indeed! Bryce tried, but it was damnably hard to have patience while attempting to guess what mischief Genevieve would entice Allegra into next. Or while slaving through an excruciating performance of *The Castle Spectre* at the Drury Lane night after night. Or while Genevieve radiated hatred and her fragrance lingered in his hallways to torment his dreams. But at the Four Queens one evening after a performance, when he heard himself awarded a cuckold's horns by a liquor-soaked gossip monger, Bryce knew he's reached the end of whatever little patience he had.

Livid that Genevieve had actually had the temerity to insinuate to one of her foppish friends that the normal marriage bonds didn't fetter either partner, furious at the thought that such talk might get back to his father and sister, enraged and strung tight with tension over the entire untenable situation, Bryce charged down the corridor toward Genevieve's bedroom, unmindful of the lateness of the hour, intent on having things out once and for all.

When he opened her door, her bed was empty.

His reaction was immediate, visceral. *Damnation! Whose bed is she sharing? I'll kill the bastard!*

He swore, then stopped short. A candle burned at a small table, revealing a litter of sketches and designs, crumpled papers, and broken nibs. He forced himself to take a deep, calming breath. Taffy was charged with keeping Genevieve safely within the confines of the house at night, and he would not be derelict in that duty. Then where the hell was she?

Ripping off his cravat, Bryce stormed out of the room, then stopped, his senses expanding. The only sign of life within the quiet house came from *his* chamber. Something painful twisted in his gut. What was the witch up to now?

He found her standing at his desk, clad in a diaphanous muslin night rail and lace-flounced dressing gown, poring over a sheet of paper. The light from a single candle illuminated her rapt expression and spangled with red-gold lights the unruly curtain of her hair, held back with a girlish ribbon.

Leaning his shoulder against the door casing, he allowed himself the luxury of watching her, acknowledging that he still desired her even while he despised her for her duplicity, the falseness that had made her choose a traitor's path. She had brass, he had to admit, trying to spy on him. Luckily, there was nothing more important in that desk than—oh, hell! He realized what she was reading and decided it was definitely time for diversionary tactics.

"Good evening, General," he drawled from the doorway.

Startled, Genevieve jumped guiltily. "Oh! I didn't see you there." She waved the sheet. "I ran out of paper, so I . . ."

Bryce crossed the room, and she involuntarily stepped

backward, her eyes growing wide. He took the sheet from between her fingers, glanced at it, then tossed it aside. His gaze raked her from tousled head to satin-slippered feet.

"Some men might take this as an invitation, you know."

High color graced her cheeks, but she gave a delicate, disdainful snort. "You know better."

"It seems fairly clear to me." One eyebrow cocked at a lazy angle. "A woman who comes to a man's bedchamber must be looking for something."

"Paper, I said!" she snapped. Then her irate expression modulated, became speculative. "But I find your supply as depleted as my own. I didn't know you wrote."

"I don't. What I do is penance."

She didn't know what to make of that for a long moment, then said grudgingly, "The part I read is very good."

Bryce frowned. "Scribblings, that's all."

"It's a play. Even I can see that."

"Not worth a Grub Street hack's attention."

He could see that the urge to argue with him was strong in her, but after a brief, silent struggle, she shrugged and went to move past him. "As you say. Good night."

His hand closed over her upper arm, and his voice was suddenly silky. "Oh, no, General, not so fast. You don't invade a man's privacy and then expect to escape unscathed. And there's the matter of your recurring disobedience."

"If you're not happy with my conduct, you can always let me go," she returned sweetly.

"Would that I could, General, but Huxford would have my head." He bent closer, and his breath whispered along her cheekbone. "But if I hear another murmur that this so-called marriage is an arrangement of convenience, and it chances to find its way to my father's ear, I'll throttle you."

"You dare not," she retorted shakily. "I'm too valuable to the crown, remember?"

"A true warrior, defiant to the end." He cupped her

cheek in his palm and lifted her face to his, hovering only
a breath away from her quivering mouth. "It will profit
you nothing, Genevieve. Push me once more, and I'll take
great joy in taking my convenience on your lovely body.
Then surely we'll be wed in fact, even though churched
in fiction."

Her eyes flashed with emerald fire. "Cad! Your threats
don't frighten me!"

"Then this should."

Lowering his mouth, he kissed her, not as his anger
demanded, but coolly, with all his expertise, seductively
wooing a response she would have been able to withhold
had it not been for his gentleness, stealing her hate and
causing her to forget for a breathless span that it had ever
existed.

When he released her, his half smile was born of malice
and triumph. "See? You are a traitor—even to yourself."

Something fragile in her expression shattered, the shards
slicing through the remnants of her innocence forever.
With a wordless cry of pain, she fled the chamber.

His mission accomplished, Bryce sat down at the desk
and picked up the sheet of paper on which he'd written
about the agony of war. With an oath, he crumpled the
page in his fist. This was another kind of war, but the
agony was just as acute—for both sides.

If only he hadn't kissed her, Genevieve thought, then
she might not have risked Bryce's fury so soon. Seated in
the middle tier of boxes at the sumptuous Drury Lane
Theatre, she rubbed her damp palms on her black velvet
skirts and wondered if she had gone too far.

Recklessly, she'd browbeaten Taffy and appealed to Allegra to be included in the outing to view a performance
of *The Castle Spectre*. Her utter failure to withstand
Bryce's most subtle form of punishment the previous night
had demanded an immediate response, something to prove
to him that she was not yet completely vanquished. But
more importantly, something to prove it to herself.

Now, while the gothic melodrama unfolded almost unregarded on the stage below, Clorinda and Allegra avidly watched all the doings of society, from the lowliest members of the *ton* to the highest nobility and foreign dignitaries. Beside Genevieve, Sir Theodore looked uncomfortable but dignified in austere evening dress. On her other hand, Jules Chesterson, attired in his usual riotous costume, plied her with outrageous compliments she only half heard through a haze of misery and trepidation.

Why had seen been so foolish in her defiance? Bryce would certainly spare a glance at the box his family occupied sometime during the evening's proceedings. When he saw her, there was no doubt in Genevieve's mind that he'd take her presence as a declaration of all-out war. And suddenly she was not certain that she could withstand an escalation of hostilities, nor survive the punishment Bryce was likely to exact.

Lord, how she hated him for that kiss! How she despised him for reminding her of the glorious fantasy that had briefly been hers. It shook her confidence and undermined her determination, the warmth of his lips melting her defenses and the icy shroud of hate that had numbed all the hurt. What was she thinking, challenging him with her presence here? Perhaps it wasn't too late to leave . . .

"Look, there's Bryce!" Clorinda exclaimed in a loud whisper.

A surge of applause from the audience marked his entrance onto the stage. Clorinda leaned over the confining wall of the box and waved her fan to catch his eye, while Genevieve cringed backward in her seat. With an almost imperceptible nod, Bryce acknowledged Clorinda's salute, then his features froze. Genevieve could feel the chill of his frosty stare paralyzing her. Desperately, she turned to Jules, chatting and flirting with forced vivacity until the action of the scene demanded Bryce's attention again.

"My dear, are you all right?" Jules asked. "You're very pale."

"I'm a bit light-headed." She smiled her reassurance

while briskly fluttering her ebony fan. "It's so close in here."

Jules immediately offered to go for a cup of water, and gratefully she accepted, welcoming the reprieve from the necessity of making conversation. However, she was soon heartily sorry to have sent him away because now her attention focused fully on the stage and Bryce's performance. It was easily apparent to her critical eye that he was wasted in the part of the dimensionless hero, especially after having played the tormented Othello with such skill and insight.

And she was responsible. But for her, he'd still be re ceiving the accolades he deserved in his own theater, instead of prostituting his craft in this badly staged melodrama. But for her, he might one day have even produced his own work—a great loss for the world of the theater if she was any judge of the portion of his script she'd read. Pressure built in Genevieve's chest, the burden of unshed tears, monumental regrets, and shattered dreams.

"Excuse me, sir," she murmured to Sir Theodore. "I— I must have some air."

Scooping up her cloak and ridicule, she left the box before he could frame a protest, threading her way through the clusters of theatergoers loitering in the circular saloon, seeking escape from the emotions threatening to suffocate her. Vaguely, she thought she heard Jules's voice, but she was focused only on the stairway leading down to the ground level and the hackney coach she might find to take her back to—where? St. James Square? Maebella's? Strung tight, her composure slipping, she nearly laughed aloud. There was no safe haven for her.

The thought was so blackly condemning she drew up short at the top of the wide staircase and was suddenly jostled by a gentleman walking behind her.

Her apology was automatic. "I beg your—"

"Keep walking." A hard hand clamped her arm, keeping her close to the curving wall while pushing her toward the steps, and the silver shimmer of a small, lethally pointed dagger appeared in his hand.

Terror abruptly replaced all other emotions. Genevieve had an impression of dark hair and cold slanted eyes, but nothing else registered, except the will to live. With a strength born of fear, she screamed and lunged away. Fire lanced through her side, and then she was falling, tumbling out of control down the long flight of stairs in endless, thumping cartwheels until finally, blessedly, she reached the bottom and all was still.

Stunned and bleeding, she might have heard her name over the roaring in her ears, but the world was contracting into blackness, growing smaller and smaller until only a pinpoint of light remained and a single oddly satisfied thought.

Won't the earl be vexed?

Chapter 12

"She's bleeding again."

"Yes, I know." Sir Theodore Cormick's hazel eyes were compassionate as he watched his son pace. The corridor of the Cormick manor house, though well appointed and spacious, was scarcely big enough to hold a man whose distress had him circling outside Genevieve's sickroom door like a caged tiger. "Sit down, Bryce. You're exhausting me."

Bryce didn't seem to hear the silver-haired man whose features so matched his own haggard face. A two-day shadow of beard and a wrinkled shirt still stained with brownish-red smears of blood was mute testimony of his distraction. "I shouldn't have risked moving her."

"You thought it was best to leave London."

"Maybe I was wrong." Bryce threw himself down onto one of the pair of fiddleback chairs lining the hall and stared wearily at his father. "Maybe Genny wasn't really the target."

"Could you take that chance?" Sir Theodore asked, his tone reasonable, soothing. "If your wartime enemies sought to do you harm through your wife, what was there to stop another attempt? Genevieve will be safer here at Clare Hill. You both will."

"Safe?" Bryce laughed with bitter self-recrimination.

242

"I couldn't protect her before. What makes you think I can protect her now?"

"You're too hard on yourself." Sir Theodore squeezed Bryce's slumped shoulder briefly, then sat down in the other chair. "You always have been, even as a boy."

Alice, an older servant skilled in nursing, bustled past with an armload of fresh linens and bandages. Her brow knit with worry, she spared neither man a glance before joining Allegra and the attending physician behind the paneled door of the sickroom.

Bryce stared blindly after the servant, his thoughts a jumble of self-loathing and guilt. He'd pushed Genevieve into her recklessness with his brutal assault on her pride. Why had he felt the need to strip her of every vestige of defiance? What if his desire to punish her cost her life?

Jules Chesterson had been the first to reach Genevieve after the attack, but he had seen nothing, and in the tumult that had stopped the performance and drawn Bryce from the stage in terror to Genevieve's side, the assailant had escaped. Huxford had deemed it prudent for them both to quit the city immediately, and Bryce had done so, canceling all his theatrical commitments indefinitely in light of the seriousness of Genevieve's injury. But though they'd taken every care, the hellish journey had exacted its toll on her, and now doubts about the precipitousness of that decision nagged him.

"Maybe I've already killed her by bringing her here," Bryce said in a raw tone.

"Compose yourself. You're overwrought," Sir Theodore ordered sternly. "You'll do neither yourself nor Genevieve any good if you try to fix blame for this. Count yourself fortunate the blade glanced off her stays as it did, otherwise the wound might have been immediately fatal."

Bryce swallowed hard and buried his face in his hands, overcome by the memory of Genevieve lying in a pool of blood, her pierced back and side a ghastly imitation of his own wounds from Lyons. Huxford thought there was even a remote possibility that Genevieve's attacker had been the same assassin who had come so close to finishing Bryce in that French city, but all Bryce knew was that the nightmare of Lyons had been resurrected in all its clawing, tearing, soul-shredding agony by this assault on Genevieve.

Lyons. Images he's tried hard to suppress battered the inside of his head.

The little plaster house standing shoulder to shoulder with its neighbors on the narrow Rue de la Fleurs. The tiny courtyard, filled with sunshine, children's laughter, and pungent herbs—rosemary, thyme, basil. Marie, her soft smile transforming a plain face that had suffered too much, grown old before her time, but who in her generosity had offered for a fleeting span unquestioning succor and surcease that he'd sorely needed.

It had only been meant to be a brief respite for a man traveling the underground roads, a resting place in the humble home of a woman who had no love for the emperor and the wars that had cost her husband his life on the frozen French retreat from Moscow. Bryce was headed for the Swiss border with stolen information about troop strengths and movements, the whereabouts of artillery and generals, but for once he underestimated the persistence of his pursuers.

Perhaps it was because he was so tired, so sick of the things he'd had to do to complete his assignments and endure. The senseless slaughter, the stench of the battlefields, the faces of the men he'd killed—they hardened a man, made him feel hollow. The soldier's high ideals and his initial desire to revenge his friend Cal had long since been reduced to mere survival. One more assignment, he promised himself time and again, and then he'd stop to regain the humanity he'd lost along the way. But Huxford always had one more job for the Griffin, and then another after that . . .

He needed the rest, and it had been so damned long since he'd allowed himself any sort of feminine comfort. Had it been any wonder he couldn't resist lingering there in that tiny way house? Waking to the odor of fresh-baked bread, allowing himself the simple fun of tossing Marie's two little boys into the air to hear their delighted giggles, finding the softness he'd yearned for in the comfort of her arms? It hadn't been love, at least for him, but a coming together of two hungry souls. He'd known better. And it had cost him.

Bryce clenched his fists in his hair, then rose from the fiddleback chair with a muffled exclamation, and, ignoring Sir Theodore's questioning expression, resumed his pacing. But he couldn't outrace his galloping thoughts now that the floodgate had been opened.

If only he hadn't stayed that extra day in Lyons. If only he'd been smarter, more on his guard. But the very softness he'd craved had dulled his edge, and so when the tall, narrow stranger with the oddly tilted black eyes appeared at Marie's door, no alarms went off. Bryce had been pulling weeds from Marie's herbs, enjoying the warmth of the late-setting sun on his bare shoulders while she put her children to bed. He hadn't seen the reptilian gleam of hate, or the flash of the man's stiletto until too late. But as he'd plunged face first into Marie's basil plants with the burning agony of a knife wound in his back, he'd heard the assassin's epithet.

"Traitor!" The words hissed past the killer's thin lips. "Swine! You'll never harm mother France again."

With the tang of crushed basil in his nostrils and the metallic taste of blood in his mouth, Bryce saw him lift the knife again to finish the job. But Marie's terrified screams split the air, and the killer went after her instead.

No. Blood gushing from his wound, Bryce teetered on the edge of consciousness, unable to move, unable to help. *Run.* Children crying, screams gurgling to nothing, and neighbors that came too late.

Bryce wanted to die then.

His punishment was that he did not.

Bryce stopped before the bedchamber door, and a muscle in the side of his jaw worked with tension. With the help of Marie's neighbors, he'd recovered enough to eventually make his way across the border where Taffy had been waiting. But the disaster in Lyons had been all his fault, Marie's murder the result of his own selfish weakness, and he hated himself for it, knew he was forever past redemption for allowing his own needs to cause the death of a good and innocent woman.

And now that same weakness was the reason Genevieve lay so desperately hurt behind that paneled door. He'd forgotten something vital during that brief, magic time when they'd been happy lovers. Somehow, she'd made him forget he'd never deserve the kind of happiness other men seemed to achieve effortlessly. While it might be irrational to think anyone he let close to him would suffer Marie's fate, he knew in his gut that it was a fact, because deep down, he wasn't any damned good. And no matter what Genevieve had or hadn't done, she'd never in a million years come close to equaling his villainy.

His caustic thoughts and utter helplessness left him on the brink of a violent explosion. "What's taking that cursed physician so damned long!"

Dr. Joshua Mundy, the silver-haired village practitioner, stepped into the hall and wearily closed the door behind him. He spoke with the gruff, familiar affection of a man who'd attended many a wild young boy's hurts and broken bones. "Cease your prattle, bantling. You disturb my patient."

"Dr. Mundy—" Bryce's throat closed.

Sir Theodore squeezed his son's arm in encouragement. "Joshua, how is she?"

"Very weak, I'm afraid. The bleeding's stopped, but she lost a great deal of blood."

"Will she live?" Bryce croaked.

Dr. Mundy's kind gray eyes clouded with compassion. "With care, yes, I believe so . . . but there was nothing I could do to save the child."

Bryce's cheeks blanched. "The what?"

"You did not know? Well, 'twas early days, fortunately." Dr. Mundy nodded to himself. "I suspect your lady did not realize it either until the spasms overtook her and the babe began to slip. 'Tis oftentimes like this in the case of a grave hurt. The injury itself, and then the fall she took . . . To survive, the body gives up what it cannot support."

"Oh, God." The words ripped from Bryce's chest in an agonizing paroxysm of remorse and loss.

Allegra opened the door and joined them in the hallway, her face composed but as pale as the practical apron she wore over a simple skirt and blouse. She faltered at the awful sight of her brother's stricken expression.

"You must think of it as a blessing," Dr. Mundy continued in a low, earnest tone. "She'll need every ounce of her strength for herself. You might well have lost both mother and child otherwise."

"I see." Bryce looked into a wasteland that once had been his soul and found nothing but desolation. He forced himself to go through the required motions, offering his hand to the older gentleman. "Thank you, Doctor."

"I'll leave you then. Give the lady every care, and I feel certain she'll respond. But do not hesitate to send me word in case of hemorrhage or fever."

"I'll see you out, Joshua," Sir Theodore offered, and escorted his friend down the corridor.

Allegra hugged Bryce in a spontaneous gesture of comfort and support. "I'm sure there will be other babies," she murmured.

His big hands clenched spasmodically on his sister's shoulders, but his throat was so full he couldn't answer for a moment. Swallowing harshly, he finally asked, "Can I see her now?"

Allegra hesitated. "She's resting."

"I'll just sit with her until she wakes."

Gently, Allegra disentangled herself, and her elegant features tightened with regret. "I—I don't think that would be wise."

"But she's my wi—" Bryce broke off with a muttered

curse. He couldn't even make that claim on Genevieve. God, what a tangle! "I need to see her."

"No, Bryce." Allegra was firm. "I—I don't know what's happened between you, but she doesn't want you at all just now. Even barely conscious, she became almost hysterical when I asked."

"But—"

"We can't risk upsetting her while she's so weak. What if it brought on a fever?" Allegra touched Bryce's clenched fist, trying to uncurl his tense fingers. "Perhaps in a few days when she's better."

Bryce took her hand almost desperately. "It won't do any good, Allegra. First Everett, now this. God help us both. The general will never forgive me."

"Surely you're wrong. She's just hurting right now. With your patient care and sympathy, she'll soon be well again."

Bryce looked at Allegra's earnest expression and wondered briefly when his little half sister had changed from a hoydenish tomboy, the bane of a hundred governesses, into such a wise and lovely lady. "I pray you're right."

Allegra smiled sweetly, but her innocent words were like salt in an open wound. "Take heart, Bryce. I know Genevieve loves you very much."

The sudden bleakness behind Bryce's eyes was a terrible thing to see. "Sometimes, Allegra, love just isn't enough."

Over the long autumn days of her six-week convalescence, Genevieve discovered that it was possible not to think at all. If you did not entertain thoughts, then you did not have to deal with the fact that your beloved grandfather was gone or that you had almost died yourself or that you'd carried a child only to have your own body betray you by expelling the babe like so much unwanted flotsam. If you were careful, it was possible to glide through the endless routine of rural days without disturbing your protective cocoon of disinterest, without having to take any but the most fleeting notice of the shadowy people floating beside you in the treacherous stream called life.

They were invariably kind, of course, Sir Theodore and Allegra, Jack and Taffy, Alice and all the servants. Even Bryce spoke softly now, always deferential, always considerate and helpful. Strangely, Genevieve didn't even care. It was as though she viewed everyone through a slightly distorted mirror so that she had to strain to recognize their faces and understand their words. And for the most part, it wasn't worth the effort.

As her strength returned and her body gradually healed, she moved from bed to chair to her first cautious steps around the perimeter of her chamber with equal apathy, vaguely curious that Allegra should be so pleased with her progress when she cared so little about it herself. It was simply easier to rise, recline, eat, dress, walk, or rest when told, for to question or disobey might shatter her protective shell, letting thoughts in, and, above all, she never wanted to think or *feel* again.

"There was a frost again last night," Allegra said one morning. Standing behind Genevieve's chair, Allegra pulled a brush through Genevieve's curls and gave the burnished locks a final satisfied pat. "There! I think you're ready to venture downstairs. We can brave a walk through the garden. It's a bit brisk, but the sunshine will do you no end of good."

"If you like." Genevieve's weight loss made her look like a lost child in Allegra's loose green velvet house robe. Gazing off into some hidden distance, she radiated an ethereal, rather fey quality of unworldliness. A letter lay forgotten in her lap.

Allegra stifled a sigh, then set the brush down on the polished dresser and smiled brightly. "What has Miss Smythe to say to you? Clorinda was most pleased with her Almack's gown, you know, and spoke kindly of Mr. Chesterson's attentions to her there. Her Great Aunt Tullimede is sponsoring her come-out ball before Christmas and was absolutely in raptures to have Madame Bella produce another creation.''

''What? Oh, I beg your pardon, Allegra, I'm afraid I wasn't attending.''

''Your letter?'' Allegra proded gently.

Genevieve looked down into her lap in surprise. ''Oh. Maebella is well. Busy, too, by her account. She'd like me to do some new sketches.''

''Why, that's wonderful!''

Genevieve rubbed her temples. ''It's so hard to think about these things . . .''

''Posh and poppycock!'' Suddenly exasperated, Allegra placed her hands on her hips. ''Dr. Mundy says you're nearly whole again, needing only extra rest to find all your old strength. You can't tell me you're not going to help your dearest friend when she needs you!''

For the first time in over a month, Genevieve was taken aback by Allegra's unexpected vehemence. ''No, of course not. That is, I could try.''

''Try, indeed! Genevieve, I know you've been through much, but it's past time for you to leave this melancholia behind. You must see how Bryce suffers. He follows you with his eyes, and then spends hours in the saddle or locked up scribbling. Why, it's as if you are two strangers, not husband and wife! You should be a comfort to each other, but the distance between you is so unnatural, and you don't even try—''

''That's enough, Allegra,'' Genevieve said, white-lipped and trembling. ''You've been very kind to me, but you have no right to say these things. There are some things you can't possibly understand.''

''You think you are the only person ever to lose someone?'' Allegra cried. ''The man I loved died on the Spanish Peninsula.''

Genevieve heard the anguish in Allegra's voice and drew a sharp breath. ''Calhoun North?''

''Yes.'' Allegra's violet-blue eyes filled.

''Oh, Allegra, I am sorry,'' Genevieve said, contrite.

"Cal was so good and funny and kind. If it hadn't been for him, I don't know that Bryce would ever have adjusted to life here. I was small when Bryce came, but I remember how wild he was. He scared me at first with all that black hair. He ran away, so many times! Father had no idea what to do with him. And then Cal met Bryce one day on the North family woodlands."

Despite herself, Genevieve was intrigued. "What happened?"

Allegra sniffled and smiled. "It must have been a terrible mill, for they both ended up with bloodied noses and black eyes, but from that day they were inseparable. Sometimes it was hard not to be jealous of how close they were."

"Did Calhoun know how you felt?"

"We would have been married when he returned." Allegra took Genevieve's hands. "As hard as it seems, you can go on, too. You and Bryce still have each other, and if only you'll try . . ."

"I've reached an end to trying," Genevieve said stonily. "It only hurts more when the dreams die."

"But Genevieve—"

Bryce's deep voice interrupted his sister's protest. "Perhaps I'd better continue this conversation, Allegra."

Genevieve looked up at the man filling the doorway, massive and masculine in his country riding clothes, a thread-picked blue coat and scuffed boots. She tugged her hands free of Allegra's, and though she made no other move, her withdrawl into herself was complete and totally frustrating to those watching.

"Perhaps you should, at that," Allegra said thoughtfully. "You may take Genevieve for her turn around the garden."

Bryce crossed to Genevieve's chair and offered his arm. "Shall we?"

Docilely, she accepted his help and made no demur when he took the heavy cloak waiting on a nearby stool and swept it about her shoulders. She didn't really need his supporting arm as they walked through the spacious rooms of the manor and out the bank of doors into the rear terrace and gardens, but she bore his help patiently, as if humoring him.

It made Bryce grit his teeth. Walking down the pebbled paths past the bare twigs of dormant rose bushes, he tried to think of something suitable to say, but her silence was so serene and impenetrable that his tongue felt tied in knots. Nor did she stop to examine the bits and pieces that littered the path as she once would have, ignoring the jay's feather and the horse chestnuts that in other days would have delighted her and joined her collection of treasures. That lack of interest hurt as much as her silence.

They reached the lower border wall of the garden, but when she would have turned to retrace their steps, he forestalled her. For a time he simply stared out over the panorama of fields, orchards, and fens while the brisk wind whipped his hair and the edges of Genevieve's cloak. It would be All Saints' Day soon, and harvest was nearly complete for another year, the hay ricks stacked and turnips gathered. From the paddocks came the shrill cry of his father's stallion and the nickering of the brood mares Allegra had so carefully chosen in the hope of producing a superior crop of foals come the spring. The pastoral placidity belied the uncertainty in his heart.

"There are some things we need to discuss," he said at last.

Genevieve didn't look at him, and her unresponsiveness infuriated him anew. Determinedly, he clamped down on his anger, knowing that it was not her to whom his ire was directed, but himself.

"Aren't you interested in your future now that you're better?" he asked in a gentle tone.

"No."

"General, this isn't like you," he chided.

She stared out over the stubbled pastures and fallow fields. "The hard lesson I've learned of late is that nothing

I say or do will alter one whit whatever path you choose for me.''

So she could still be difficult! Bryce grimaced, but plunged ahead. ''It's not safe for you to go back to London.''

Her response was dry. ''I believe someone made that abundantly clear.''

''Until Huxford has need of either of us or else deems the entire enterprise an exercise in futility, it seems best that you continue on here for a time, especially considering our—er, unusual circumstances.''

''I see.''

''It's a matter of your protection, you see, keeping up the appearance of a marriage.''

''That doesn't make it right or honest.''

Bryce stirred uncomfortably as she put an unerring finger on the most salient point. Damned if this wasn't the most awkward mess he'd ever encountered! She was neither mistress nor wife, but duty and shared tragedy bound them, and hate and vengeance served no purpose.

''No, but neither of us has much choice in the matter. In light of that, I thought . . .'' He hesitated and cleared his throat. ''Perhaps we should both try to put the past behind us.''

''Are you saying I've done enough penance for my sins?''

''I'm saying we need to begin again.''

''At what, Bryce?''

He made a helpless gesture. ''Finding a way to exist peacefully so long as we're together.''

''That's very forbearing of you, considering everything.'' The wind lifted the coppery tendrils wisping over her forehead, and she turned to meet his gaze for the first time. Her eyes were hazy with indifference. ''I assume existing peacefully means I will share your bed again?''

He choked. ''That's not what I meant!''

''If that's what you want, I can't object.'' She shrugged. ''There's no profit in it, is there?''

"Damn you, Genny!" He scowled ferociously. "I'd never . . . Just what kind of man do you think I am?"

A flicker of infinite sadness crossed her face, almost instantly replaced with her now ever-present abstraction. "When did that ever really matter?"

With that she left him, slowly retracing the path back up to the mellow red-brick manor. Bryce stared after her as though she were a gorgon risen from a dragon's tears. What she had become out of self-defense against him was a monstrous creation, a lifeless parody of the vibrant woman he'd first known.

Bryce sank down on the low stone wall and buried his face in his palms, clashing emotions rocketing him in every direction. He knew he should still condemn Genevieve for her crimes, but she'd paid dearly already. Who was he to require more? Perhaps he'd been too willing to believe the worst and accept the most damning evidence, while ignoring the truth of what she was that lay in the experience of his own heart. That much, he could admit now, was his failure, not hers. Their relationship had been twisted by the deceptions they'd both perpetrated. How could he say any longer that her motives were less pure than his own?

Somewhere under that lethargic armor was the real Genevieve Maples. And somehow, Bryce vowed, *somehow* he'd find a way to release her, to bring her back to her true self so that when all of this was over she could take up her life again. He couldn't expect more, not after all that had happened, but at least he could do that much for her.

And for myself, his deepest heart whispered. Because despite everything, he missed the little general like hell, and he wanted her back.

But Bryce's determination was destined to be frustrated over and over again by Genevieve's cool indifference. He was somewhat heartened by Allegra's report that Genevieve had begun a new portfolio of designs for Maebella Smythe, but despite his repeated efforts to draw her into a meaningful discussion of their problems, to somehow break down the barriers she'd erected and find common ground again, she remained as aloof and untouched as a princess in a tower.

Still, he refused to let her merely sit staring out a window every day, insisting she come watch him work the horses, or join Sir Theodore in a game of hazard, or give Jack Potts a drawing lesson. She was even stoically unconcerned when he arranged a simple reinternment ceremony for Everett Maples's remains in the Cormick hilltop plot. With Jack Potts, Genevieve was more herself than anyone else, so when the lad asked her to come with him to the November fifth Guy Fawkes bonfires and celebrations in the village, Bryce decreed that they'd all go so she would have no reason to decline.

The evening's high celebrations in the village of Clare had already begun when the inhabitants of Clare Hill arrived in carriage and wagons. The music of pipe, tabor, and fiddle clamored from every lane, and impromptu dances took place under the flambeaux on each corner. Bands of children carrying straw-stuffed effigies of the infamous Guy Fawkes, who'd tried to blow up Parliament and King James with it in 1605, raced from house to house begging for treats and wood to add to the pyres to be lit at the end of the festivities. Fortunately, after two days of rain and blustery weather, the night had turned fair and chill, just right to bring roses to one's cheeks and an appetite for hot brandy toddies to warm the blood.

Like Allegra, Genevieve was bundled in bonnet, cloak, and mittens, and she held Jack's hand tightly and listened to his animated chatter as they followed Sir Theodore and his daughter through the whirl of parades, speeches, and dancers. Though the village lay only a brisk walk from the manor, it was the first outing Genevieve had made away from Clare Hill since her arrival, and her distraction was shaken by an edgy nervousness, as if she expected someone from the crowd to leap at her with a knife. Seeming to sense this, Bryce never strayed far from her elbow, but in his new caped greatcoat, he seemed more ominous than reassuring.

They walked down winding lanes past charming old pargetted half-timbered and pink plaster houses to the site of the bonfires. In another frame of mind Genevieve might have enjoyed the tiny shops and tidy gardens, but her black humor and weltering anxiety bubbled and churned within her, so she took little note of the sights. Jack urged them on, unwilling to miss even a moment of the pyrotechnic displays, most of which had been donated by Sir Theodore himself.

They took positions in the circle of spectators around the largest bonfire, and Jack joined the cordon of excited children dancing inside the ring with their straw effigies. The first explosion of fireworks evoked shrieks and "ohs" of appreciation from the lively crowd, but Genevieve jumped and covered her ears. She felt Bryce's massive presence directly behind her, and he leaned forward to speak into her ear so that he could be heard over the crowd.

"Are you all right?"

Genevieve's bonnet bobbed affirmatively, but her shoulders under the heavy cloak shook with tension. In her overly sensitive state, she felt bombarded from every direction with myriad sensory impressions. Happy shouts sounded like a banshee's screams. Burning powder from the fireworks scorched her nostrils with a battle's stench. The flare of torches blinded her, and the press of bodies was smothering, forcing her to take shallow breaths through her mouth to fight her rising nausea. It was suddenly more than she could take, and she turned abruptly.

"Where do you think you're going?" Bryce demanded, blocking her path.

Bonnet brim lowered, eyes to the ground, she shook her head. "I've had enough."

"By God, so have I!" he snapped, suddenly infuriated. He grabbed her arm and swung her back around to face the bonfire now being lit by a group of villagers with torches. "You and your megrims have been coddled long enough, General. A month and a half is sufficient time to at least pretend you're recovering, and I won't have you spoiling the others' fun with a fit of temperament."

"It's not that," she protested weakly. Allegra and Sir Theodore continued to watch the festivities, oblivious to the sudden tension erupting between the couple next to them.

"What is it other than pure damned selfishness?" Anger darkened his tone. "You're in love with self-pity. You want everyone to think you're fragile and treat you like a crystal doll."

"That's not true," she said, her breath coming shorter with growing agitation.

"I know how strong you really are. This weakness of heart has all been another act, hasn't it?" he demanded harshly. "A war of nerves to play on our sympathies!"

Sparks from the crackling flames of the bonfire leaped skyward into the darkness, scattering like her fleeing composure. With a series of wild yells, the children began to pitch their Guy Fawkes effigies onto the pyre. Genevieve tugged at her captured arm, and her voice rose. "You can't know how I feel."

"I know you've been acting about as alive as one of those straw men. Your own grandfather wouldn't know you!"

"Leave Grandpapa out of this," she cried. "You're not fit to say his name!"

It was the first sign of her fighting spirit Bryce had seen in weeks. Encouraged, he pressed harder. "That crazy old reprobate. What did he ever do but get himself killed?"

"He saved my life!"

"For what? This living death you're leading? You're wasting the sacrifice he made. Maybe you should have died instead of him!"

Genevieve jerked out of his grasp with a strength that surprised him, and her expression beneath the demure brim of her bonnet was a mixture of livid hate and stark despair. "Damn you! I wish I *had*!"

She plunged into the gyrating circle of dancing children and was swept around the towering bonfire before Bryce realized her intent. He darted after her, but suddenly Jack was swinging on one hand, slowing him down. Bryce shouted her name, straining to see through the flickering yellow light. Orange and red flames leaped and danced, crackling and consuming the pile while music and drums and laughter filled the air like the billowing smoke. There! He spotted a flurry of dark cloak disappearing into the crowd.

"Jack!" Bryce bent and shouted in the boy's ear. "Tell my father I'll take care of Miss Genny."

"Aye, Cap!" The boy gave a saucy salute just as he'd seen Taffy do and hurried to obey.

But it wasn't as simple a matter to catch up with Genevieve as Bryce expected. The boisterous crowd of merry-makers slowed him at every turn. Growing more and more anxious each minute she was out of his sight, he pushed through the throngs, hurrying toward the spot where they'd left the carriage, only to find it unattended. Now his concern redoubled. Though unlikely, what if the Abbot still had someone watching for just such an opportunity? Upset, Genevieve might do anything foolish. Bryce cursed his stupidity. Had an arrogant miscalculation placed her in jeopardy again?

He found her bonnet on the path to Clare Hill. Sweating, he prayed it had only been her headlong flight that caused her to lose the headgear. Running now, he followed the path home, leaving the light and merriment behind in the village, climbing the gently sloping pathway toward the manor just in time to see a shadow pass across the lawns.

"Genevieve! For God's sake—Genny!" he roared and charged after her. He caught up with her on the steps of the entrance portico and grabbed her arm, his breath gusting from his lungs in great gulps. "Damnation, Genevieve! Are you quite daft? Why did you run away?"

Her hair had fallen from its pins sometime during her

flight and now spilled down her back in a wild tangle that matched her mood. She turned on him with the fury of a madwoman, digging her nails into his hand and shrieking. "Leave me alone, you cur! You blackguard! I hate you!"

He grunted as her nails scored his skin. With an oath, he hauled her inside, pausing at the base of the staircase in the manor's central hall. A single lamp flickered on a side table, but all the servants had gone to the festivities so the house echoed strangely, the sounds of their labored breathing and scrabbling heels expanding to fill the eerie hollowness.

"Hen-witted female!" he said, pulling her close to control her struggles. "What if the Abbot's men had been waiting for a chance to find you alone?"

She glared at him, her eyes jade-green with rage. "I'd have welcomed them, for they're sure to do me less harm than you!"

Her words struck home, and he winced. Holding her still with one arm around her waist, he gently cupped her wind-cooled cheek with the other hand. His voice was husky with pain of his own. "I don't want to hurt you . . ."

"You're a past master at it!" Her lashes fanned down, shutting out his hateful visage, but he held her close, and the familiar scents of bay rum, wool, and musky male skin mingled with the lingering freshness of the chill night wind and surrounded her, beckoned her into the realm of things she had tried so hard to forget. She moaned softly. "Why can't you leave me alone? I don't want to feel this way. I don't want to feel anything!"

"You can't hide from it forever."

Her eyes flew open, and defiance glittered there. "Don't tell me how I can feel!"

"You don't have a monopoly on suffering, Genevieve." Bryce's mouth thinned into an angry slit. "But you're only hurting yourself this way."

"You have no right—"

"After everything we've been through, I'm probably the only one in the world who does."

His gaze fell upon the trembling outline of her mouth, and his blue eyes clouded. Slowly, he lowered his head, sealing her lips with his own. It was bittersweet, that kiss, fraught with insecurities and possibilities, old hurts and new pleasures. Dazed, Bryce had but one thought. *She feels like home.*

When he lifted his head again, they both shuddered.

"That's one thing you can't deny," he said unsteadily. "God help us both, it's still there."

"No!" She pushed away from the seductive warmth of his bulk. "It doesn't mean anything!" she spat, trapped and desperate. "All 'sound and fury, signifying nothing'!"

Angry frustration etched creases beside Bryce's mouth. "Genevieve—"

"*Nothing*, do you hear?"

He released her suddenly, and she staggered back at the blazing contempt in his eyes, coming up short against the edge of the staircase.

"All right! Bury yourself alive! Entomb your heart and soul with your grief! I'm sorry about Everett, but he's gone. It's easier to languish behind that icy shell than to deal with that or anything else! Well, I can't fight you anymore; you're stronger than I am in this. But I want you to remember one thing, Genevieve."

Shaken by the naked emotion on his voice, she retreated up the first tread of stairs. "Wh-what?"

His features tightened with an awful constriction of sorrow. "It was *my* child, too."

Something shattered within Genevieve, and a strangled cry ripped from her throat as the babe had been ripped from her body. Her hands flew to her mouth, white-knuckled fists pressing against her lips to stifle the sound, but it was too late. Like the trumpets of Jericho, Bryce's bald statement of the one thing she'd never allowed herself to contemplate or accept sounded the collapse of all her defenses. Prickling moisture collected in her eyes and a giant weight pressed her chest, stilling her breath, stopping her heart. A silver tear slid down her cheek.

Bryce regarded her strangely. "You didn't think it mattered to me. Damn you, woman! Of course it did. Only you matter more."

With a sob, the dam of Genevieve's denial ruptured, and the grief, terror, and fury that she had been holding back all these many weeks spilled over and became a raging torrent of scalding, cauterizing tears. She sank down on the stairs, her face in her hands, her slender body convulsed in a paroxysm of racking sobs that devastated the man watching with their sound of utter hopelessness and heart-wrenching despair.

"Genny." His own throat thick with tears, Bryce went to her, pulling her unresisting form into the haven of his arms. Seated on the steps, he held her and rocked her as she wept, murmuring disjointed phrases of comfort into her hair.

"You haven't cried . . . It's all right . . . Cry all you want . . ."

He released the fastening on her cloak and shrugged out of his greatcoat, sitting in the puddle of garments for a long time while she keened her grief and his shirtfront became a sodden rag. She clutched at him almost desperately, as if afraid that he, too, would be taken from her at any moment, and for Bryce that was a true measure of her defeat and the cruelest twist of all, because he knew he was the last person she would ever need or want.

Still, he held her, nuzzling her temple, inhaling her heady woman fragrance, rubbing her quaking shoulders until the painful, cathartic sobs eased. She clung to him, her breath shuddering unevenly, limp with exhaustion and the healing release of emotion.

"Grandpapa," she whispered, anguished. "Oh, God, I miss him!"

"I know, I'm so sorry," Bryce said, rubbing her back. "Someday I hope you'll forgive me for my part in that accident. Neither Huxford nor I ever wanted the old man's death."

"He loved me, and now there's no one . . ." She hiccoughed on a lingering sob. "Why did he do it?"

"Because he loved you. He chose a hero's death, Genny. We should all be as fortunate when our time comes." Bryce looked off in the distance, still tortured by memories of Lyons. "It wasn't wasted like some deaths are. You're still here."

"How can you say that? You should hate me."

He jumped, then shook his dark head. "No, I only hate what you've had to go through."

Her tears began again. "We made a child together, and I didn't even know it until it was too late."

Bryce gently brushed her hair back from her flushed face. "Don't fight it, Genny. You have to grieve to heal."

Her breath caught sharply. "It hurts."

"Aye. But sometimes hurting is the only way to know you're still alive."

His fingertips wiped away the moist tracks of her tears, and he followed their path with his lips, brushing soft kisses across her cheekbones, along the delicate angle of her jaw, to the tremulous corners of her mouth.

With a soft moan, Genevieve turned her head, instinctively seeking the solace of his touch, the reaffirmation of life's most basic truth, to somehow fill the emptiness of the loss they'd both experienced. Bryce responded to that unspoken need, taking her mouth, tasting the essence of her sorrow and sharing his own.

Somehow, comfort changed, transmuted into the undeniable hunger that never failed them, leaping like wildfire through their veins. Genevieve's hands crept around Bryce's neck, and the touch of her fingers against his nape set off explosions of arousal in his brain and his loins.

Breathing harshly, he drew back, and the apology on his lips died as he saw the longing in her soft green eyes. There was peace here, for both of them. He threaded his hands into the springy mass of her hair, holding her gaze intently.

"Genny?"

"Yes."

That simple word of surrender forked through Bryce like a bolt of lightning. He swallowed hard. "I'm not Darcy, Genevieve."

"No."

"I'm not your soldier hero, come to rescue you. It would be a mistake to believe that."

"I know who you are, Bryce." Her mouth—her wonderfully soft, perfect mouth—trembled, and her absolute vulnerability and naked need undid him.

"Help me feel alive again," she whispered in a voice that made him ache.

To Bryce, caught in a mire of need, passion seemed the surest path to atonement, and denial was impossible. Scooping Genevieve into his arms, he carried her upstairs, and it was only much, much later that he wondered at the paradox of her words.

Had he brought her back to life only to hurt her yet again?

Chapter 13

Waking slowly, Genevieve lay quiescent in her sleeping lover's possessive embrace and drowsily examined the complex geometries of the silver frost spangling the windowpanes. Bryce's warm, steady breathing fluttered the tendrils on the nape of her neck, and his arm curled around her waist, tucking her bottom, spoon-fashion, against his hair-dusted thighs. Passion spent for the moment, they cuddled beneath the covers against the room's chill in a homey, tender intimacy while the early-morning clatter of chores drifted from the kitchens and harnesses rattled in the yards outside.

If only we could stay just as we are, she thought, but the impossibility of that wish only made these moments of contentment more precious. Soon the consequences of their actions must be faced, for although they'd found solace and some peace in the release of their bodies, nothing had essentially changed. She still wore the brand of a traitor, and Bryce's honor demanded retribution. Genevieve feared the pleasure she knew he'd found would flay his guilt anew, perhaps start them again on the bitter cycle of cause and blame. Her own desire for vengeance was dulled by her trials, but was forgiveness truly possible for either of them? Genevieve could not guess. She only knew that despite all that had gone before, she'd never really stopped loving Bryce Cormick.

Closing her eyes against the brilliance glittering from the windows and a betraying sting of tears, she prayed for a way to redeem herself in Bryce's eyes. She beseeched the Almighty for a second chance to prove her loyalty. She prayed that Bryce would love her.

"*Mon ange*, don't cry." Bryce's sleep-husky voice was a deep murmur as his lips found the curve of her shoulder.

She drew a shuddering breath. "Last night that's what you wanted."

"What you needed." His hand splayed across the angle of her hipbone, exploring. "There's a difference."

She jumped as his fingers grazed the still-tender welts of tissue on her lower back. "Bryce, don't—"

"Let me see." Adamantly, he drew the covers back, holding her still while his gaze skimmed the puckered pink scar.

Flushing all over, she grabbed at the bedclothes. "Not a pretty sight."

"No, but a worthy one." Dipping his dark head, he laved the ridge of healing flesh with his tongue, making her shiver uncontrollably. Turning her to face him, he retrieved the blankets, enveloping them again in a cocoon of warmth. "Now we're both marked, General."

Hesitantly, she touched him, seeking and finding his old wound. "Yes."

"Once a soldier's prowess was marked by his battle honors, but there are some scars you cannot see." Fingers spread, his palm came to rest over her womb. "Though undoubtedly a complication, I would have spared you this loss if I could."

She bit her lip. " 'Twas your loss as well. Forgive me for not seeing that."

"We both paid the price of our passion." He sighed and traced the lush outline of her perfect mouth with his forefinger. " 'Tis I who should beg forgiveness, for now I repeat the injury."

Peachy color dusted her cheekbones. Looking down,

she focused on the hard delineations of his chest. " 'Tis no injury," she admitted softly, "but a healing."

"If in my greed for you I plant another babe—"

"I'll love and care for it as I would have the other, whatever comes."

He frowned, his mouth grim. "I would never abandon a child of my own body."

She swallowed, afraid he was about to sacrifice the only common ground they had left. "This is the only honest thing we've ever had. Can you turn away from it now?"

His arms tightened around her, and his voice was low and gravelly. "Christ help me in my weakness, I can't."

"Nor can I."

"My beautiful witch." He groaned and kissed her hard. "I promise—"

A ruckus in the corridor interrupted whatever pledge Bryce would have made. Taffy's strident protest split the peace.

"See here, m'lord! You just can't—"

There came the briefest of raps, and the bedroom door burst open.

"What, Bryce, still abed at this hour? What an old woman you've become." The Earl of Huxford strode into the bedchamber as if it were his right. "Come, man, I didn't ride all night to—Well, what have we here?"

"Get the hell out, Hugh!" Bryce snarled, rolling to a sitting position in the bed.

"Didn't realize you were—er, occupied," the earl said, his avid glance taking in Genevieve's bare shoulders and tumbled hair as she struggled to an elbow. He smiled. "But I see that no introductions are necessary."

Genevieve's face flamed with mortification. Bryce swore darkly and pulled the bedclothes up to her throat.

"I'm warning you, Hugh . . ."

"Just as well you're together anyway," the earl said, looking around for a chair. "My news concerns you both. When's breakfast? I'm devilish empty—"

Bryce sprang from the bed with a roar. "Goddammit! That's enough!"

Magnificently nude, primitively enraged by an intrusion into his exclusive territory, all semblance of propriety or obedience to a superior forgotten, Bryce grabbed Huxford by the collar and booted the flabbergasted lord into the hall. The earl landed in an undignified heap at Taffy's feet.

"Feed him, Sergeant!" Bryce barked, then slammed the door with a force that resounded throughout the manor. He turned back to Genevieve, his chest still heaving with the magnitude of his ire. "Damned arrogant aristocrat! Fine thing when a husband can't even make love to his wife in the privacy of his home!"

Genevieve peeped from behind the shelter of the covers. "But you're not my husband, and I'm not your wife," she observed cautiously.

Bryce planted his fists on his lean hips in an attitude of deep chagrin. "Bloody hell! Whatever path has brought us hence, it amounts to the same thing."

"It does?"

His mouth firmed stubbornly. "Yes, it does. And if you think there's any going back for us, you're wrong."

She looked at him in astonishment. It was the closest thing to a statement of commitment she had ever heard from him. Then a tremulous smile tweaked the corners of her mouth, and she giggled.

"The earl's *face* when you—" She flopped back into the pillows, trying to stifle her merriment with little success.

"He deserved it, the ass." Bryce sat down on the side of the bed with a rueful grin, then leaned over and kissed her, chasing away her giggles and replacing it with breathless excitement. "I'm sorry he embarrassed you, *chérie*."

Sobered, she touched his cheek. "He wouldn't have come all this way himself unless it was important."

"No."

A chill ribbon of fear uncurled within her, and she shivered. "The Abbot?"

"Maybe."

She took a deep breath, then climbed out of the bed and reached for the now-familiar paisley robe. "We shouldn't keep him waiting, then."

Bryce caught her close, tilted her chin, and kissed her again. "Try not to worry, General. Everything will be all right."

Strangely calm, she almost believed him. After all, for the first time, Bryce had taken her part over another. It was a small victory, but one to cherish.

From the sideways glances and barely suppressed grins, it appeared no one in the household was unaware of the Earl of Huxford's ignominious expulsion from Bryce's bedchamber or the fact that Genevieve had spent the night in Bryce's bed. Although Allegra was too delicate to mention it directly, Bryce's sister was beaming when she inquired of Genevieve's health as they met in the corridor a short time later. Even Sir Theodore, headed outdoors for his morning ride of inspection, appeared in excessive high spirits as he informed Bryce and Genevieve the earl waited on them in the dining room.

"I don't know whether to be embarrassed or touched by everyone's evident relief that our 'marriage' has resumed," Genevieve muttered, delicate apricot color dotting her cheeks.

Leading her toward the dining room, Bryce tightened his fingers on her elbow. "Their interest is a compliment, an indication of how much everyone here has come to care for you."

She bit her lip, and her gaze clouded with guilt. "How will we ever untangle this coil?"

She was already regretting the passion they'd shared, Bryce realized with a pang. In her black bombazet gown and sedately coiffed chignon, she was slim, elegant, and composed, a far cry from the emotional woman she'd been the night before. No one would ever guess this demure lady was capable of turning a man inside-out with desire, fueling his hunger with a sensuality and responsiveness that banished all doubts. Though she'd begun this subterfuge, he now welcomed it as a method to keep her close in all ways, and if he did not question his own motives, he told himself it was because the earl's arrival demanded immediate attention.

"You concern yourself with trivialities when there are larger matters at stake," he dismissed gruffly. "The legalities will sort themselves out. Come, no doubt Hugh is waiting to rebuke me for my impudence."

But the earl, having dined well on sausages, boiled eggs, and porridge, was in a frame of mind to forget any offense to his illustrious person.

"Ah, there you are!" Huxford said, waving a piece of freshly baked bread dripping with golden honey. "Join me, won't you? I say, Sir Theodore's table is as excellent as ever. Must have something to do with the freshness of country provender."

"Your appetites will eventually kill you, Hugh," Bryce warned amiably, guiding Genevieve to a chair at the table. He walked to the laden sideboard and began to fill two plates. "That is, if I don't do it first."

"No hard feelings, are there?" The earl's jovial tone was belied by the assessment in his flat gray eyes as he took in Genevieve's high color and downcast face. "I do apologize for my abrupt arrival, but 'tis a matter of some urgency." He raised a languid hand. "The door, if you please?"

Bryce set the plates down on the table and wordlessly shut the double doors of the simply decorated room, ensuring their privacy. Seating himself at Genevieve's side, he poured them each coffee and reached for a napkin, deceptively unconcerned. "I gather there's trouble?"

Huxford dropped the unfinished heel of bread onto the empty plate before him and pushed it aside, all affectations of affability erased from his countenance. "Before its usefulness expired, the mark of the Abbot's Seal paid off handsomely. I was able to expose a damned tricky French agent running a Dover tavern, and we broke a code the Abbot's men had used to feed information to the Serbian resistance. Not to mention intercepting several very interesting messages out of Gibraltar and even Elba itself.''

''Not bad. But that's all over now?''

''We knew it was only a matter of time before the Abbot substituted another signature with which to contact his minions.''

''And?'' Bryce prompted around a bite of bacon.

''And we were lucky. From the last missive we received, we deduced the Abbot has quit the country.''

Genevieve made an involuntary sound of surprised relief, her fork poised over the barely touched contents of her plate. She blushed as the earl's charcoal gaze swung to her. ''That's good, isn't it?''

''Not at all. He's plotting an assassination.''

A deadly blue light ignited Bryce's eyes. Quietly, he set down his utensils. His very stillness unnerved Genevieve. ''Who?'' he demanded.

''The only man capable of foiling Bonaparte's return should he attempt it.''

Breath hissed between Bryce's teeth. ''Wellington.''

''Exactly.''

A silent pall hung over the table. The magnitude of the potential devastation not only to Britain but to the entire European community should the greatest military hero of the past decade be eliminated was overwhelming.

''You see how diabolically clever the Abbot is,'' Huxford continued after the pregnant pause. ''Murdering the duke would serve a twofold purpose: a signal to Boney that the time to move is right, and the removal of the only other military mind who could thwart a campaign to return the emperor to the throne.''

''But . . . but now that you know of the plot, cannot measures and safeguards be taken to protect the duke?'' Genevieve asked in confusion.

''Of course, but that is insufficient. It's imperative we

uncover the conspirators before they put their plans into action.''

''What can be done? Isn't Wellington in Paris?'' Genevieve asked.

''All the world's in Paris, my dear, including the Abbot himself now, somewhere among all the émigrés, courtiers, sycophants, diplomats, fashionable English visitors, and opportunists,'' Huxford answered. ''Which makes our charge that much harder, rather like plucking the proverbial needle from the haystack. No easy task, even for the Griffin.''

''What are you suggesting, Hugh?'' Bryce demanded.

Shrugging, Huxford plucked an object from his waistcoat and slid it across the table. Genevieve's fork clattered against her china plate, and she stared in horrified repugnance at the glittering pink gem slithering on its tarnished chain across the shiny wood. Bile rose in her throat at the sight of the Abbot's Seal, the originator of all her troubles, and nausea coupled with a building dread.

''You said the seal was worthless now,'' Bryce said, his eyes narrowing suspiciously.

Huxford turned his genial smile toward Genevieve. ''Except as bait.''

The blood drained out of Genevieve's face, and she caught her breath.

''You've lost your mind, my lord,'' Bryce said flatly.

''Consider first, my friend,'' the earl continued. ''The lovely Genevieve is the only person known to have outwitted the Abbot and lived, and his memory is notoriously long. Should she appear at some of the more lavish functions of the court of Louis, sporting this mysterious antiquity, the symbol the Abbot most desires—well, she'd be irresistible, wouldn't she?''

Bryce scowled. ''And as defenseless as a lamb led to the slaughter!''

''With the Griffin at her side?'' Huxford made a disbelieving moue. ''You never did give yourself enough credit. Remember, the Abbot once intended to present the seal to Bonaparte. You know the legends. Glory, success, and power belong to the one who holds the gem. I tell you, the Abbot will be compelled to retrieve the token, and then we'll have him!''

"You don't believe that superstitious drivel, do you, Hugh?''

The earl chuckled. "I have to admit things have been going extraordinarily well since it's come into my possession, but we have only to remember poor Mr. Maples to see the fallacy of any such mystical belief.''

Bryce's mouth firmed into a straight, grim line. "It's too dangerous. I won't allow it.''

"It's not your decision, Bryce," Genevieve said quietly.

"Nor is it his!''

"You're right." She folded her hands on the table and stared at them. "It's mine.''

"Genny—''

Ignoring Bryce, she raised her troubled gaze to meet the earl's. "You need a larger panorama to display your *bait*, my lord. The stage, for example.''

Huxford nodded, his expression calculating. "Very good. Very good indeed.''

"Cormick and Maples are well-known names in the theater," Genevieve said slowly. "Perhaps a European tour, beginning in the French capital?''

Bryce vaulted to his feet, and his fist hit the table. "Dammit, no!''

Stretched taunt, Genevieve's temper flared. "I'll do it without you if I must!''

"What you're contemplating is suicidal!" Bryce said between gritted teeth. "You don't have to prove anything.''

"Don't I?" She laughed without humor. "Do you think I want to spend the rest of my life hiding from some faceless threat who wants to kill me?''

Bryce dismissed her question with a sharp gesture. "There are ways . . .''

"And no matter what you think of my actions until

now," Genevieve continued relentlessly, "how can I ignore the chance to bring my grandfather's murderer to justice?"

She watched the silent battle on Bryce's face with her heart in her throat. *And how will you ever come to truly forgive me and love me if I cannot prove myself a patriot instead of a traitor you despise?*

"You must admit the plan has merit, my friend," the earl interjected.

A shiver of stage fright tingled down Genevieve's spine. She had never performed except under heavy makeup and costume, and the thought of acting a part without the protection of a disguise was a frightening one. She lacked the talent, the know-how, the magic a truly great performer needed. She would botch any role and make a fool of herself, but she had no choice. To attract the Abbot's attention in a city of millions, to prove herself to Bryce, she *had* to do it.

"I know I'm not capable of much," she said, screwing up her courage, "but surely there is some minor play or perhaps a series of vignettes that my lack of talent might not spoil?"

"What the devil are you talking about?" Bryce demanded. "Woman, you've played the varied parts in our own personal drama with such realism no fictional character is beyond your reach. Kate the shrew, Juliet, Desdemona—I daresay Mrs. Letchfield would quake in her slippers should you become her competition."

She was taken aback by this high praise, but still hesitated. "Then you think it could work?"

"With B. D. Cormick as her coach," Huxford said, "how could it not?"

"I said Genevieve possessed the talent to handle dramatic roles, not that I'll allow her to take part," Bryce growled. "And I'm certainly not going to lend my assistance to such a prize bit of insanity!"

"Then you abandon me to my fate." Even without Bryce's help, this was the chance she'd prayed for just that morning. She knew now that the Lord answered prayers, though sometimes in frightening ways, and though her blood ran chill with fear, she dared not miss the opportunity. Resigned, yet adamant, she turned to Huxford. "What would you have me do, my lord?"

"Well, we'll have to hire a troupe to support your performances," the earl mused, steepling his fingers under his chin and raising his eyes to the ceiling beams. "And of course, there's the matter of a bodyguard—"

Bryce swore roundly and jammed a hand through his ebony hair in agitation. France, again. He had thought never to return to the country of his birth and the wrenching dichotomy of loyalties, certainly not in a resurrection of the Griffin and all the hell that persona entailed. Yet how could he let Genevieve face the Abbot alone? He'd almost lost her once, and though their relationship was a welter of confusion, he couldn't take that chance again, no matter what it cost him personally. He looked at Genevieve.

"You're determined, are you, General?"

She lifted her chin stubbornly. "My future depends on it." *And whatever happiness we may find together.*

"It's your life we're talking about," Bryce said, frustration darkening his visage.

Genevieve drew a deep, shuddering breath. "I know," she whispered, repeating the appeal she'd made the night before. "Help me."

"Hell!" His shoulders slumped, and he looked from her to Huxford and back again. "I suppose it's the only way to keep you out of trouble."

Her half smile was tremulous with relief. "Probably."

"I can always depend on the Griffin," the earl said, well satisfied. "Now, let us formulate a plan . . ."

Just over a fortnight later, Genevieve stood at Bryce's side on stage at the Odèon Theater off the Rue de la Seine receiving, quite to her surprise, a thunderous ovation for a performance that until that moment she had not been quite certain she could pull off. True, a goodly portion of the audience was upper-class British whose appetites for entertainment had been jaded by a long season of Parisian delights, but the vignettes of famous Shakespearean lovers that had been the core of the newly formed Cormick-Maples Company's performance was a crowd-pleaser, a reminder of things English for those who would be spending the upcoming holiday season as exiles, as well as a novelty for the French themselves and other foreign drama aficionados who had flocked to the capital. To all appearances, the Cormick-Maples duo were also newlyweds, a romantic fact that only increased ticket sales.

Exhilarated, flushed with success, she curtsied her thanks, then accepted from the manager a bouquet of hothouse lilies, a symbol of the Bourbon restoration. The heart-shaped bodice of her glimmering ivory satin and rose silk gown framed the pink gem hanging around her neck, and though it weighed little, it felt as heavy as a hangman's noose. Holding hands, she and Bryce stepped back together as the curtain slid shut a final time. The moment the two edges of fabric met, she turned and threw her arms around his neck.

"Thank you," she murmured, quite overcome. She nuzzled his smoothly shaven cheek, crushing her flowers but not even caring. "Thank you for giving me this. I had no idea . . ."

His fingers tangled in her hair, held high with strands of pearls, and he pulled her even closer, sharing her victory for a brief moment. "You shouldn't be so surprised. You're a fine actress, and you worked hard. That's why they loved you."

She leaned back, smiling up at him in wonder. The chemistry between them on stage had been truly magic, from the hilarity of the shrewish Kate and her lusty Petruchio to Juliet's poignant suicide over her dead Romeo.

"Both in front of the curtain and behind the scenes, you make of me more than I am, Bryce Cormick. It was like a dream."

Bryce's expression sobered, and he hooked his forefinger under the chain hanging around her neck. "It's no fantasy, General, but a deadly game. You can't ever forget it."

Blinking as if splashed by shower of icy water, she nodded. "I know."

"Come." Bryce drew her toward the wings, nodding in Taffy McKee's direction. The Welshman was never far these days, for the former sergeant was the first perimeter of defense in ever-increasing circles of bodyguards and watchmen designed to protect Genevieve and snare the Abbot. "We're to be on display at Lady Oxford's reception, and we can't be late. After all, that's what we're here for, isn't it?"

Swallowing, she nodded again, her euphoria draining away.

It had been a difficult transition from Suffolk to Paris, even with the earl to expedite matters and arrange for a premier performance at the Odèon. Allegra and Sir Theodore had been mystified at the sudden decision, but Bryce had merely told them that he needed whatever money he could raise. Since he hadn't accepted his father's offer of financial help, the story rang true enough to answer most questions. And since it was more than evident that he and Genevieve had reconciled their differences, it was also perfectly reasonable that they would not wish to be separated.

But their farewell to those at Clare Hill had been emotional, with Genevieve clinging to Allegra and Jack Potts until the last moment. The black-eyed lad had been a bit put out at being left behind in Suffolk, but Genevieve knew that he'd be fine under Allegra's protective wing and tried not to worry, though she'd waved at the boy from the carriage until he was too small to see.

After that, everything had been a mad rush. Choosing a production format, hiring a small company of players, selecting an eye-catching wardrobe from Maebella's growing stock and making sufficient explanations of her old friend, then facing a rough channel crossing and an excruciating journey to Paris over muddy roads had been difficult and trying, especially coupled with the pressure to memorize lines and rehearse with a man whose disapproval and cool aloofness grew in reverse proportion to their distance from the French capital.

Not that he had ignored her completely, Genevieve thought. But the difficulties of the five-day overland journey and the rush to ready their stage production had presented few opportunities for privacy, and out of consideration for her fatigue, Bryce had made no "husbandly" demands, merely holding her as she slept or else avoiding her bed altogether on the pretext of standing watch. Genevieve tried to appreciate his thoughtfulness, but she feared the distance he seemed to be trying to place between them again almost as much as the increasingly frequent glimpses of a frightening individual she knew as the Griffin.

His demeanor was at once abstracted and watchful. She saw how he must have been during his assignments in the war—suspicious, hard, living on nerve and instinct. And as soon as they'd reached the shores of France, Genevieve was certain he'd gone to war. On more than one occasion during their journey, he'd stopped the coaches in order to scout ahead on his own, and he'd had no patience with anything less than his own exacting perfection in vigilance, snapping at everyone around him, including his old friend, Taffy.

Now, as she entered Lady Oxford's glittering salon on Bryce's arm a short time after leaving the Odèon, she wondered who he really was. Certainly not Darcy. Probably not even B. D. Cormick. No, she decided, it was the Griffin whose eagle's eye scanned the elaborately dressed and perfumed crowd sipping Bordeaux wines and nibbling *gâteau*. He was searching for some clue, *something* that would identify the Abbot before he could set his nefarious plans in motion. Involuntarily, Genevieve shuddered. They were deceivers all, and only the cleverest would survive.

"Another performance, General," Bryce murmured, sensing her tension as they moved forward in the receiving line to be presented to their hostess, "and a more demanding one. Have you reconsidered this lunacy?"

Genevieve straightened her spine. "You may watch me captivate this crowd as well," she said loftily, then gritted her teeth and proceeded to do so.

Lady Oxford, a youngish matron with ostrich plumes in her carroty hair and a penchant for dramatic attitudes, was effusive in her compliments to both Bryce and Genevieve.

"My friend Lord Huxford said you were both rare talents. And what a thrill to finally have some civilized entertainments in the city," she said. "Paris has its charms, I'm sure, but I must admit sometimes I pine for home, or at least for proper sanitation. How do you find the city, Mrs. Cormick?"

"I confess I've seen little of it," Genevieve said. "We only just arrived, and then the rehearsals, you see . . ."

Truthfully, Genevieve was both fascinated and appalled by what she'd seen of the capital, mostly from the safety of a carriage or the window of the suite of rooms Huxford had arranged for them at the Hôtel des Étrangers. While the boulevards were wide and lined with parks and elegant dwellings, just behind them lay confusing narrow warrens of canted buildings and twisting, turning lanes with open sewers down the center, little changed since the city's medieval beginnings. While the eye found much to delight, the nose was constantly assaulted by odors best left uninvestigated.

King Louis resided in the Tuileries Palace, and further down the River Seine on the Îsle de la Cité, the Cathedral of Notre Dame rose over the city with its distinct flying buttresses and incredible stained-glass windows. But the November rains had transformed the parade grounds of the Place de la Concorde into an ocean of mud, and it was difficult to see how even the advent of spring might transform the dismal landscape. Still, there were the cafés and the opera and the gaieties of the upcoming holiday season, the king's Sunday receptions and countless balls, so much activity, so many people, and somewhere among them, a spy plotting murder. Genevieve thrust the thought aside to continue her exchange with Lady Oxford.

"I'm sure I'll enjoy exploring the city when time allows. I've an especial interest in taking some of the latest French fashions back with me."

"I'll be most happy to take you around to Madame Yvonne's, but my dear, I hope you'll take it as a compliment when I say that you don't dress at all like an English-woman anyway!"

Modestly, Genevieve refrained from explaining the gown was of her own design, though the comment pleased her, for French fashion still set the standard for modern taste. "Thank you, I am fortunate to have the services of Madame Bella in London."

"I must have her direction when I return home, for she is undoubtedly a genius. Your gown sets off that most unusual jewel to perfection."

Genevieve's hand flew to her breast, touching the cool pink gemstone. Self-consciously, she lowered her hand, forcefully reminded of her mission here. "It's a very old piece I . . . I received from my grandfather."

"Well, you make a charming picture, my dear." Lady Oxford tapped Bryce's forearm with her fan in a flirtatious manner. "You must be on your guard at all times, sir. There are many Parisian swains who would steal away your lovely madame. Ah, and here are some of them now."

Lady Oxford swept Genevieve into a circle of society bucks, diplomats, and military attachés, ardent theater lovers all, introducing her to Chevalier du Roche, a slender royalist of middle years attached to the prince royal's household; Colonel Breshnell of the Fifty-Second Dragoons; and Prince Deter Deberg of a minor Baltic state, among others. But Genevieve was especially delighted when she saw a particular apple-cheeked face among the group.

"Baron von Throder!"

"My dear Miss Maples—or should I say Frau Cormick? It is a pleasure to see you again." The portly Prussian diplomat bowed over her hand, his light-colored eyes twinkling with humor.

"How kind of you to remember me."

"But of course I remember!" The baron shook his well-groomed silver head, and his expression sobered. "I was saddened by your illustrious grandfather's passing. A great loss for the theater. But you own performance tonight was wonderful, and a living and fitting tribute to Everett Maples's great talent."

Genevieve's throat tightened, and she squeezed the baron's thick, short-fingered hand fervently. "Thank you. I only hope to be worthy of Grandpapa's legacy."

"Indeed you are, my dear. My congratulations."

Genevieve would have liked to discuss her grandfather further, but Lady Oxford was already urging her toward the next group. With a final grateful glance at the baron for his kind compliments, she drew a deep, fortifying breath and continued her foray into society.

For the remainder of the evening, Genevieve sparkled and scintillated, keeping up an amusing flow of witty conversation, playing the flirt to such perfection she was constantly surrounded by a circle of admirers, while at her side Bryce grew more and more silent. When supper was announced, he reclaimed her from the earnest British Colonel Breshnell, and they lingered for a moment's respite in the ornate salon as the guests in their peacock raiment migrated toward the dining room.

"If you are quite finished captivating every man here, General," Bryce said, "there's someone who wishes to meet you."

The demanding role Genevieve played was so exactly opposite her temperament and mood that she was drained and shaky, and Bryce's snide tone rankled her nerves. "I'm merely following the earl's orders. Aren't I being conspicuous enough?"

As he drew her through the door of a small antechamber, Bryce's lean cheeks flexed with irritation. "You've half the émigré population sniffing up your skirts, from the youngest fuzzy-cheeked boys to the most aged roués, if that's what you mean. How will I tell the difference between the Abbot and someone expecting to tumble an actress?"

"Use your imagination!" she snapped, pricked by words that touched a nerve. She'd never meant to become a demimondaine, but the role matched her situation. Living with a man without benefit of clergy made her only a mistress, and it was never what she'd envisioned for herself. Guilt made her touchy, but on the point of giving Bryce a piece of her mind, she paused, struck by a woman's instinctive understanding. "You're jealous."

His look was contemptuous. "Don't be ridiculous. I know where you sleep."

She was stunned; her momentary gratification evaporated. Would he always reduce their relationship to that elementary level? With a flash of insight, she realized that it was his way of denying any deeper emotional commitment. He could reap the pleasures of her flesh without having to admit to himself he cared for a traitor. He could pretend that he simply used her as she deserved, and never know what he denied himself.

But she was trying to prove herself, wasn't she? Risking her life as bait in Huxford's spy trap. What would Bryce do when he no longer had that excuse to keep her at a safe emotional distance? Doubts assailed Genevieve. Maybe Bryce wasn't capable of love as she knew it, as she needed it. Maybe he'd find some other reason to reject her. And maybe she was a fool to dream of more than he could give. Helpless, she knew only time would tell.

A door opened opposite, and she hastily composed her features just as a tall gentleman in a plain blue frock coat entered the anteroom, followed by two aides.

"I would speak privately," he said, dismissing the aides with a wave. They bowed back out of the room as he turned to Bryce. "Mr. Cormick?"

Bryce made a leg. "Your Grace."

A ripple of shock raced through Genevieve as she recognized Arthur Wellesley, the Duke of Wellington himself. Quite larger and much handsomer than she had expected, he carried his middle years well; his step was youthful, his carriage and bearing military and erect. His deep-set blue eyes and strong profile accentuated the air of authority he wore as naturally as the simple coat. He shook Bryce's hand, eyeing him narrowly.

"You were at Vitoria."

"You have a long memory, my lord."

The duke smiled with a glimmer of the self-deprecating humor for which "Old Nosey" was justifiably loved by his men. "Perhaps just an eye for a fellow campaigner. I've heard of your service to the crown, Cormick. An estimable record. And here I shall be in your debt."

"I'm honored to do what I can, sir." Bryce drew Genevieve up beside him. "And this is—"

The duke took Genevieve's hand and bent over it. "Lord Huxford has already explained Mrs. Cormick's valiant part in this. It is my pleasure, madame."

"Thank you, Your Grace," she said, her eyes wide as she sank into a curtsy.

"Nay, it is I who should thank you." The duke shook his head ruefully. "Although I cannot say I approve. Indeed, I vastly regret the risk you take for my sake."

"My lord, I am well acquainted with the Abbot's viciousness," she replied softly, touching the cool weight of the Abbot's Seal without thinking.

"So this is the bauble?" Wellington examined the gem closely. "Intriguing. Another of Boney's eagles. But to risk an antiquity is one thing, while a lady's fate is quite another."

"The nation owes you a debt that cannot be repaid," Genevieve replied. "If only I have the means to dislodge this villain before irreparable harm is done, how can I be less courageous than you?"

"Well said, madame!" The duke chuckled and caught Bryce's eye. "She makes a good soldier, eh?"

"The general makes up in courage what she sometimes lack in sense."

That produced a full-fledged grin. "Are you a thorn in the Griffin's side, my dear?"

"On occasion, my lord, I am the entire rosebush," she answered honestly.

Wellington's heavy lids drooped to cover his amusement, then he sobered. "I'm still of the opinion that my Lord Huxford has overreacted to this so-called plot. There have been plots against me before and doubtless will again. I know I am much hated here in France, but I have duties to perform as ambassador, and I cannot become a recluse. But it rankles that Huxford wants to hide me behind this lovely lady's skirts. I've a mind to call off the entire enterprise."

"I have a personal interest in catching the Abbot, as well as a patriotic one, my lord," Genevieve said. "You cannot dissuade me in this."

"Every precaution is being taken to safeguard Genevieve, I assure you," Bryce said. "And I have sources from the lowest strata to the most elite. Sooner or later some whisper of the Abbot will come to my ears. I will keep you informed of any developments."

Wellington nodded. "Then let us see how we go on for a time. We will meet again. And Cormick?"

"My lord?"

"See that you take damned good care of your rose, eh?"

Shortly after their interview with the duke, they made their farewells to Lady Oxford. Genevieve was so fatigued after the long and eventful evening, she could hardly climb the stairs to their suite at the hotel. Nevertheless, she smiled at the image of Bryce as her gardener. As everyone knew, roses needed a lot of love to flourish. Dared she hope Bryce might eventually see that, too?

"The duke was most gallant," she murmured as Bryce inserted the key in the lock.

"You charmed him as easily as the other besotted fools at Lady Oxford's," Bryce replied sourly, ushering her into the small but well-appointed salon with its Savonnerie carpets and decorative Thomire bronzes. A fire crackled in the marble fireplace, dispelling some of the November chill, and between the doors leading off to the bedrooms and dressing closets a small filigree lamp burned on a narrow Empire-style table whose top was already littered with a ball of old yarn, a perfectly preserved aspen leaf, and three round pebbles—the beginning of Genevieve's newest collection of magpie finds. While her eccentricity might amuse him and surely served as a barometer to chart her moods, tonight Bryce had no patience with it. "And must you collect this trash?"

She sighed at his belligerent tone. "Spare me your complaints, Bryce. I'm too tired, and that's not what this is really about anyway."

"Perhaps you're right. But I'm not complaining. I'm simply amazed at how you relish the role of simpering flirt. Give me the damned seal so I can have Taffy take it to the vault."

Her temper frayed by too much tension, Genevieve removed her cloak and long kid gloves, then pulled the chain over her head and practically flung it at him.

"Here, take it. You know how I hate the feel of it against my skin. It's cold and insensitive, just like you!"

Bryce stared at her, impatience hardening his features. "This assignment is going to be difficult enough without your enticing every lusty beau you meet, you know."

"Since you have such an obvious disgust of me," she returned heatedly, "there's certainly no reason for you to continue to share my bed!"

Bryce's fist clenched around the Abbot's Seal, but his features remained impassive. "As you wish."

"Fine!" Hiding her hurt at his lack of resistance to her impulsive statement, Genevieve hugged herself and stared into the coals glowing in the fireplace. She was suddenly fiercely glad no further intimacy had been possible since leaving Clare Hill. Passion's ties would only destroy her in the end.

"I'll take this to Taffy," Bryce said quietly. He seemed to hesitate. "Shall I send the maid up to help you?"

She shook her head in stubborn silence, keeping her back toward him. She only relaxed when the latch clicked shut behind him, and then it was to take a deep shuddering breath to prevent the tears stinging behind her eyes from falling. Setting her chin, she went into the bedroom, so dejected she didn't even bother to take the lamp, making do instead with the long panels of golden light that fell from the doorway into the airy chamber.

She felt her way to the side of the bed, working at the concealed ribbon of her bodice, wondering how or even if she could take back her hasty words. A black shape stepped out from the depths of the window drapes.

The Abbot!

Abject terror ripped a scream from Genevieve's lungs. She lunged away, shrieking, scrambling for the lighted doorway. A distant part of herself marveled that he'd found her after only a single showing of the seal. The irony was that she didn't even have it now, and he would surely kill her for nothing!

"No, my dear—"

A hand tangled in her gown. With another terrorized scream, Genevieve pulled away and felt more than heard the delicate fabric rip. The light flickered in the doorway, and suddenly there was another deadly shadow, sinister in its utter silence, falling upon her assailant with a murderous frenzy of blows. Released, Genevieve fell to the carpet, sprawled among a shower of fragrant, leafy stems. A final, resounding crack and all was still, except for a man's ragged breathing.

"Genny," Bryce croaked. On his knees, he straddled the other still form. "Are you hurt?"

"N-no." She was amazed she could speak at all.

"Bring the lamp."

Scrabbling on her hands and knees, she staggered to her feet and ran to bring the light. She returned at once, her ruined gown falling off her shoulders, dreading what she would see. Lifting the lamp high, she swallowed and forced herself to look.

A corn-yellow head lying on a bed of strewn lilies.

Wisps of green florist's tissue.

A swollen face with one eye rapidly turning the exact shade as a shocking violet-colored waistcoat.

"Oh, my God!" Genevieve gasped. "Jules!"

Chapter 14

"You damned imbecile! You're lucky you're not on your way to hell!"

Murderously angry, Bryce paced back and forth while Genevieve applied a cool compress to the side of Jules Chesterson's puffy jaw and discolored eye.

"Just wanted to surprise Genevieve," Jules mumbled, wincing as she gently blotted his bruised face. He still seemed a trifle groggy from the blow that had rendered him unconscious. "Gave the maid a franc so I could deliver my bouquet in person, but I guess I fell asleep waiting."

Bryce swore softly, virulently, crushing the remnants of Jules's floral offering under his heels and filling the bedchamber with the cloying scent of lilies. "You hen-witted peacock! I may have to beat some sense into you yet!"

"Bryce, calm down," Genevieve pleaded, tugging at the paisley robe she'd thrown over her ruined gown. "It's all over now."

"Meant no harm, truly," Jules said, aggrieved. "Just wanted to see you. Congratulate you on your recovery and your performance. Better than King Harold by far!"

Genevieve hid a smile while dabbing at a split on Jules's lip. "That's very kind of you, I'm sure. Now hold still."

"Missed you something terrible. When Miss Smythe

told me you were in Paris, I had to come. Never meant to give you such a fright, you know.''

"Yes, I know," Genevieve soothed. "It was a lovely gesture. It's just that my nerves have been rather over-wrought of late.''

Bryce snorted and jammed his trembling hands into his pockets. When he'd heard Genevieve's scream, he'd moved on instinct. Thankfully, Chesterson's ineptness at self-defense had produced insensibility before the Griffin's lethal hands had throttled the very life out of the coxcomb, but it had been a near thing, and inside, Bryce shook with reaction.

Jules commiserated with Genevieve's delicate nervous constitution. "This wretched city is enough to bring on the vapors in anyone. For a beaten people, I've never seen such belligerence, such defiance! Bonapartist slogans scrawled everywhere, and French officers challenging our own good English soldiers to duels on the slightest pretext! Why, I was in Tortoni's just yesterday when a lieutenant of the Garde du Corps insulted a pair of dragoons, and the skirmish that followed left three lying dead in the filthy gutters!''

"Dreadful," Genevieve agreed, fussily wringing out the compress again. "I'm afraid you're going to look like you've been brawling, too, Jules.''

The dandy gingerly examined his damaged visage with his fingertips, horrified at his distorted features. Losing his patience completely, Bryce grabbed the young man's arm and jerked him to his feet.

"Be thankful your vanity is all that suffered, Chesterson," Bryce growled, dragging him toward the front door. "Now get the hell out of here. And stay away from my wife!''

Jules bristled. "Now see here—''

Genevieve hastily intervened. "Yes, Jules, dear, you'd best go. Will you be able to make it back to your lodgings, or should we call someone to assist you?''

"I can manage," Jules said sullenly.

"Good night, then. Be sure to apply cold packs for the next day or so," she advised, ushering him out. She closed the door, then swung on Bryce. "You didn't have to be so hard on him!"

Bryce was taken aback by her sudden attack. For an instant he had seen open up again the black bottomless place inside himself where a killer lived, and she was worried about that witless fop! His anger exploded.

"Damn you, Genny! What if he'd been the Abbot?"

She took a cautious step back. "He wasn't."

"Can you be sure? Is it coincidental that Chesterson's been hanging around since all of this began?"

"Are you suggesting that *Jules* . . ." She shook her head. "That's ridiculous! He's just very fond of me, that's all, and foolish. Your suspicious nature is warping your judgment."

"Luckily for you. But I still say he bears watching."

"I'm not listening to this!" She turned away, but he caught her arm and drew her up against himself, staring down angrily into her mutinous expression.

"Can't you see what I'm up against here?" he grated. "I thought we were secure, but then that clodpate simply waltzes into your chamber! Goddammit! I can't even protect you from a dandified twit like Jules Chesterson! I'm terminating this charade as of right now. Pack your things. You can go back to Clare Hill—"

"No! Don't you understand? This is something I must do, no matter what. If you can't stomach it, then *you* go."

He glared at her. "Damnation, you're stubborn!"

"Some things are worth fighting for," she said obliquely.

"No matter what the cost?"

"No matter what the cost."

Whether she was speaking for herself or for him, Bryce knew the die was cast. To protect Genevieve, he couldn't wait passively for the Abbot to act. He had to unleash the part of himself he both feared and detested. He had to let the Griffin loose on the squalid underbelly of the city, to somehow find the Abbot and his conspirators so that Genevieve would be safe. And then he had to hope that after that descent into hell, somehow he could find his way home again.

"Witch!" he whispered, bending toward her perfect lips as though drawn by a magnet. "Kiss me, so that I may count the cost well spent."

Their mouths met, melding sweetly, disclosing heated secrets and dark, primal yearnings, all earlier conflict forgotten. Murmuring her need, Genevieve melted, freely bestowing her response, gladly receiving and returning the thrust of his tongue, shattering him with the utter completeness of her acceptance. Groaning, he carried her to the bed. Feverish, exultant, they came together with a fierce joining that melted flesh and dissolved fears. He lost himself deep, deep within the silken depths of his woman, and in the instant before the stunning completion of their striving, he knew the world was well lost for this fleeting glimpse of paradise.

Genevieve learned over the following days it was possible to live on nerve alone. She also learned that making oneself an attractive piece of bait was hard work, for she was busier than she had ever been in her life.

After verbally flaying a strip of hide off Taffy and the rest of the guards, then instituting tighter security measures, Bryce seemed satisfied that the Jules incident would not be repeated. Genevieve and Bryce continued to perform every third evening at the Odèon, and spent the rest of the time making a conspicuous round of parties at the British embassy and Lady Oxford's, dining in great splendor on *suprême de volaille* at Beauvilliers in the Rue de Richelieu and savory *tomats au poisson* at the Trois Frères Provençeaux. They even visited that mecca of frivolity, the vast building and gardens of the Palais-Royal with its array of shops and cafés, bold-eyed prostitutes, and any number of uncharted pleasures.

There were occasions to suit every taste. Card parties

and excursions to see the Russian soldiers still bivouacked on the Champs-Elysées. Concerts and dumb shows, *levers* and receptions, and always the gossip flowed. The king had had a contretemps with the minister of the horse, the Duchesse du Montange reported. Over delicate cups of pitch-black coffee, fashionable misses repeated tales about Talleyrand and Metternich, while their beaux considered the multinational intrigues taking place at the Congress of Peace in Vienna. And hadn't one heard the remarkable rumor that Marie Louise, the former empress, had taken the handsome Count Neipperg as her lover barely two days after leaving Paris on her way home to the court of her father, the emperor of Austria?

Genevieve's circle of admirers grew with every event, and boxes of candied fruit and marzipan and vases of hot-house flowers inundated their suite. The Prussian Baron Heinrich von Throder was an especial favorite, lavishly kissing her hand each time they met, then offering grand-fatherly advice and amusing anecdotes from his long dip-lomatic career to entertain her. The cosmopolitan Chevalier du Roche, the portly Duc de Maille, Prince De-ter, and countless others vied for her attention, a flattering state of affairs for a female who'd missed out on the joys of flirting and courting because of an unorthodox youth.

Through it all Bryce played his role of jealous husband without further comment or complaint, their passion-filled nights reassurance enough. He even tolerated the reap-pearance within her circle of Jules Chesterson, somewhat subdued but still adoring. Sometimes when Genevieve caught Bryce's eye on her over a crowd of bucks and swains, it was all she could do not to take his hand and lead him back to their rooms then and there to find for-getfulness within his arms. Despite the gaiety of their schedules, it was impossible to forget the reason that armed bodyguards shadowed their every move.

But more and more she was disturbed by Bryce's intense preoccupation and a sense of imminency that strung her nerves to the breaking point. He left her in Taffy's safekeeping to pursue the Abbot in his own fashion, seeking out the lowest classes, losing himself among the most villainous dregs of French humanity. She did not question him about his absences, or about the copious notations he seemed always to be making in his small leather journal, sensing his need to keep a part of himself inviolate, but it was these times that frightened Genevieve the most, for when he returned he seemed a stranger.

But after two weeks of soirees, gatherings, outings, military reviews, musicals, and dinners, with the Abbot's Seal on full display, *still* no one nibbled at the bait Huxford had so carefully set. Intolerable frustration and the need for action were the reasons Genevieve reacted so precipitously at yet another cosmopolitan gathering when she found herself in the midst of a conversation that was decidedly pro-Bonapartist.

An orchestra played at one end of the candlelit ballroom, and dancers circled in a kaleidoscope of colorful costumes and glittering gems while pockets of guests conducted animated conversations around the margins of the shiny parquet floor. Sipping champagne from a crystal flute, Genevieve listened to Lady Holland call the exiled emperor a "poor, dear man." It was a curious fact that many upper-class English were fascinated with Bonaparte, admiring him almost as much as his own countrymen.

"For all his faults," one gentleman said, "it cannot be denied that Bonaparte is responsible for sweeping changes in French society. Why, his code is already a model of law."

"Unfortunately, monsieur," the Chevalier du Roche replied, lifting his slim shoulders under his severe black suit in an expressive Gallic shrug, "it already appears the aristocracy—alas, even the king himself—has been so long from their homeland they have no way of understanding the new French way of thinking. That is, as serfs no longer, but as free citizens of the Revolution."

It struck Genevieve odd that a man employed in the royalist camp should voice such a thought. Perhaps Bonaparte's sympathizers were more widespread than she knew. Maybe they'd been going about this all wrong, expecting the Abbot's need for revenge to draw him out. But if he was too involved in his plot to eliminate Wellington to worry about such a petty grievance now, perhaps she might pique his curiosity another way. With the certain knowledge that gossip would circulate, mayhap she could send another kind of message to the Abbot.

"All that bodes ill for King Louis, does it not?" Genevieve asked du Roche with an airy laugh. "Many, including myself, have long admired Bonaparte's genius. How dull and thick anyone else appears when contrasted with his fire and powerful drive."

"I swear I cannot abide the thought of him locked away in such a dismal place as Elba." Lady Holland sighed. "I think I shall send him some books to cheer his exile."

"I believe the emperor would prefer a battalion of his finest troops," Genevieve murmured mischievously to du Roche. Idly, she twisted the chain bearing the Abbot's Seal around her forefinger, drawing the chevalier's sharp-eyed attention. "I, myself, would welcome the diversion."

"Madame, it is a chancy thing to wear an imperial eagle these days."

"Truly? I'd understood that the bees and eagles and initials of the emperor still adorn the state apartments at the royal palace, monsieur. Why would anyone begrudge my simple token of admiration?"

"Such a blatant symbol might be misconstrued."

"And perhaps not." She met du Roche's dark-eyed gaze blandly. "The bauble came into my hands by accident, and someday I would like to return it to its rightful owner. I'm sure I would find such a transaction very . . . rewarding."

"I had no idea you were such an ardent fan of Bonaparte's," Lady Holland said. "Would you like to include your token when I ship my package of books?"

"Perhaps that won't be necessary, my lady," Genevieve said, turning a smile on Prince Deter, who had just appeared to claim a promised dance. As the prince led Genevieve away, she called back over her shoulder, "If fortune smiles, something else may prevail to relieve the emperor's boredom."

She spun into the dance on a wave of reckless triumph, her blood rushing with the excitement of this dangerous game.

There, *that* should get the Abbot's attention!

"Bless me, Father, for I have sinned . . ."

"What is your need, my son?" Reeking of ancient incense, beeswax, and penitence, the heavy curtain dividing the confessional muffled the Abbot's husky voice into anonymity.

"The actress, Monseigneur. I have watched as you directed. She bears the sacred seal like a battle standard, yet speaks of reward."

"Fascinating. Avaricious and deceitful as Eve. I misjudged her."

"The cause, Monseigneur—"

"—may yet be served by this woman. Praise God that Leclerc's attempt in London was so clumsy. Wellington's head *and* the Abbot's Seal on one platter. The emperor will be generous."

"But the woman, Monseigneur?"

"She could provide the knowledge to secure the duke's fate. Patience and timing are all. We shall recover the seal in good time, but first, to see if her unspoken offer is genuine, tell her this . . ."

Whispered instructions rustled like old paper through the curtain's folds.

"It shall be done, Monseigneur."

"Bless you, my son. *In nomine Patris, et Fílii, et Spíritus Sancti . . .*"

On the west bank of the Seine between the Rue Mazarine and the Rue de la Harpe, the old city was a congested maze of houses, shops, cafés, schools, billets, taverns,

brothels, chapels. The area lacked the pretensions of its
more urbane neighbor, the Faubourg-St. Germain, but
what it missed in splendor was more than made up by the
earthy intensity and patriotic fervor of its inhabitants. It
was into these warrens that Bryce had gone in search of a
conspiracy. He had not been disappointed.

"This way, D'Arcy."

Bryce followed the young man he knew only as Philippe
down a dark alley that stank of urine despite a layer of
grimy snow. A lantern strung between the overhanging
buildings cast a feeble circle of light, revealing the faded
sign of the Café de l'Orange. Philippe furtively looked
over his shoulder, shivering as the bitter wind howled down
the alley, then led Bryce into the café.

A welcoming blast of warmth hit Bryce's beard-stubbled
cheeks, and he inhaled with relish and a staggering nos-
talgia the scents of wine, sharp cheese, and garlic simmering in the kitchen stock pot. He took in the heavy,
age-blackened tables and benches, the clusters of drinking
and vociferously arguing patrons, workingmen with the
smell of sweat and fish upon them, and the saucy laugh
of a buxom serving wench. Underneath his coarse wool
coat, his heart beat faster.

Memory thickened his throat with painful recollection
of his boyhood, of nights spent huddled on the hearth of
rooms just like this as his mother disappeared up the stairway to entertain a new *cher ami*. It was a lifetime away
from Clare Hill and his father, that gentle soul who hadn't
known what to do with his son except to attempt to remake
him into an Englishman. The fates had brought Bryce full
circle to confront his honor, his roots, his identity. French
or English, which? A man of two nations, but no homeland.

"Allez-vous." In the language of Bryce's youth, Philippe bade him come. *"Jacques est ici déjà."*

"Oui," Bryce grunted and followed him through the
thick blue haze of pipe smoke to a group at a table in a
dark corner. At the sight of a stranger, all discussion came

to an abrupt halt, and suspicious eyes raked his workman's breeches, rough coat, and bulky knit cap. Bryce's casual inspection was just as thorough. Ordinary men, yet hardened by war and disappointment and privation. Desperate, dissatisfied, they sought to remedy what they saw as a vast injustice, and their method was murder.

"Who's this, Philippe?" The growl came in French from a burly individual with oily black hair and the stained apron of a butcher tied around his massive belly.

"A friend of mine, and of the cause," Philippe replied, eagerly sliding onto the bench next to the butcher and reaching for an earthenware cup of wine. "D'Arcy, this is Jacques Subierre."

Blue eyes narrowed against the pall of gray smoke, Bryce nodded, suffering the man's scrutiny unperturbed. It was critical that he be accepted as one of their own. But then, it was not difficult. After all, the Griffin was half French.

"D'Arcy, eh?" Jacques grunted. "You're not from Paris."

"Marseilles."

"Soldier?"

"Gunner. Neuchatel Battalion."

"Saw action?"

"Enough."

"*Sacré!*" Jacques squinted at Bryce, tucking his chin into the rolls of fat on his neck to show his annoyance at Bryce's laconic replies. He turned to Philippe. "This one, we have no need of. What are you thinking, imbecile, to bring a stranger here?"

Philippe's lower lip jutted sullenly. "He's a good man. I can vouch for him. Saved my life when two British officers jumped me. Besides, you said to recruit all the help I could get."

Bryce maintained an impassive countenance, showing nothing that would indicate he'd carefully set up the situation to befriend young Philippe just to have this opportunity for entrée into this circle.

Jacques turned his scowl back to Bryce. "What else do you have to say for yourself, Gunner D'Arcy?"

Bryce considered, then one corner of his mouth twitched in a half smile. *"Vive l'empereur."*

Grins broke out around the circle, and immediately a place was made on the bench for Bryce and a cup pressed into his hand. Muttering, Jacques acceded to the decision of the group.

"As I was saying," Jacques began importantly for the benefit of the newcomer, "I've had word from the Monseigneur."

"And?" a stringy fellow with sallow skin and a fanatic's burning eyes prompted impatiently.

"And Leclerc will be here soon, if the weather cooperates."

"It smells like more snow to me," a red-nosed imbiber commented, lustily slurping at the lip of his cup.

"Silence, dunce!" Jacques thundered. "What do you know? You smell only grapes! May as well be drinking the swill the cellar masters are selling to the English bastards these days."

A collective snicker circulated the table at the trick played on the detested visitors.

"But this Leclerc," Philippe said, picking up the thread again, "will he tell us when it is to begin?"

"Mais oui, mon frère." Jacques rubbed his hammy fists together in anticipation, then his look turned furtive. "But enough! The walls have ears. Continue your preparations as planned, and say nothing. When the time comes to act, you will know it." He raised his cup. "Napoleon!"

The toast was drunk round the table, then the talk turned general about the abuses of the English, the spinelessness of the grossly fat Bourbon *couchon* now seated on the throne of France, and reminiscences of the war.

Bryce sipped the fruity wine and relaxed imperceptibly. After weeks of painstaking work, it was as simple as this. Yet only he knew the price he paid for becoming the Griffin night after night. It was an insane paradox, that to live up to his notion of honor he must act dishonorably, deceiving these earnest men with his lies of French patriotism in order to betray them. He accepted the burden, for a greater good must come of it—protecting Wellington for future duty to the crown and revealing the Abbot so that Genevieve might be released from the dangerous duty she demanded of herself.

Hiding a grimace, he raised his cup again and drank deep. She was stubborn, that woman, taking on this challenge when she'd already more than paid for her mistakes. In his clumsy way he'd tried to tell her that, but she had something to prove, and he knew it was his fault she took these risks. When she'd confessed several days ago that she'd added a little honey to the trap with a new bit of playacting as a Bonapartist, he'd laid into her royally for her rashness, provoking a tearful defiance that waylaid his heart.

God, it had hurt, castigating her when all he really wanted was to bury himself in her softness, watching the hurt accusation growing in her vulnerable green eyes when he would have given anything he owned to be able to take her someplace safe. But all he had to offer was the doubtful haven of his arms.

He wondered if she thought about them being together after this was over. It was so hard to see past the *now* of their existence, when they both had to put all their concentration into this exercise in survival. It didn't pay to think about how, with her sweet mouth and passionate acceptance, she'd become as necessary to him as his next breath. It broke a man's concentration to realize that they were gradually rebuilding the tenuous strands of trust that had been sheared the night of Everett's death.

But they both had jobs to accomplish before anything permanent could be settled between them. Even now, as he sat here in this low tavern, she played her part as bait at Lady Holland's ball. And he might make a fatal mistake if for one unguarded second he allowed himself to hope . . .

Shaking off the miasma of unattainable dreams, Bryce

forced himself to join in the genial debate going on at the table, to build the trust and camaraderie that he must ultimately betray. Fighting off the loathing that gnawed at the bloody edges of his self-worth, he tried to remember why he'd become a soldier—and couldn't.

Genevieve wondered if this was what it was like to be a soldier—long periods of bored inactivity interspersed with intense spurts of terrifying action. It was a ridiculous life, she decided, and if Bryce wanted it, he was certainly welcome to it. She supposed it was different for a man mingling with who knew what kind of dangerous conspiratorial types this very evening. But as for her, if she had to smile at one more vacuous compliment or endure one more excruciatingly clumsy waltz with Lady Holland's pimply nephew, she would be forced to scream for mercy. Lord Huxford had never told her that acting as bait would be like this.

Deftly disentangling herself from the nephew, Genevieve made a grateful escape, limping past the powdered and perfumed guests circulating through the spacious ballroom. She smiled graciously to those she knew and fluttered her Chinese silk fan, taking care to call attention to the gem that dangled in the daring cleavage of her lavender and silver-lace gown. She was also thoroughly sick of the Abbot's Seal. Since nothing she'd said or done seemed to be of any interest to that nefarious but still elusive spy monger, she wondered how much longer the earl would expect them to keep up this charade.

Behind a stand of potted palms, she found a deserted card room and collapsed onto a satin sofa. She was easing her abused and aching toes from her slippers when a genteel voice startled her.

"Madame, do you believe in Jesus?"

Genevieve's hand flew to her throat. "Oh, Chevalier! Sir, how nice to see you. Do join—"

She broke off to stare in stunned amazement as Bertrand du Roche's words sank in. As always, he made an elegant figure in black evening attire, his continental grace, manners, and breeding wafting from him in waves as he approached. But it was his unusual greeting that astounded her, for it was a Bonapartist catchphrase, designed to identify one sympathizer to another!

"What did you just say, sir?" she asked carefully.

Seating himself beside her, the chevalier lowered his voice. "I repeat, madame, do you believe in Jesus?"

"I am as devout as any good Christian." Heart pounding, Genevieve met his gaze directly, knowing they were not speaking of Christ, but of Napoleon Bonaparte. Du Roche was undoubtedly a sympathizer, but where was this leading? There was one way to find out. "In fact, Chevalier, you may say I await the second coming with all eagerness."

A slow smile of satisfaction lit the chevalier's patrician features. "Then perhaps a lady of such devotion would welcome an introduction to my confessor? Monseigneur is a man of vision, an *abbé* most concerned for his children—" Du Roche paused at Genevieve's involuntary gasp, then continued slyly, "Especially a daughter who lost her *grandpérè* in an tragic accident the Monseigneur deeply regrets."

"It—it was an old man's foolish gesture that cost my grandfather's life. I hold no one responsible," Genevieve lied. She tightened her fingers around her fan to hide their trembling, but she could scarcely breathe with excitement and fear. The Abbot himself had sent du Roche! She could not let this opportunity slip away, not before Bryce and Huxford could spring a trap. How could she convince the chevalier and thence the Abbot that she was no threat and might indeed be useful to him?

She licked her dry lips. "I regret that my meeting with your Abbot—your Monseigneur, I mean—was interrupted in such an untimely fashion. We might have dealt well together—for a price."

"So he thought as well, madame."

Encouraged, Genevieve impulsively pulled the chain she

wore over her head and pressed the Abbot's Seal into the astonished chevalier's hands.

"Then take this to the Monseigneur for me. It has always been his, and"—she took a deep breath—"and I am his willing servant."

Chapter 15

"You won't like what I've done."

"Very likely, General, especially if it's something so dire as to keep you up until dawn."

Bryce shut the door of the apartment behind him. He'd changed after leaving Philippe and the rest, and was glad he'd taken the trouble. He smiled at the picture she made, waiting for him in her night rail and shawl before the cold hearth with her tumbled hair shining in the pearly light and her little collection of treasures in her lap. "Have you been there all night?"

"Most of it."

She was lovely in her dishabille, and desire darkened his gaze. "Then let's both go back to bed."

"But where have you been all this time?"

Bryce wanted her to think more of him, not less. How could he say he'd been drinking with potential assassins whom he would surely betray if he could? "You don't need to know."

Rising with a grimace for the stiffness of her muscles, she carefully set aside her small prizes, the pebbles and feathers and yarn that seemed to bring a touch of familiarity and comfort to each new place she found herself. Her voice held a betraying wobble. "You think you're protecting me, but you only frighten me more by shutting me out. Don't do this, Bryce. I need you."

The simplicity of those last words lanced through him like a bolt of lightning. He placed his hands on her shoulders and brushed a kiss beside her ear. "I need you, too, *chérie*."

"Then tell me I did right by giving the Abbot his seal."

Bryce stiffened. "You did *what*?"

She told him.

When she'd finished, Bryce raked a hand through his hair and shook his head in consternation. "Jesus! What will Hugh say?"

"That I traded a relatively worthless trinket for the chance we must have," Genevieve answered earnestly. "I had only a moment to prove myself, and it worked. Du Roche was impressed with my spontaneous gesture of good faith, and knew his master, the Monseigneur as he calls him, would be also."

"And in return?"

"The misunderstanding is cleared up, so I need not fear the Abbot's retribution. Indeed, I have the promise of his generosity, according to du Roche." Shrugging, she gave a harsh, self-mocking laugh. "Oh, I'm becoming so skillful at deceit! After only one performance I am suddenly the coldest, most mercenary and traitorous bitch in Paris, willing to sell my own grandfather's life to the highest bidder! You should have heard the wicked lies that rolled off my tongue with such ease—even about you."

"Me?"

She tapped his starched shirt front with her forefinger, giving him a mock-coquettish look. "My oh-so-boring husband. I told du Roche I needed the means to leave you and the theater behind. I would do *anything* the Abbot asked to secure my freedom."

Bryce's brows drew together in an expression of furious calculation. "And he believed you?"

She nodded, tension thinning the lush curve of her mouth. "All I have to do to cement the relationship is meet the Chevalier at the Palais-Royal to pass on whatever

gossip and information I can glean from the English del-
egation.''

''About Wellington.'' Bryce's scowl darkened even
further.

''He is the Abbot's main objective, is he not?''

''Dammit! I'm not sure of anything anymore!'' Dragging her close, he tangled his fingers in her bright hair and
tilted her face up to his, inhaling the sweetness of lavender
soap and warm female skin. ''You took a damned crazy
chance, General.''

''Then make the most of it,'' she challenged breath-
lessly. ''Force the Abbot out in the open and finish this!''

''The danger—''

''—is no greater now that it has been. If I am the means
to conclude this, then use me, and swiftly!'' Her voice
broke, lowered to a mere whisper. ''Because I—I can't
take much more of this, Bryce, and I couldn't stand to fail
again.''

''Courage, *mon coeur*,'' he murmured.

With an unintelligible cry, she dropped the shawl and
looped her arms around his neck, her cheek pressing
against his broad chest. He felt her shivering beneath the
thin stuff of her night rail and pulled her closer.

''I'm sorry I'm such a coward,'' she said in a choked
tone.

''Don't be foolish. Never has there been a woman as
brave as you.''

''I don't feel brave.'' She nuzzled her cheek against his
starched shirt, savoring the outline of rocklike muscles
beneath the fabric, seeking unconscious comfort in the
tactile sensations that made up her total impression of this
man. Tonight other nuances clung to him, wine and cheese
and a not unpleasant tang of garlic. She wondered where
he'd found such homey things and envied him. ''I'd like
to run away from this place.''

''Not enjoying your sojourn into society?'' he teased,
his mouth grazing the top of her head.

''It's a splendid show, but . . .''

"But what?"

"It's not home, is it?"

They both knew it was the dream of home that called her, for she'd never had the real thing. At that moment Bryce would have given anything to make that simple dream a reality for her . . . and for himself. But duty came first.

"Chin up, General," Bryce said huskily. "All soldiers must go where they're sent."

"Yes, but—" She sensed a sudden stillness within him and looked up in puzzlement. "Bryce?"

"I think that's it, General," he said slowly, thinking, his gaze calculating.

"What is?"

"The way to force the Abbot's hand." His eyes lit with growing excitement, and he drew her down beside him on the sofa. "I've heard the duke speak of the ministry's desire to remove him from the dangers of Paris. They've offered him an assignment in the American conflict. He'll never agree to it, but it could be useful . . . Can you meet with the Chevalier again?"

Bewildered, Genevieve nodded. "I'm to send him a message anytime I learn something of importance."

"Perfect." Bryce dropped a quick peck on her astonished mouth. "Listen, General, these are your orders. When you meet du Roche again, this is what you must say . . ."

"You say Wellington is to leave for the Americas!"

"*Oui,* Monseigneur."

"My God!"

Bertrand du Roche tried to peer through the confessional screen to no avail. His knees ached from the wooden kneeler of the prie-dieu, and his nostrils burned from the acrid incense smoldering on the altar. Muffled by the heavy curtains, the sung Latin of High Mass was indecipherable, but the clump and rustle of worshippers as they knelt and stood guaranteed the conversation in the confessional would go no farther.

"And how does our new friend come by this startling news?"

"Monseigneur, she says the Duchess of Wellington has placed a large and very confidential order with Madame Yvonne, a certain modiste of her acquaintance. All traveling clothes, suitable for the wilderness of America. To remove the duke from possible threat without losing face, they must find him a suitable post, *n'est-ce pas*? Commander-in-chief of the British forces in the New World would surely be a fitting opportunity for one of such stature."

"The negotiations at Ghent—"

"—falter, Monseigneur. War between Britain and the Americans continues. The British need their ablest commander there."

The voice behind the screen was tight with frustrated rage. "No! The emperor's plans must not be thwarted! This act must be a signal to the world. When? When is the appointment to take place?"

"That she did not know, Monseigneur," du Roche said regretfully, "only . . ."

"Oui?"

"Only that the modiste had complained loudly that a week wasn't nearly enough time to finish the work, but still it must be done."

"Only a week! *Sacré!* The proper time, the exact place—how can that be chosen in only a week? But it *must* be!"

"How can I assist you, Monseigneur?"

"See what else the woman can learn, Chevalier. Appointments, engagements, everything."

"She will expect payment."

"Let her prove her worth first."

"She could have sold the seal. Instead, she returned it to you with no demands."

"Are you besotted with the woman, Chevalier?"

"Of course not!"

"Good. Eve and the serpent were one in the same."

"But it is my duty to advise my master—"

"It is your duty to obey me!" the awful voice thundered from behind the screen.

Du Roche quailed and crossed himself. "Forgive me, Monseigneur."

"Watch her carefully, my son, and bring me anything you learn."

"It shall be done, Monseigneur."

"Then go with God, my son. The second coming is near."

"It's not right for them to keep us in the dark like this," Philippe muttered angrily, pacing the dank warehouse. The icy wind blowing off the River Seine whistled through the cracks in the walls of the dilapidated wooden structure, causing the flickering, smoky lamp to throw eerie shadows over the litter of bales and boxes, barrels and crates, and the grave faces of the handful of zealots gathered there.

"Patience, my young friend," Bryce advised. "We'll learn our mission soon enough."

"Yes, but what if something's gone wrong? What of our earlier plans? We are not ignorant peasants! And we are loyal to the man. If we are willing to risk our lives for the emperor's cause, Jacques should tell us to what purpose without all this secrecy."

Discontented muttering sounded the group's agreement to Philippe's complaints.

Perched on the lip of a hogshead, Bryce stretched out his long legs and crossed his ankles with an air of indolent ease, but inside his coat pocket his fist clenched around a pebble he'd filched from Genevieve's collection of Parisian treasures. Touching something she'd found and admired helped him focus on his mission and control the tension threatening to explode.

This hastily called council of conspirators had to be a direct result of the information Genevieve had passed to du Roche only days before, confirming Bryce's belief that the Abbot directed this plot. Now, if only haste would produce carelessness, there was a chance not only to dismantle the scheme, but also to uncover the Abbot himself.

"Leclerc will have our instructions," the sallow-faced man avowed. "Subierre is often a pompous fool, but Leclerc—now there is a man!"

"This Leclerc," Bryce muttered to Philippe, "is he a hero, then?"

"*Oui*, with a reputation for deadliness," the young man returned. "Once crossed, it is said many find themselves—" He made a cutting noise and drew a thumbnail across his throat in demonstration.

"A man to respect."

"He served credibly during the war in numerous secret capacities where his skills were invaluable." Philippe's voice dropped even lower with awe. "They whisper he is an assassin who enjoys his work, especially with a knife."

"And this Monseigneur who directs Leclerc's labor as well as our own, will he present himself as we begin his glorious work?"

Philippe shrugged. "Who can say? Sometimes it is safer to know nothing, D'Arcy."

Bryce grinned. "Then we are as sheltered as in our mother's arms, *mon ami*, for Subierre keeps us ignorant as newborns."

"That *couchon*! I only pray he does not lead us into disaster. Ah!" Philippe nodded toward a rickety door suddenly filled by two figures, one instantly recognizable as the corpulent butcher. "They're here. Now for answers."

Jacques Subierre carried a large bundle under one arm, and he cast a furtive glance over his shoulder, pulled the door shut, then gestured for his companion to follow him into the circle of light.

"*Mon vieux*," Jacques said, acknowledging his compatriots with a grim nod, "I have brought you Leclerc."

"What is the word, monsieur?" the sallow-faced man asked deferentially.

Leclerc stepped into the light, revealing a wiry figure

nearly Bryce's height in nondescript peasant's garb and a floppy wool hat that shaded his thin face. "Show them."

"*Oui,* monsieur." Eagerly, Jacques unrolled his bundle, tossing garments at each man, mid-length blue coats with colored undercollars, gray trousers, and soft cloth caps with black leather brims and white metal cross insignia.

Bryce examined the uniform while covertly watching Leclerc. The rest of the coven of Bonapartist conspirators were amateurs, but some instinctive inner alarm warned Bryce that here was a truly dangerous adversary and, for the first time, a direct link to the Abbot. Apprehension and alertness prickled along his spine, and he welcomed the weight of the blade concealed at the small of his back. Beside Bryce, Philippe sputtered his confusion.

"*Prussian* uniforms? What is this?"

"Landwehr Infantry," Leclerc answered shortly. "They are always ill-dressed, ill-supplied, nothing the same. Use your own boots and muskets and you'll blend right in with no trouble."

"But why Prussia?"

"Because, my impatient young fool," Jacques explained, "when we execute the English bastard Wellington, we want the world to think it was his own allies who did it!"

Only the wind whistling through the warehouse disturbed the stunned silence.

"Wellington," came one awed whisper. "*Mon Dieu!*"

Bryce's fists tightened in the coarse wool of the Prussian coat, willing the conversation to go on. He had to know what they planned!

"The Monseigneur believes we can do this?" Philippe asked.

"We cannot fail," Jacques insisted. "*L'empereur* is waiting for this sign. And since everyone knows Prussia sits in Czar Alexander's hip pocket, who do you suppose they'll blame for this act?"

"Russia!" the sallow-faced man cried. "We'll make

them pay for what they did to us on the march from Moscow.''

"Exactly. And the Alliance in Vienna that is presently carving up Europe into tasty chunks will explode in flames of war.''

It was a diabolical plan, worthy of the Abbot's Machiavellian manipulations, and it just might work. Bryce remained motionless and silent as the other men clamored for details, explanations, directions.

Dramatically, Jacques waited until the questions subsided. "The Landwehr Infantry will take part in a military review at the Champs de Mars in two days' time. Wellington will be there—and so will we.''

"That's too soon!'' Philippe protested. "We can't be ready!''

Bryce wanted to echo Philippe's words. It would be difficult to put an Allied trap in place on such short notice. But knowledge was the best armor. Just as soon as he could leave this place, it was imperative that he inform Wellington.

"Gutless *poltron*!'' Jacques snarled at Philippe. "We will do as Monseigneur orders. There isn't time to quibble, for the bastard Englishman plans to quit our country like the coward he truly is. The only way we will let him go is in his coffin!''

There was a general nodding of heads and murmurs of agreement.

"Our lives are Bonaparte's,'' one man stated. "What must we do?''

"Our assignment is to create a general disturbance,'' Jacques replied. "Monsieur Leclerc will do the rest.''

Leclerc raised his head, a malevolent half smile twisting his thin lips and a reptilian sheen glittering in the Mongol tilt of his black eyes. In that instant of recognition, the pungent odor of crushed basil and the echo of Marie's screams flooded Bryce's senses with fresh horror. The assassin from Lyons!

Memory relived the hot brand of a knife slicing through

his side, innocents destroyed for helping him, help came too late. Suddenly drenched in cold sweat, Bryce arched against the imaginary pain, then cursed inwardly at his own weakness and fought to control the impulse to fling himself at Leclerc's throat.

Rage and hate and bloodlust burned his gut like acid, but he couldn't afford the luxury of revenge. At least not yet. Not when keeping his cover intact meant protecting Wellington and finally removing the Abbot. He averted his gaze and inspected the Prussian Landwehr uniform for the tenth time, purposely slumping, melting into the group when every instinct urged him to howl like a mad dog and send Leclerc straight to hell where he belonged. His muscles vibrated with tension, tight as springs, ready to uncoil into a killing frenzy. Using every ounce of his will, he forced the red haze out of his brain and compelled himself to attend to Jacques's instructions to the conspirators.

"We are agreed then?" Jacques asked. "We meet at the Café de l'Orange at dawn, two days hence." This elicited nods of assent and murmurs of understanding. "*Bon.* Enough said. Leave now, *mon frères,* and remember the fate of *l'empereur* rests on you."

Solemnly, the gravity of this charge weighing heavily on each man, Jacques and Leclerc led the group out of the warehouse, stepping onto the quayside dock and into the darkness of the chilly Parisian night. Ten feet below the edge of the wooden dock, the black river lapped at the pilings, filling the nose with an overpowering stench of sewage and rotting fish. As the rest of the group drifted away, Bryce hung back behind the two leaders, who paused for a last earnest word. He tugged his knit cap low over his brow, unwilling to risk exposure, yet reluctant to let Leclerc out of his sight when the unavenged souls of Marie and her children cried for justice.

"*Allez,* D'Arcy," Philippe urged, shivering in the frigid wind. "There's still night enough to find comfort in some soup and a warm bed."

Bryce nodded, tucked his Prussian uniform under his

arm, and with head ducked as though against the brisk breeze, strode past the two leaders. He was close enough to hear Jacques's jocular prediction.

"No doubt, Monsieur Leclerc, this bit of work will please Monseigneur.'

"No doubt, Subierre."

Jacques's tone grew sly. "A joy for you, especially after your failure in London with the actress."

Bryce's step faltered badly, and his blood thundered in his ears. Were they speaking of Genevieve? Was Leclerc also responsible for the attack that had nearly killed her? It had to be. Damnation! Huxford was right!

Leclerc's voice was smooth and unconcerned. "I am assured I will have another opportunity with the woman when her usefulness to Monseigneur is through."

"No!"

With the suddenness of an eagle swooping to capture its prey, Bryce sprang at Leclerc, roaring defiance—all caution, Wellington, *everything* forgotten at the horrifying mind-picture of Genevieve suffering Marie's ghastly death. He caught the man full in the chest with his entire weight, sending him sprawling, then flung himself after the assassin. Jacques screeched in surprise, but his strident demands to desist rose unheeded into the night. Members of the group hurried back to witness the surprising attack.

"Murderer!" Bryce spat, grappling with his victim, pounding him with his fists, uncoiled now in a killing fury that knew no limits or discretion.

The blade appeared between them in the flash of an eye, slicing through the thick fabric of Bryce's coat sleeve to pierce his upper arm with a searing heat. He jerked back, but realized his mistake before Leclerc could press his advantage to deadly effect. Made strong by desperation and years of guilt, Bryce's fingers bit into Leclerc's wrist, holding the bloodied tip of the knife away as they rolled and bucked, coming ever closer to the edge of the dock.

"He is a madman!" Jacques shrieked. "Stop! Someone help, *vite*!"

Footsteps pounded down the planks, hesitated. How did one go about stopping two hellhounds bent on mutual destruction?

In the brief moment of respite before intervention became inevitable, Bryce forced Leclerc's hand backward against the splintery planks of the dock. Muscles locked, poised motionless for the barest instant, Leclerc got his first clear look at his assailant. His black eyes dilated.

"You!"

Two sets of hands grabbed Bryce, jerking him roughly to his feet. The wound in his arm tore further, and agony ripped him as blood gushed down his arm to drip off his fingertips. The rough treatment left him gasping and light-headed, cursing Leclerc and the ultimate disaster of his own undisciplined folly.

Others wrestled the blade from Leclerc and helped him up. Lip bleeding, one eye already swelling, he shook them off, hissing vicious epithets. "Traitor! Unnatural son of mother France! Why aren't you feeding worms?"

Bryce's rage ignited again, and he smiled, his eyes burning with an unholy light that unsettled all observers. "You slaughtered the lambs, Leclerc, but you didn't slay the lion."

"What is this nonsense?" Jacques demanded. "There is no room for petty quarrels here."

"Is there room for treachery, monsieur?" Leclerc snarled. "I know this foul *chien*, this Griff—"

With nothing left to lose, Bryce charged, taking the men holding him by surprise, hurtling squarely into Leclerc and taking them both over the edge of the dock to plummet into the icy black water of the Seine. They slammed into the surface and disappeared in a tangle of arms and legs. Disoriented, stunned, they were immediately captured by the current, which sucked at them like a ravenous predator as it carried them off into the darkness. The excited shouts on the dock above diminished and finally faded away completely.

Clawing at each other as though scrambling up a ladder,

they at last bobbed to the surface in search of air. Flapping numbed limbs, blinded, gasping, Bryce spun in the tide, but Leclerc's fingers sank into his hair, pushing him under, choking on only a small mouthful of oxygen.

Bryce struggled, eyes open in the frigid medium, only Leclerc's darker shadow visible in the black water. But the assassin had the advantage of breath and leverage, and with a vicious twist he managed to kick Bryce's wounded arm. What was left of his air exploded from his lungs as the pain took him to new limits of blackness. From a vast distance, it dawned on Bryce that the bastard intended to drown him!

Angels beckoned; seraphs with Marie's worn face, cherubs with Genny's luscious mouth . . . Genny! And Leclerc alive and free to carve her to ribbons! Ears ringing, lungs exploding, Bryce forced his numbed hand beneath his cumbersome coat, praying.

He could hardly feel the hilt of the weapon in his hand, but there was no time left. Calling on the last of his strength, he swung—and plunged his blade deep into Leclerc's chest.

For an interminable instant, nothing happened, and Bryce knew he'd failed. Then Leclerc jerked, writhing violently, and released his hold on Bryce to grapple with the deadly knife instead. He drifted down into the darkness in a whirlpool of silvery bubbles. To hell, Bryce hoped.

Freed at last, Bryce fought one-armed for the faraway surface. It was a million miles away, and somehow it hardly seemed worth the effort now that Genny was safe. Deep down, he knew he'd never been any different from Leclerc, so why should he fight it? He should have died in Lyons, but he'd cheated death that day. Wouldn't it be simpler now to let the torrent suck him under and under . . .

Bryce broke the black surface of the river in a burst of spray, breaching like a wounded whale, gulping down huge gusts of the blessed air. The current picked him up, whirling and spinning him, carrying him down to the sea, past the shadowy outlines of docks and barges, and to oblivion, he hoped. The weight of his clothes pulled him under again, and he choked on a mouthful of wave, then came up again coughing and cursing.

His arm burned. His face hurt. His lungs ached. Damn, but this dying was hard!

He thought, *To hell with it.* And out of habit or the will to live or sheer perversity, he began to swim for shore.

"It's been two days, Taffy! Where could he be?"

Dressed to go out, Genevieve paced the length of the gilded salon, twisting her yellow kid gloves into knots at each turn. The bright morning sunshine slanted through the narrow windows, highlighting the gold braid of her forest-green walking gown *á là militaire.*

"Now, ma'am," the shiny-pated sergeant said uncomfortably, "the Cap knows what he's doing."

"Then why doesn't he let us know where he is?" she demanded. Spiders danced an apprehensive gavotte within her stomach. "Surely he could send some word. I'm frightened, Taffy. Something's happened. I just know it."

"You're exciting yourself for nothing, ma'am. Many times he had to work alone for weeks at a time. There's a reason for this absence, you can bank on it. The Cap's got a way of doing things . . . You just have to trust in him."

"The Griffin's way," she said bitterly. "Scarcely reassuring."

Taffy's cheeks ballooned in surprise. "Well, yes. Ma'am, you oughtn't to know about such as that."

"If I knew more, perhaps I could come to better understand Bryce," she said, turning her complete attention on the flustered sergeant. "I care deeply about him, but he's so hard to reach. That damned Griffin in him gets in the way!"

"The war does strange things to a man, ma'am," Taffy replied solemnly. "The Cap was trying to put it all behind him when this started up again."

A pang of guilt made her wince. "The Earl of Huxford and I have done him much evil."

"Here, now, ma'am, don't take on so. The Cap never doted on a lady the way he does you."

Heartened, Genevieve gathered up her courage. "Tell me about the war. About the Griffin."

"You can't ask that of me, ma'am," Taffy said, shaking his bald head. "That's for the Cap to tell, if he can. After Captain North was killed . . . Well, you'd best ask the Cap."

"I will—if he'll just come home."

"If it'll ease your fears, I'll scout around a bit."

"Would you?"

"Aye. But don't get your hopes up. If the Griffin don't want to be found"—Taffy shrugged—"then he won't."

"Perhaps I should wait here, then." Chewing her lip, she wrung her poor abused gloves into a wrinkled clump. "Mr. Chesterson is taking me driving, but I have no interest in it."

"No, you go ahead, ma'am," Taffy interrupted. "It'll do you good to get out on so fine a day. I'm sure when you get back the Cap will have returned, too."

Taffy left with that, and when Jules Chesterson presented himself at her door moments later, colorfully arrayed in puce inexpressibles, yellow embroidered waistcoat, and plum tailcoat, Genevieve was reconciled to following the sergeant's recommendation. After all, she could worry as easily outdoors as in, and she hated to disappoint Jules, for his pleasure at having her company all to himself for a change was evident in his shining countenance.

As they descended the wide steps of the Hôtel des Etrangers toward the rented curricle Jules had secured, the dandy happily expounded on the possibilities of the morning's itinerary.

"Shall we go to the Bois, my dear?"

"You decide," Genevieve said, holding the brim of her bonnet as the breeze gusted around them, the air chilly despite the brilliant sunshine. Her fingers brushed the plume of dyed duck feathers gracing the band, their soft-

ness instantly recalling another sunny day beside a certain
stream. So much had happened since a girl and a soldier
had walked beneath the willows. With one last regretful
stroke, she drew her hand away, forcing herself to concentrate on Jules's cheerful chatter.

". . . or I hear there's to be a splendid military spectacle for the Duc de Angoulême and—"

"Madame, please!"

A grimy-faced urchin of undetermined sex darted from
the curb and tugged urgently at Genevieve's skirts. She
reached automatically for her ridicule.

"Little beggars are everywhere," Jules muttered irri-
tably. "No, don't give him a sou. Only encourages them."

"Really, Jules, there's no harm—"

"Your husband, madame! Come, fast!" The ragged
child pointed violently at a rough two-wheeled fishmon-
ger's cart parked in the gutter with an ancient crone standing at its rear.

"Husband?" Genevieve repeated uncertainly, then
gasped and ran down the steps to the street.

"Genevieve!" Astounded, Jules followed her. "Whatever are you doing?"

She flung herself around the tail of the cart only to come
up short at the sight that awaited her. "Bryce!"

Filthy, clad in damp, unfamiliar garments that reeked
of the river, Bryce half lay, half sat on a mound of nets,
his eyes shut, clutching his rudely bandaged left arm. His
stubble-shadowed cheeks were unnaturally flushed, and his
mouth was clenched and grim. Genevieve bent over him
anxiously, repeating his name, touching his clammy hands.

"Genny?" Bryce roused reluctantly, as though with the
greatest effort.

"Yes. Dear God, what happened?" Genevieve felt the
heat of his skin through her gloves. The old crone tugged
her ragged shawl over her gray head and launched into an
explanation in a river patois that was all but indecipherable
to Genevieve's schoolroom French, while the urchin joined
in with an occasional high-pitched addition to the tale.

"Genevieve," Jules said, marching to her side, "you have no business dealing—My word! Cormick!"

"Help me, Jules," she said, frantic. She lent Bryce her arm as he struggled upright, and felt his inaudible groan. "He's hurt! We must get him inside."

"Good Lord, he's filthy!" Jules said in distaste, recoiling from the overpowering stench of fish. "I'll call someone."

With surprising strength, Bryce grabbed a handful of Jules's coat. "Damn you, you frivolous bastard, help me up!"

"Well, really!" Jules huffed, but at Genevieve's look of appeal, he added his weight to hers and assisted Bryce off the back of the cart.

"Where have you been? What's happened?" she cried.

Swaying on his feet despite Jules's assistance, Bryce shook his head, trying to clear it. "Madame Aiguille and her grandson plucked me out of the river . . . I don't know when. Damn! What day is it?"

Jules told him in an impatient tone. "Although what difference it makes if you've been brawling—"

"The review!" Bryce grated. "Has it begun?"

Jules caught Genevieve's eye. "Let's summon a physician. He's obviously out of his head."

Suddenly savage, Bryce shook off their assistance with a roar. "The military review in the Champs de Mars, you fool! The Bonapartists will make an attempt on Wellington this very morn!"

Thunderstruck, Jules could only stare. "My God, I've never heard such rot!"

"A Prussian regiment, only most of them will be French," Bryce muttered. He raised a practiced eye to the angle of the sun. "There's little time."

"Jules." Genevieve touched Chesterson's arm. "Believe him."

"But my dear Genevieve!"

She swallowed. "He's in a position to know."

The dandy blinked, then looked at the couple before

him in an entirely new light. Bryce gave a disdainful snort, dismissing him.

"Have you any money?" Bryce asked Genevieve.

Disconcerted, she nodded. "A bit."

He grabbed her ridicule and tossed the whole thing to the crone. "*Merci beaucoup,* madame." Without pausing to acknowledge her grateful shrieks, Bryce hauled Genevieve toward the curb, leaning heavily on her. "Find me a conveyance. It may already be too late!"

"You're in no condition to go anywhere!" she protested. "I'll send word—"

"No time."

"Let me help." Jules caught up with them, taking Bryce's weight off Genevieve, then assisting him to the waiting curricle. "As one Englishman to another, I demand it, sir!"

"Hurry," Bryce said, gritting his teeth as he settled into the seat. "I think—hope—I eliminated the central assassin, but they can take it forward anyway . . . No, Genny, stay here. It's too dangerous"

"Don't waste time arguing," she snapped, squeezing into the seat beside him as Jules hastened around the vehicle to take the driver's place. "I'm coming, too!"

From the firmness of her mouth, Bryce knew better than to attempt to dissuade her. "Go, Chesterson."

"Like a bat, sir!" Jules slapped the reins down on the backs of the pair of spirited bays, and the curricle shot forward at a breathtaking speed. "I may not be good at a damned thing else in this world, but, by God, I'm a whip hand when need be!"

Chapter 16

❦

They heard the martial music of drums and trumpets and the enthusiastic roar of spectators long before Jules's curricle reached the boundaries of the Champs de Mars. With a reckless skill that amazed Genevieve, Jules threaded the vehicle through the narrow Parisian streets in a mad race toward the parade ground. So fast and furious was their pace that no conversation was possible. Genevieve anxiously watched Bryce's countenance grow more and more pasty under the fever-flush, but she could do nothing but hang on and pray. More than once, only Jules's adeptness and the grace of God kept them from overturning or running down a pedestrian.

Finally the banners and flags rising above the grounds came into view, and they were forced to slow their velocity by the multitudes who had turned out to see the spectacle in honor of the Duc de Angoulême, nephew to the king. Although the parade grounds were wet and muddy from the autumn rains, the sunshine lifted spirits and the crowds were in a holiday mood. Jules drew the vehicle to a halt on the far edge of the parade grounds.

"There." Bryce croaked the single word and pointed.

Across the flat expanse of the Champs de Mars stood a pavilion sheltering the honored guests. Before the illustrious dignitaries passed cordon after colorful cordon of French and Allied cavalry, foot soldiers, and artillery;

French Hussars, Saxony Grenadiers, Russian Cuirassiers, French Garde de Corps, British Dragoons, in a rainbow array of spanking bright parade dress, their proud pennants and streamers snapping in the breeze in time with the cadence of marching feet and clopping hooves.

"Looks peaceful enough," Jules began.

Genevieve gripped the tufted leather side of the curricle, breathing a quiet sigh of relief. "Maybe it's all right."

"Take us around," Bryce ordered in a tight voice. "Wellington will be with the Duc de Angoulême. We must warn them both."

Obediently, Jules clucked to the lathered horses. "What are you looking for?"

"A Prussian unit. Bonapartists in disguise. Blue coats. A shabby lot—Jesus! There they are!"

Straining forward, eyes narrowed like an eagle's, Bryce picked out the Landwehr Infantry, searching—yes! Jacques's rotund silhouette brought up the rear. He calculated the distances.

"Go across," he said. "They'll pass in front of the reviewing stand before we can drive around."

"Across?" Jules looked aghast at the crowded field, marked like a chessboard with square after square of soldiers and cavalry. "But—"

"Go, damn you!" Roughly shoving Genevieve down to the floorboards, Bryce snatched Jules's whip and laid it across the backs of the heaving bays. Whinnying at the ill treatment, the horses shot forward, and the curricle lurched and bucked into the marital milieu, scattering foot soldiers and horse troops before it like ducks on a pond.

"Holy Mother, Cormick!" Jules bellowed, scrambling for the ribbons while holding on for his life. "Are you trying to kill us all?"

"Bryce." As she thumped against the floorboards, Genevieve's voice was a mere squeak of fright.

"Stay down, General!" he barked. "Jules, drive straight for that unit!"

"What?" Jules's squeak matched Genevieve's.

"Just do it!"

Something in Bryce's adamancy conveyed itself to Jules, and his youthful countenance grew set and grim. Without further comment, he stood up in the jouncing vehicle and whipped the horses into greater effort, ignoring the outraged cries and angry shouts of the soldiers bailing out of their path on either side.

They bore down on the Landwehr unit just as it marched into position before the reviewing stand. The disturbance their progress created finally registered on the corpulent rear "soldier." Jacques cast a glance over his shoulder, and his eyes nearly popped at the out-of-control carriage hurtling at his group, its blond driver bellowing like a Roman charioteer. But it was the black-haired, savage-visaged ghost beside him that caught Jacques's wild-eyed attention.

"*Sacré! Le diable!*" Just as the others in the platoon realized something was very wrong, Jacques swung his musket and fired.

The parade ground was reduced to instant chaos. Jules toppled off the curricle like a felled oak. Panic struck, and the ranks of the Landwehr broke. Bryce stood and grabbed for the ribbons, catching one, and the team spun in a tight circle, spraying clots of mud and sodden grass. More shots rang out from the frustrated Bonapartists. As bullets whizzed past their ears, the tall Englishman and the short French duke on the reviewing stand both forgot their dignity and dove for the ground. In the bottom of the curricle, Genevieve gulped back a scream as one wheel of the vehicle completely left the earth.

The disorder didn't last long.

By the time Bryce had drawn his frenzied team to a halt, the remnants of the counterfeit Landwehr Infantry had dispersed in all directions, with quick-thinking officers in the Duc de Angoulême's green and gold livery hot after them. Panicked horses stirred up quantities of mud, but red-faced noncommissioned officers roared their charges back into order.

Angry generals and irate colonels with pistols drawn surrounded Bryce. They were nonplussed yet again when Genevieve's chestnut curls peeked over the side of the curricle. A plethora of furious demands in a bevy of languages assaulted him, but Bryce merely lifted one hand in a typically Gallic shrug that spoke more eloquently than ten thousand words.

"Mr. Cormick!"

Lips clamped together so hard they appeared almost blue, Bryce turned stiffly toward the imperative voice. "Your Grace."

The Duke of Wellington strode across the muddy expanse between the curricle and the pavilion with absolute indifference to the confusion roiling on every side. He waved aside the angry circle of onlookers. "It appears we must be grateful for your sudden, if rather unorthodox, appearance and intervention. Would you care to explain?"

" 'Twas Bonapartists, Your Grace," Genevieve gasped, wobbling up from the floor of the curricle, bruised in every portion of her anatomy. With a businesslike air, she resettled her battered bonnet on her head. "But explanations later. Mr. Cormick is injured, sir. Where's a physician?"

"Send for my surgeon," Wellington ordered, his blue eyes amused. He gestured to an aide-de-camp. "Help them down."

Eager hands hastened to obey, assisting Genevieve from the vehicle. "Where is Mr. Chesterson? He could be badly hurt—"

She regained her feet just as a member of the German Legion escorted a badly shaken Jules into the circle. A bullet crease bloodied his cheek, and he cradled his right wrist close to his chest, but otherwise he seemed unharmed. Genevieve rushed to him.

"Jules, thank heavens! Are you all right? You were wonderful, absolutely heroic!"

Despite his painful grimace, Jules's expression was rather wondering. "I didn't do too badly at that, did I?"

Bryce climbed stiffly down from the curricle, and Genevieve hastened back to his side, touching his sleeve, searching his strained face, caught between panic and elation. "Is it over? Bryce, tell me!"

"General . . ." Bryce smiled regretfully—then crumpled into an ignominious heap before her and the conqueror of the Conqueror of the World.

"Genevieve?"

In the upstairs hall of the British ambassador's residence one week later, Genevieve quietly pulled the sickroom door shut behind her and looked up. "Jules."

Clad in a severely elegant French-cut suit, yellow curls brushed into strictest order, a half-healed scrape on his cheek, Jules hardly looked like himself. "How is the patient?"

"Sleeping at last." She pushed the loose chestnut ringlets from her tired face and gave him a wan smile that was all she could manage after a week of nursing and worry. "You're so good to inquire every day."

"I could do no less." Steadying her elbow with his left hand, for his broken right wrist was encased in a splint, Jules drew her into the little window-seated alcove at the top of the landing. "And the arm?"

"They think now they can save it." Genevieve's tremulous smile wavered, then her breath caught, and she burst into tears.

"My dear!" Awkwardly, Jules placed a comforting arm around her shoulders and urged her to a seat on the cushioned bench. "But that's wonderful news!"

"I know." Hiccoughing, she gratefully accepted Jules's pristine linen handkerchief to mop her streaming cheeks. "The surgeon drained the putrefaction, and Bryce's fever is down, and I don't know why I'm such a watering pot."

"You love him, that's why."

With her cheek resting on his shoulder, she heaved a sigh. "Oh, Jules . . ."

"Mr. Cormick is a fortunate man, and I'm not really heartbroken, you know."

Her small laugh was rather watery. "No?"

"It was part of the costume, you see, being enamored of a beautiful actress."

"So you can put your affection away as easily as you have that truly awful canary waistcoat?"

"What? You never said—" He saw her teasing smile and broke off, laughing. "It *is* awful, isn't it?"

"Excruciating." She wiped her eyes a final time then returned the handkerchief to him.

Jules's expression grew serious again. "You know I could never totally abandon my feelings for you."

"But perhaps they've changed?" She clasped his hands in hers. "Friends are so much more comfortable than lovers, and I do value your friendship, dear Jules."

"And I yours." The corners of his mouth curled upward. "Though I would never have imagined my *tendre* for you to lead me into the eye of a storm of espionage!"

"Where you accounted for yourself with great valor, my friend. The duke expressed his gratitude, did he not?"

"Very graciously, too, but at the same time sealed my lips. Imagine my chagrin! I'm sworn to keep the details of my adventure to myself and cannot laud it over my fashionable confederates."

"But *you* know the service you performed for your country," Genevieve pointed out softly. "And that's what is important."

Jules raised her hand to his lips. "Lovely and wise."

"I cannot take credit for what has been within you all along. Now that you've discovered your own worth, it is up to you to make the most of it."

"Actually . . ." Jules cleared his throat. "I had thought I might go home soon. Haven't seen my parents for a time, you know. I hesitated to leave with your husband so ill, but now that he's improved . . ."

"Though I'll miss you, that's an excellent plan," Genevieve said warmly.

"And you are well cared for here," Jules continued as though to reassure himself.

"His Grace has been most accommodating and has overseen Bryce's treatment himself."

It was hardly worth mentioning that although most of the conspirators had been imprisoned, Chevalier du Roche had gone off missing immediately after the debacle at the Champs de Mars, and though it was thought his ring in Paris was smashed, the Abbot himself was still at large. Considering these facts and the seriousness of Bryce's condition, the duke had deemed it prudent to eliminate any extra notice by immediately removing them from the Hôtel des Étrangers and establishing them in rooms within the embassy house.

Of course, all their obligations at the Odèon and elsewhere had been immediately canceled, and word of the events that had transpired forwarded to the Earl of Huxford. Genevieve could only hope that the earl would be satisfied with what the attempt had accomplished as well as its cost. As far as she was concerned, her obligation was at an end.

"I feel certain that we will follow your example as soon as Bryce's condition allows," Genevieve continued.

"Splendid! I rather fancy keeping Christmas in the country this year," Jules admitted, "but we will surely meet in town after the New Year."

"I'd like that very much indeed."

Jules rose. "Then I will take my leave of you, my dear Genevieve, and wish you *bon chance.*"

"Good luck to you also, Jules," she said.

The young man who'd taken on such an air of maturity in such a short space stared at her, then, with great temerity, kissed her cheek. "If ever your luck deserts you, come to me—for anything."

Long after Jules had disappeared down the stairs, Genevieve sat smiling to herself, touching the place on her cheek, wondering why she hadn't done the sensible, uncomplicated thing and fallen in love with him. But that answer was moot in the face of what she felt for Bryce Cormick, and little by little, the tension that had engulfed her since his collapse began to be dispelled by a sense of enormous relief and quiet rejoicing. Bryce was going to recover, the Abbot's plan had been foiled, and now there was time to hope for a future with the man she loved.

"*Bon chance*, Genny," she wished herself aloud, and went back into the sickroom to watch Bryce sleep.

A man could only sleep so long before his mind gave him a boot in the arse and told him to get back to reality. Or at least that's what Bryce came to believe after waking a few times to find himself swimming in his own sweat and his heart pounding like a drum from the terrifying images his darker self had thrown at him in the form of nightmares. Whether it was caused by the damnable ache in his arm, or the laudanum the physician was feeding him, or the soul-stultifying knowledge that he was one step lower than a rabid cur, the effect was the same.

As soon as he could think, he turned the Griffin's formidable powers of concentration to the problem. As soon as he could sit up, he sent for Wellington.

"You're determined in this, are you, Cormick?"

"Yes, Your Grace."

"I see."

The duke stood before the long window of Bryce's convalescent chamber, staring into the Parisian night, watching the street lanterns flicker to life one by one. Dressed for one of the numerous preholiday fêtes, he rocked back and forth on his well-shod heels, his hands locked under the tails of his severe evening dress coat, waiting while his personal surgeon adjusted the bandages on Bryce's arm with Taffy McKee in stoic attendance.

Dr. Fergus made a neat knot in the end of the bandage and pulled it tight, ignoring Bryce's wince. "You're a lucky man, Mr. Cormick. Damned lucky. Thought for sure you'd lose that arm when I first saw it."

"I appreciate your efforts, Doctor," Bryce said. Gingerly, he slipped on the clean shirt Taffy produced, tucking it one-handedly into the waistband of his trousers. In the mirror over the fireplace he caught a glimpse of himself, and for an instant it wasn't his own haggard features he saw, but the cool slanted eyes of a hell-bound murderer. Suppressing a shudder, he sat back down in the uncomfortable Empire-style chair.

The physician shrugged. "I can't take credit for a strong constitution and expert nursing."

"Mr. Cormick is fortunate in his wife," the duke said, turning back to face the trio. "But however much I welcome your appointment to my staff, I'll not be the one to break the rest of the news to her, sir."

From his seat, Bryce nodded while ignoring Taffy's disapproving glower. "That is my duty, Your Grace."

There was a knock at the door and a soft feminine inquiry.

"And I believe this is a perfect opportunity to perform it," the duke replied dryly, then waved Taffy and the doctor toward the door. "Come, gentlemen."

Attired in a dove-gray gown and carrying Bryce's napkin-covered supper tray, Genevieve flushed a peachy tone when the eminent statesman-soldier opened the door for her and ushered her into the room. Easily brushing off her apologies for disturbing their conversation, he inquired of her comfort, complimented her appearance, and then he and his companions quit the room forthwith.

"Well!" Genevieve laughed, a trifle breathless, and set the tray down on a small table before Bryce. "Small wonder His Grace turns so many feminine heads!"

Bryce watched her fuss over the tray with a sharp pang of longing. Not for him the tender, homey intimacies, the loving services. He couldn't let his innermost needs supplant what was best for Genevieve. He owed her that much. For once in his godforsaken life, he was determined to do the right thing or die.

"Is something the matter?" Transfixed by Bryce's pained expression, Genevieve poised over a steaming soup tureen. The aromatic blend of bay leaf, marjoram, and bouillon swirled through the air. "The doctor hurt you!"

The corner of his mouth twitched at her accusing, indignant tone. "No, but leave that. I'm not hungry."

"You must eat to build up your strength." She ladled a bit of the broth into the bowl and then coquettishly waved it under his nose. "The duke's chef is truly a miracle worker with a joint of beef."

"Not now. I want to talk to you."

"Act the child, and I'll be forced to feed you like one," she warned, advancing on him with a loaded spoon.

"Dammit, General! Not now, I said!"

She stared up into his blue eyes and was suddenly mystified and alarmed. "All right."

Swearing under his breath, Bryce swung away from her while his hand made tunnels in his dark hair. It wasn't going how he'd planned. Dammit, *nothing* had gone as planned since Genevieve Maples had come into his life!

"You're going back to England," he said abruptly. "Tomorrow. You'll be traveling with a British party. I've spoken with the duke, and it's all arranged."

"Wh-what?" She staggered back, as though physically shoved by the onslaught of words. "Home?"

"Yes, home." The word had a bitter taste. "Back to Miss Symthe, and your dress patterns, and a normal life."

"And you?"

He made a negligent gesture. "This attack on the duke has solidified the government's position regarding the need to remove him from Paris. He dislikes an assignment to the New World, especially since the negotiations at Ghent will soon resolve the American conflict, so as a suitable substitute he will take Lord Castlereagh's place at the Vienna Congress in the new year. In the meantime, he's reactivated my commission so that I may join his staff as added security until he leaves the city."

"And then you'll come to London?" she questioned carefully.

"That remains to be seen."

"What about your career?"

"The theater will still be there whenever I return."

She licked her dry lips and abandoned her pride. "I would prefer to stay with you."

"That's impossible."

At the cool implacability of his words, icy tentacles of fear more powerful than any she'd yet experienced constricted her heart. She sank into a spindly-legged chair and clasped her hands to hide their trembling. "Why is it impossible?"

He cast her an impatient glance. "My duties to the duke . . . and your safety demand it. The Abbot—"

"Don't use *him* as your excuse! He has the seal now, so there's no reason for me to fear reprisal any longer, and even if there were, London would be no safer than here."

"You'll have to let me be the judge of that."

"Ah, yes," she said, laughing softly, bitterly. "I suppose that is what this is really about. *Judgment.* In spite of everything I've tried to do to redeem myself, you still haven't forgiven me for what happened to the Athena or for my involvement with the Abbot."

"Don't be ridiculous."

"Then why are you still punishing me?" she cried. "Why are you sending me away?"

Bryce's eyes looked haunted. "Genevieve, you don't understand. I'm not trying to punish you. I'm trying to do what's best."

"For whom? Certainly not for me." She blinked furiously, fighting back tears. "I love you, Bryce. Don't do this to us."

He closed his eyes on the torment that shimmered in her anguished expression, steeling himself. It would be so easy to succumb to the tender vulnerability of her perfect mouth, to lose himself again in her arms. But she was still an innocent, and the depravity and corruption within him would only destroy her in the end if he let his weakness rule. He tried to tell her.

"I can't give you what you want."

"I only want you." A tear escaped form her lashes and

glistened down her cheek. "Not some dream of a cottage with roses in the garden."

He shook his head, and his voice was hoarse. "You have no idea what I really am, General."

"I know more than you think. After all we've been through together, how could I not? We're neither perfect; we've both made mistakes. But I can accept you as Bryce, or Darcy, or even the Griffin because they're all part of who you are. Why can't you accept it, too?"

"Because I don't want to hurt you again!" he said savagely.

With a brittle laugh, she dashed the tear off her cheek. "Pray, then, what is this?"

"This is the way it has to be." Walking up behind her chair, he slipped his hand under the ringlets at her nape, his thumb tracing the delicate bones of her spinal column. His voice was thick. "Christ, Genny! Why do you have to make it so damned hard?"

Her lashes fluttered, and she swallowed, the convulsion transmitting her distress through his fingertips resting on her throat. "You *do* care. I know that."

He wished he was man enough to deny it, to tell her that it was only lust with no finer emotions involved so that she could rekindle her hatred and banish him with the fire of a cleansing anger from her heart and mind forever. The cruelty would have been kinder, but this was a farewell for him, too, and he wasn't strong enough.

Bending, he kissed the gentle curve of her neck, feasting on the ivory-toned skin. His husky murmurs were the truest words he'd ever uttered. "I adore you."

With a small cry, she stood and flung herself against his chest, taking care not to jostle his injured arm, but holding on to him as though her life depended on it. Bryce resisted the temptation only momentarily, then he pulled her fully into his embrace, cradling her shuddering form in the sweetest torture known to man while he whispered soothing nothings into her ear.

"I have no pride left," she half laughed, half wept,

"but I'll beg if I must. I ask nothing but to stay at your side."

"Oh, God, Genny," he muttered into her hair. "You deserve better than that, better than *me*."

"How dare you!" She gripped the linen of his shirt in both fists and shook him. "How dare you presume to make that decision for me? I'm a woman full grown! I'm prepared to live with the consequences of loving you."

"But I'm not." Regretfully, he disentangled her hands and set her away.

Devastated, she looked at him with a mixture of pity and rage, desperately casting about for some argument to make him see what he so blithely sacrificed. "What about your family? What will you tell them? Though it began as a game, you're the one who made our 'marriage' real to them."

"A bit of the truth will suffice—that I'm the one responsible for our separation. No one will blame you." Rubbing his jaw, he met her accusing gaze, then glanced away again. "And don't worry about finances. You won't lack, I'll see to that. You'll have your couturiere salon with Miss Smythe just as you wanted."

She grew paler with each word he spoke. "Dreams change. Why can't you see that?"

"I want you to be happy."

She choked and pressed the back of her hand to her mouth. "Liar. You were never of so noble a bent as that. Why don't you admit your freedom means more to you than I do?"

"Freedom is not the issue."

"No, only getting clear of the unwelcome encumbrance of a clinging female the instant her usefulness is over! Well, don't worry, I think I understand you at last. I won't be an embarrassment to you any longer."

Bryce took a step toward her. "Genny—"

"Your soup is cold." She snatched up the tray, rattling crockery with the suddenness of her capitulation, already in full retreat as she backed toward the door. "I'll have Taffy bring you some more."

"That's not necessary."

"Oh." For an instant she looked as though he'd struck her, then she raised her chin defiantly. "In that case . . ."

With perfect deliberation, she dropped the entire tray flat on the floor, shattering tureen, bowl, and lid, spilling broth everywhere. Despite the cold misery in his gut, it made him smile.

Her soft green eyes were cloudy with unshed tears, but her voice was firm. "I don't want you to see me off tomorrow."

His smile disappeared. "I understand."

"No, you don't. If you had the faintest inkling of understanding, instead of running away from love you'd be doing everything in your power to make me stay."

His words were raw. "I wish I could."

"You have only to say it," she replied softly.

Silence hung like a curtain between them for the span of a heartbeat. Chin quivering, Genevieve turned toward the door. With her hand on the knob, she looked back at him one last time.

"The night we met, you told me you were a coward, Bryce Cormick. How I wish I'd had the sense to listen."

December 4, 1814

. . . most grieved that I increased your apprehension, my dearest Maebella, but my decision to remain in Paris yet awhile was an impulse of the moment, as I'm sure you determined by the state of my hastily scribbled note which Lady Meadows and her niece so kindly delivered. In truth, I fear my companions thought I had quite lost my mind, for our carriage had reached the outskirts of the city before the resolution settled upon me, causing quite an uproar when I insisted on being let out. Lady Meadows was most upset at the thought of turning back as we had made a late start that day, but I assured her I could well handle the situation (which proved to be absolutely the case), and they were much relieved both of the obligation of escorting my person back to the embassy and bearing with my most disagreeable company all the way to London itself.

Of my separation from Mr. Cormick, I will have much to explain when I finally find myself again in your comforting presence, but I find the topic too painful to express in the written word. Suffice to say, I am comfortably settled in Madame Yvonne's garret (for even so great a couturiere could not find fault in my offer to work for only room and board in exchange for her tutelage), and I am applying myself assiduously to learning all that I can about French fashion for both our future benefits . . .

December 13, 1814

. . . received your missive with the greatest affection and appreciation, but I beg you not to be overly concerned about me. Though my confused emotions wax and wane like the moon, from disappointment to anger to the tenderest felicitations for Mr. Cormick, I am certainly *not* wasting away with melancholia. My pride would not allow it, just as it would not allow Mr. Cormick to arrange my departure from Paris to suit his own whim. Taking control of that small decision has done much to restore my confidence, and having a purpose of my own (in educating myself at Madame Yvonne's skillful hands) makes me feel that I can command my own fate again.

I am pleased at your clientele's response to my sketches and enclose more of the same. Madame Yvonne has me rendering her designs now, and we are equally satisfied with the results. As the crush of holiday orders is upon the salon, I find I could not possibly desert her at present, though I long to see you. At least the burden of long days causes me to fall into my cot in nightly exhaustion so there is no chance to think about other things . . .

December 25, 1814

. . . and so all the compliments of this holy day, my dearest Maebella. The third seamstress, Angelique, took me to the most beautiful and moving midnight services at Notre Dame. And no, there is no reason to inform Mr. Cormick that I am still in the city, for he undoubtedly has his own sources to apprise him of the news. At any rate, I expect no contact, for he was explicit and vehement in his resolution to dissolve our relationship, such as it was. Though my heart was very much engaged, I am determined to win over any moments of bleakness. I would not be even so foolish as to waste a Christmas wish on a hopeless cause, but I confess I am never on the streets without finding myself looking for a particular tall, ebony-haired man. No doubt I will soon outgrow such fancies, but do not think this is the reason I've elected to stay another month . . .

January 9, 1815

. . . so busy I rarely miss the stage, and society not at all. It is especially interesting to see society inside-out as it were, for Madame Yvonne caters to the most influential ladies, and whereas only weeks ago I counted myself among those ranks, now I have the wonderful attribute of perfect anonymity again. Such a relief! The triumph I enjoyed in Paris was entirely due to Mr. Cormick, and without his support I have no heart for acting. The vagaries of the dramatic life have finished heartier players than I, dear Grandpapa included. Concentrating on my own proclivities for design and fashion offers a much more stable future. I miss you terribly, Maebella, and long for home with all my heart, but Madame Yvonne is depending on my help with her spring designs . . .

January 20, 1815

. . . the news is that the Duke of Wellington will leave the city shortly to take his position at the Congress of

Vienna. I understand it is a glittering city with many diversions, especially for unattached gentlemen (and gossip has it that His Grace's marriage has disintegrated as fully as my own relationship with Mr. Cormick). I suspect the duke may well expect Mr. Cormick to accompany him, and I wonder if Bryce has sufficiently recuperated to withstand such an arduous journey, as the winter weather has been especially inclement . . .

February 8, 1815

. . . nearly finished with the spring portfolio, and feel certain that the agreement struck with Madame Yvonne to supply her exclusive designs to our London clients as well as my own will be propitious for all concerned. Reports say Wellington took only young Lennox and Colonel Fremont with him . . .

February 19, 1815

. . . remainder of Wellington's staff left for the Austrian capital yesterday. My arrangements have been made, and, as there is nothing left for me in this city, I am coming home . . .

Genevieve carefully negotiated the narrow, icy treads of Madame Yvonne's back stairs, then turned down the rear alley, picking her way through the grimy slush. Overcast skies made the alley dim, and a frigid February wind bit at her nose and pierced her tobacco-brown spencer. But her letter to Maebella, its wax seal still warm, rested inside her ridicule right next to her precious coach tickets and transportation papers, and she was determined to post the letter this very evening. Whatever she'd meant to prove to herself about independence, vain hopes and loneliness and an aching heart had taught her more. It was time to go home, and Maebella would be glad.

"Madame!"

The beggar's sibilant whisper made Genevieve jump. Crouched against the crumbling brick wall in a filthy coat and misshapen hat, he was little more than a bundle of skinny bones and dirty rags. She ducked her head and hurried past.

"Please, madame, you must help me!"

Something in the familiar cadence of the voice brought Genevieve up short. She turned back uncertainly. "Who. . . ? Oh, my God—Chevalier!"

Genevieve stared in recognition, aghast. He'd lost weight, and his face was lined and aged with privation. That the urbane Chevalier Bertrand du Roche should be reduced to such penurious circumstances seemed unbelievable. Then fear replaced amazement. This was the Abbot's man! What did he want?

"Please, madame, I mean you no harm. I am a desperate man, a hunted man," the former courtier said pitifully, tears streaking his begrimed face. "It is a miracle of *le bon Dieu* that I saw you on the quay. Have compassion on me."

"What do you want, Chevalier?"

"Your help. You see what's become of me. I've been running since the Champs de Mars."

Genevieve took a wary step backward. "Why come to me? Surely you should seek your master's aid?"

The Chevalier spit on the ground and swore. "That devil, that Abbot—bah! He is the cause of this. Did I not serve him well? And he leaves me behind. Abandons me to my fate, blaming the bungling attempts of a few ill-trained boys on me. The royalist dogs are closing in. I'll hang if I am found, madame."

The weight of her responsibility in his dire situation pricked her. She sighed, weary of intrigues. "You knew the risks, Chevalier."

"I only want to leave the country." His expression turned sly. "If you help me, I will tell you things you may find useful. A clever woman could turn a profit, reap a dozen times over the small amount I require."

"I have no use for such things anymore." He looked so defeated, she felt a stirring of pity. Whatever his poli-

tics, he was still a human in need. "Come, I have bread
and some wine upstairs. You may have that and the few
francs I have left, then you must go."

"You are a saint, an angel!"

Grimacing, Genevieve led du Roche back up the narrow
stairs to her single room. He wolfed down the bread and
cheese she set before him and gulped the wine, his continental manners forgotten with the sharpness of his hunger. She dug in her ridicule for the franc notes, and when
du Roche made an involuntary sound of distress, she
looked up to find his gaze riveted on the coach tickets.

"You're going on a journey, madame?"

"Home to England, Chevalier." She thrust the franc
notes at him. "This is all I can do to help."

He took the notes in his trembling hands, his face
twitching. "A trade, madame. Valuable information for
your passage."

Genevieve considered. "All right. Tell me the Abbot's
true name." Du Roche's face fell, and she laughed. "You
don't even know that, do you, Chevalier? You were no
less a pawn in this chess game than I. Bonaparte is still in
exile, the Abbot's attempt on Wellington failed miserably,
and it's all over."

"You think so? Then you underestimate the Abbot,"
the Chevalier said furiously. "Why do you think he fled
to Vienna? *To make another attempt on the duke.*"

Genevieve's hand flew to her mouth to stifle a horrified
gasp. "Oh, no!"

"*Oui!* And this time there will be no Griffin to interfere
by removing the Abbot's assassin at a crucial moment.
Why else would the Abbot's so well-laid plan explode in
disaster? But they fished Leclerc out of the Seine, and
before he died he told his master . . ."

"Wh-what?" The blood drained from her face, leaving
her cheeks the color of alabaster. "Told him what?"

"You see?" he asked, his expression cunning. "I do
know something of value."

"I'll give you whatever you want—just tell me!"

Du Roche leaned closer. "A bargain, then. Though you've already guessed. Leclerc told the Abbot the Griffin's *name*."

"Pox and perdition!" Genevieve whispered, stricken with horror.

"*Oui*, madame. 'Tis your husband, Bryce Cormick, Leclerc named. And the Abbot knows. Perhaps not now, but sometime, the Griffin will pay."

Genevieve's head swam. Wellington was again a target, and Bryce, his identity uncovered but suspecting nothing, was headed straight into the Abbot's murderous and vengeful hands! A shudder racked her slender frame. She wanted no more of these things, only to go home to Maebella's simple kindnesses and dream innocent dreams again.

But that was impossible now. Swallowing, Genevieve knew what she had to do.

"Madame?" Chevalier du Roche's prematurely wizened countenance twisted hopefully.

"Take them, Chevalier." Genevieve pushed the coach tickets into his grasp.

"Ah, *merci*! You are so generous, so beautiful—" He tried to kiss her hands.

She shook her head. "No thanks are necessary, monsieur. It is the ticket to your freedom, not mine, and you have earned it well this day."

Chapter 17

"**T**hey're still out there, Cap."

Frowning, Bryce held his restless mount in the black shadows of a stand of snow-capped firs overlooking a mountainous valley between the Salz River and the Austrian Danube. The quartet of British privates making up the rest of the escort waited some distance behind the rocky outcropping.

"You're certain they're the same ones?" he demanded.

"Yes, sir. See for yourself." Taffy passed his field glass to Bryce. Though the sun was so brilliant it hurt the eyes, the air was bitterly cold, biting the lungs with every breath, and his words formed white puffs of condensation in the frigid air.

Bryce lifted the glass to his eye, and the circle of the lens revealed the same two horsemen who'd dogged their trail for the past day and a half, slogging their weary horses through the slush of rocky mud and icy snow that was all that indicated the roadway up this incline. The way the muffled and cloaked duo spared neither their mounts nor themselves hinted at an urgency that boded no good.

The hair on the back of Bryce's neck prickled against the fur collar of his heavy cloak with an instinct he'd learned long ago not to ignore. An occasional glimpse of fellow travelers wasn't so unusual, but now, on the sixth day of their trek toward the Austrian capital, a torturous journey in which they'd ridden hard and slept rough, Bryce had steered his party off the main highway, detouring upward into the snowy foothills of the Styrian Alps at Huxford's direction, toward holy ground and perhaps some answers to mysteries still unsolved. That the two below followed them into this relatively untraveled region was definitely suspicious, and Bryce took no unnecessary chances.

"Perhaps we'd better have a closer look at our companions," Bryce said, handing Taffy the glass again.

"Aye, sir. 'Twas just in my own mind to say as much."

Bryce smiled to himself at the prospect of a confrontation. He'd been spoiling for a fight since the day Taffy reported Genevieve hadn't left Paris at all; itching for a contest the many weeks it had taken every ounce of his self-control not to go to her; clamoring for a brawl to release the accumulated tension, rage, and frustration since the day he learned she had bought herself passage back to England, and he'd known the battle of wills was finally over.

He'd won. He could go on now to Vienna and Wellington's work. He'd done the right thing. But the victory was as empty as he was, and he'd been ill-tempered and glowering ever since. A two-fisted altercation with a pair of ruffians was just what he needed to improve his disposition.

An hour later, Bryce had backtracked with his men, positioning them on either side of a forested curve of the road. When the two horsemen galloped around the turn, Bryce's signal whistle mingled with the thunder of pounding hooves. The second rider's head jerked up in a listening attitude, slowing momentarily, but it was too late.

Instantly, six mounted men sporting sidearms and rifles sprang from behind the snowy appendages of the drooping firs, surrounding the riders, cutting off all avenues of retreat or advancement. The first horseman reined in sharply at Bryce's shout to halt, but the second horse panicked at the unexpected attack, reared, and tossed his rider into a snowbank.

Taffy grabbed the leader's bridle, but things had happened too quickly, and he put up no fight. The soldiers' grins were wide as Bryce climbed down to inspect the bundle on its back in the snowdrift. He nudged the figure with the toe of his boot.

"Arise, *mein Herr,* and explain yourself!"

A low moan was all the answer he got. Impatiently, he bent closer, pushing aside the brim of the fellow's enveloping hat—and stared into the softest gray-green eyes in the world.

"Genny!"

Giddy, lurching with vertigo, for an awful instant Bryce spun somewhere between heaven and hell, then plunged to earth again with the fiery rage of a dying star. Cursing, he set her up and jerked off the misshapen hat, then unwound the knitted muffler covering her nose and mouth until her pale face was fully revealed and there was no doubt of her identity. Her snow-covered garments were a boy's rough working garb, but the chestnut curls spilling over her shoulders and the luscious, trembling mouth certainly belonged to the female who'd bewitched his dreams all these many lonely weeks.

"Damnation, woman!" he roared. "You could have been killed! Are you all right?"

"I—I—" Shaking with cold and trepidation and shock, Genevieve nodded, unable to form the words around her chattering teeth.

Bryce's curses redoubled as he dragged her to her feet and brushed the worst of the snow from her back and shoulders with ungentle hands. He gestured sharply for the soldiers to put away their weapons and fetch the skittish horse, then lit into Genevieve again.

"Of all the imbecilic tricks—what in Christ's name do you think you're doing?"

She managed a faint answer. "F-following you."

Bryce gawked, his anger growing by the minute. "You came after me *alone*?"

"With Michel. I hired—" A tremendous shudder made her clamp her teeth together. She pointed. "There."

The young man at Taffy's side sported the well-worn coat and wraps of a hoslter. He was barely out of his teens, still peachy-cheeked, hardly someone Bryce would have chosen as a guide across Europe.

"This is the man you seek, mademoiselle?" Michel asked.

"Yes. *Merci*, Michel."

Michel's round face puffed with the satisfied pride of arrogant youth. "A hard ride, *oui*? But I promised we'd catch up to them, didn't I? *Vraiment*, I am a tracker *extraordinaire!* Now we rest at last."

Swaying on her feet, Genevieve managed a shaky smile for the youth. " 'Tis well deserved, my friend."

Bryce's expression ran the gamut of every emotion: mystification, bewilderment, grudging admiration, elation, fury, joy, desire. Anger was the only defense that gave him any security.

"You deserve a sound flogging for this piece of insanity, General. Of all the clodpated stunts!"

Pale as she was, twin spots of rosy color blossomed on her cheeks. "I had to come, you see . . ."

"All I see is an idiotic woman!" He cast an irritable glance in the boy's direction. "Do you ride with us, Monsieur Michel?"

"*S'il vous plaît, monsieur.* The roads are dangerous for a solitary traveler, and I have a mind to see Vienna."

Bryce scowled. "Very well. Let's go. Between the two of you, you've made us waste enough time as it is. I'd hoped to reach our destination by dusk, and if we don't hurry it will mean another night sleeping on frozen earth for us all."

He dragged Genevieve toward his horse, paying no attention to her feeble protests or her stumbling gait.

"My horse . . . I can ride," she began.

"The hell you can! Look at you! You're so nearly done in you can hardly walk. Were you trying to kill yourself?"

"Of course not!" she denied, indignant. "If you'll just—"

"Never mind your excuses!" He lifted her across his saddle, then vaulted up behind her, pulling his heavy cloak around them both.

"But Bryce—" she wailed softly.

"Shut up, General," he snapped, closing his arm around her middle and pulling her shivering form into the shelter of his body. "I'm not responsible for what I might say or do right now, so take heed."

She subsided meekly, but Bryce was certain it was not because she was cowed by his threats but because she was near exhaustion. At his signal, the party moved on, the pace such that more conversation was impossible, for with Genevieve in such a fatigued state it was more imperative than ever to reach the haven he sought.

Bryce was relieved when he felt her shivering subside, and humbled by the trust she placed in him when she eventually dropped into a light doze. The pliancy of her body and the floral scent of her hair were sheer torture, alleviated only when he gave in to the urge and buried his lips against her temple. Even then, she didn't stir. It had cost her dearly to pursue him in this fashion. Why? The question rattled around his head without answer as they continued to climb into the heights.

It was nearing dusk when they reached the final span of their journey. They rode in shadows through a narrow valley, but high above, the last rays of sunlight still blazed on the distant snow-capped peaks. As Bryce kicked his weary mount around the last bend, he felt Genevieve's soft gasp.

"Genny?" He wondered how long she'd lain awake and quiescent in his arms. *And if she'd enjoyed it as much as he had.* "What is it?"

"I dreamed this once," she whispered, spellbound at the scene that lay before them.

On the next pinnacle, rising as if part of the living stone of the mountain itself, was an ancient and intricately designed Romanesque building with vaulted arches and onion-domed spires, inspired by the minarets of the Turkish legions who had conquered this region so many centuries earlier. And circling above the towers, in the space between a monument dedicated to man's pilgrimage on earth and the snow-covered mountain aerie rising to touch heaven's sunset-tinted vault, eagles soared.

"I've seen this," she marveled, her words soft and awe-struck. "But how can that be?"

"Perhaps you're dreaming again," he said gruffly. They passed through the cluster of straw-thatched huts crouched at the foot of the monastery complex, heading toward the heavy arched main gate.

"Perhaps." Cuddled against his warmth, she glanced back over her shoulder, dazed with wonderment, smiling slightly at his unsuspecting irony, for lying again in his arms was indeed a longed-for dream. "In my vision, when I saw the eagles, I thought of you."

"You mean to make me into a Bonapartist symbol?"

"You know better. No man is more loyal to England. How many times over have you proven your devotion? I simply mean it as it sounds."

Despite himself, Bryce was drawn into her moment, this bubble of time when there was only harmony between them. "And how is that?"

Her eyes sought again the distant swooping flight of majestic birds. "That your nature is free and proud, but somehow always searching."

"A Griffin is part eagle, too." He lifted his gaze to the sky, and his mouth tightened in self-recrimination. "The part that is a predator."

"There is an order and balance to all things."

"And your fatigue gives you fancies."

She smiled at the utter irrelevancy of such a practical conclusion to their mystic discussion. Rather than pursuing it, however, she examined her surroundings more closely. "What is this place?"

At that moment, the sun disappeared completely behind the peaks, and cold shadows fell across Bryce's face. "The Abbey of the Holy Word."

She stiffened. "Your Abbot has nothing to do with these holy men, does he?"

Bryce shrugged. "We'll see."

By sheer effort of will she pulled herself free of the fantastical cocoon that had enthralled them, called back to more urgent concerns. "Bryce, there's something I must tell you—"

"All in good time, General," he interrupted, not unkindly, as he led his small band through the open gates. "Rest first, then talk."

Benedictine monks in heavy black robes and cowls hurried across the wide, clean-swept interior courtyard to welcome their unexpected guests. Worship, the preservation of scholarship and civilization, and hospitality had long been the hallmark of the religious communities of this region.

Within short order, the travelers had collected their meager baggage from the horse's packs and were then escorted through the echoing, stone walks of arched colonnades to the wing of simple, spacious accommodations set aside for the visitors who often came to examine the illuminated vellum volumes in the order's immense and ancient library. The odors of smoke and cooking food mingled with the exotic scents of incense and beeswax candles, and the bells above the chapel tolled deeply, calling the brothers to vespers.

Leaving Genevieve in the capable hands of a smiling village matron employed by the brothers for woman's work, they separated to refresh themselves. As soon as Bryce was presentable again, he went to pay his respects to their hosts and speak of his mission, obtaining a promise that on the morrow the reverend father himself would be happy to receive him.

The aching harmonies of prayer chants being sung in the choirloft drifted to every corner of the compound, petitions and thanksgiving, penitence and praise borne on the wings of the abbey's eagles to the gates of heaven. Bryce paused before the chamber to which Genevieve had been assigned, listening to the haunting chorus as if it might give him some inspiration of how best to face the woman waiting beyond the door, some modicum of strength to do again the hardest thing he'd ever had to do— give her up. Taking a deep breath, he rapped on the heavy timbers, and at the soft answer went inside.

This guest chamber was one of the best, long and spacious, with high narrow windows and a stone fireplace at one end. A table holding a lit branch of candles and the remains of a meal stood in its center, and beyond that a well-draped bed piled high with eiderdown coverlets. A tall settle stood beside the fireplace, and as Bryce advanced into the room, Genevieve rose slowly from the shadowed seat.

She'd changed into a simple, high-necked gown the color of moss and smoke, and her shining hair fell unfettered to her shoulders like a medieval chatelaine's. But as Bryce met her gaze, and her power invaded his senses like a glowing sun, he knew that she was more sorceress than mortal, a siren with the face of an angel and the mouth of a pagan princess.

Oh, God, I want to kiss her!
Please, God, let him kiss me!

Genevieve felt Bryce's look like a touch, the whisper of unseen hands caressing her body, making her heart pound and her blood rush. Involuntarily, her lips parted, swollen and aching from kisses still unreceived, yet desperately desired. An invisible connecting current vibrated between them like a plucked bowstring, drawing Bryce across the room in a trance, his beautiful blue eyes hooded, but the hunger in them as he stopped before her undeniable.

Trembling, Genevieve felt hope flare within her, but then something in Bryce's eyes changed, darkened, and she watched him withdraw into a place within himself she feared she might never be able to reach. But she had to try, and like a true general, she knew a frontal attack might be her only hope.

"Don't think you will send me away this time," she said.

Bryce shook his head, and a lock of ebony hair fell across his forehead. "What did you hope to gain from this rash act? Coming all this way, in such weather, with only that boy—it was not only foolhardy, but madness itself!"

She almost smiled. Madness was a perfect description of the whirlwind that had begun the night they met, but if loving Bryce was insanity, she could not fear it as Grandpapa had, but rather embrace it, for this, too, was a part of life, and one she would never choose to miss, regardless of the outcome.

It took all her strength not to reach up and smooth back that rebellious lock of hair. "I had to stop you."

A muscle in Bryce's jaw flexed as he fought an incredible urge to weep, and his voice dropped to a husky timbre laden with weariness and defeat. "Nothing's changed, General, except you've had a long ride for nothing."

"I count your life *something* whether you do or not!" she cried, suddenly fierce. "You mustn't go to Vienna. The Abbot is ahead of you, and he knows who you are!"

Bryce's head snapped up, and he gripped her cold hands. "Tell me."

"Du Roche," she said, nearly overwhelmed by the familiar texture of his skin against her own. "He came to me for help, told me everything. The Abbot will try again to assassinate Wellington in Vienna."

"Damn! Are you sure? Can you trust the Chevalier?"

"Yes, I think so. He was desperate, bitter at the Abbot's desertion. I helped him, and he was grateful. The duke is a target still, but now so are you!"

He was stunned, not by this news, but by the courageous way in which she'd acted on it. "And you put yourself in who knows what kind of danger, just to warn me?"

"I had to," she said simply. "I love you."

"Ah, Genny!" He closed his eyes, swallowing back a thickening in his throat. No one had ever cared enough to risk everything for him. It was humbling. But it was impossible. He released her hands and began to pace. "I can't believe you! You could have sent word. Why, it may not even be true at all. Du Roche was probably lying."

"I was afraid a message might come too late, and you'd have no warning. Would you have taken such a chance?"

"No."

"Then do not berate me for what I had to do. Now you may send word to the duke—"

"I deliver my own messages, and I can't shirk this duty. It's time to finish with the Abbot."

"Even though you could be in terrible danger yourself with no idea of its source?" She gripped the tall edge of the settle for support. "That's more foolhardy than my following you, or anything else I've ever done!"

"Except for falling in love with me." He touched her cheek, and regret etched creases beside his mouth. "Genny, understand. I'm the best at what I do."

She saw his determination and nodded slowly. "I was afraid you'd say that. So be it, then, but I'm coming with you."

"The hell you are!"

"I was excellent bait once before," she argued. "Even without the Abbot's Seal, I expect I can generate some interest."

"I absolutely forbid it! You're going back."

Releasing her grip on the settle, she stepped toward him, lifting her chin at a haughty angle. "How do you propose to arrange that? I've come this far already, and I'll follow you all the way to Vienna if I must!"

Bryce gave a bark of reluctant laughter. "You would, too, wouldn't you, General?"

Her chin angled up another notch. "Just try me."

Frustrated, tempted, torn, he shook his head. "Go home, Genny. You belong in England."

"My home is wherever you are, because I belong with you, you great lunkhead! Haven't you learned *anything* over the past months?"

"Self-control mostly," he said in a dry tone.

"Oh!" Turning her back on him, she faced the fire, digging the heels of her hands into her eyes, swaying with weariness, yet far from retreating. "I'm not going to cry. I promised myself I wouldn't cry!"

Bryce crossed to stand behind her, fighting an urge to stroke her bright hair, but instead closing his hands on her shoulders. "If you come, tears will be all you find, Genny. I can't risk it."

"Risk! You're the one who refuses to be reasonable about that. Someone who knew you as the Griffin told the Abbot your name. Someone called Leclerc—"

Bryce's grip tightened painfully, and he whirled her to face him again. His eyes were so dark they appeared almost black, and his voice was vicious. "What of Leclerc?"

"He's dead." She sighed imperceptibly as Bryce's vise-like hold eased, but did not flinch from the hellish joy that burned suddenly in his eyes. "You killed him, didn't you?"

He hesitated, then nodded curtly. "An old debt repaid in full."

The baldness of his answer made her catch her breath. "I—I see."

Dropping his hands, he stepped back, his look laden with bitter challenge. If ever there was a way to make Genevieve regret the folly of giving her affection to him, this was it. He grabbed at the chance, barehanded, as if turning the blade he'd used on Leclerc on to himself in well-deserved retribution.

"Look well, General, and witness the ugliness of the Griffin. You want no part of him."

Her gaze flicked to his left arm, and the new scar she knew lay there. She took a deep breath and let intuition be her guide. "If you did this thing, then it was necessary. He tried to kill you. And it wasn't the first time."

"In Lyons—" He broke off, turning abruptly to stare into the fire, his mouth twisting with a shudder he could not control.

"Tell me what happened."

"You don't want to know."

Anger sharpened her voice. "Don't dismiss me like a child! If you can give me nothing else, at least give me that much respect. If there's a reason for the choice you force upon us both, I'm entitled to know what it is."

He turned on her, his look savage. "It's death, don't you understand? I took bloody revenge on Leclerc, not only because I had no choice, but because *I wanted it.* I even enjoyed it, after what he'd done to sweet, gentle Marie, after I saw . . ."

He choked to a stop, and Genevieve froze, for it seemed he looked into hell. "Saw what, Bryce?"

"Her two little sons, lying dead with their throats slashed because of me—and I could do nothing to save them! I didn't even have the grace to die myself! God, they've haunted me."

The fire crackled and popped, the only disturbance in the silence that lay like an open wound between them. She swallowed. "You must have tried to save them."

"I never had the chance." He sank heavily into the wooden seat of the settle and buried his face in his hands. "I shouldn't have stayed. That's what killed them, my selfishness. But I was so tired, and it was so good there, so peaceful in that little house with the sweet basil and the rosemary perfuming everything in the garden. It was just supposed to be a rest stop. If I hadn't stayed, then nothing bad would have happened . . ."

"You cared for her." It was not a question.

"She was a gentle woman, and kind to me at a time when I needed it desperately. If only I'd gone on, then Leclerc wouldn't have found them, wouldn't have done what he did." Bryce looked up at Genevieve, and his eyes were tormented. "He left me for dead, Genny, but Marie and her poor babies . . . I heard . . . I heard it all . . ."

Genevieve went to him, compassion and love welling up within her like an overflowing fountain. "Oh, Bryce, I'm so sorry . . ."

With a ragged sound, he reached out and pulled her between his knees, wrapping his arms around her waist, laying his head against the womanly softness of her breasts, shuddering with the horror of his memories. Genevieve threaded her fingers through the black silk of his hair and rubbed his stiff shoulders, murmuring wordless solace, finding her own comfort in her ability to comfort him.

"You can't blame yourself," she whispered against the top of his head. She stroked his jaw, reveling in the feel of hard bone, and taunt, freshly shaven skin, then tugged his face upward so that she could brush his brow, the slant of his cheekbone, and finally his mouth with gentle, healing kisses. "You mustn't."

With a muted groan, he caught her lips, and everything that was between them flared to instant life. Standing, he pulled her closer, bending his head to deepen the kiss, taking her sweetness with fiery sweeps of his tongue. Her response was everything he'd ever dreamed of, the melting pliancy of her body, the heat of her mouth, bewitching, drowning, life-giving—and the most terrifying thing he'd ever known.

"No." Breathing heavily, he pulled back, and there was real fear in his eyes. "I won't do this to you."

She nearly sobbed with disappointment. "Have I asked you for anything? There are no conditions."

"Goddammit! Why can't you understand? If we're together, anything can happen. Anything . . ." His expression was both haggard and beseeching. "Be merciful, Genevieve, and let it go. It's the only way. I'll only hurt you again."

Genevieve knotted her fingers in his shirt and refused to let him run. "Look at me, Bryce! *I'm not Marie!*"

A hard flush rolled up from his collar to stain his cheeks

the color of old brick. "What the hell is that supposed to mean?"

"It means I'm not going to leave you like she did!" Gulping for breath, Genevieve fought to bring the tremor in her voice under control. "You're afraid to share your life with me because you think somehow I'll leave or die or stop caring, and you'll be responsible because you just aren't good enough or worthy enough or strong enough."

"That's not true."

"Isn't it?"

At her quiet but infinitely disturbing question, Bryce pulled away, and she let him go. Thoughts roiling, he inspected her—the slender, defiant figure in a simple gown, the fire of her burnished curls brushing her shoulders, the stubborn curve of her jaw speaking volumes about her determination. She was all that was valiant and courageous, indefatigable and vigilant, plucky and loving, risking her own life to protect his. But he was equally determined to protect her from her most dangerous assailant—himself. If he had to wound her yet again, the least she deserved was his honesty.

"Perhaps it is true," he said at last, his voice raw with the effort it took to bare his soul. "I'm not too proud to admit I'd prefer to spare myself more grief."

The admission that he had suffered and would suffer only partially gratified Genevieve. "So you'll let fear sacrifice our chance at happiness?"

"How could anything between us last when you've plenty of reason to learn to hate me? I've certainly done enough damage to your life so far."

"It's absurd for you take responsibility for everything that's ever befallen me. I've made choices, too."

"What's happened that I didn't have a hand in?" he demanded harshly, bent on having the entire ugly truth out in the open where neither of them could ignore it. "Think, Genevieve! I've taken your virtue, your grandfather, your control over your own destiny. I must go to Wellington, and if you're with me, your very life will be at stake! If you had any sense you'd run and keep on running.''

The color fled from her cheeks, but her chin remained at a belligerent angle. "You're too hard on yourself. I forgave you what little there was to forgive long ago, and I'd hoped you'd done the same for me. Perhaps I was wrong. Perhaps you can't love a traitor.''

"Dammit! Don't say that. You're no traitor, never have been! It's just—"

"What, Bryce? That sometimes circumstances move you in unexpected paths? And it's really no one's fault?"

"Yes.''

"And that maybe all your guilt, all those many reasons you use to keep punishing yourself, to keep the people who care about you at a distance, are without substance, because you're a good man who's had to do hard things, and you did them the best you knew how.''

Bryce grimaced. "That pretty picture is as different from the truth as ice from fire.''

She made an impatient gesture. "After what we've endured together, how can you think that I don't know you? And when are you going to understand that knowing the truth isn't going to drive me away? No matter what you've done or haven't done, Bryce Darcy Cormick, I love you. And nothing is going to change that.''

The utter simplicity and sincerity of her words pierced the armor he'd erected so long ago, and arrowed straight into his battered heart. He wondered what he had ever done to deserve the regard of a woman like Genevieve Maples. The answer hit him like a cannon blast—nothing.

And she loved him anyway.

His last defenses crumbled and crashed in irretrievable pieces. In spite of all the pain and deception, she loved him enough, trusted him enough to accept him just as he was, with all the foibles and flaws and sins of an imperfect, mortal man. There was no abhorrence in her soft green gaze, only complete acceptance, and it fed a need within Bryce that he had never confessed to anyone, even himself.

To finally admit that need was liberating. To know that this unique woman wanted to meet that need filled him with awe. Blue eyes blazing, he took a step toward her. "Ah, Genny . . ."

"Love's a gift, Bryce," she said softly. "All you have to do is take it."

He framed her face in his hands. "You make it difficult to refuse a gift like that."

Her fingers covered the back of his hands, holding him to her, and her eyes filled. "I want to make it impossible."

"Don't weep, *mon ange*," he murmured, his voice husky with swelling emotion. "You already have."

With a strangled cry, she launched herself at his neck, and Bryce took her fully into his arms, burying his mouth against the sweet curve of her throat, trying to absorb all the nuances that were uniquely Genevieve. He knew it would take a lifetime. He trailed his lips across her jaw, across her cheeks to sip the salty moisture from her lashes, then kissed her with all the tenderness and passion of a man newly freed from a lifetime's bondage.

"*Je t'adore*. With all my heart, I adore you. Stay with me. For all time, I love you. *Je t'aime*."

Genevieve sighed, breathless with relief, and smiled through a misty haze of tears. "Yes, forever."

Bryce drew her fingers to his lips, kissing each one. "I've seen you fashion beauty with these small hands. I've seen you make something wonderful out of practically nothing. But I never dreamed I'd be so lucky as to be transformed by your witch's magic."

"If we're together, then that's enough."

His expression changed, and he drew back. "No, it's not. God help me, it's not nearly enough, but I can't let you go again. I need you too much. I'll never deserve your devotion, *chérie*, but there is one thing I can give you. Come with me."

Taking her hand, he led her from the apartments, brushing aside her mystified questions and marching her through the windswept colonnades and across the dark courtyards and finally into the main chapel. Though the thick stone walls did much to keep out the bitter winter cold, the air inside was cool and scented with the waxy odor of candles burning on the gilt and white rococo main altar. A multitude of reflected flames danced in the jewel-toned panes of the stained-glass windows nestling within the nave of the building, while statues of saints smiled benignly from the alcoves that hid secondary altars. While Genevieve gaped at the splendor, a tonsured monk appeared, looked surprised by Bryce's low request, then nodded and scurried away.

Bryce turned to Genevieve, threaded her fingers between his own, and raised her knuckles to his lips. "Well, mademoiselle? Might you consent to be wed in a place like this?"

"W-wed?" Her eyes grew large.

"Yes, wed. Married. To me."

"Bryce." Her look was confused, pained. "This isn't necessary. I never meant to force you into something you don't really want."

"I thought you wished to marry your soldier." There was a sudden note of insecurity in his voice. "Or was it only Darcy you wanted that way?"

"No, of course not." She licked her lips. "Only . . . only it can't be just for me."

Bryce's face was solemn. "It isn't, my love. I want you so much I surprise myself, and for so many reasons it will take years to fathom them all. But I still have a mission to accomplish, and no time to delay. I want to give you my name to protect you and to prove that for once in my benighted life, I truly mean what I say."

She looked down at their clasped hands. "I never doubted that."

"Then do me the honor of becoming my wife. It's time

to turn the deception we've lived into the truth that's been between us all along.''

Suddenly there wasn't enough air for Genevieve to breathe. ''Now?''

''Now. When next I take you to my bed I want us properly churched. I'm determined this marriage will start off right.'' His tender smile was half serious, half teasing. ''And perhaps then I will be able to command your obedience when the need arises.''

The fire in his eyes made her breathless; the happiness that sang in her veins, bold. ''I promise to be a model of wifely docility, sir, so why do we delay?''

He laughed softly, and squeezed her hand. ''As ever, General, you know how to take command of a situation. Come.''

They crossed the open space before the main altar under the watchful eyes of the saints and martyrs depicted in the colorful windows. The monk who'd met them at first appeared again at a side door. He escorted the aged prelate, who looked almost as mystified as Genevieve felt, to a seat on the dais and then arranged missals and vestments in hasty prepartion. It seemed a fantasy to Genevieve to be beside the man she loved, preparing to exchange vows of love and commitment when only a short while ago she'd known only despair.

As they knelt on the cold flagstones before the smiling priest, she whispered a prayer of thanksgiving. As they made their vows in a halting mixture of English, French, and German, Genevieve held Bryce's hand and began to believe in their future. And when her new husband bent his dark head to place a wedding kiss on her trembling lips, she understood that her love was returned in full, and she knew joy.

The old priest bestowed his final blessing over their bent heads, then offered his congratulations with a beatific smile that smoothed wrinkles and years from his face. Bryce helped Genevieve to her feet, and with all solemnity, they affixed their names in a book of records and thanked the good father.

When Bryce placed a guiding hand to her back and turned her toward the aisle, Genevieve looked everywhere but at her new husband, searching the stained-glass visages of saints and archangels as if for advice and blessings. Though they were scarcely strangers, she felt unaccountably shy, struck by the enormity of the change that had taken place so quickly and made breathless by the thought of what lay ahead. Her gaze locked on a particularly beautiful window that hadn't been visible until they'd reached the apse, and her eyes widened in shock. With a startled cry, she clutched Bryce's arm.

"Genny? What is it?" Her suddenly ashen countenance made him frown. "*Chérie,* it's too late for second thoughts . . ."

"Look." She pointed a trembling finger at the glass portrait of a man with a serene face in a bishop's robe and miter, surrounded by his faithful flock and the bounty of a full harvest and a peaceful nation.

"There," she choked, "around his neck—the Abbot's Seal!"

Chapter 18

"**D**rink this, Genny. You're still too pale."

Seated once again on the settle before the fire in her own quarters, Genevieve obediently sipped from the small goblet of peach brandy Bryce pressed into her hands. The sweet and fruity flavor of the liquor blossomed on her palate, and warming fire filtered through her numbed system. She took another fortifying taste, but as she passed the glass back to Bryce, her voice still held a betraying tremor.

"I'm being childish. I'm sorry."

Bryce inspected her strained features, then drained the remaining brandy himself, and set it aside. "It's understandable. You've been through a lot."

"It's not that, or even wedding nerves." Consumed by a sense of foreboding, she bit her lip and the liquid crystal of threatening tears glittered in the firelight. "But to have that *thing* overshadow the happiest moment of my life . . ."

"Don't." Bryce sat on the settle beside his wife and took her gently into his arms. "Proving Hugh's hunch about the origin of the Abbot's Seal in such an unexpected manner was a shock to me as well."

She burrowed her forehead against the pristine linen of his shirtfront, soaking in the tactile sensations of crisp, starched fabric over hard male muscle. "I could not fol-

359

low all Père Florien said when you explained we'd once had the seal but lost it again.''

"The good father was philosophical. The Abbot's Seal comes and goes from the abbey according to God's will, he said, and when the time is right again, it will return.''

"So the legends are true?''

"In some respects. The founder of the abbey—the man in the window—was a Roman soldier who turned to Christianity. What we thought was a chunk of glass appears to be one of the finest rose diamonds in existence.''

Genevieve's head fell back, and she gaped up at Bryce. "Diamond?''

"Indeed. Its value is unsurpassed, and has been used over the centuries as collateral for the construction of cathedrals, as the ransom of popes, as the price of peace, as a way to put food in the mouths of the poor in times of famine. The holy monks took the pride of a Roman emperor and turned it to the work of God, but now that work is perverted by our self-styled Abbot.''

"Who will surely harm you if he can,'' she added, shuddering. "Was Père Florien able to offer any help at all as to the Abbot's identity?''

"Only that the seal was last in the abbey's possession over forty years ago and disappeared after a novitiate was forced to leave the order under a cloud of scandal. Unfortunately, for his heinous sin the erstwhile monk's name was obliterated from all records, and Père Florien himself had only the vaguest recollection of the incident.''

"So we are no closer to the truth than before.'' She laid her trembling fingers against his cheek. "I'm beginning to believe in fate, Bryce, and it frightens me.''

He caught her hand and pressed a fervent kiss into her palm. "Rest easy, *chérie*. The seal has no supernatural powers.''

"Yet we will surely leave for Vienna with the sun's rising, and then . . .'' She shuddered.

He kissed her gently, his tongue laving away the last perfumed drop of brandy coating her perfect mouth. "We will both do our duty. After that, the future is what we make of it.''

''Yes,'' she murmured, her mouth seeking along his jawline. ''Tell me about our future.''

''After Vienna, I'm retiring the Griffin, no matter what Huxford wants.''

''It's time for you to have some peace.''

He stroked the underside of her chin, then deftly unfastened the buttons of her bodice one by one. ''We'll go to London first if you like.''

''Yes.'' Her breath quickening, she tugged fretfully at his shirt. ''You can work on your play.''

''And you'll design delightful gowns for Maebella.'' His heart hammered at the little wicked wonders her fingers wrought on his flesh.

''We'll rebuild the Athena.'' She arched against him with a sigh of pleasure as his hand slid beneath her chemise to cup her breast boldly and tease the puckered nipple. ''B. D. Cormick will make a triumphant return to the stage, and I'll supply wonderful costumes.''

''Wonderful,'' he echoed, nipping at the delicate cords of her neck, moving across her heated skin with kisses that left her shivering and expectant.

Pushing her gown off her shoulders, he let his hands roam, experiencing the silken texture of her skin, inhaling the sweetness of her fragrance, steeping himself in the totality of her, his wife, his mate. Their coming together was familiar, yet completely new, for between them before there had always been doubt, but now there was confidence in the commitments made, and this newfound freedom filled Bryce with awe and exultation. He hadn't sacrificed his freedom by committing himself to this woman. Instead he had been liberated from the fear that prevented true intimacy.

Their lips met, clung in exploration and renewal and welcome, tenderness and desire and an aching need building, building . . .

She tugged his shirt off, giving free rein to the urge to

touch him, the crisp whisper of dark hair whorling his chest, the hard sinews and blue veins of his arms. And always there was the dark splendor of his mouth on hers, taking her breath, giving her passion. Releasing her lips, he bent to suckle a nipple through the fine fabric of her chemise. She cried out with the ecstasy of it, her fingers mapping his face, guiding him to the most sensitive spots.

"Tell me more," she said, gasping. "Tell me everything."

"We'll go home to Clare Hill."

"Oh, yes." She squirmed as his supple fingers slid down her ribs and hooked on her hipbones. "Sir Theodore will be glad."

"You'll help me learn to know him, I think." Heart pounding, loins aching, Bryce drew back, framing her face between his palms. His voice was husky, and his eyes burned like incandescent sapphires. "And we'll raise horses and children until we are both very, very old."

Joy shone in her gaze, and an unexpected, yet delightful mischief. "Which ones first?"

With a growl, Bryce lifted her in his arms and carried her to the heavily curtained bed. "Definitely the children!"

She gave him a sultry look through her lashes. "I can hardly wait."

Laughing exultantly, he laid her on the bed and covered her with his body, kissing her neck, her shoulders, her pouting mouth. "Witch! *Je t'aime.* You'll have it all, I promise—"

She covered his lips with her own to still the words, suddenly fearful. "Don't say it. It's like a dream, too wonderful to believe. I'm afraid to hope too much when everything—our future, our plans, even our promises—must wait until after Vienna."

His gaze darkened. "At least we have tonight."

"Yes," she breathed, reaching for him with hungry desperation. "Give me tonight."

Flames kindled with gentle seduction leaped to passionate life as their lips met again and need consumed them. Discarding the remainder of their garments with feverish movements, they explored each other with wondering, seeking hands and avid mouths, awakening needs long hidden, secret vulnerabilities now revealed to love's tender and healing fury.

To Bryce, she was slender, delicate, strong, a woman with satiny skin blushed with the tint of peaches and the softest mouth in creation. To Genevieve, he was hard, powerful, commanding, this man of hers with his beautiful blue eyes and secret hurts. When they came together at last, they were filled, completed, made whole.

She felt like home.

He was her homecoming.

With long, slow movements, he worshipped her, telling her with his body of his adoration, whispering his love in French, then English, watching the tension building on her lovely face until her eyes widened and she crashed over the edge of pleasure. Holding her until her quivering subsided, he began to move once more, bringing her back again and again to the brink of madness.

She went wild beneath him, digging her fingers into the lean muscles of his hips, pulling him deeper, pouring her spirit into lingering, ardent kisses that stole his soul, glorying in their joining with fervent whispered vows of need and love that touched his hidden heart and finally destroyed his control. Forgetful of everything but the woman in his arms, spasms of pulsating delight shattered his senses, spiraling him into a realm beyond all knowing. And as the universe exploded about him, Bryce heard Genevieve cry out and rejoiced, for he understood then that this was only the beginning of their journey together.

The four-day journey to Vienna was arduous and urgent, a race against time and the Abbot's plotting. Bitter cold hampered them, even when they reached the main highway again and the track improved. Fatigue was a constant enemy, but Genevieve would have walked barefoot across glaciers to stay with Bryce, so she hung on doggedly, conscious of his anxious eye on her and determined not to lag behind no matter what it cost. Sometimes he took her before him on his horse as he had that first day so that she could rest, and the loving words of desire and encouragement he whispered warmed her heart and her body.

Dazed by the pace he set, she was more dazed by the stolen moments of blazing passion they shared, under a blanket in a makeshift tent during the four hours of sleep a night he allowed, in the musty bed of a tumbledown inn where they exchanged horses, in the loft of a barn offered by a friendly farmer. It was as if Bryce was trying to store up sensations and memories against an uncertain future. And while she understood, she also feared.

What if they came too late to prevent tragedy for Wellington? What if they arrived in time? Would the Abbot take his vengeance on the Griffin instead? And now that she and Bryce had truly found each other again, how would she survive if she lost him?

They reached the wide valley of the Danube in record time, and much to their relief, the weather moderated as they traveled through the ever more gently sloping hills, covered with dormant vineyards. From this high vantage Genevieve had her first glimpse of Vienna itself and was amazed that this European cultural and artistic center, the third largest after Paris and London, was still a fortified city, with buildings crowded behind the ramparts of a medieval walled fortress, now converted to pleasant walks and promenades. The walls were encircled by a wide band of open country planted with linden trees, and in the spring the spacious lawns would form an emerald ring about the inner city. High above it all gleamed the Gothic spire of St. Stephen's Cathedral.

Their exhausted, ragtag party finally entered the city proper on a brisk March Sunday morning, cantering through the narrow, roughly paved streets past palatial residences of surpassing grandeur while the deep voice of St. Stephen's bell tolled the faithful to Mass. Michel took his leave of the party there. At the same time, Bryce dismissed the escort to find their billets among the military contingent, then led Genevieve and Taffy straight to the British mission on the Minoritzenplatz, an elegant square not far from the imperial residence of the Hofburg. The young aide who greeted them in the sumptuous anteroom looked down his aristocratic nose at their unkempt appearance, especially Genevieve's breeches, and was further mystified by Bryce's urgent demands to see the duke.

"But Captain Cormick, sir! You weren't expected, and His Grace has many pressing obligations."

"Nothing untoward has occurred, then?" Bryce asked tightly. "He's come to no harm?"

"Certainly not!" The aide was astounded. Relieved, Genevieve sank gratefully onto a low bench and tried to finger-comb her unruly hair into some semblance of order. Taffy stood at rigid attention beside the door, but Bryce glowered at the hapless aide.

"Then where is His Grace at present?"

"I believe he and a party of guests have gone to a performance at the Spanish Riding School."

Bryce cursed under his breath and ran his palm over the dark four-day growth of stubble on his jaw. "Just the type of damned thing he must avoid!"

The aide looked at Bryce uneasily. "Perhaps Lord Clancarty could be of assistance? He should be arriving soon. There's a reception planned for the plenary committee just day after next and I confess we're all a bit frazzled, so—"

Bryce cut into the aide's speech with an impatient gesture. "Look—er, Mr. Milke, is it? We require accommodations, and my wife needs a place to rest until I return. See to it, will you?"

"Accommodations? Sir, with the town so full of delegates, there's hardly a room to be had in all of Vienna!" Milke protested.

Bryce paid his blustering no attention, turning instead to Taffy. "Come along, Sergeant, we'd best find His Grace immediately. If not even minimal precautions have been taken, we could well be in for trouble.''

"Wait a minute!" Genevieve cried, jumping to her tired feet. "I didn't come all this way just to be left behind now!"

Bryce shook his shaggy head. "Do I have to call upon those vows of obedience you took, Mrs. Cormick?"

"Must I remind you that I'm as much or more a part of this mess as you, Mr. Cormick?" Throwing her hair over her shoulders, she tucked her muffler around her neck and headed for the entrance. "So don't dally any further. No doubt His Grace will want to hear directly what I learned."

Nonplussed, Bryce stared after her, then his lips twitched. Damn, if she wasn't stubborn! His married life might be turbulent, but it sure as hell wouldn't be dull! Bryce jerked his head at Taffy. "Well, Sergeant? You heard the General."

The home of the Spanish Riding School was a colossal vaulted hall the size of a city square attached to the Hofburg itself. Within minutes, they were hurrying up the wide marble steps to the elevated box seating with the strains of a Mozart symphony and refined applause filling their ears. Genevieve gave an involuntary gasp at the sight of the huge arena, decorated with elaborate pediments and carvings, lit by crystal chandeliers, and circled by a double balcony of box seats separated by white Corinthian columns.

But the splendor of the surroundings faded in comparison to the magnificence of the pure white Lippizaner stallions in their scarlet and gold liveries, ridden by trainers in brown coats and white deerskin pantaloons, showing the epitome of the classical riding art in intricate quadrilles, great leaping *coubettes* and countless other "airs above the ground."

"This is not good." From a vantage of a turn in the balcony stair, Bryce searched the vast auditorium, automatically noting all the places in which a potential assassin could hide. "Not good at all."

"Cor, Cap!" Taffy muttered. "Every nabob in Austria must be here. How the devil will we find His Grace in all this?"

"There he is!" Genevieve pointed across the arena. The Duke of Wellington sat in full view in the front of a center box with a company of fashionable ladies and other distinguished gentlemen.

"God, this is perfect," Bryce said. "If the Abbot doesn't make his attempt here, he's missing a hell of a chance. Let's go."

"What do you mean by a chance?" Genevieve asked, skipping a little to keep up with Bryce's long strides as they circled the concourse. In their incongruous garb, they drew stares from the liveried footmen stationed around the corridor between the openings to the boxes.

"I mean there's any number of places a sniper could just pick him off. See that upper balcony?" He jabbed a thumb in the direction of the opposite wall. "If I were planning it, I'd put a sharpshooter up there and—"

Bryce drew up so abruptly that Genevieve stumbled against him. His gaze focused across the arena, and he caught her arm to steady her without looking. "See it, Taffy?"

The Welshman narrowed his eyes. "Up there, Cap. A flash."

"Off the barrel of a carbine?"

"Damn me, Cap, I couldn't tell."

Confused, Genevieve stared across the way, but saw nothing unusual.

Bryce passed a hand across his eyes. "Maybe I'm seeing things. Wait, there it is again—oh, *hell*!"

"Bryce?" she faltered.

"Someone's there, and up to no good," he said, giving her a shove. "Run, General! Get the duke out of that box any way you can! Come on, Sergeant, the stairs!"

Alarms buzzed in Genevieve's head, and fear chilled her veins. So it started like this, with no warning. Heart in her throat, she called out after him. "Bryce, be careful!"

"At ease, General," Bryce said grimly. "He doesn't know I'm coming. Now hurry!"

She turned obediently and sprinted around the curve of the concourse, darting past ladies in high bonnets and men in tailcoats, searching for the duke's box. Dodging around a portly figure, she was brought up short by a stubby hand on her arm.

"Why—why it's my dear Mrs. Cormick! Whatever are you doing here in Vienna?"

Genevieve looked up at a round Father Christmas face, now pursed with concern at her flyaway hair and flushed countenance. "Baron von Throder!" She tried to smile and at the same time extricate herself from his grip. "How do you do? We've only just arrived as you see . . ."

"Delightful! But you must need refreshment." The baron's look said she appeared in dire need of *something*. "I have a house in the Wallnerstrasse . . ."

"Thank you!" Too harried to be coherent, Genevieve tried to smile. "I'm in a rush. So nice . . . another time . . . I must go. *Auf wiedersehen!*"

She left him frowning after her in bewilderment, but she was too busy searching each box for the duke's familiar profile to worry about the older gentleman. *Where* was Wellington? She almost shouted for joy when she heard "Old Nosey's" robust laughter drifting from the next box.

"Your Grace!" She darted into the opening, only to find her way blocked by two footmen.

"Nein, Fräulein." Shaking their heads, they shooed her back, indicating in German she could not translate and gestures she could that this was a private box and she was not allowed past them.

"But you don't understand!" Frantic, Genevieve tried to explain. "It's vital I speak with him. Your Grace!"

Several of the fashionable ladies seated in the rear of the box turned to register their annoyance at the ruckus she was kicking up.

"Please, someone!" Genevieve bobbed on her tiptoes,

trying to see over the footmen's heads. "I must see the duke!"

One of the ladies gave a sharp command, and a footman instantly reached to forcibly remove Genevieve from the scene. Panicked, she ducked under his arm and into the seats, and as she plowed her way through the astonished observers, she screeched the most outlandish thing she could think of.

"Uncle Arthur. It's me, Genny! Don't you know me?"

The Duke of Wellington swiveled in his chair, completely baffled by the abrupt advent of a chestnut-haired "relation." Genevieve scrambled over the remaining seats, occupants and all, leapfrogging across the knees of a tall, strawberry-haired man in a high-collared military tunic and tight kid breeches. She threw her arms around the duke's neck with apparent delight but made certain that it was her back that was presented to the threat from the upper balcony.

Struggling to preserve his dignity while battling her stranglehold, Wellington blinked, then his face went slack with recognition. "Good heavens! Mrs. Cor—"

"Uncle Arthur!" She bussed him on the cheek, whispering fervently under her breath. "Sir, come with me, please! You're in terrible danger!"

"Er—ah, Genny, dear! What a surprise!" he answered loudly, then muttered under his breath, "This is highly irregular, ma'am. What the deuce—"

Out of the corner of her eye, Genevieve caught a glimmer of movement high in the opposite balcony. Had Bryce eliminated the threat? She couldn't take the chance!

"Oh, Uncle, I feel faint!" she cried, and promptly wilted into what she hoped was a convincing swoon.

Consternation swept the company, but the duke and his strawberry-haired companion reacted chivalrously, catching her before she actually hit the floor. Forcing herself to act as a dead weight, Genevieve kept her eyes closed while they shouted for air and space, then carried her out of the box. It was only when they reached the relative safety of the inner concourse and a small concierge office that she could really breathe again anyway.

Propped in a chair, she was plied with glasses of water and vials of sal ammoniac as restoratives until eventually the duke himself ordered the room cleared so that his "niece" could recover away from curious gazes. As soon as this had been accomplished, Genevieve cautiously opened one eye and found the duke patting her hand and gazing at her with sharp speculation.

"Perhaps you'd like to tell me what the devil's going on here?" he asked mildly.

She sat up straighter, gulping back her embarrassment. "Your Grace, I do apologize, but I could think of no other way!"

In a rush of words she explained about du Roche and the Abbot, about the trip from the Abbey of the Holy Word, about Bryce's instincts in the arena and the imperative need to remove the duke from such a precarious situation even if there wasn't a gunman in the balcony.

Wellington pinched his lower lip thoughtfully all through her discourse, his expression growing more grave. On learning Bryce and Taffy had gone after whoever had lurked upstairs, he opened the door to demand a contingent of footmen, only to find Bryce and Taffy approaching, stern faced but empty-handed. "It appears your companions had little luck," Wellington remarked laconically.

"Bryce!" Genevieve flew into her husband's arms the moment he came through the door.

"Calm yourself, General," Bryce soothed. "There's no harm done, and you deserve an award for that performance! Have you ever thought of government intelligence work as a calling?"

"I haven't your fortitude," she choked, and buried her face in his shoulder.

The duke watched with interest, but refrained from any remark except to demand if Bryce had found what he was looking for.

"The sergeant and I must have scared off whoever it was," Bryce explained.

"It all seems quite nebulous, you know, Mr. Cormick," Wellington said, his brows beetling down to form a straight line. "How can we be sure this new threat is genuine?"

"We found this." Bryce opened his palm, revealing the shiny brass casing of a carbine slug. "I'd say that whoever was up there had more on his mind than all the king's horses, sir."

The duke accepted the bullet with a snort of disgust. "Seems this pretty well eliminates all doubt. From what Genevieve tells me, it's clear this felonious Abbot is a tenacious fellow."

From the haven of Bryce's embrace, Genevieve nodded her agreement. "Yes, and unfortunately for us all, the Abbot is now privy to Bryce's role as the Griffin. I fear he is in just as great a danger as you, Your Grace."

Wellington's visage darkened with calculation. "That knowledge could certainly curtail the Griffin's effectiveness."

"In some areas but not all, Your Grace," Bryce replied. "Until this villain in apprehended, it's imperative you stay low and out of sight."

"Nay, Mr. Cormick, that's impossible. The work of the Congress is at a critical stage. Only in the last days have I neared completion of the work Lord Castlereagh began on a proviso denouncing the slave trade." The duke shook his head. "I cannot disappear at this vital juncture."

"I understand, Your Grace, but certain precautions can and must be taken, if you'll allow me to advise you."

The great man's lips twitched. "As I have no desire to become a dead example of Bonapartist thinking, I'm forced to agree, Mr. Cormick." He indicated the door, and Taffy jumped to open it. "Perhaps we should make our way back to the embassy house—very cautiously, of course— to discuss this? Between the two of you, I have very able champions in my corner, and I thank you both."

"I'm sorry again about that scene, Your Grace," Genevieve said. "I hope it won't be too awkward to explain to your guests."

"I'm sure they'll understand my free-spirited niece was simply exuberantly glad to see her uncle again."

"That's a bit of a relief." She gave a wobbly laugh. "And please, I'd like to thank personally the other gentleman who helped me. I'm afraid I nearly trampled him, and I don't even know his name."

"Do not concern yourself, ma'am," the duke drawled with a twinkle. "It was only Alexander, the czar of Russia!"

"It is impossible, Monseigneur." The renegade Cossack cursed blackly and aimed a vicious kick at the base of a wooden wine rack. The brick arch of the dank, deserted cellar dripped with moisture, and his accented words were a guttural counterpoint to the high, melodious rattle of the dusty bottles. "First all schedules are changed, and now they double the guards on the English dog."

"Not possible, Grigor, just more difficult."

The Abbot's voice was mild, but it masked a terrible rage and frustration. At each turn, the Griffin thwarted him, even appearing out of thin air at another crucial moment with the red-haired bitch at his side! But Leclerc had proven valuable one final time, and now the Griffin had a name. He briefly pressed his thick fist over the lump concealed beneath his cravat. The Abbot's Seal was never off his person now, and he vowed by all the powers of hell to settle Bryce Cormick's doom, as well as Wellington's, once and for all.

The Cossack, one of a number of deserters recruited by the Abbot especially for their ferociousness and willingness to perform any atrocity for a price, continued to curse—ill luck, the czar, the woman who'd spoiled his aim at the horse show.

"It is too much thinking, Monseigneur, all these plans! One disturbance and it all goes wrong. Let me ride and shoot as I was trained on the steppes.'' Grigor bared his blackened teeth in a murderous hiss and pounded his deep chest. "I will kill the English lord the first time he sticks his long English nose out his door—I am not afraid!"

"I question not your courage, my son, but your empty head. As the eagle flies from his cage, Wellington's death must be a public execution for all the world to see. There must be no more mistakes, no more delay."

The Abbot grimaced at his own words, knowing time was running out. *L'empereur*'s patience was not unlimited, and the secret missives that came from Elba were daily more imperative. The time for action was nigh if he hoped to win Bonaparte's favor and the control of a clutch of German and Austrian duchies, particularly one belonging to an abbey that he'd vowed to dismantle brick by brick.

The Cossack lifted a magnum of wine from the rack, smashed its neck, and guzzled the liquid straight from the broken bottle. Wiping his mouth on his wrist, he cocked his head and stared at his master. "What you want is impossible," he repeated sullenly.

"There is always another way." His eyes narrowed, and a sinister plan, a delicious, ironic scheme of unsurpassed diabolicalness, began to form within the Abbot's mind.

The Cossack belched. "Since the dogs stand guard over the bone, no one can get close enough for your purpose, Monseigneur."

"You are wrong, Grigor." A slow, feral smile touched the Abbot's lips. "There is one man, and also a way to bend him to my will . . ."

"Watch your step, ma'am."

"Thank you, Sergeant." Genevieve settled into the carriage seat and tucked her velvet cloak over her iridescent blue-green skirts. Thankfully, the tapestry gown she'd designed for the Victory Gala had survived its trip across the Continent in a saddlebag without serious harm, so she hadn't had to forgo the duke's invitation to an elegant dinner at the Austrian chancellery. "I'm certain I'll be fine from here."

"The Cap told me to see you all the way back to your rooms for the night, and that's what I'll do, ma'am."

Taffy climbed into the coach, and they set off, rocking and swaying back and forth as the wheels rolled over the ancient cobbles of the Ballhausplatz toward their accommodations of the past two days, a shabby two-room apartment behind the opera house they'd felt fortunate to find in the current housing shortage.

"Cap said he's sticking close to His Grace tonight," Taffy continued, "and since the committee's negotiations could go on until two or three in the morning, he just don't want his lady taking any chances on her way home."

"It's not I who's still taking too many risks," Genevieve said. Chewing at her lower lip apprehensively, she shivered and placed her slippers on the hot box of coals provided to keep the passengers warm in the cold March dreariness. "Why must he always go the extra measure? It's as though he still has to prove his loyalty, to somehow pay for the fact that his mother was a Frenchwoman."

"It's just the Cap's way, ma'am. He sees his duty, and nothing or no one will stop him from doing it—even at the risk of his own neck." Taffy saw her expression change, and his shiny pate grew red as he made hasty amends. "Not that there's a chance of anything happening! You heard the duke's plans from his own mouth. Double guards, no open events, and Baron Hager's Viennese secret police have increased their surveillance to the point where a gnat couldn't sneeze without someone saying gesundheit!"

Genevieve laughed. "I hope you're right."

Taffy nodded sagely. "Now that they know what they're looking for, I wager the Abbot is a goner right enough."

With her fingers tracing patterns in the nap of the velvet cloak, Genevieve sobered again. "I know Bryce feels he must use his expertise as the Griffin to protect His Grace, but there's still so much we don't know. It could be Paris starting all over again, and what that might demand of Bryce frightens me.''

"It's not the same. This time he's letting others be his eyes and ears while he stays close to the duke. He even has the excuse of doing a dramatic recitation at the next reception to cover his actions. Nobody'll question that His Grace invited a famous dramatist like B. D. Cormick to entertain his guests.''

"I suppose you're right, but I wish this was over and we were home again.''

"Aye. I miss that little scrapper Jack gettin' into mischief. Won't we have some stories to tell the young scamp!''

"Starting with how I left my footprints on the czar's pantaloons?'' she asked wryly.

Taffy slapped his knee and chortled. ''Now there hangs a tale for certain!''

Genevieve tried to compose her features, but her eyes sparkled with a glint of irreverent hilarity. "I'll have you know the czar was most charming when I offered my apologies this evening. He even recommended the schnitzel at dinner. And he and Baron von Throder included me in an extended discussion about the boundaries of Saxony and Warsaw.''

"Aye, there's a lot of familiar faces here,'' the Welshman remarked, peering out the carriage window as they approached the opera house, made the turn into a side street, and drew to a halt before the ramshackle house where their rooms were located. "Though I suppose it ain't such a curiosity that diplomats congregate wherever great deeds are taking place.''

"I suppose not,'' she replied slowly, struck by the observation.

As Taffy handed her down out of the vehicle and turned to pay the driver, she paused on the dark street, considering. The Abbot had been active in London, Paris, and now Vienna, shadowing Wellington's movements. Who else had made these journeys? Behind what face lurked the novitiate who had stolen the Abbot's Seal from the Abbey of the Holy Word so long ago? Someone who'd once wanted to be a priest, now turned away from that holy calling to a life of espionage, treason, and murder. She had the awful feeling that if she could just *think*—

A ridiculous thought struck her, and she suppressed a giggle at her own fancy. There was one man whose Father Christmas face kept popping up everywhere, but surely that theater-loving Prussian diplomat couldn't be— or could he?

Genevieve touched the tapestry bodice of her gown, and at the softly textured feel, Victory Gala night at Covent Garden came back in a rush of memories and sensations. Bryce's wonderful performance, the duke with Prinny, Jules leading her down the saloon, showing off, introducing her to—to a little man who'd rather attend the theater than a seminary!

"Oh, my God!" Genevieve gasped and grabbed at Taffy's arm.

"Ma'am? What is it?"

"Quickly, Sergeant! We must go back. About the Abbot. I may be wrong, but I think I know who—"

A trio of horsemen galloped around the corner at that instant, bearing down on them with a thunder and spark of hooves on cobbles, the wild war calls of the eastern steppes, and the lightning flash of sabers. In a moment, the first fur shako–topped rider swept the coachman from his perch and sent the carriage team snorting and rearing down the street.

Taffy shoved Genevieve toward the building's doorway. "Run, ma'am!"

Hooves flying, nostrils distended, the second and third horses were on top of them in the blink of an eye, and in that brief but endless moment, Genevieve saw a blade slash across the night sky straight at Taffy.

"Sergeant!"

Her horrified scream came too late. Crimson splattered. Taffy rolled into the gutter and lay still. Genevieve made an involuntary move toward him, aborted in mid-stride as a massive arm reached down and swept her up and across the saddle of a grinning, bearded, rotten-mouthed murderer.

She shrieked and struggled, using nails and teeth on the sour-smelling ruffian, but he only laughed, shouted something in an unknown language to his friends, then bundled her own cloak over her head and charged off into the night.

Smothered, jounced to within an inch of her life, terrified, Genevieve cursed and prayed, struggled and strained, all to no avail. After an interminable, agonizing ride, the torment ended, only to be replaced by excruciating terror as steely arms closed around her and carried her to an unknown fate.

She heard the clang of metal hinges, then dripping water, and a dank, yeasty mustiness penetrated her cloak to clog her nostrils. Exhausted, half suffocated, she fought to stay conscious. Her captor dumped her unceremoniously into a heap on the damp brick floor, and it was all she could do to lift the enveloping velvet from her face and take great gusty breaths until the ringing in her ears subsided and the black sparkles behind her eyes disappeared.

A brutish hand tangled in her hair and jerked her face up. The bearded ruffian showed his black teeth and said something that would have been lewd in any language. Genevieve quivered at the salacious gleam in his black eyes.

"Enough, Grigor," a voice said. "You did well. When I'm done, you may have her, but not yet."

Reluctantly, the Cossack released her, his eyes narrowed with an anticipation that made Genevieve's skin crawl. With a hand on her abused scalp, she staggered to her feet and peered at the shadowy figure standing behind the Russian. She did not have to look hard, for she already knew what she'd see.

"What is it you want of me, Monseigneur?"

"You know me, my dear?"

"I know you, Baron von Throder!" she said, her voice venomous with hate. "Or should I name you the Abbot, instead?"

The Prussian diplomat with the cherub's face stepped into a column of light leaking from a shuttered lantern on the wine cellar's arched wall. "You are too clever for your own good, my child."

"Villain! Vile spawn of Satan!" Genevieve choked, curling her fingers into fists of impotent rage. "Your men have killed Taffy!"

"A lesson to all who stand in the *l'empereur*'s path."

"Just like Samson Baggart and my grandfather," she returned bitterly. "And for what? Bonaparte is finished, his dream of the eagle's return dead, and you are a fool to believe otherwise!"

The back of his hand caught her across the mouth. She staggered against the Cossack, instantly pulling away in abhorrence as the salt-sweet taste of her own blood exploded against her tongue.

"We shall see who is the fool when Wellington is dead and *l'empereur* sits again on the throne of France and all Europe," von Throder said coldly. "The true believers will be amply rewarded for their loyalty."

Genevieve touched her bloodied lip and shook her head in defiance. "Do you think the Abbot's Seal makes you invincible? You delude yourself, Monseigneur, with this fantasy of a priesthood you never earned. Bonaparte has nothing to give you, and Wellington is beyond your puny reach."

The baron's jovial smile gleamed. "Mine perhaps, but not the Griffin's."

Genevieve eyes dilated with horror. "No!"

"Oh, yes, my dear. Wellington must be eliminated. And to preserve your pretty neck, your lover will perform the deed for me!"

Chapter 19

❦

T he warm, sweet odors of cream and apple tarts and
freshly brewed coffee assaulted Bryce the minute he
walked through the glass doors of Kluger's fashionable
coffeehouse. Patrons in elegant morning dress that matched
his own subdued attire read the newspapers as they
munched cinnamon cakes and sipped espresso or "a small
brown one" with globs of whipped cream floating on the
surface.

The cloying atmosphere made Bryce want to puke. Bile
churned in the back of his throat and acid burned a hole
in his middle, but he swallowed his nausea just as he had
before every battle in his life. He took an unhurried seat
at a small round marble table in the rear of the bustling
establishment, just as if fear and desperation hadn't been
his constant companions since Genevieve's abduction the
night before.

Retrieving a letter from his pocket, he reread the imperative summons for the thousandth time, then traced the
imprint of an eagle's talon on the wax seal with a trembling fingertip. Dammit! The bastard had Genny! And
loyal Taffy lay dying in the hospital of the Sisters of Mercy.
Bryce had come as directed, alone and unarmed, to face
Genevieve's kidnapper, and never in all his career had he
felt so helpless.

"Is this seat taken, *mein Herr*?" Without waiting for

an answer, Baron Heinrich von Throder slid his pudgy form into the opposite chair. He signaled a waiter to bring coffee for two and then beamed at Bryce. "Allow me to recommend the Sacher torte. It's very good here."

Bryce leaned back in his chair and looked down his long nose at his nemesis. "So it's you. I congratulate you, Monsieur Abbot."

"The Griffin has been a worthy opponent, Mr. Cormick. But, since I have your queen, it's now checkmate."

The waiter arrived with the coffee and a plate of pastries, and the conversation ceased as the baron poured thick golden cream from a silver pitcher into his cup then took an appreciative sip. Bryce ignored his own cup, his gaze on the older man as cold as glacial ice.

"I did not come here to exchange pleasantries, Baron. Where is Genevieve?"

"Far from here, so do not bother to set your spies after me, *mien Herr*. But she is safe, for the moment, as long as you cooperate."

"I want my wife. And if she has come to any harm—"

"Now, now, Mr. Cormick!" von Throder protested, licking a dot of cream from his upper lip with the delicacy of a kitten. "We are both civilized men. I'm sure we can reach an accord without resorting to threats."

Bryce hung on to his temper with all his strength, but just under the surface a wild, snarling creature snapped its beak and flexed its claws, waiting for the chance to rip out von Throder's black heart.

"What do you want?" he growled.

"Only your assistance in a small matter that has been troubling me for some time." Von Throder smiled genially. "Since you've been the instrument that disrupted my plans on too many occasions in the past, it only seems fitting that you now have the chance to do penance for your transgressions."

Bryce's stomach churned, but his face remained a tight mask. "How?"

"Remove Wellington—permanently."

Bryce's gaze grew even colder. "I see. When?"

"Tonight, at the British reception so there will be plenty of witnesses, including myself."

"And in return?"

"I'll release your wife unharmed." The baron shrugged. "Of course, whether you're alive to be reunited with her will depend on your skill, won't it? However, I have great hopes for you, Mr. Cormick."

"And if I don't agree?"

"Why, then she'll die, of course."

"Why should I trust you to let Genevieve go afterward?"

"Because you have no other choice, my estimable opponent!" Von Throder chuckled in delight.

Bryce swallowed, tasting the bitterness of gall. Wellington's life for Genny's. He would, no doubt, be hanged as a traitor, and in exchange his wife would live. God, what a choice!

Everything he'd worked and sacrificed and suffered for out of devotion to country mocked him. Could he turn his back on the beliefs on which he'd based his life, make meaningless everything he'd stood for to become the thing he despised most—a traitor to both friend and nation? But what of the woman he professed to love? To protect her, he'd give his last breath, his immortal soul, but could he give his honor? Genevieve's love and faith had wrought enormous changes in him, given him peace and life again. How could he turn his back on her now—even if it cost him everything?

The baron watched Bryce closely, saw the tension and vacillation in his expression, and with precise calculation made a casual comment that pushed Bryce over the edge of rationality.

"I might add, Mr. Cormick, that your wife's guard is a rather animalistic Cossack who has eyes for the lady in question. Should you falter, I'm afraid I'll simply have to give her to Grigor before I kill her."

"No," Bryce said, his voice hoarse and tortured. "That won't be necessary. Just tell me what to do."

Genevieve knew what hell was now. It was a day that was a thousand years long. It was the rasp of a voice made raw from a million vain cries for help through the narrow cracks in a locked cellar door. It was knowing the man you loved was at Satan's mercy and that you were the instrument of his ultimate destruction.

Genevieve prowled the dim, damp confines of her prison for the hundredth time, circling the long, cluttered space, tiptoeing past the dusty, rickety wine racks, poking into every empty corner and dead end, rattling the bolted door in another futile display of fury. She'd watched the day pass through those tiny cracks and the sun fade again to the black of another overcast night, and wondered how long the Abbot intended to keep her here.

She supposed she ought to be grateful they'd left her alone during this interminable day. It could have been much worse than being cold and hungry and thirsty. Shuddering at the memory of Grigor's lascivious expression, she determinedly pushed that fear to the back of her consciousness. She had larger worries.

What was Bryce thinking? Had the Abbot set forth his nefarious scheme? Surely Bryce would never agree to murder the duke! But what if he didn't? Would she die at the filthy hands of a lecherous Cossack? What if he did? How would either of them ever live with the consequences of such an action?

Shivering, Genevieve pulled her velvet cloak closer. She'd pried open a wine bottle when thirst had grown unbearable, using nails and teeth on the stubborn cork, and now she picked up the flagon and took another cautious sip. She didn't think she was drunk, but the spirits burned within her empty stomach with a heat that was at least falsely reassuring. If there was only something she could do! Some way to escape to prevent Bryce from having to make such an awful choice!

She frowned and hefted the thick glass bottle thoughtfully. As a club, it wouldn't be much of a weapon, but it was better than nothing. A bubble of hysterical laughter caught in her throat as she tried to picture herself bludgeoning the huge, hulking Cossack into submission.

Taking a deep, steadying breath, Genevieve prayed for calm. As agonizing as the situation was, she knew Bryce, knew his love, knew his lightning-quick intellect, his courage, his ingenuity. If there was a way out of this dilemma, Bryce would find it. She just had to trust and be ready to take advantage of any opportunity to help herself and him.

The rumble of voices and the rattle of the lock made her look up in alarm. Irrationally, she didn't want her captors to think her so weak that she'd turned to drink. Moving quickly, she shoved the damning bottle into the nearest rack with such force the ancient shelving creaked and swayed dangerously, as if drunk under the load of hundreds of bottles of choice vintages. She darted back out of harm's way, but the rack settled again under its burden like a prehistoric beast only momentarily roused from a millennium's slumber. With her heart thumping in her chest at this near-escape, she turned to face a more dire threat.

"Ah, Genevieve! I trust you've had a pleasant day, my dear?"

In the light of the lantern held aloft by a grinning Grigor, Baron von Throder was resplendent in elegant evening dress, even sporting a red satin sash with the Order of the Star of Prussia across his chest. His mood was entirely too jovial for Genevieve's peace of mind.

"You don't really care whether my day was pleasant, so why ask?" she demanded, her voice raspy with tension and too much shouting.

"You wound me, my dear!" The baron gestured toward Grigor, who held a flat basket in his other hand. "I'm not really so heartless. Why, I've even brought you a repast. You may serve, Grigor."

The Russian hung the lantern on a beam, then slid the shallow basket onto the dusty lid of a wooden barrel and removed the napkin. The yeasty odor of fresh bread and the sharp tang of cheese and spicy sausage rose in a wave, and saliva puddled in Genevieve's mouth. Grigor took a small knife from his belt and chopped the sausage into hunks, but suddenly it wasn't the food on which Genevieve's avid gaze focused, but the shiny weapon. She tore her glance away, only to find Grigor showing his black teeth in a mocking smile.

"You want it, eh?" He offered a bit of sausage on the tip of the dagger. "Here, mam'selle. Take it."

Genevieve knew he was taunting her, daring her. She lifted her chin in haughty disdain. "I don't dine with vermin." Ignoring his growl, she turned back to von Throder with a demand. "How long do you intend to keep me here, Monseigneur?"

"Not long. In fact, by the end of the evening I feel confident that everything will be concluded to my satisfaction."

"You can't mean—no!" Genevieve stifled a gasp of disbelieving horror. "Bryce would never agree to be your weapon!"

"Love makes weaklings of even the strongest men. Right, Grigor?"

The Cossack snarled something unintelligible, bit the sausage off the blade himself, then jabbed the knife back into his waistband. The Abbot merely laughed.

"Your husband was most cooperative, my dear. In exchange for your freedom, he will execute the dog Wellington this very evening, before all the illustrious guests gathered at the British mission to hear the great B. D. Cormick perform."

"I don't believe you."

He shrugged. "Indeed, 'tis true, for I'll be there as well to remind your husband of his duty."

"Bryce answers to a higher call than that of a rabid madman!"

Von Throder's round cheeks brightened with irritated color, though his voice remained mild. "You are an annoyance, my dear, that I no longer need. Kill her, Grigor, and make certain the body is never found."

Rooted in place, Genevieve felt the blood drain from her face and her belly clench with fear. From a great distance a part of herself remarked the Abbot's typical treachery—he'd never had the least intention of releasing her despite the terrible bargain he'd exacted from Bryce. The cold chill of fright gave way to an even more icy fury.

Grigor's face split with an evil grin of anticipation. "Your promise, Monseigneur?"

"Oh, very well." Von Throder waved an absent hand and started for the door. "Take the bitch first if you must. Just remember what I said."

"Thank you, Monseigneur."

"And you wanted to be a man of God!" Genevieve sneered contemptuously. "Small wonder they expelled you from the abbey!"

Von Throder jerked around as if stung, and his roly-poly features contorted in a gargoyle's grimace of his true nature. "I had visions, but the monks called it blasphemy. The Abbot's Seal holds the power of God. It only wanted direction. My direction."

"A vicious madman's?" Genevieve's expression was disdainful. "What good could *you* have done with such a godly relic?"

A dull red flush crept up von Throder's neck. "I could have built that abbey into a new Rome, so powerful all nations would have stood in fear of my dominion! I could have been pope, but for the monks' unbelief. Instead, they forced me into the secular realm where I've had to be more patient. But my talents and my seal have been useful even in this sphere, and when Bonaparte rewards his faithful, I'll control that duchy. The monks will pay for the insult they did to me, and when I'm finished there won't be a stone upon a stone where once rose the Abbey of the Holy Word!"

Genevieve stood her ground, her eyes flashing emerald with scorn. "Satan will hang those stones around your neck and drown you in eternal hellfire for your sins!"

Von Throder's face grew even more grotesque. "Kill her, Grigor," he repeated. "And do it slowly."

"You can rely on me, Monseigneur."

The door slammed behind the baron. Grinning like a wolf, Grigor took a step toward Genevieve. Panicking, she turned to flee, knowing there was no way out but compelled by fear to run, helpless as a mouse cornered by a cat. Grigor, for all his mass, was swift and caught her in two steps, dragging her into his embrace, the stench of his sour sweat choking her, his big hands easily controlling her frenzied struggles.

"Ah, now we have some fun, little cat!" the Cossack said, laughing at her puny efforts. He ripped off her cloak and plunged his fingers into her bodice, pinching her painfully beneath the tapestry fabric, and his hot mouth, stinking with decay, covering hers in a wet assault that made her vomit rise.

Frantic, terrorized, she pushed at him, her mind screaming for Bryce. Oh, God! Had it come down to this—rape and death in a squalid cellar? Her fingers closed over the handle of the knife at Grigor's waistband, and with the last ounce of her strength, she ripped it loose and spun free.

"Get back!" Gulping ragged breaths, she sidled away, sweeping an arc through the air with the tiny blade.

Grigor placed his hands on his hips, threw back his bearded face, and roared with laughter.

"Ha! Think you to kill me with *that*, mam'selle? Why, it's no more to Grigor that a mosquito's bite!" He pulled a horn-handled pistol from the depths of his coat pocket and displayed it proudly. "It would take ten of *these* to knock me down."

In her despair, Genevieve knew he was right.

But there was still one way to avoid defilement and shame, to spare herself the agony of suffering that awaited her at the Cossack's brutal hands. Turning the blade, she placed the point against her own heart.

"Mam'selle, no!"

"Stay away!" she ordered, gathering her courage. A feeling of *déjà vu* overwhelmed her, for she'd played this same scene out as the distraught Juliet to Bryce's Romeo in Paris. But this was no mere playacting. Though her hands shook with trepidation, it was easier to die swiftly, mercifully, at her own hand than endure the death Grigor planned.

Easier, yes, a part of her argued silently, but Juliet's Romeo was gone, and Bryce was still alive, and the defilement of his honor was a fate worse than either his death or hers.

"You make a grave mistake, mam'selle," Grigor growled. "You have only to please me, and I may let you live. The Monseigneur isn't the only one who can keep secrets."

Genevieve stared at the tip of the blade, felt its prick against her tender skin, mesmerized by the possibility of release. Even if she survived Grigor's assault, how could she come again to her marriage bed a ruined woman? But as long as she drew breath and there was even an infinitesimal chance that she might live to help Bryce escape the Abbot's sentence of eternal damnation, how could she take the coward's way out? Wasn't what she felt for Bryce Cormick worth *any* sacrifice?

The answer was yes.

Shuddering, she dropped the knife. It clattered against the wet bricks like a death knell. Raising her eyes to the waiting Cossack, she forced herself to take a step toward him.

"Please don't hurt me. I'll do my best."

The Russian's black mouth opened in a feral grin of satisfaction at her abject fear and complete humiliation.

"A wise choice, mam'selle," he said, jamming the pistol in his pocket. He grabbed her and brutally mauled her mouth against his own.

"Please," she gasped when he lifted his head to examine the effects of his lovemaking. "I've had no food, and your passion makes me dizzy. A morsel, I beg, a drop of wine. Or else I cannot hope to properly please a man of your great strength."

Grigor puffed up at the compliment, and, like a lord granting a boon to a serf, nodded solemnly. "A fine idea. There's no hurry and many bottles here. Which do you want, mam'selle? Grigor can be generous. You choose."

"That." She pointed to the top row of the wine rack. "The champagne."

Grigor's laughter boomed. "Yes! The champagne!"

Releasing her, he reached for the dusty bottle. Genevieve moved on instinct, grabbed the rack itself, and pulled with all her might just as the Cossack clenched his hammy fist about the neck of the bottle. His weight did the rest.

Creaking, the teetering rack shifted, then toppled in slow motion. Genevieve danced out of the way, and Grigor bellowed in consternation, but it was too late. Bottles catapulted from their cubbyholes like missiles launched on a battlefield, raining down on the hapless Cossack, pelting him with heavy blows of Bordeaux and sauterne and claret. He was senseless before he hit the glass-littered floor, falling into a puddle of liquid grape like a drunkard while bottles smashed and rolled in abandon around him. Genevieve ducked and jumped as the rack itself groaned and splintered, then crashed down on the fallen man.

It was over so quickly, she had no time to think about what might have happened if she hadn't moved fast enough. Picking her way through the broken glass and splintered boards, she gingerly approached the Cossack. A purple goose egg the size of a small cantaloupe was already raising up on his forehead where the champagne bottle had struck him.

Forcing herself to breathe through her mouth so she wouldn't disgrace herself by losing the contents of her stomach, she gritted her teeth and reached into Grigor's pocket for the key. Retrieving his pistol as well, she grabbed her cloak and scampered for the door.

Fresh air had never been like this. The fetid atmosphere of the squalid alley was ambrosia to her, and she gulped it in great gusts, stumbling over her own feet as she fled. How long Grigor would be unconscious was a question she couldn't answer, and at this very moment Bryce might be performing a heinous act, thinking he was saving her life!

She reached the cobbled main street with its occasional street lantern and desultory traffic, spinning in circles as she tried to orient herself. Where was she? Which way was the Minoritzenplatz? The Gothic spire of St. Stephen's rising majestically over the city gave her the answers. Breathing a silent but heartfelt prayer, she turned up the street toward the British mission and ran.

Another time, Bryce would have reveled in the fact that he had his audience in the palm of his hand.

Though the small dais on which he stood at one end of the ornately decorated reception room was only the suggestion of a stage, the guests seated in graceful gilded chairs arranged before it or standing along the crimson silk-covered walls were as enthralled as if this were the grandest Covent Garden production.

A selection from Sheridan had been greeted with enthusiastic laughter.

Hamlet's soliloquy moved many of the viewers to tears.

When Bryce began Mark Antony's oration from *Julius Caesar*, he could have heard the proverbial pin drop, so completely did he control the assembly.

And, seated in the front row beside the beautiful Duchess of Sagan, one of the premier hostesses of Viennese society, whose name had been linked romantically with Metternich's earlier in the fall, the Duke of Wellington sat as unsuspecting as a newborn babe.

" 'Friends, Romans, countrymen . . .' "

The familiar lines rolled from Bryce's tongue, his deep

voice mesmerizing, every gesture and action focusing all eyes upon himself. He was vaguely surprised he could still get the words out past a throat that was threatening to close up at any moment. His neckcloth seemed to strangle him, but he resisted the urge to tug at it, for what was physical discomfort compared to the agony that was torturing his soul?

Genevieve. The vision of her lovely face haunted him, and longing of an intensity he'd never known consumed him. Was she safe? Hurting? Fear and desperation knotted his gut, and involuntarily he looked up, spotting again the portly figure of Baron von Throder lounging in apparent ease near the rear of the hall. But the Abbot's pale eyes gleamed, and meeting Bryce's look, he nodded imperceptibly, imperatively.

Bryce knew what that look meant: *Do it, or she dies!*

The oration complete, applause thundered as Bryce took his bow, then died down again when he struck a pose, hands in pockets, seeming to acquiesce to both the audience's and Wellington's demand for another selection.

"I am sorry I cannot oblige Your Grace," Bryce announced for all to hear, "but as Brutus remarked of Caesar, 'joy for his fortune, honour for his valour, and . . . death for his ambition.' "

Pulling a pistol from his coat, Bryce fired point-blank at the duke's heart.

Heart pounding, breath coming in labored shreds, the muscles of her abused legs on fire, Genevieve stumbled around the corner of the Minoritzenplatz and into a scene of chaos.

Carriages clogged the street. Pedestrians stood in anxious clots before the British mission. Hysterical women in the arms of their ashen-faced escorts swooned down the front steps. Soldiers and police lined the curbs, holding back the curious. Grim-visaged gentlemen of the medical and diplomatic corps fought their way inside through the throngs spilling out of the carved and crenellated front entrance.

"Oh, no." Genevieve lurched to a halt, pressing her fist against her mouth to stifle a scream of anguish. *She was too late!*

In a horrified daze, she pushed through the maddened swarm, struggling to reach the entrance. Snatches of conversation confirmed her worst fears.

". . . blood everywhere—His Grace's shirtfront, the Duchess of Sagan's gown . . ."

". . . damned monstrosity! God blast these Bonapartists!"

". . . the actor did it!"

". . . guards fell on him immediately . . ."

". . . no doubt at all—Wellington's dead!"

". . . hang the bastard!"

Genevieve's steps faltered as her world shattered and her dreams crashed down around her head. Half hidden by a knot of bystanders, she hadn't the strength to push the remaining few feet to the staircase. Shuddering violently, chilled despite the warmth of her recent exertion, the Cossack's pistol weighing down the inner pocket of her cloak, she swayed on her feet, near total collapse. Wellington was dead, and Bryce as good as executed for the crime if he hadn't already been killed by zealous guards! Stars danced behind her eyes, and her ears rang with her own dreadful words of condemnation and destruction.

"Too late . . . too late! Oh, Bryce, forgive me. I'm too late."

What to do now? Her husband had become a traitor and a murderer because of her. Could she plead for mercy for him? Even her dire circumstances would not be an excuse for destroying the most revered military statesman in England's recent history. And what of Bonaparte? The Abbot had said this news would signal the emperor's return to power. Might the Sicilian tyrant flame unchecked across Europe again, this time with no Wellington to stop him?

These repercussions bespoke tragedy for many besides herself.

Genevieve squeezed her eyes closed and struggled for control. If only she could see Bryce one last time!

"A very great tragedy, indeed," a familiar stentorian voice said from the crowded doorway.

Instantly, Genevieve's eyes popped open again, and they filled with virulent green hatred. The Abbot himself! His face set in the very throes of grief, Baron von Throder made his ponderous way down the staircase just as the policemen decided the crowd had grown too volatile and abruptly ordered the streets cleared.

Pushed back by the multitude, Genevieve saw von Throder lift his hand to summon his carriage, and her own hand reached into her cloak for the secreted pistol. It might be too late to save Bryce, but it wasn't too late to complete his work. Determination surged through her, giving her strength, restoring her vitality. While there was still a single solider on the field, this general would not admit defeat!

One look confirmed that it would be too risky to innocent spectators to chance a shot at the Abbot here. But as he disappeared into the green-lacquered coach supplied by the Austrians for visiting diplomats, Genevieve realized it could no more than inch forward through the chaos for some time to come. It would be enough.

Racking her brains, she came up with the street name she needed: Wallnerstrasse. On asking directions from a nearby policeman, she had reason to thank God again for making Vienna such a small and tidy city. Ignoring the ache in her legs, she set off at a brisk pace, focusing only on what she had to do, not on the ruins of three lives. For to contemplate that would be to lose heart, and she refused to let Bryce down in this last desperate battle of the Abbot's war. She could risk all now, because it had already cost her everything.

Genevieve reached the Wallnerstrasse well in advance of the Abbot. The houseman who answered her knock found a woman with a halo of wild chestnut curls in a wrinkled evening dress who had no qualms about threatening him with a pistol. As if her veins flowed with ice water, she calmly backed the startled servant inside the rather shabby foyer, before a gentleman taking his evening air on the opposite street corner could observe anything amiss.

Closing von Throder's door behind her, Genevieve locked the houseman in the coal cellar after making it clear, despite the language differences, that she'd blow his head off if he made a peep. Then she crept into what could only be von Throder's office-library, a room that smelled pleasantly of leather and tobacco, filled with bookshelves. Over the marble mantel, a pendulum clock beat a steady rhythm and showed it was still a quarter hour before midnight. She selected a chair in a dark corner and waited impatiently to exact a cold-blooded vengeance.

The opportunity was not long in coming.

She first heard the jingle of carriage harnesses echoing along the quiet street, then the irritated muttering of the master of the house having to let himself in. She'd removed her cloak and placed the cocked pistol in her lap. With every nerve wound as tight as a watch spring, she raised the pistol.

A spate of muttered German obscenities preceded the Abbot's entrance into the library. Shoving open the door, he stomped to the wide desk situated before the window, lit a lamp, then reached for a decanter of brandy. With his broad back to Genevieve, the baron poured a generous portion into a cut-glass tumbler and tossed it down. His stubby hand closed around the decanter's neck again.

"One would think you have something to celebrate, *mein Herr*," Genevieve said softly. "You're mistaken."

The baron's back stiffened, and he turned slowly, his colorless eyes widening at the sight of the pistol trained on him. "I congratulate you on your ingenuity, madame. I see I've underestimated you."

"You may keep your compliments, Baron." She rose,

ignoring the unsteadiness in her knees, keeping the weapon pointed at him. "I have no need of them, and since you will soon be in Hades I suggest you turn your thoughts in that direction."

"An enterprising woman such as you settling for mere revenge? Madame, you disappoint me!"

"For all the evil you have done me and mine, for my grandfather, Bryce, Taffy, and Wellington, I will eat this tasty dish and savor every morsel." Determinedly, she raised the pistol.

"Wait!" The baron's round forehead glistened with sudden beads of perspiration.

" 'Tis not so pleasant being on this side of the threat, is it, *mein Herr*?"

"Think of what you do, Genevieve."

"I have, Baron, very carefully. You've taken everything from me but this, and if I go to hell, at least I'll have the satisfaction of having sent you there first."

"Perhaps I'm not making myself clear," he interjected hastily. "Why should you settle for so little when you could have so much more? Just name your price. Money? A written confession? Maybe it's *this* you really want."

Von Throder dug beneath his cravat and extricated the tarnished chain and rosy gem she'd first seen in her grandfather's hands, holding it up before her horrified gaze. Genevieve recoiled as if it were a cobra.

"The mystic promise of the Abbot's Seal is waiting for you," he said slyly.

Though her teeth chattered with nerves, her look was contemptuous. "I want nothing tainted by your villainy."

"And yet you become a part of it by this very act." He saw her hesitate and smiled kindly. "Go now, my dear, and we'll cry truce. This was never your fight, was it?"

"You made it mine," she choked, striving to control the suddenly wavering pistol barrel. The ice water in her veins had dried up, leaving her dangerously weak and cowardly. Did she have it in her to do it? She must!

At a sudden disturbance in the foyer, her glance slid

momentarily away from the Abbot, and her pistol wobbled. He took a lightning-quick step toward her, but she lifted the weapon again, hanging on to her determination by the most gossamer of threads.

"Don't move!" she ordered in a shrill voice.

"That will be my men returning," the baron explained with a lift of his round shoulders. "You're too late again, so put down your weapon, my dear."

Gulping, grasping for courage, Genevieve tightened her finger on the trigger.

"Do as he says, Genny," Bryce drawled from the doorway. "Though I appreciate the gesture, I really don't fancy sleeping with a murderess!"

Chapter 20

"**B**ryce!" Genevieve's mouth dropped open, and the pistol careened at crazy angles.

"Easy, General." Bryce crossed the room and gently removed the weapon from her nerveless fingers. "Better let me have that."

"An excellent move," boomed another voice. "After all the trouble we've gone to, we certainly don't want the lady putting a hole in the baron before we've had a chance to ask him a few questions!"

"Your Grace!" Genevieve gulped and swayed with shock.

The Duke of Wellington, appearing quite hale and whole except for a brilliant crimson stain on his chest that made him look as if he wore a scarlet waistcoat, strode into the room, followed by a handful of armed guards. At the desk, the Abbot staggered backward with a German oath of incredulity.

Keeping the pistol trained on von Throder, Bryce placed a supporting arm around Genevieve's waist, and she looked up at him with mystification. "But how? Oh, God! I thought . . ."

Humor crinkled the corners of Bryce's mouth. "An actor deals in illusion, *chérie*. You know that."

Relief washed over Genevieve in giant, crashing waves, bubbling through her like spindrift and leaving her so breathless and giddy her knees dissolved beneath her. She clutched Bryce's lapels to prevent herself from sliding to the floor.

"Dammed fine plot, too." Wellington grinned. "A pistol loaded with blanks, a bladder filled with sheep's blood under my shirt, and a word to my guards were all it took. I rather thought my performance added a certain panache to the overall scene, didn't you, Bryce?"

"Should you ever desire a change of career, Your Grace, I can guarantee you a warm reception on the London stage."

"Hoaxed!" Von Throder was so red-faced with frustrated fury, he appeared on the verge of an apoplectic fit. "By Satan, 'tis impossible!"

"You should not have underestimated the Griffin," Wellington retorted, a grimly satisfied smile tilting his mouth. "Your blunder was threatening his lady."

"I didn't expect the bastard to release you before the deed was done," Bryce said to Genevieve. "Gave us all quite a turn when our man watching this place reported your appearance. It's just like you to try to organize everything yourself, General, but you'd have spared me a few anxious moments if you'd come to me first."

"Knowing nothing of your plan, how could I?" Dazed, Genevieve shook her head in bewilderment. "And the baron didn't release me. I escaped before Grigor could carry out his orders to kill me."

"What!" Bryce's hands tightened on her urgently, and he went pasty under his tan. "Are you all right? Genny, they didn't hurt you?"

She shuddered at the memory of how close it had been, then shook her head. "I'm all right, truly. I outfoxed Grigor before he could . . . before he . . ." She couldn't finish.

"Jesus!" Bryce's eyes darkened to the wrathful blue of a seething thunderhead, and his features set once again in the Griffin's chilling, deadly mask. He pointed the gun at von Throder's forehead. "I stayed your hand too soon, General."

Clutching the Abbot's Seal, the baron cringed backward, whimpering in fear. Wellington and the guards froze.

"Bryce, no!" Genevieve grabbed for his arm, her expression beseeching.

"You beg for this *couchon*'s life?" he snapped.

Genevieve's eyes filled. "I beg for *yours*. God knows the Abbot deserves no mercy, but it's got to end somewhere. We've come so far, my love. Don't jeopardize it all with one rash act."

For a terrible second the line of Bryce's mouth remained implacable, then Genevieve felt the tension drain from his body. Uncocking the weapon, he jammed it in his belt and pulled her to him, burying his face in her hair.

"*Mon ange*, my soul!" he whispered. "Again you tame the Griffin. Only God knows what I'd be without you."

Von Throder collapsed against the desk, relieved at this reprieve. With a contemptuous glance, Wellington retrieved the Abbot's Seal from the shaken Abbot and gestured to the guards. "Remove this criminal. The courts will deal with him as he deserves, beginning with the murder of Everett Maples."

"The Church will rise in outrage at my martyrdom," von Throder mumbled. An insane light burned in his eyes. "Blasphemous unbelievers! You'll see the power of my visions! They'll build cathedrals in my name. I know things you're too blind to see. War, pillage, death, and more—it's coming for you. You'll all see . . ."

As the guards led the raving baron away, Genevieve trembled in Bryce's arms, unnerved by the almost prophetic tenor of the Abbot's lunacy, yet enormously relieved to have this confrontation behind her. "I can't believe this. Is it truly over at last?"

Bryce threaded his fingers through the curls at her temples and gently kissed the tears from her spiky lashes. "Thanks to you, *mon brave*."

"You are a most courageous woman, Mrs. Cormick," the duke said, idly swinging the seal by its chain. "We'll have to decide what should become of this bauble, won't we? No doubt when we interrogate von Throder and examine his files, we'll have the true story of the Abbot's complicity in a number of plots, enough to send him to the gallows lawfully or at least keep him incarcerated for the rest of his worthless life."

Genevieve smiled unsteadily from the haven of her husband's protective embrace. "For the first time in a great while I feel free again, Your Grace. The Abbot caused much suffering, and—oh, no—Taffy! Bryce, how could I forget. . . ?"

"The nursing sisters have the sergeant in their capable hands, my love," Bryce assured her gravely. "The rest is with God. But you know Welshmen—they're too tough to kill."

Genevieve raised a shaky hand to her forehead, dizzy with the news that Taffy was still alive and apparently fighting to stay that way. "I pray you're right."

"Speaking of bloodshed," the duke said, looking down at his own stained attire, "I'd better see to my garb and look in on the late meeting of the plenary committee to squash a certain nasty rumor concerning my recent demise. Bryce, I'd suggest you take your valiant lady home to bed before she faints in your arms."

"I've never swooned in my life!" Genevieve said, straightening indignantly. She immediately wilted again. "Perhaps I am a trifle fatigued . . ."

Laughing, the duke took his leave.

"Come, *chérie,*" Bryce murmured. With great solicitousness, he placed her cloak about her, then led her out of the house to a waiting carriage. As he settled her onto the seat and pulled her against his shoulder, a wicked twinkle shone in his eyes. "I believe we'll take His Grace's excellent suggestion—especially the part about bed."

"Rogue!" she chided with a tired smile. Her breath hastened with the familiar pace of rising passion, but she could not stifle a yawn of both physical and emotional exhaustion. "I have been through an ordeal, remember?"

Bryce swallowed hard. "I will never forget how I feared for you, my love."

"I was frightened, too," she answered softly. "But mostly for you."

"Me?"

"I knew what a terrible choice the Abbot forced you to make, and I couldn't bear to be the cause of your dilemma. Deep down, I knew you could never betray your country in that way, but for a time I believed you had. I'm sorry I doubted you, Bryce. I should have known your ingenuity would see you through this trial."

"Genny." He shook his head in disbelief. Would he never cease to be amazed at this woman's faith in him? It exalted and humbled him. "God knows what I would have done if it hadn't worked as I planned. I love you beyond everything, and if it had taken the sacrifice of my honor and my life to save you, I'd have gladly given them both."

"My existence has no meaning without you, so 'tis fortunate my darling Griffin is a master at his art." Touching his cheek, she raised her mouth and gave him a loving kiss. "You see, Bryce? There is a purpose to everything you are."

"Since you're safe again, I suppose I should never again begrudge that portion of myself," he answered gruffly. He stroked her hair, then paused as a sudden question made him frown. "How did you free yourself from this Grigor fellow, anyway?"

Feeling utterly safe and protected, Genevieve snuggled against her husband's massive chest, her lashes drooping. "Oh," she said drowsily, " 'twas nothing. I merely bashed him with a champagne bottle."

"What? Genevieve—"

But she was already asleep in his arms, and the utter trust of that simple action warmed him and freed him from the awful constriction that had plagued him since her disappearance. Kissing her temple, he murmured the words in his heart. "I love you, Genny."

At last they arrived at their accommodations near the opera. There was plenty of hot water on the hob and food in the small pantry. Washed and fed, Genevieve made no demur when Bryce promptly tucked her into bed, and he was content simply to hold her as she slept out her fatigue. When in the wee hours he finally succumbed to the lure of slumber himself, his dreams were unmolested by old ghosts.

The midmorning sun splashed across the drab counter-pane of the old poster bed when next he opened his eyes. From the cobbled street below came the bustle of traffic, and the calls of vendors floated through the crisp air to mingle with the fragrant hint of spring wafting in from across the Danube.

Bryce turned his head to find Genevieve propped on her elbow, smiling at him. Her hair fell in a shimmering tumble across her shoulders, and the thin lawn of her night rail was little impediment to a man's appreciation of her womanly charms. His pulse quickened.

"Well, wife? What makes you smile?" he asked, his voice husky with sleep and something else.

"I'm happy, husband." Smiling even wider, she leaned over and kissed him.

"You are, eh?" Reaching out, he wrestled her playfully onto his bare chest, his hands sliding everywhere his eyes had been.

"Yes." Laughing, she squirmed under his tickles. "Gloriously happy!"

"Then give me a proper kiss to prove it."

She gave him a sultry pout, pursing her perfect mouth in a perfectly luscious bow that plucked at his control. "As you wish, husband."

Bending, she gently melded her lips against his, sweetly plying her wiles, hinting at hidden mysteries and unfolding intimacies. With a groan of impatience, Bryce caught her nape, holding her still as the kiss deepened with a feverish exchange of tongues that left them both breathless.

"Did you know this is the first time we've ever awakened together that there hasn't been some conflict between us, trying to tear us apart?" she asked, tracing patterns with her fingertips down the lean plane of his stubbled cheeks. "No pain, no anger, no danger. It's like a miracle."

"Or a dream come true." Catching her flushed face between his wide palms, Bryce looked at Genevieve in wonder. "God! It's incredible how much I love you! I never knew I could feel for anyone the way I feel for you, Genny. Your merest touch makes me tremble like a green lad."

"And I blush like a schoolgirl at your every look." She sighed. "The Abbot robbed us of the time we should have spent holding hands beneath the willows."

"Our salad days." He caught her hand and pressed an aching kiss into her palm. "Innocent courting games and wooing you as a proper suitor should. I wish I could have given you that, my love."

"Perhaps this is our time now."

"We'll make it our time," he murmured. "I want to give you all the good things you deserve—a home, a family, everything."

"Then love me, Bryce, for that's all I've ever needed."

"Forever, *chérie, je t'aime.*"

With the air of a man making a solemn pact, he pulled her down, capturing her mouth in a kiss that sealed all promises, past, present, and future. Genevieve trembled in response, murmuring her pleasure and need wordlessly and igniting the answering need that smoldered within Bryce. With a growl, he rolled her beneath him, pulling at her gown, wanting nothing to separate them ever again.

Breathless, Genevieve stirred against his weight and helped him remove her garment, sighing with delight when his hard, hair-dusted body covered her softer form, dizzied by the rush of erotic tactile sensations loving this man evoked. The sandy-rough rasp of his tongue stroking the cavern of her mouth, the tenderness of his callused fingers kneading the curve of her buttocks, the hot shock of his erection against her inner thigh. She was drowning in sensation and gloried in it.

Bryce feasted on the apricot-tinted delicacy of her skin, smiling at her shivers of delight, then shuddering in turn as her teeth grazed the puckered coin of his male nipple and her tongue explored the indention of his navel. Boldly, freely, she stroked him, surprising and pleasing him with her curiosity and initiative, wringing gasps of pleasure from his tortured lungs.

Purified by the fires of trials surmounted, refined by bonds of intimacy and commitment, their passion was perfected in the physical act of love they shared. Protected by their trust in each other, they abandoned all control and came together in a conflagration of the senses.

As Bryce entered her, Genevieve cried aloud for the sheer joy of his possession. When his wife arched beneath his penetrating thrusts, taking him deeper within her silken depths than he'd ever dreamed possible, Bryce groaned with the exquisite pressure of completely belonging to the woman he loved. In a communication that surpassed mere words, they strove to show each other the true measure of their feelings with each drugging kiss and every lingering caress. Giving, sharing, loving: these were the only realities that mattered as the universe shattered and dissolved, hurling them into that blissful abyss that only true lovers know.

When at last they could both breathe again, Bryce and Genevieve looked at each other and laughed softly, joyfully, gratefully. Lassitude weighed their limbs, but they were equally reluctant to part. Even when Bryce finally withdrew, they lay together in a tangle of damp limbs.

"For a married woman, that is a remarkably silly smile you're wearing," Bryce teased.

"You're completely responsible, sir." She rubbed the pads of her fingers against the notch in his collarbone,

dipping into the moisture that pearled there. Teasing him
back in her own way, she stroked her fingers against her
lower lip, then, like a gourmet, sampled the salty essence
of him with her tongue and watched his beautiful blue eyes
ignite again.

"Madam," he growled, moving his hand to cup the
velvety fullness of her breast, "keep that up and you'll
have reason to grin."

"Mmm, a promise I can't wait to collect!"

Chuckling, Bryce punished her sauciness with a kiss
that quickly escalated out of control. "God, I love your
mouth! I never again want to be farther away from you
than at this moment."

Flushed and breathless, she touched the black silk of
his hair, and her smile turned impish. "It might prove
rather awkward in polite society, but I'm willing to try it
if you are."

Laughing, he reached for her, kissing her neck and
shoulders, whispering loving words and suggestive promises. She giggled and blushed, overcome with happiness,
but then Bryce stiffened and lifted his head. An imperative
knocking sounded from the entrance of their rundown
abode.

"Hellfire and damnation!" Bryce's look was rife with
disgust. "Just when I've got you where I want you, another damned interruption. I can't think when we've ever
had the leisure to enjoy each other without interference!"

"You'd best go see, Bryce," Genevieve said anxiously.
"It may be someone with word about Taffy."

"You're right, of course." He crawled from the rumpled bed and reached for his trousers. "But I'm warning
you, General, when we get to Clare Hill, I'm liable to
lock us both in my room for a month."

"Now there's something to look forward to."

Laughing, Bryce grabbed up his shirt and left the room,
and Genevieve snuggled back against the pillows to contemplate such a pleasant eventuality. When Bryce returned

with a letter in his hand and a strange look on his face, however, she sat straight up again in alarm.

"Bryce? What is it?"

'I'm summoned to wait upon the duke in a matter of great urgency . . .''

Foreboding gripped Genevieve's throat. "Now? Why?"

"Word just arrived by courier. All the Abbot's plots were for nothing." With an eerie fatalism and ironic calm etching his countenance, he handed her the missive. "Ten days ago, Napoleon Bonaparte escaped from Elba. The eagle has flown!"

"But why must it be *you*? Haven't you done enough?"

Bryce gazed into his wife's tear-washed eyes and wished to God he didn't have to hurt her again. "Genny, we've been over it and over it. Please understand. This is the only way."

"I don't care!" Beneath the brim of a new chip straw bonnet that matched her traveling costume, Genevieve's green eyes flashed with pain. "I know you think I'm being childish, but it isn't fair! I don't want to leave you again."

"Dammit, Genny! Do you think I do?"

Stalemated, they stood glaring at each other beside the coach waiting to take Genevieve back to England. It had only been two weeks since news of Bonaparte's escape had come, and with it so many complications! Now reports flew that the former emperor had reached Grenoble and that his old army was flocking to his standard by the thousands. Even Marshal Ney, sent by Louis to block the road to Paris, had defected to the emperor's camp, and soon, if he hadn't already succeeded, Bonaparte would again be in Paris before the violets bloomed, just as he had promised. An exodus of panicked royalists and British visitors already flooded the channel ports as they fled before the threat.

Bryce raked a hand through his hair. "You know what's happening and what's at stake. The proclamation the Congress signed declaring Boney an outlaw beyond the pale doesn't mean a thing. It will take an army to stop him now, and there's no doubt that Wellington will be the man the Five Powers appoint to lead it.''

''But you've fought your war! Let someone else do it this time!''

''How can I desert His Grace at this crucial moment? Czar Alexander told Wellington it was up to him to save the world again, but his staff has been dispersed, mostly to the New World, and he needs every able officer, especially in intelligence. You don't really expect me to shirk my duty now, do you?''

Genevieve drew a shaky breath and gave a sharp negative shake of her head. ''No. You wouldn't be the man I love if you could.''

''Then come here, General, and kiss me. I don't want us to part in anger.''

With a small, anguished cry, she flung herself into his arms. ''I'm sorry! I'm not angry at you, just so afraid.''

''I know, *chérie*.'' He inhaled her scent, memorizing the feel of her in his arms, imprinting memories for darker days. ''Since I cannot, I want you to go home to Clare Hill for me.''

''This is the hardest thing you've ever asked me to do. I couldn't stand it if I lost you now.'' Her words wobbled betrayingly. ''Please let me stay with you.''

Bryce's heart twisted, and his voice was husky with regret. ''It's impossible. I'll be traveling fast as the armies mass in the Low Countries. Knowing you're safe at Clare Hill is the only way I can concentrate on what I must do. If I'm distracted with worry about you, I could make a mistake and . . .''

She gave a watery snort. ''You don't play fair, Bryce Darcy Cormick.''

''War is notoriously unfair.''

''Just you make certain the Griffin keeps his wits about him,'' she said sternly.

He smiled. ''Of course.'' Dipping his head, he kissed her gently, thinking about the first time he'd tasted her luscious mouth, so long ago in a carriage crossing the Epping Forest, and how he'd like to untie her bonnet now as he had then and hold her forever. But duty—that bloody bitch!—called him yet again. Only this time, there was more than ever to come home to.

"I'll be most vigilant," he murmured when he raised his head at last. "Do something for me?"

Lifting her misty gaze to his, Genevieve blinked back new tears. "Anything. You know that."

"Hold on to this for me." He gave her a small leather-bound book.

"Your journal!" Her expression was awed that he would entrust his most private thoughts to her. "But—"

"I'll fill another one for you during this enterprise. And there's something else. See this is restored to its proper home." From his coat pocket he drew the Abbot's seal and folded it into her palm.

"Oh, Bryce," she breathed, transfixed anew at the glistening pink stone with its eagle's talon.

"It doesn't belong to the world. Greed and ambition and power pervert its real purpose. Take it back to the abbey so that it can do God's work again."

"Yes." Her fingers closed over the talisman. "Pray God, it will be an offering for your safe return to me."

Bryce smiled at that, watching as she reverently placed the seal and his journal into her ridicule. He then turned to the man waiting inside the coach. "You'll help her return it to Père Florien, won't you, Taffy?"

The former sergeant was still pale as milk, his right arm sported a sling, and a dashing new scar graced the top of his cheekbone, a feature which no doubt would soon prove a favorite among the ladies. Despite his convalescent status, Taffy grinned his assent and saluted with his left hand.

"Aye, Cap. Just as you say."

Bryce assisted Genevieve into the coach, leaned in through the door, and offered Taffy his hand. "Take care of her for me, old friend."

Using his left hand, the Welshman shook hands with Bryce and swallowed hard, his eyes glistening suspiciously. "The missus can count on me. You watch yer back, Cap."

"I will." Bryce shifted to gather Genevieve's gloved hands into his own. "Give Maebella my best and kiss Allegra for me, Genny, and tell my father—"

He broke off, staring at their clasped hands. Genevieve tilted her head to peer into his face. "Yes?"

"Tell the old man I love him." Bryce's mouth twisted, and he gave a careless shrug. "I don't think he's ever heard it from me, even indirectly. It may mean something."

"Of course it will mean something!" she said, her face going pale with alarm. "But it sounds so final. You come home and tell him yourself, do you hear?"

The corner of Bryce's mouth lifted at her command. "Yes, General."

"Swear it!" she said fiercely.

"I swear."

Drinking each other in with their eyes one last time, they spoke together.

"I love you, Bryce."

"*Je t'adore,* Genny."

With a singularity of desperation, their lips met again, clung, then parted. A muscle ticking in his clenched jaw, Bryce stepped back, slamming the carriage door, and nodded to the coachman. With a slap of the reins, the vehicle started forward, and he had a fleeting glimpse of misty green eyes that he knew would haunt him, even after death.

Heart pounding, he damned his man's duty as the best part of himself disappeared into the Viennese traffic.

Chapter 21

"Here, Miss Genny! Lookit what I found you."
Genevieve roused from a bout of glassy-eyed
abstraction and returned her attention to Jack Potts and the
other companions enjoying this fine late June afternoon on
Clare Hill's rear terrace. Sir Theodore pored over his paper while Allegra carried on a desultory conversation with
Jules Chesterson. Genevieve set aside her sketchbook and
vowed to curtail the spells of preoccupation that had become such a habit during the two months since she'd returned to Bryce's Suffolk home.

"What is it, Jack, dear?" she asked, smiling. He'd
grown taller and filled out on good country fare during her
absence.

The boy's black eyes danced as he proudly presented
her with a spray of white goose feathers. "Will these make
good quills for your drawings?" he asked.

"Excellent quills, Jack." She stroked the soft feathers
to show her admiration. Nearby, bees sang among the fragrant trailing roses, pinks, and marigolds that surrounded
the terrace. "No doubt with these I shall make my finest
designs ever for Maebella. Now there is no reason for me
to further delay filling her latest orders. Thank you."

"Taffy said you'd like them."

"Now, Jack," Allegra Cormick chided gently from a
perch on the low rock wall bordering the gardens. "I hope

you aren't overtaxing Mr. McKee with your shenanigans.''

In recent weeks Allegra had taken Genevieve's subtle recommendations and simplified her style of dress. She looked cool and elegant in a simple lavender gown, not at all the frumpish horsewoman or awkward spinster, though her relaxed attitude still showed a careless but totally unselfconscious flash of well-turned ankle.

"No, miss, o' course not!" Jack looked indignant. "Why, Taffy says he's fit as a fiddle, and if he hadn't promised the Cap to look out for Miss Genny, he'd be on his way to fight Boney, too. Can I go with him if he does?''

"Indeed you may not, young man," Sir Theodore said sternly. He leaned back in the wooden lawn chair and straightened his newspaper with an authoritative crackle. "Besides, if this dispatch from Wellington published in the *Times* is any indication, the entire conflict might well be over. Isn't that right, Chesterson?''

"That was the word when I left London three days ago, sir," Jules replied. "For all accounts it was quite a pounding match.''

While the knot in his neckcloth was still perfection, both the height of his collar points and the vibrant colors Jules had once affected had been replaced with an elegantly conservative suit of plain blue worsted. Now he sent Genevieve an anxious glance. "I'm certain you'll hear from Mr. Cormick very soon.''

For a naked moment, the faces of the three other adults in the group reflected their anxiety for the safety of son, brother, husband.

Though Bonaparte had taken his time before making his move from Paris, once he'd marched, he'd engaged the Allied armies in short order on the Belgian frontier. Now everyone knew the names of obscure villages like Thuin, Enghien, Quatre Bas, Waterloo.

They knew that the Life Guards and King's Dragoons had mounted a crucial cavalry charge, only to be almost totally destroyed when the French infantry cut off their line of retreat. They discussed the valiant defense of the garrison at La Haye Sainte where only forty-one survived. And everyone knew the twenty-seventh Foot was dead to a man.

Casualties on both sides ran to tens of thousands, and the carnage had been devastating, but the French lines had been irretrievably broken and Bonaparte was in retreat, no doubt to face another abdication or worse. It would take weeks to bury the dead, to account for the missing, to care for the massive number of wounded. And though the finger of providence had been on Wellington, making him seemingly invulnerable as well as invincible as he raced from crisis to crisis in the thick of the battle, personally exhorting the troops, there had been no news at all about Captain Bryce Cormick.

Genevieve valiantly swallowed back her trepidation as she had during the past torturous weeks. "Yes, Jules, I'm sure you're right. And it's kind of you to visit so often to bring the latest news."

"I very much enjoy your gracious hospitality," Jules replied.

"As well as the company of a certain Miss North?" Allegra teased. Mischief sparkled in her violet eyes as she took blithe advantage of the friendship that had sprung up between her and the former dandy.

Jules's ears reddened, and his smile was sheepish. "Miss North is charming, of course, but she is not the only reason I come."

"Oh, certainly," Allegra said, nodding knowingly. "There is also the matter of your helping my sister-by-marriage find a publisher for my brother's play. But surely those negotiations could be conducted by post?"

"I prefer doing business in person," Jules said, tugging at his collar as his face turned an even brighter shade of crimson.

"Oh, do not plague him so, Allegra!" Genevieve begged, laughing. "Jules, you may keep your protestations, my dear friend. Your fondness for the lady does you credit. And, if I'm not mistaken, that's her pony just coming over the hill.''

Jules brightened at the sight of Clorinda North's dappled mare topping the knoll. "So it appears. I'll just go meet her, shall I?"

"Go, by all means!" Allegra said, waving him away. "Clorinda is just as sickeningly besotted, so you make a fine pair of lovebirds. Go on, and you go with him, Jack, to see to the lady's mount. We excuse you both."

"Yes, miss! Thank you!" Beaming at this rare opportunity to show his growing expertise with horses, and at Allegra's uncommon confidence in him, Jack ran down the terrace steps.

With a grin, Jules followed, forgetting his dignity so far as to vault over the low wall to reach the visitor before Jack did. Sir Theodore set his newspaper aside and shook his head in wonder as Clorinda dismounted straight into Jules's waiting arms.

"Extraordinary! They may very well suit."

"I think you can count on choosing a wedding gift for Clorinda from your stable before the summer is out, Father," Allegra said.

"Hmmph. I'd as lief see my own daughter settle on some fellow so I might plan a wedding as well," Sir Theodore snorted.

"What nonsense!" Allegra rose to place an affectionate peck on his cheek. "Who'd want an ungainly bluestocking like me? I fully intend to remain a spinster so that I may plague you in your old age, Father."

Sir Theodore's mouth twitched, and Genevieve hid a giggle behind her hand. She knew full well that they played out this little farce for her sake to take her mind off Bryce, and she loved them for it.

"Try to talk some sense into my daughter's head, will you, Genevieve?" Sir Theodore asked plaintively. "You recommend the married estate, don't you?"

"Oh, assuredly, sir," Genevieve said. Rising, she set aside her sketchbook and reached idly for his discarded newspaper. "But only if love is present. I am sure Allegra will one day meet a man who will steal her heart as surely as your son stole mine."

Old pain twisted the curve of Allegra's lips. "I already have . . . and lost him. Sometimes that's the way life works."

"Allegra!" Sir Theodore snapped in horrified admonition as the blood drained out of Genevieve's face, leaving her pale as chalk.

Allegra gulped in dismay at her unfortunate choice of words. "Oh, Genny, I'm sorry! I didn't mean—"

"I know. It's all right." Genevieve gave a shaky smile, shrugged, and folded back the newspaper. "We're all a bit on edge."

"Don't." Allegra's hand closed over her sister-in-law's wrist.

"What?"

"You're going to read the casualty lists. I know, I used to pore over them endlessly before Cal died. It's morbid, Genny, and it doesn't do any good. Father's already said that Bryce's name isn't there."

"Yes, I know. But some of the officers I knew in Paris might be, and . . ." She trailed off at Allegra's pitying look. "I feel I must do something! It's not knowing anything that's so hard!"

"You're right, my dear," Sir Theodore agreed heavily. "I wonder if that damned friend of Bryce's—Huxford, isn't it?—could make inquiries for us."

"Yes, that's a good idea," Genevieve said eagerly.

She hadn't heard from the earl since receiving a note from him on her return to England thanking her for her participation in efforts to bring the Abbot to justice. He'd also taken the opportunity to chastise her for what he called her impulsive decision to return the Abbot's Seal to the Abbey of the Holy Word. When she read that, she'd laughed, knowing the earl was too worldly ever to understand the reasons she and Taffy had traveled out of their

414 SUZANNAH DAVIS

way on that godly mission. Just knowing Père Florien and all the monks prayed for her husband was reward enough.

"I'll write the earl," she said. "If anyone knows where Bryce is, he will."

"Damme, I'll go to London tomorrow and see him in person!" Sir Theodore said.

"And if nothing comes of it," Allegra added, "then we can go to Brussels! I hear most of the wounded are there."

As Jules and Clorinda climbed the terrace steps arm in arm, Allegra and her father launched into a spirited discussion of the preparations that would be necessary for his trip. Feeling better, Genevieve folded the newspaper in half, then gave a startled cry.

"Oh, no!"

"Genny?" Allegra frowned as she saw that Genevieve was holding the paper open at the casualty lists, but her voice was soft with compassion. "Someone you know?"

The drone of the bees roared in Genevieve's ears. The sweet aroma of roses sickened her. The brilliant sunshine faded into eternal darkness. Genevieve touched a trembling finger to a single name on the long list of dead officers: *Captain Griffin D'Arcy.*

"Dear God, that's Bryce!" she whispered and fainted.

"Genny, you must try to eat some breakfast."

Allegra stood beside Genevieve's bed holding a tray of tea and toast, and although her eyes were rimmed with red from weeping, her attitude was adamant. "It's been three days now, and you're not going into a decline if I can help it!"

The reply was muffled by a mound of pillows and bedclothes. "That sounds suspiciously like a threat."

Disconcerted, Allegra slid the tray onto the rumpled foot of the bed and sat down beside Genevieve. "Genny, please . . . for Bryce's sake, don't grieve so. You'll make yourself ill."

Genevieve threw her tumbled hair out of her pale, tear-streaked face and rolled over to face her sister-in-law. "No, I won't. Trying to hold my feelings inside is what would kill me."

Allegra bit her lip uncertainly. Though grief-stricken, Genevieve was calm, perhaps too much so. "Are you all right?"

"Nothing can ever be completely right without Bryce." Genevieve sat up against the headboard, and rested her chin on her upraised knees. "But I'm not hiding from what I feel as I did before. I've earned the right to weep for my husband."

"I hate to see you like this."

Genevieve carefully tucked the thin lawn of her nightgown over her toes, then met Allegra's look gravely. "Loving Bryce taught me that you can't build a wall between yourself and life just because things are hard or painful. Every experience, every emotion has to be faced."

Allegra's chin trembled. "It's hard, isn't it?"

"Bryce told me once that hurting is sometimes the only way to know you're truly alive." Genevieve's voice broke, and her eyes filled. "Well, I hurt, Allegra. God, it hurts!"

"You can't give up hope," Allegra protested around a sympathetic thickening in her own throat. "There could be a mistake. I know Father will demand that Huxford get to the bottom of it."

Genevieve shook her head sorrowfully and wiped away the moisture on her cheeks with impatient fingers. "Griffin D'Arcy was a name Bryce used. He . . . he knew his duty, and his honor as a soldier demanded he follow his conscience. I know that however he died, he conducted himself valiantly, as a hero. We both knew the risks, and despite everything, loving Bryce was worth any cost—even this one."

"Oh, Genny," Allegra said, swallowing hard. "I know he loved you, too."

"That is my solace."

Bryce's journal lay beneath her pillow, a testimony to his talent as an observer of humanity, and a legacy of his passion and love for her to cherish. She'd read his thoughts, his dreams, his fears, and wept a thousand tears for each one that would be unfulfilled now. But it had been a cleansing and a healing, a chance to truly treasure what they had shared and to gather her courage for what lay ahead.

Rising from the bed, Genevieve picked up a piece of toast, eyeing it with determination if not appetite. "The certainty of Bryce's love will give me the strength to do what I must."

"What you must?" Allegra repeated blankly.

Palm open, Genevieve stretched the fabric of her gown over her flat abdomen and met Allegra's curious gaze with a tender smile.

"For our child."

It was the knowledge that Bryce's babe grew within her body that sustained Genevieve through the sultry days of a Suffolk July. By the end of that month, Bonaparte was in British custody aboard the *Bellerophon*, soon to be on his way to permanent exile on faraway St. Helena Island. Waterloo survivors trickled back into the country, but not even the Earl of Huxford's redoubtable talents unearthed anything past the report of Bryce's death on the field of battle. In death, even as in life, as Taffy had said, "If the Griffin don't want to be found, then he won't."

The loss of his son had aged Sir Theodore overnight, and it was only with the greatest diligence that Allegra managed to persuade her father to forego a trip to the Continent himself. The sheer number of dead had necessitated mass burials, and there was little hope of locating Bryce's remains among the thousands of casualties. They would have to be content with a marker as a memorial in the Cormick family cemetery.

"Do you think you could bear having a Griffin for company up here, Grandpapa?" Genevieve asked aloud one humid afternoon in early August.

She'd brought a bouquet of red roses and ivy to lay on

Everett's stone in his corner of the Cormick plot here on the shady hillside overlooking the willow-lined bank of the River Stour. "Allegra feels such a symbol would be appropriate, but I'm not so sure . . ."

Oblivious of the grass stains she was making on her sprigged muslin gown, she knelt to lay the flowers on the stone and reached for a few scraggly weeds. She'd found walking the countryside in her broad-brimmed straw sun hat both healthful for the growing infant and tranquilizing to its mother, though only a slight thickening of her waist hinted at her delicate condition as yet.

Her walks often brought her to this peaceful graveyard and one-sided conversations with her grandfather. Fanciful though these talks might be, she took comfort in them, somehow sensing that Everett knew and understood her need. And he didn't hover in too-solicitous concern when she felt the need to weep.

"They are so kind to me here, Grandpa, but even though Clare Hill is the home I thought I always wanted, it means nothing without Bryce. He was the only home I ever needed, and I miss him dreadfully. I miss you both."

She pulled a dandelion, wrinkling her nose at its acrid odor, then reached for another. "What Allegra would say if she could hear me talking to you, Grandpapa, I can't imagine! But since she's gone to Newcastle to purchase breeding stock for Sir Theodore, we need not worry about interruption."

Dusting her hands, she sat back on her heels, smiling slightly at herself. Bringing Everett up to date on all her news helped her to sort out things in her own mind, to set the stage for the next scene about to unfold in her life.

"Did you know Mr. Kemble himself has expressed an interest in producing Bryce's play? *Two Soldiers* is quite a success already, but then I had no doubts about that. Perhaps Bryce would not approve of my having it published, but the profits have already cleared the Athena's debt, so he could not argue with that—although I'm sure he would accuse me of too much organizing! I wonder if this babe will inherit his theatrical bent? Or perhaps an artistic temperament?''

Rising, she withdrew her sketchbook from her workbasket, then took a seat on the sun-warmed stone of the cemetery wall. She continued to chat, bringing Everett all the news from Clare Hill as she made a few rough drawings. Maebella planned to visit soon, and Genevieve wanted to have a portfolio of fall designs to send back to London, for Madame Bella's salon continued successful and was all the go with the fashionable set. Today, however, despite the pleasant warmth of the sun and the fresh scent of the hot grass, nothing Genevieve drew appealed to her.

She took off her hat to fan her warm cheeks, studying her work with a critical eye, then, with a sound of disgust, set the hat aside and ripped the pages from the book. Giving in to her restless mood, she selected a new sheet and began to sketch the scene spreading out down the hill before her. In the little valley, the silver ribbon of the Stour unfurled between banks of willows, and complacent cattle grazed on Sir Theodore's lush pastures. On a whim, Genevieve added an observer to the pastoral scene, a thick-set man with a beakish nose and mane of flowing hair.

She smiled to herself as Everett's features took shape beneath her pen. She would have to do a larger portrait of him, she decided, perhaps as Falstaff, something to show his great-grandchild when she recounted the vast dramatic talent of Everett Maples. In this sketch he appeared to be pointing something out, so she gave him an audience—a small child with a shock of black hair to hold Everett's hand and hang on every word of his tall Irish tales.

Her pen faltered, and she drew a tremulous breath, shaken by a sudden notion. Could this be the child she and Bryce had lost? In her need, had she produced a fantasy, placing that child who'd never had a chance at life in the loving care of his great-grandfather? Irrationally, she looked up, but the hillside was empty, the somnolent riverbank deserted except for late afternoon shadows.

Genevieve smiled at her fancy, but could not shake a deep sense of certainty. As sure as there was a heaven, then her beloved grandpapa and that first child shared it together. The thought calmed her and gave her peace.

Almost of its own volition, her pen began to move again, filling in the object of the pair's interest. With just a few strokes, another figure emerged in the drawing, a tall, ebony-haired man in an officer's coat climbing up the hill from the river. Genevieve knew that it was Bryce, but she hesitated when she came to fill in his features, uncertain whose expression he would wear—Bryce the actor, Darcy the soldier, or the Griffin?

With a small sound of pain, she dropped pad and pen into her lap, unable to finish. Eyes brimming, she lifted her head at the soft sound of whistling—and her heart stopped.

Below her, a tall figure with a cane limped up the willow-lined path. Genevieve shaded her eyes with her hand, squinting, but the slanting bands of sun and shadow made the man seem like some phantasm of her distraught senses, some ephemeral ghost, an otherworldly angel wrenched from her innermost dreams and needs. Just as in her drawing, she couldn't see his face, but there was something she recognized, something she *knew* . . .

Genevieve leaped to her feet, pens, sketchbook, and drawings flying. Papers fluttered in all directions like birds taking wing—like eagles! With a cry, she flung herself down the grassy slope, her feet pelting, her lungs bursting, her arms outstretched, her wild chestnut curls streaming behind her like the banners of a victorious army.

"Bryce!"

"General!" He lifted his cane in salute and was nearly bowled over by his wife's headlong rush into his welcoming arms.

"It is you!" Sobbing for joy, she clung to him, kissing every part of his face she could reach, murmuring in incoherent gratitude. "Thank God. Oh, thank God!"

Staggering slightly under her ecstatic onslaught, Bryce

held his wife tight, perilously near tears himself. "Who else, *chérie*?" he asked gruffly. "Or do you think I am a ghost?"

"If you are, then take me wherever phantoms dwell, for I never want to be parted from you again."

"Never again, Genny, I promise."

Their lips met in tender greeting, in the promise of sweeter passion, in the glorious salute of true homecoming. Trembling, Genevieve touched his cheek in wonder. He was thinner, paler, than he should be, but beautiful to her eyes.

"Dear God in heaven, am I dreaming?"

Bryce stroked her bright hair, and his large frame shook with the rush of honest emotion she'd taught him to trust and cherish.

"This is what dreams are made of," he said in a husky voice.

"Yes, yes!" She laughed joyously through her tears, wanting to share her happiness. "Your father. Does he know?"

Bryce nodded. "I saw him and Taffy at the manor, but surprising Allegra will have to wait upon her return. Gave the old man a shock, coming unannounced as I did, but I had no patience to wait. He actually cried, Genny. All this time I thought he was simply doing the right thing by his bastard son, but he really loves me for myself."

"I know. Many of us do."

"You're the only one who's ever been able to make me believe that." He kissed her again, sweeping his tongue over her lower lip as if tasting her for the first time. "God! How I've missed you! You'll never know."

"I have an idea." Tears slid from her lashes. "They reported you slain at Waterloo. How can this miracle be?"

"It must have been your prayers, my love, for it was a bloody pounding. I rode as one of Wellington's aides-de-camp, and my horse was shot out from under me near the end of the melee."

"You were wounded?" She looked him up and down for signs of injury, finally noting the cane. "Your leg!"

"Easy, General. The ball went right through my thigh, and laid me up properly, but I was luckier than most."

Bryce tucked her close to his heart, and they moved along the path beside the glittering river. The wind tossed and tumbled the scattered sheets of Genevieve's drawing papers down the hill after them in celebration.

"I can't see how getting shot should be counted lucky!" she said shakily.

"Again, your prayers must have been with me. I ended up with the Prussian wounded, out of my head with fever for a time. That's what took me so long to get back to you. Couldn't even get a damned letter out until I was well enough to travel to Brussels, and then I came across the channel and there was no point . . ."

"But Griffin D'Arcy was on the casualty list—I don't understand."

Bryce's lean face darkened, and his hand tightened on her shoulder. "I was handling sensitive intelligence for a time, so an alias seemed necessary. I guess someone who knew me by that name saw me fall. I'm sorry you had to go through that, love, but maybe the Griffin did die that day."

They paused beneath the curtain of green willow strands on the path toward Clare Hill, and Genevieve examined his face uncertainly. "What do you mean?"

"I don't know exactly." His blue gaze searched an inner distance she could not see, the bloodiness of a battle she could only begin to imagine. "There were many heroes that day. Just men trying to do their best for causes they believed in. That's all I ever tried to do. I've hated so many things for so long. The way Cal died, the way I had to work, the guilt that ate at my gut because deep inside I felt like a traitor to both my countries."

"Oh, my dear," she murmured. "What a burden you carried!"

"No longer, Genny, It's as if somehow all that's been

purged from me. Letting go of the hate means I can forgive myself and finally set the dark part of the Griffin to rest.''

"Then for your sake," she said slowly, shaken by the knowledge of whose face belonged in her drawing of ghosts, "I'll be glad it happened like this, but I never want to lose you in such a way again."

"Lose me?" He pressed her against the trunk of a willow tree, nibbling at the side of her neck. "Madam, you'll never be able to get rid of me!"

"Thank God." She sighed, happiness flowing like the waters of the river as she clasped her arms around his neck. The wind clattered the willow fronds and tossed the paper drawings around their ankles and into the stream.

"Belonging to you is the greatest freedom I've ever known, *mon ange*. Not even death could change that." He kissed her with incredible tenderness and heart-stopping need, murmuring against her perfect mouth, "*Je t'aime*, Genny, forever."

There was so much to tell him about, so much to share. The success of his play, the child they would have, all the plans they'd made together on their wedding night. But that could wait, for Genevieve's heart was so full, her head so giddy with the miracle of his resurrection that she could only whisper the most important things.

"I love you, Bryce."

Floating in the river, the drawing of the faceless specter dissolved until nothing remained but the flash of Everett Maples's smile. As that, too, melted away, Genevieve reached up to kiss her husband again.

"Welcome home, my love. Oh, *welcome home*."

Now that you've enjoyed
Suzannah Davis'
DANCE OF DECEPTION,
sample another of Avon Books'
Romantic Treasures—
ONLY IN YOUR ARMS
by Lisa Kleypas

Will circumstances require that the innocent Lysette Kersaint consent to wed her mysterious handsome protector Maximilien Vallerand . . . ?

There was a noise behind her. Lysette spun around, bumping her hip on the corner of the chest of drawers, but she didn't feel the pain. Max had entered the room and was watching her.

"I gather you feel my marriage proposal is not worthy of consideration," he remarked.

"Get out of my room!"

"It's not your room. This house—and everything in it—is mine."

"Everything but *me.*" Nimbly she tried to slip past him. Max caught her around the waist and closed the door with his foot. At the touch of his hands, she shrieked and tried to kick him. Her toes glanced off his booted shin. "Stop it," he said, and shook her once, lifting her until her soft-slippered feet were barely touching the floor. "We are going to discuss your rather short-sighted approach to the future."

"Let go of me!"

The corner of his mouth tilted mockingly. "My sweet, just what do you think you're going to do if you *don't* marry me?"

"I–I have alternatives."

"Such as?"

"I could teach—"

"With your reputation? No one would have you."

"Then the convent—"

"They won't take you in. There is no place you can go where I won't be able to ferret you out and bring you back here. And you can discard any hope of returning to the bosom of your family. In the estimation of any decent family, placing yourself in my custody was choosing a fate worse than death. You are ruined, my innocent, for any man but me. You face only two alternatives—to be my wife . . . or my mistress."

Lysette stared at him in shock. "I can't," she finally said. "I won't marry you, and I certainly won't be your . . ." She stopped, unable to say the hateful word.

"In actuality, there would be little difference between the two. Wife or paramour, you're going to be mine." His hand lifted to her face, and the backs of his fingers drifted along the curve of her jawline. Lysette's entire body tensed. "There's no need to cringe so fearfully, sweet. The arrangement might turn out to be pleasant for you."

"Pleasant?"

"You'll be the wife of a wealthy man. I'll dress you in clothes and jewelry that will properly display your beauty. I'll give you whatever you desire."

"I don't care about money."

"I'll be a considerate husband in all ways." Max paused, and let the silence draw out. "You'll be well satisfied, Lysette."

"It does not matter how considerate you would try to be," she said through dry lips. "I don't want . . . I–I don't like you at all—"

"You won't have to like me." He drew her closer, his arm taut around her waist.

Lysette was paralyzed as his hand moved down the side of her throat and smoothed over her breast. Her nipple ached at the light touch and contracted into a hard peak. Shocked by the intimate gesture, she stared up at him, while a surge of tingling warmth seemed to collect underneath his hand.

"Don't," she breathed, red with shame. "Oh, stop it!"

Ignoring the feeble protest, Max cupped his hand over her breast, then brushed his thumb against the sensitive bud. "You enjoy my touch, don't you?"

"I . . . I don't . . ." She faltered, and her voice caught in the back of her throat.

His warm, teasing mouth moved over her face, traveling to the corners of her lips, the curve of her cheek, the tiny space between her eyebrows. Lysette tried to turn away, but his arm tightened around her back, and his hand slipped inside her bodice. At the touch of his hand on her naked flesh, she gasped weakly and felt her knees wobble. If not for his supporting arm, she would have collapsed.

Max smiled against her forehead, while his fingers continued their gentle play. "You're not indifferent to me," he said . . . "Say you'll be my wife."

Lysette was stubbornly silent.

"Then I'll make you my mistress. Tonight." His head bent closer, his features half-concealed in shadow. "No, now," he said gruffly, and lowered his mouth to hers.

Her gasp of protest was smothered as his mouth crushed hers relentlessly. His arms confined her against his hard, insistent body. She couldn't move . . . couldn't breathe. Pressing her lips together, she made an imploring sound . . . and then his hand came to the side of her face, and his fingers stroked her cheek with startling gentleness. Dazed, she relaxed against him, unable to help herself.

Slowly Max broke the kiss and stared down at her. Opening her heavy-lidded eyes, Lysette felt herself swallowed in the depths of amber fire.

"Open your mouth," Max said huskily, his lips brushing against hers.

"W-what?"

"Open your mouth when I kiss you."

"No—"

Max bent over her again, assaulting her senses with a slow, sultry kiss, his tongue thrusting gently between her lips. Lysette gave a small cry and tried to retreat, but she was anchored firmly against him. There was no use in fighting him—he would not let her go until he was finished. Her head fell back against his arm, and her hands flattened on his shoulders.

And then all too soon, shamefully, there was no need for coercion. Her own senses betrayed her, responding to the touch and taste of the man above her. She reached out for him, her slender arms curving around his back, her spine arching until her breast was urged deeper into the confinement of his hand.

When she had surrendered completely, Max lifted her in his arms and carried her to the bed. Impatiently he nuzzled past the perfumed cluster of ribbons that concealed her cleavage, and buried his mouth in the valley between her breasts.

Suddenly Lysette realized what was happening. She tried to push him away. "P-please, Max," she stammered. "I need to rest," she said timidly, longing for him to go away. "I . . . need to be alone."

"Of course." Max did not move. "As soon as you consent to my proposal."

"I cannot think—"

"What is there to think about? You know it's pointless to deny me."

"You are cruel!"

"Only when I don't get my way." Max shifted his position, making certain his elbows bore the brunt of his weight. "Tell me you'll marry me."

"I would consent to your proposal," she said haltingly, "if . . ."

"If what?" Max asked swiftly.

"If you would allow me some time before . . ."

"Before we consummate the marriage," Max finished for her, seeming unsurprised by the request.

"Yes."

Max was quiet for a moment. When he spoke, his voice was oddly gentle. "I won't be generous with your reprieve." His loins throbbed, his body urging him to pull up the twisted hem of her gown and continue what they had begun. "It all depends," he continued, "on how sorely you test me."

"Yes, Max," she whispered.

"And as long as we are being honest with each other, *enfant*, tell me . . . are you harboring any suspicions that I will attempt to dispose of you as I did my first wife?"

Lysette gave him a startled look. "You said you didn't kill her!"

"What a trusting creature you are," he said.

"Sh-should I be suspicious of you?" she dared to ask.

Suddenly Max grinned. "Yes, my sweet. Just a little."

FREE BOOK OFFER!

Avon Books has an outstanding offer for every reader of our Romantic Treasures.
Buy three different Avon Romantic Treasures and get your choice of an Avon romance
favorite—absolutely free.

Fill in your name, address and zip code below, and send it, along with the proof-of-
purchase pages from two other Avon Romantic Treasures to:

AVON ROMANTIC TREASURES
Free Book Offer
P.O. Box 767, Dresden, TN 38255.

Allow 4-6 weeks for delivery.

- -

(Please fill out completely)

AVON ROMANTIC TREASURE FREE BOOK OFFER!

Name_____

Address _____

City_____ State_____ Zip_____

Please send me the following FREE novel:
____ 76214-5 SPELLBOUND   ____ 75673-0 DEVIL'S DECEPTION

____ 75921-7 DREAMSPINNER   ____ 75742-7 BLACK-EYED SUSAN

____ 75778-8 CAUGHT IN THE ACT ____ 76020-7 MOONLIGHT AND
                                                                MAGIC

I have enclosed three completed proof-of-purchase pages.

76128

0 71001 00450 2

ISBN 0-380-76128-9

Proof
-of-
Purchase